VIAL
THOUGHTS

Vial Thoughts copyright © 2023 by Van Essler

Published by Raw Dog Screaming Press
Bowie, MD

First Edition

Cover: Daniele Serra

Printed in the United States of America

ISBN: 978-1-947879-54-6
Library of Congress Control Number: 2023931013

RawDogScreaming.com

Van Essler

RAW DOG
SCREAMING
PRESS

For my husband, who somehow found my babble about fictional people and incessant typing endearing.

For my kiddos, who brought me steaming cups of tea and gave me the best excuse to take breaks.

And for my mother. I'm forever grateful for every encouraging word and sheet of paper you gave me for my strange, little stories.

All your love keeps my imagination wild.

Acknowledgments

Once upon a time, in the early 1990's, a wise teacher read my very first chapter book then foretold a future for me as an author. Ms. Alexander, I doubt you realized what you unleashed on the world in that moment, but I thank you immensely.

Honestly, a horde of educators showered me with their expertise and guidance over the years. To the whole of Seton Hill's MFA program, I remain eternally grateful—you not only helped to shape this novel but helped me discover myself as a writer in a clearer sense. I had some of the most amazing critique partners—Chad, Stephanie, Eowyn, Victor, and Lucas—your comments and insight were vital to bringing this story to life. Thank you to Scott for your RIGs and being such a welcoming ambassador for the horror community. Timons, I appreciate your willingness to share your thoughts with me whenever I sought you out and treating me like an unofficial mentee.

To my official mentors, I couldn't ask for more wonderful people to guide me. Paul, your enthusiasm and encouragement got me through some rough times. I hope you know how much light you bring. Heidi, I can't thank you enough for all that you've done for me. In an industry that feels like endless closed doors, you were steadfast in reminding me that persistence would open one. You never failed to convince me I was up for every challenge.

Joe-la, thank you for fielding all my gory questions with grace and giving me support. As much as I appreciate your medical expertise and willingness to chat about blood and bone, I value your writerly support all the more.

My dear Virg, you have been an angel in more ways than you can ever know. Thank you for talking me down from every needless panic and lifting me up from every low. You deserve the moon.

Thank you to my amazing publisher, Raw Dog Screaming Press. Jennifer, you are a true treasure. Your patience and kindness have been more than I could ever hope for in my debut.

Most of all, thank you to my dear family. You believed in me from the very beginning, back when this book was merely a little cluster of ideas. You gave me space and time for my writing, and you listened to my rants about characters and writer's blocks. A book requires a community behind it, so this is as much your baby as mine.

P.S. To ye ole goth crew, the fishnets and overly done black eyeliner may be gone, but I still got it. Thanks for the inspiration and countless memories.

ONE

To inject is to know, and to know is to be wise, and to be wise is to contribute to the Age of Awareness.

The proverb dripped from Lenora's lips, slurred and small, in a repetitive loop. She hovered in the void between the waking world and the nonsensical realm of the mind, trapped. There had been no dreams. No visions or tedious lists of business accounts. Not even shape or sound. A chill graced her fingertips and thoughts rushed back in. The flat black of unconsciousness slunk back and her own voice rang clearer in her ears. *To inject is to know...*

Splattered dashes of color waltzed across her vision. She blinked. The rough outline of a man developed in the foreground—his eyes seemed impossibly small behind his glasses. The face hovered, familiar. *Dr. Wallace.*

Behind him, the shelves of Aqua Peritia vials covered every inch of wall space in the shop. The pigmentation of each vial cast its hue into the room in a kaleidoscopic effect. The vibrant saturation overwhelmed and added to her dizziness, making the world uncertain. The colors must serve some purpose. Perhaps blue for poetry and green for science? She managed to focus on the label of the nearest mustard colored vial. *Bloodletting for Health.*

She twisted her head away in disgust.

An acrid yet sweet taste, like rotten banana blended with paint thinner, made her mouth water. *Ether.* She would have to take several long strolls amid the garden lavender to dissipate the nasty scent. Ether had a tendency to cling, to haunt.

Worse, her wrist throbbed. With the procedure completed in her etheric slumber, the pain hit her in strange waves as her body was gradually waking to sensations. Swollen, but probably no longer bleeding. The groggy heaviness in her bones kept her arm at her side, but she could feel the fruits of the surgery—her Aqua Peritia Cuff. Each moment, she became more aware of the bracelet's foreign feel against her skin.

"Do you recall where you are?" Dr. Wallace poured two cups of tea.

"Your Peritia shop," Lenora answered.

Aqua Peritia—the foundation of the Age of Awareness.

A smoky herbal aroma swirled upwards with the rising steam. *Strong tea.* Mixed with the ether reek from her pores, it became a noxious force churning her stomach. She wiggled away from the cup until her bustle bumped the armrest.

The wave of nausea rolled over her. The aftereffects of ether were well documented, but reading about something and experiencing it were two different beasts. She let full breaths fill her corset to the seams' limits in a calming rhythm. After a few minutes, the worst of it seemed to pass.

"I do hope you find the cuff acceptable. I strive to prove my reputation for personalized pieces is justified." When Wallace chuckled, his nose scrunched up against his glasses.

It took some effort to lift her arm, but she had to see it for herself. The thick bracelet, her Peritia cuff, was gorgeous in its intricate design. A leather strap housed the sleek cogs. Delicately wrapped wires flowered around a gold-leaf port while red gems that matched the cherry hue of her hair concealed the anchoring screws that bit into her like ticks. Each part had been polished to a blinding gleam. She flipped her shaking hand palm up. A tube, the width of a dandelion stem, snaked from the tiny clockwork device into the vein of her wrist. The pink flesh rose around the rubber and throbbed outwards.

"It's… exquisite," she said.

Lenora turned her wrist in every direction. A garden setting root in her skin. She had planted herself into the Age of Awareness, and this was merely the beginning. She could taste all the potential on the tip of her tongue, a spot of sweet amidst the sour of bile wafting up her throat. With the device now implanted, the world laid at her fingertips. Anything, everything, became possible.

If only her father had been open to all Aqua Peritia offered. He forbid any in his employ to wear a cuff. He may have been a brilliant man, revered for his handling of the expansive Leahill business empire, but that didn't mean he knew everything. She insisted again and again that a device could not be good or evil, only used by a person in such a way. Her intentions were noble.

"Will Homer do?" Wallace crept along the shelves of vials. His glasses slid down his nose to the bulb at the ruddy peak.

"Homer?"

"I generally prefer the classics for the test injection. My clients know the work well and can remark on any irregularities. However, if you find Homer dull, I have countless other choices. Perhaps something more factual?"

"Actually, Shelley, please. Mary Shelley. I just read Frankenstein last week." She tried to quell her quivering nerves by sitting up straighter, as all the governesses had insisted was becoming of a lady.

He set the oceanic blue Homer vial down and spied her with his pinprick eyes anew.

"The fiction about the pieced together man?" he said without hiding his disgust.

"Yes, that one."

There was no time to delve into the many merits of Shelley's work. Let him think as he pleased. Something far more daunting consumed her at the moment—the initial injection.

Any leak, no matter how minute, could cause irreparable damage, poisoning her muscles or organs. Days or weeks of illness would follow. Death was exceedingly rare, but agonizingly brutal and drawn out when it did happen.

Mr. Wallace retrieved a new vial from the shelves for her. Rich orange sparkled with flakes of gold when agitated. He rotated it in the light, thoroughly inspecting it. Lenora tensed as he pulled his chair close to her.

"Rest assured, I am here to guide you through all the necessary steps…"

As Dr. Wallace droned on about how to prepare for injection, apprehension closed in on her. The vial, so mesmerizing to watch, conjured dread at the realization its contents would be coursing through her.

What if something goes wrong? She nibbled her lip. *What if I'm one of those rare cases that spend months slowly withering away in bed for a shiny new trinket?*

Surely that fear was merely an echo of her father. The last gasp of his defiance against the device successfully used by practically everyone in Elsothe, from the ash sweepers to Council members.

To inject is to know, and to know is to be wise, and to be wise is to contribute to the Age of Awareness. The words replayed in her head, the familiar cadence a comfort. She focused deeper on her mantra to give her shaky hand to Wallace when he asked for it. The vial snapped into place, sending the orange Aqua sloshing around in the glass.

"You hear that snap? That's how to be sure it's inserted correctly. Now, to inject, twist the vial counterclockwise. It will click when you have turned it enough. There is typically a brief period, maybe a few seconds, before the Aqua Peritia takes effect," Wallace explained.

The vial had an unexpected heft. The extra weight sent a shot of pain to her tube-punctured flesh, the physical discomfort a welcome distraction from the flares of anxiety. If her emotions showed, Wallace didn't seem to notice.

He continued in his monotone manner. "I recommend closing your eyes, as it can be unsettling to see the world while injecting. Make sure you are stable and comfortable. Any questions?"

Countless questions but none she could manifest in that instant. "No."

"Then, at your leisure, Miss Leahill." He motioned towards the cuff.

Light bounced off the lenses of Wallace's glasses onto the vial. A spectrum of warm peach to orange flame whirled inside the Aqua Peritia. That same fire-like hue would flash in her father's eyes if she so much as mentioned cuffs or vials. She could feel him, as if his spirit stood behind her, staring down her defiance. She closed her eyes to banish him. *To inject is to know…*

Twist.

Click.

The Aqua Peritia stung. Rolling waves of intense prickly pain rode up her arm only to fade into a thick pressure as if amber were solidifying her vein, clogging the blood flow.

Then she went numb, and the concoction blossomed.

Not merely Shelley's words but the meaning behind them, the images they conjured. Frankenstein's creation stood beside her in such clarity that the stitched lines of his features had texture. Henry Clerval's corpse flashed upon her psyche, as solid and grotesque as the story itself. Gloom and guilt tainted the countryside a dismal grey. The towering Frankenstein estate loomed on the horizon. Elizabeth's scream echoed sharply in her mind. The terror tangible, choking the air as if the creature's hand had her throat. Escaping. Persuing. Her limbs burned with the panicked sprinting. The entire tale rushed through her in a torrent of detail, sound, and understanding—she could all but taste it. Each moment frozen in perfection like an artist's masterpiece, while flowing to the next moment concurrently.

Beginning, middle, and end, all in sequential order, yet all simultaneous.

The creature confronting Frankenstein on the mountain pass sent a chill through her. She couldn't catch the individual words; they scattered and fled as soon as they grazed her ear. Still, the intimidation and desperation lingered, hanging like icicles on her mind. The song of Justine weeping in innocence. The blazing copper and scarlet of the cottage in flames. The heat heavy. The smoke snaked around her limbs. His face—the tattered bits of flesh assembled into a malicious grin framed in a darkened window. The story receded into a distant intangible phenomenon. Some points stuck to her while others vanished within the fog of the whole, as if it were a nightmare she could remember in only a few ways rather than in its entirety.

Her eyes snapped open with a jump in her heartbeat. In hindsight, maybe Homer would have been a wiser choice.

Dr. Wallace swiftly reacted to her distressed appearance. He detached the empty vial and then lifted her hand to examine the tubing. "Everything alright? Any pain or sickness? The story in proper order and detail?"

"It was…" Lenora willed her heart to slow to a more regular pace. "Impressive."

And it had been, yet the experience had not been what she expected. She'd read Frankenstein dozens of times before. The injection version, detailed and intense as it was, did not align with her own imaginings. In fact, it had been far more frightening than the lovely prose she delighted in. More immersive than reading but at the same time it felt as if she hadn't been party to the creation of the story. Instead, like she had been whisked through another's interpretation of the work. The difference vexed her more than she wished to acknowledge, making her fidget in her seat.

After giving her another thorough examination, Wallace relaxed.

"Good. Good. Everything seems to be functioning properly," he said.

She handed him a thorough list of Aqua Peritias she had compiled over the last few years. More classics, of course. Goethe's *Faust*, Dante's *Divine Comedy*, the collection of children's tales by the Grimm Brothers Claire used to read to her as a child, and dozens of non-fiction works.

Dr. Wallace fetched each title with minimal searching. He darted around the stock only pausing to push up his glasses. A splendid leather Peritia case was provided for her as well, each vial carefully inspected before being tucked into a slot. He directed her to return the empty vials to him once finished. *Nothing goes to waste.*

"Before you depart, I wish to express my condolences on your loss. Your father was a well-admired man, and Canimere is poorer with his departure." The tinted glints from the vials around them softened the room like stained glass but his expression remained flat. "I'm afraid I'm not certain which of your gentleman relatives has been entrusted with managing the estate. Whom shall I contact regarding the charges?"

"I am managing my estate."

Dr. Wallace gave her a nasal laugh that finished in a snort. "I was unaware you had such a bold sense of humor."

"I don't." Lenora gathered up her wide-brimmed hat and ash mask.

"With respect, such things shouldn't be burdened on a lady like yourse–"

"My father was a great man, Dr. Wallace, revered in both business and social circles. He had many talents, especially for dealing with money." She clenched her hand to direct the anger away from her voice. "It stands to reason that I, his sole heir, will be equally talented, does it not?"

He said nothing more, his desire for payment more pressing than his need to preserve his outdated beliefs.

A signature scribbled, then their business was settled. With the fresh surge of confidence from the experience, she dressed to depart with sure movements, her frail state from the procedure flung to a distant memory.

Lenora loathed the necessity of the ash mask in Canimere, especially on such a sticky, humid day. The barrier kept the soot from invading her mouth, but the smell of the city still permeated the filter. The street clouded with the blight of a dying trash fire, all old smoke from rubbish. The last blast of summer heat roared through the city before autumn took the reins. The rubbery edges of the leather suctioned to her face. She might as well have an octopus latched on as adornment, for she certainly felt as if her face was being attacked.

Above her, the mammoth stem of ash shot upwards from the industrial districts, mushrooming out into a giant umbrella—the combined pollution of countless factories. Anything beneath the dark mass was showered with a constant flurry of descending embers. Most days, the fall was so thick it obscured the sun, making it a dull orange glow in the sky. The streetlamps in Canimere ran all hours, failing to bring true illumination into the storm of pollution.

Across the street, urban children sculpted black piles trapped in the alley into a complex fortress. A battle ensued, where boys in baggy britches and girls in dainty dresses tackled each other in the soot. It didn't take long for them to blur into a species of their own, a genderless swarm of charcoal-colored goblins. Coated from cowlick to heels, the victor claimed the prized title of king or queen of the tar.

A soot-smeared sign glared down at the scene below from the building across the way. *Triumph in the Ash* illuminated with flickering bulbs around the frame. Lenora never saw such signs at Glenn Haven Academy or in the lush, rolling hills of the estate holders. Now that her position required her to travel into the city often, the abundant signs made her squeamish. It felt as if all those working for the country's advancement, in the constant flood of the suffocating ashfall, had the Council's words constantly watching from above.

The Age of Awareness wasn't fully realized—not yet.

The winds remained in her favor, and the sootfall was light on the north side, with the bulk of the filth landing in some other sad neighborhood. Sparse rays of sunlight streamed in from the late afternoon sunset.

She was tempted to rip off the binding straps of her mask. Indeed, it appeared several of the pedestrians on the street had the same inclination. They carried their masks at their sides while their simple Peritia cuffs caught the few ribbons of sunlight. Enticing, but the removal would risk ash up her nostrils and inking her eyes. For those dwelling in the constant bleak snow, the risk was worth the reward.

A couple of the sweepers also chose to go barefaced as they gathered the accumulated ash into piles and then pushed it into the dump vessels at each corner. Even with the thin slices of light, they toiled cheerlessly in their dismal labor. The ash would never cease so their sweeping carried on without end. With a distinctly high whistle and then a whoosh, the vessels sucked the waste downward. The complex maze of piping running under Canimere would force the pollution out of the city.

Why the Council had spent the effort and income to dispose of the soot instead of discovering a way to stop it from falling, Lenora couldn't guess. Perhaps she could work on that issue, a side project of sorts.

Her carriage driver, Jacob Dudfield, leaned against her Wilthiem steam carriage and puffed on a hand-rolled cigarette. At a lanky nineteen, Jacob had been a bold choice for the post of private driver. The flock of suits—old fashioned men of a former era her father had accumulated to handle the accounts—scoffed at the young lady who was driven around the hazardous city by an even younger servant.

They were unable to realize Jacob's skills in steam carriage construction and upkeep outweighed his inexperience. He constantly improved upon the carriage in some manner. She noticed a new steam stack or smoother ride each trip into Canimere. *What a shame not everyone can see his brilliance.*

"Jacob," she called from across the street. She lifted the Aqua Peritia case at her side for him to see.

She cradled the case like a delicate treasure. There was much to be done. With her Peritia cuff finally in place, she could devour books and articles at an accelerated pace, even the dull topics. With her inheritance of the estate and all the knowledge at her fingertips, surely she would discover the best path to propel Elsothe forward to the Age of Awareness—whether that be supporting other formidable women or devising a new beneficial product. Something so remarkable no one could ever again say "that was good—for a girl," or "your father must have spent a great deal of time helping you with this." She squeezed the handle as if embracing it.

Jacob dropped his crude cigarette and stepped on it in his rush to meet her.

Two Enforcers patrolling the cobblestones cut him off. Their brass helmets and masks, splattered with soot, appeared strikingly similar to bits of old ship wreckage dredged up from the sea. Their air-tight suits seemed more fitting for exploring some deep underwater chasm than for policing the narrow streets. They frightened her as a child, causing her to hide behind the nearest adult. All she could do now was hold the Peritia case like a weak shield.

Jacob stiffened then sprinted over to her once the Enforcers passed.

"Think it's true what they say? That they're machines?" Jacob whispered.

"I don't know," she replied in a whisper.

Complex clockwork devices in human shape. As much as she detested gossip, the theory had merit. No man could withstand so much weight covering him, nor could he survive the heat from the coal-powered box on the Enforcer's back. It would be an impressive feat of engineering—and equally terrifying.

Surely the Council wouldn't trust heartless tinker toys with the protection of the people. The very idea sent pricks of panic up her spine.

"Let's go." She handed over her case. "I've had enough of the city for one day."

Her young driver escorted her across the road. Unsure of driver etiquette, he switched back and forth between outpacing her and lagging behind her. She was as flustered as he was in that regard. Glenn Haven taught her numerous lessons, but the nuance of public etiquette never graced the syllabus. He finally settled into step with her side by side, and that seemed the most natural for both of them. He quickly opened the carriage door and held out his hand to steady her as she stepped inside.

She arranged herself on the velvet cushions.

With a clunky pull of one of the numerous levers, a blast of cool air circulated through the cabin, drawing all the ash up and out of the piping to the left. The air filter finished in seconds, but the buzzing sound of the vent rattled in her head longer. She tore off her hat and ash mask and threw the accessories beside her, trading the tightness of the mask for the confines of the cabin. It soothed only a touch, but she was on route to be free of the city and all its weight.

The carriage door swung open with a flurry of dark specks. She jumped in alarm. A tall man ducked into the cabin and shook off the ash from his blond hair. He plopped himself on the seat across from her, emanating a cloud of airborne soot. She covered her mouth and nose as her shock melted away. This act clearly had insult written all over it, not attack, as the man reclined in her emerald cushions as if they were his own accommodations.

Another cleansing wind rushed through the carriage as the man removed his goggles and tanned respirator.

"Dr. Brechin." She scowled at him.

"Miss Leahill, what a pleasant surprise. Do you frequent this carriage often?"

The doctor pulled a reptile from his coat. Its lime scales clashed with the four brass false legs fastened to the stubs of its absent limbs. A yellow jewel of an eye blinked to adjust to the light as the creature unraveled itself from a fetal position.

"And your lizard," Lenora added, not bothering to hide the distaste in her voice.

"He prefers Harold, if you please, and he's an iguana. Eee-gwan-na." The creature crawled up his chest one mechanical leg clank at a time until it settled onto Brechin's shoulder.

"Miss?" Jacob poked his head back from the driver's seat. "Should I… remove him? Or…?"

"No, that's not necessary," Lenora said.

Brechin took her hand gently, bowing as if to kiss her un-gloved skin. He paused before his lips touched. The iguana leaned in with its eye trained on her.

"Please don't tell me you had one of those ridiculous things attached to you. Those concoctions are full of harmful chemical compounds. Each injection is an attack to the nervous system. It interferes with brain function. Didn't your father warn you of the dangers?" He pushed her hand away. "And you reek of ether."

The mention of her father stung. *Why do these arrogant men keep bringing up the dead?* The departed shouldn't be able to dictate the actions of the living, yet everywhere she turned, Father was there.

"That's none of your concern. What do you want, Dr. Brechin?"

"Elliot, if you please." He straightened his coat. "After much consideration, I have decided to indulge your request regarding my work for your father."

Their acquaintance was recent, but Lenora felt certain Dr. Brechin was the oddest man she had ever met. He appeared far too young to be the celebrated doctor and scientist he claimed to be. She figured him maybe two or three years her senior at twenty-six or so. She had the unfortunate pleasure of calling on him at his filthy office two weeks earlier. He eagerly pulled down some pictures of his accomplishments from the walls for her, a couple of which featured her father beaming proudly in the background. He had beat out celebrated doctors in their forties for several grants. Mechanical limb replacements, new surgical techniques, numerous awards for his research on skeletal structures—even with proof, it all seemed implausible for a man of so green an age.

Perhaps his age would cause less suspicion if he weren't so completely boorish and difficult. Somehow, he had managed a private arrangement with her father for a large weekly sum; however, the account lacked any documentation as to what Brechin was paid to do.

Then there were his hands—fingers long and thin like spider legs, one fingernail on each hand coated with black paint. It seemed such an untrustworthy trait, those fingers.

"Then, may I suggest you schedule an appointment with my associates at Canimere Central."

Brechin's face scrunched up as if insulted. "Why would I go to the lackeys? I would much rather discuss matters with the head of the estate."

A warm jolt ran through her. *Head of the estate.* Someone finally addressed her as such without the title dripping with sarcasm or distain. A strange man, to be sure, but at least he took her seriously.

"Is that so? Jacob, make a stop at Dr. Brechin's office on our way, please," she said. The carriage roared to life with a cracking screech of steam, then inched forward. "I'm sure the fact I cut your funding yesterday has nothing to do with the decision to come to me directly."

Brechin waved off her accusation, his black nail flapping in the air like a single speck of soot.

"Not at all." His lip curled up on one side, then drooped. "Actually, the details regarding Samuel's death were more of an incentive."

A truly odd man indeed to be a beacon of scientific advancement, yet still indulge himself with gossip. Then again, perhaps not. He didn't appear to be prodding her for more insight regarding the rumors, rather, he spoke as if stating a well-known fact.

Lenora leaned forward. "And what about my father's death? It was ruled an accident."

"You trust the Council's rulings? Their morality is as riddled with holes as their Age of Acceptance or whatever they call it."

There was still much work to do before Elsothe could be raised to the enlightened state the Age of Awareness promised; she agreed on that point. However, questioning morality flirted with treason, yet he spoke of it with such ease.

"Psshhh, an accident," Brechin continued. "Don't you think it's the slightest bit strange how Fogarty's fireworks went awry and happened to explode right into Samuel's carriage? And why did he even have his little advertising parade anyways? From what I can tell, the circus does quite well. It sells out most shows."

Preposterous to give the gossip even so much as a dusting of plausibility, but his logic raised too many questions to disregard them entirely. If nothing else, her father left her a legacy and the means for progress. Perhaps she should start making her mark by quelling the rumors about his demise. If Brechin could provide any concrete answers, she would coax them out of him.

"Are you implying this circus set out with the intention to harm pedestrians?"

"Samuel didn't confide in you much, did he?"

Lenora twitched, then straightened hoping to at least feign matching his height. "What of the circus?"

Brechin turned to his lizard, giving the animal rhythmic strokes to stretch out the silence between them. "I'm sure you're curious about Harold's legs. That's quite a story. The man who brought him to me had the ignorant idea he could live among trained hounds. Obviously, that didn't work out well considering they bit—"

"I don't have time for this. *You* don't have time for this. I'm only listening until we reach your office. Derailing me from topic to topic will not serve you."

Brechin gave the iguana another pet as an exasperated sigh escaped his lips. "The account you were reviewing… Samuel contracted me to work on the Agitated Delirium epidemic."

"The contagious lunacy? You're working on that?" Her spine frosted over as he nodded. "But the Council has nearly discovered a cure."

"Don't believe everything you hear in the city. Sometimes stories are designed to deceive. In this case, to arrest a possible public panic. In truth, the epidemic has become worse. Now, even the wealthy are becoming infected."

Lenora's hand went to her collar as if she could pull away an intangible hand gripping her throat. Agitated Delirium—a condition worse than death. Locked within their own nightmares, its victims' minds were corrupted, rotted.

Jacob twisted his neck to speak over his shoulder. "Sounds like a load of rubbish to me, Miss."

"That is a rather bold claim," Lenora agreed, but the vein of her neck pulsed rapidly under her fingers. She withdrew her hand from her throat and squared herself at Brechin. "But, still—what are your findings?"

Brechin wrapped his long fingers around the edge of the seat. Anger twisted his hunched form, or maybe frustration. Either way, the jolt of his shift to such a foreboding pose sent another spike of dread through her. He was serious.

She ran a silk handkerchief between her fingers. *The epidemic worse.* What manner of horrid place was Canimere that black eternally descended upon it, and insanity traveled about like the flu? The asylums were already overpopulated with victims; impossible to think more fell ill each day.

They came to a halt outside Brechin's office. The Wilthiem bubbled and sputtered a few minutes at the curb as they sat in silence.

"Dr. Brechin, your findings?"

He came back from whatever thoughts had consumed him. "Elliot, if you please. My findings? Those I would have to show you."

"Show me?"

"This upcoming Tuesday, at my office. I'll show you. Come in the late afternoon and expect a long evening. Full disclosure, provided I have funds, of course."

Lenora sank back into the cushions. This was a foe she hoped to never face. Still, any progress regarding the Delirium epidemic would be of immense value to Elsothe. She would be taken seriously rather than seen as a novelty with such information.

"Funds granted, but this better be worthy of them."

"It will." He put on his goggles, looking remarkably like an overgrown wasp.

A cyclone of ash rushed into the cabin when he opened the door. She covered her mouth with her handkerchief, blinking away the specks. He stowed Harold in his jacket and stepped into the grey haze outside, only to thrust his head back inside a moment later.

His voice became deep and choppy when filtered through the mask. "Oh, and Miss Leahill, it would be in your best interest to stay clear of Fogarty and his circus."

TWO

The Wilthiem knocked wildly to the left as Jacob swerved. By the dim light cast from a nearby tavern, the slumped silhouette of a man shook his cane in one hand. His other arm, ending in a stump at the wrist, extended towards them as if he could point with an imaginary finger. Whatever offensive language the man yelled muted in the rumble of the Wilthiem's flight. The carriage had narrowly missed him, but Jacob didn't slow down or look back.

Lenora rubbed her wrist beneath the cuff's tubing. *Three days and still tender.* The rocking forced her to brace herself and slam the device against the carriage wall. The wound looked faintly rose, but otherwise appeared undamaged.

"Sorry, Miss," Jacob called from the front.

"Please slow down. There's no need to be in such a hurry."

There was plenty of reason. The south district of Canimere known as Pitchdrift was notorious for being the refuge of the dregs of the city. The poor, the sick, and the weak. The lowest of criminals prowled the area openly without repercussions. The darkest pit within the confines of Canimere's miasma.

A rather dubious location, all things considered, to set up a circus.

These streets weathered a thicker fall on account of their proximity to the factories belching out filth. Mountains of soot piled up as the sweepers abandoned the crumbling cobblestones at dusk. Nightfall only compounded the district's sins. The bars swelled with patrons. Broken streetlamps were rarely replaced. Even though they merely skirted the edge of Pitchdrift, Lenora sensed a shift in the city. The buildings twisted, bowing to the factories dominating the skyline. The shadowed spaces held eyes.

She swiped her handkerchief between her fingers in rapid succession. She had to admit, it was a perfectly set stage for murder and monsters. A place where the soot concealed remains so that not even the bones could escape.

Jacob kept the Wilthiem bolting through the streets. "Just making sure you don't arrive late for the show. Besides, there ain't much you would want to look at."

But she needed to look. She had to know the facts. Her father had been on these same roads when the accident happened. What would her father have to do in a place of the broken? If she could decipher him, maybe that gooseflesh that rose whenever his name was spoken would cease. Maybe his memory would fade from the hallways, so she didn't have the sudden panic of imagining his footsteps coming.

If it happened on these streets, maybe his death wasn't an accident at all.

Disheveled wretches shuffled within the maze of crumbling brick. Some tied rags around their faces to protect themselves from the ash. They scurried through the streets like rats whose tails had been nipped off in traps. *No, not tails*, Lenora corrected herself. *Hands.* Missing hands, severed above the wrist. On some, it was the right. Others, the left. Every line in the district appeared distorted; structures crooked and weighed with soot like moss-covered ruins, human forms lacking symmetry.

She heard of these people in whispers but had never seen them before. The most pathetic of the impoverished lot, so deprived they lacked a full body.

Perhaps her father visited to provide some sort of charity to these unfortunate souls. Somehow, she doubted that.

With a quickening pulse, she counted the absent appendages as they passed by. *Fourteen, not including the angry fellow with his cane.* Perhaps a common injury from working in the factories, the hand caught in a machine and plucked from the worker? The Wilthiem rounded a corner. *Sixteen.* No, too clean of a separation. A ritual performed to prove allegiance to one of the criminal overlords of the district? *Seventeen.* Likely not, it would be rather unproductive to maim those wishing to serve you. Jacob veered right as a herd of drunken men spilt out of a tavern into the middle of the road. *Eighteen. Nineteen.* Maybe punishment from other criminals, territorial disputes? *Twenty.* They slowed as the theater came into view. *Twenty-one.*

Cardend Theater stood as a looming giant over the neighboring structures, a relic from the times of the monarchy, back when the area had been a fashionable spot on the bay. Pillars stained with tide lines of the nightly rise of soot. Angelic statues at the gate that once greeted patrons had crumbled into monstrous mockeries with broken wings.

"Are you sure, Miss? I mean…" Jacob pulled the carriage to the entrance of the theater. "Well, that doctor did say not to come."

She strapped on her ash mask while readying her umbrella. "True, but he also hinted at several irregularities regarding this circus. If Brechin thinks I'm going to sit on my hands and wait for him to be forthcoming, he is sorely mistaken. I'll figure it out myself."

"You could talk to the Council. Ask for another look at the accident?"

She thrust her umbrella out of the open carriage door but twirled the handle instead of opening it. Seeking answers from the Council should have been the first option that popped into her head—the proper protocol—however, she hadn't thought of it until he mentioned it. Even so, she already knew asking them would be a fruitless endeavor.

"They wouldn't bother," she said.

They would tell her grieving women are exceedingly sensitive and prone to hysteria. She would sooner end up in an asylum than be granted further investigation. Between the two, she would rather face the bleak of Pitchdrift than the corridors of madness.

"But Miss, you see, it's not safe here. My pa always says—"

"Don't worry. I'll be fine," she asserted through the mask then dashed out of the carriage before he could respond.

Jacob meant well, but she had to find out for herself. She needed to know if the talk around the city held any accuracy. *If it wasn't an accident.* Perhaps that's why if felt like her father lingered, following her around the manor and scowling from corners during her meetings. His memory clung to her, weighing her down.

She would have the truth of it, even if it meant stepping into Dante's *Inferno*.

Her umbrella popped open with a flap, like the wings of a bat expanding after sunset.

A long walkway wound through walls of onyx, packed three feet high, leaving no way to deviate from the path once she entered. Robed in the waste of the city, sculptures flanked the doors to welcome guests with faceless stares. Effigies of the past marring the present. Lenora hit the path in a brisk but shaky walk.

The malevolent tone of Pitchdrift gave the darkest of the rumors a solid foundation to form. A target on her father's carriage. A steady hand at the launch system's controls. The fireworks discharged with accuracy. Splinters of the steam coach slicing through the air, blending with the barrage of golden sparks and the splatter of blood. That steady hand scratching off the name Samuel Leahill from a list.

Damn her father for sheltering her from the city, for not acclimatizing her to the ash. She should feel like a warrior ready to wield her umbrella like a broadsword rather than a frightened child, but the thick sheets of ash made all in its wake seem to move. She sensed the reapers guarding the entrance clicking their brittle fingers in preparation to gouge her.

Even as she told herself there was nothing to fear, she quickened her pace, lest the ghoul statues pull her into the stygian blackness. No time to stop at the entrance; every second spent with her back exposed to this cursed district was a moment too long. She sped up, intent on muscling through the large metal doors straight ahead with one shoulder angled forward to force them ajar. As the collective breath of the district hit the back of her neck, she rammed the doors.

They gave smoothly, swinging open with surprising ease. The soft spring on the carpeted floor underfoot was the only indication she passed through them. She crashed forward like a runaway train, unable to slow herself, her hem caught underfoot. She took a waiting usher down to the carpet with her, as she tangled up in the yards of her satin skirt.

A tumble followed by a handstand and the usher landed on his feet, unfazed by their fall. His hand extended to help her up.

"Thank y—" Her voice left her as his hand wrapped around her glove, his fingers touching the bare skin of her wrist.

The fingertips felt pliable like clay. The texture sent shivers coursing through her. The flesh of his face and hands sagged with an oily sheen, as if he were a melted-down candle, all thick layers of wax covering his exterior. She found the whites of his eyes unperceivable in the shadow of hanging meat where his brows should have been. The skin at the base of his neck pulled to the side, stitches barely holding it in place. It appeared as if someone had cut away excess flesh and sewed the resulting gash closed.

Canimere held far more disturbing inhabitants than Claire's fairytales had magic, yet they strolled about as if their presence wasn't odd in the least. As if nightmares belonged, just as assured of their place as they were in her slumbers. She stood frozen, unable to decide if she should flee or curtsy to the usher.

"Welcome." The melted wax man pulled off his hat to bow, revealing a mop of horsehair plastered crookedly on his skull. He motioned at the inner door. "This way, please."

Lenora swiftly made her way inside, not daring to look back.

The interior of Cardend Theater blinded with its opulence. Warm hues of yellow wallpaper and scarlet draperies. Plush red carpets. The vents blew warm cinnamon-spiked air while the mass of finely dressed patrons chatted below. A fancifully carved oak ticket counter lined the wall where several of the wax men served the swarm in attendance. The centerpiece of the room, a chandelier that sprayed beams of light in all directions, hung before an elegant double staircase. *Such a feast for the senses.*

The dreadful exterior of Cardend fell into distant memory as the twinkle from the chandelier sparkled down on every distinguished guest. A refuge from the spoilage; a promise of future splendor.

Surely such grandeur could not be associated with murderous plots.

Lenora gave the usher her coat and hastily dusted herself off. Not the way she had planned to make her grand entrance as head of estate, but she might as well make the best of the situation. With a quick cup of her hand in front of her mouth, she nervously checked her breath. The pungent ether smell was weak, nearly gone. Once she neatly adjusted her grandmother's emerald necklace and earring set, she ventured through the crowd towards the ticket counter.

She strode among the posh crowd, perfect posture with her cuffed hand poised to whisk away imaginary stray hairs. She twisted her wrist slightly to accentuate the new addition to it, catching beams from the brilliant chandelier. Her debut as an independent woman of society, with her personalized cuff polished for admiration.

"Is that Lenora Leahill?" she heard one woman ask.

"I do believe it is. In green? Isn't she in mourning?" spoke another.

A man chimed in, "To be in society so soon after such a tragedy in the family? And without an escort? One would have thought her upbringing was better."

"I heard she decided to manage the estate herself. Can you imagine, a *lady* in business? Distasteful."

The jubilant tone of the crowd decreased while a whispering buzz rose. Women lifted their fans only to peek out at her from over the top. Some men glanced at her sideways and turned their backs, while others stared directly, shaking their heads.

Lenora dropped her hand to her side as her corset once again seemed to collapse in on her. Hardly the reception she hoped for but a familiar one. Her first step into Glenn Haven had been the same. As the sole female student, all the boys gawked at her as if she were some attack on common decency. She stiffened. That instinctual pull in her gut cramped. Always that unease, that heavy uncertainty when all eyes were upon her.

She would not play the frail, frightened damsel; she refused to appear that way to them. She tilted her chin up, even as the rest of her body shook.

The Council boasted all could rise to great heights with the tools of mechanical advancements, yet the old traditions twisted these people into adorned vultures. Obviously, these were not the true people of the Age of Awareness; these were impostors.

"Allow me to express my utmost gratitude," a voice announced from the top of the stairway.

The room fell silent.

A well-built man in blazing crimson—from boots to top hat—stood at the apex of the stairs with a woman in dazzling sequins and slender torso on his arm. The crowd's attention shifted to him, but the piercing gaze beneath his manicured dark brows centered directly on Lenora.

His face, from the bridge of his nose down, was polished brass. The mechanical pieces jointed together into the lower half of his visage. The replacement clicked sharply as the gears next to his ears moved around. His mouth ticked open into a smile too wide to be human, displaying two perfect rows of silver teeth.

He tapped the long-waisted woman's arm and said, "Excuse me, Birdy." She gracefully withdrew from the spotlight but managed a quick glare at Lenora as she retreated.

"To accept my humble invitation and apology is more than I ventured to hope for." He descended the staircase as he spoke. His voice carried a ring on the vowels that slightly echoed. "It truly speaks to one's character by the manner in which they act towards those who've unintentionally wronged them."

The crowd gawked at her anew like they would some exotic creature in a menagerie. A small, caged thing, soon to perish in its confinement.

As if by instinct, the audience parted when he walked into them. The man stood before her and removed his hat. Spinning it on his fingers, he bowed.

"I am honored to have the presence of such a remarkable woman. Welcome, Miss Leahill."

The lobby exploded with applause. Now they were celebrating her? Was all it took for acceptance the approval of a man? *Then why hadn't Father done so?*

Once the clapping died down, one of the wax men announced to the guests, "Showtime in ten minutes."

The flock strolled toward the open doors of the theater between the two staircases.

The man replaced his crimson hat while taking her arm and led her towards the stairs. "It truly is a pleasure to have you attend our little show, Miss Leahill."

"Thank you, Mr...?"

"My apologies. I am Fogarty. Johnathan Fogarty." Behind his ear, a tiny whistle of steam sprang out as the jaw repositioned to a more natural-sized grin.

"Thank you, Mr. Fogarty. I'm afraid I did not receive the invitation you spoke of," she whispered as they climbed the stairs.

"Shhh. What society doesn't know is better for the clever among us. Besides, I was considering extending such an invitation soon, though I feared you would decline. Now there is no need to worry as you think ahead of the game. I admire that."

"It's best to always position yourself ahead." *Father said that once, hadn't he?*

"Indeed." He paused to remove his hat then placed it over his chest with his free hand. "Allow me to truly express my sorrow at the loss of your father. Samuel was a true friend, a shining example of a philanthropist and an intellectual. Though our work together was the majority of our relationship, his warmth and kindness were at the heart of it."

Lenora scrambled to dig through her memory. Her father had not mentioned this man once.

"I am distraught the world has lost him on account of my staff's miscalculations," he continued.

Exactly what one should say under the circumstances, yet the words rolled too easily over his metallic lips. Perhaps such a man had practiced lines to the point he could speak any words with a smooth cadence. Or perhaps not.

"It was an accident," she noted as they topped the staircase trying to keep her tone even. She wasn't going to get much out of him if he could sense her suspicions.

"Yes, but I feel as if I am at fault. Forgive me." He replaced the hat on his crown. "But enough discussion of such sad events. There is business to attend to. The advancement of our venture must be examined. I'm pleased to hear you are managing the estate. I'm sure we will be wondrous partners."

Her head buzzed. *Business venture? Partners?* There was nothing on the books regarding performance art. Her father supported a handful of painters and sculptors in the past but nothing in theater. Certainly nothing of the circus variety.

"Of course."

"I have no doubt this will be of great importance to us both." He drew the curtain to reveal a private balcony box. "I hope this seat pleases you."

"Quite."

"Marvelous. I'm afraid I am required on stage, but I do hope you take delight in our performance." He bowed again. "We will speak privately after the final curtain. We have much to discuss, my dear. I can barely contain my anticipation." With that, he planted a cold kiss on her hand and departed.

She took a seat. The box gave her an elevated view of both the stage and the audience shifting about below. *Much to discuss.* Rather curious yet alarming. It was evident her father kept many secrets and colleagues she found unfitting of his reputation. The pristine image of him in her head was accumulating stains and starting to yellow with age, but that's how ghosts are meant to look—dirty and worn from the life they left behind.

With one finger, she traced the swirls of her cuff. She had hoped to come better prepared. The lack of Peritia vials on the circus frustrated her to the point she broke two empty vials by slamming them on the desk. She resorted to digging through old newspapers and catalogue books of theatrical performances. The search turned up little more than Fogarty's name and the transition from traveling show to theater act seven years ago with the purchase of Cardend.

The lights dimmed. A hush spread through the crowd. The quiet eerie in its completeness. Fogarty strode in front of the curtain with simultaneous grace and force. Center stage, he froze as the air went unnervingly still. He waited two breaths, maybe four, and then threw his arms up while producing his impossible grin. His chin blinded random audience members as it reflected the spotlight.

"Ladies and gentlemen, madams, mademoiselles, and messieurs, I present for your delight and consideration… The Sublime Spectacle!"

The audience roared with applause. He let the thunder swell to a peak then dropped his arms, and silence resumed.

"As is so often the case, we begin with chaos. Life devoid of direction. Behold."

The curtain pulled back as he flung his arm wide towards the stage, then he ducked beyond the spotlight. Chaos indeed played out behind the curtain. A flock of entertainers all clustered together yet performing separately. Music piped in from a player off stage; a jumble of high horns and rambunctious drumming. Too disjointed to be upbeat, the noise felt as if bloating the discord of the performance.

A bear boxing with a bearded lady nearly collided into the sequined woman, Birdy, who had twisted her body into an unfathomable sort of knot. Conjoined twins waltzed between the boxers, narrowly escaping a jab. On the other side of the stage, a man covered in nautical tattoos swallowed a sword. As the hilt settled on his lips, a trapeze artist swung down from the rafters. The big toe of her slipper glided centimeters from the sword's handle as she flipped around the swing. The slightest error and the man's neck would be sliced open for all to witness.

Each near miss spiked a collective panic that made the audience flinch. Lenora was not immune; her imagination brought each potential casualty to life. There would be blood on the stage, vibrant and gleaming. The meaty smack of a body hitting the polished floor. Yet the actors escaped—a spider's thread from devastation each time. The threat never receded, only burrowed deeper each moment, like a splinter worming further into her flesh.

Three elephants stormed across the stage. Lenora grabbed her opera glasses and observed the animals in further detail. *They're real.* As the elephants stomped through the acts, painted men rode tiny unicycles around the animals' legs, avoiding being grotesquely flattened in slick last-moment zips left and right. The audience gasped and shrieked at each close call. The herd managed to exit the stage, leaving everyone untouched.

Her pulse pounded in her ears erratically with the music. There were daring feats performed to exhilarate the audience and then there were unnecessarily risky maneuvers. This was the latter.

Fogarty took to the stage with his extended smile whistling steam like a teakettle. The heavy thud of his footsteps dwarfed the quieting music. The performers wound down in a wave left to right that rode the decreasing volume of the score. When all fell still, the soundtrack stopped.

"My friends," he announced, more to the audience than to the acts obscured behind him by his steam cloud. His arms folded over his chest in a mock plea that clashed with the overzealous grin from his mechanical jaw. "I implore you to cease engaging in this hazardous manner. I shall guide you, and you will find harmony together."

In an unnerving synchronization, the performers bowed to the ringleader. He returned the gesture, and the audience squealed in delight.

Fogarty took his seat in a glistening chair on a platform farther back center stage. A new song blared into the theater—some upbeat tune with heroic building violins and a marching rhythm, like the music of a triumphant return from battle tainted with the weak scratchiness of a record player. From his elevated post, Fogarty introduced each act one by one.

Three bare midriff dancers carrying brightly colored scarves graced the stage. With undulations rolling down their bellies, and scarves billowing, a fresh burst of cinnamon and exotic spices came from the vents accenting the carnal movements. Singers showed their impressive range among taxidermied oddities. Each note was repeated by some mechanism in one of the lifeless, stuffed creatures in a pitch-perfect echo. The hanging bat screeched high notes; the badger croaked low. Pinheads rushed the stage in a comical round of slapstick mishaps.

The acts went on and on, each performance a blend of tacky dazzle and panache, yet Lenora couldn't shake a growing unease. The way Fogarty sat on stage gradually set her nerves sharp as if she had bit down on a fork. He loomed above them with an air that silently implied they performed for him and him alone.

Lenora sat stunned in her seat as the lights brightened for intermission. Even if this man and his circus had meant no malice towards her father, his demeanor exuded a subtle hint of menace. His posture both flamboyant and laced with intimidation.

Her handkerchief slid between her fingers. Ridiculous that some timid place within her begged to slip out of the theater and return to the security of Foxton. She could ignore any further contact and pretend she never came. *No, that's irrational.* He was an actor; this persona could be nothing more than a well-established character. She couldn't let herself be driven by mere assumptions to be flighty and inconsistent.

As everyone settled in for the second half of the performance, a brisk chill ran through the theater. The tone of the audience changed. Their apprehension rose like smoke, flooding her box.

Fogarty made his hat twirling entrance and introduced a fencing pair clad in strange black armor covered with large buttons. Each touch on one of the opponents popped and sparked as the buttons exploded. The thick scent of gunpowder overwhelmed the lingering vented spice. Before either fencer could best the other, Fogarty drew his sword and dispatched them both in dramatic fashion, spraying red sparks over the stage.

Next, the Birdy woman performed as a scantily clad tightrope walker. She spun a web of rope from stage right to left, rotating her curves to the oohs and aahs of the captivated audience. While Birdy meticulously weaved her web, she shot knowing glances back at the ringleader in a tasteless display of debauchery. Once her masterpiece was completed, Fogarty swung his sword and the web fell. The seductress swung off stage, blowing the audience a farewell kiss.

The acts progressed in this manner, increasing in grotesqueness. Legless ankle biters spun on wheeled contraptions over the stage floor like demented vagrants. Cloaked men juggled daggers on thin stilts while they spit green fluid. Yet each monstrosity was inevitably bested by the metallic jawed ringleader.

Was this the uplifted art of the Age of Awareness? Awful displays smoothed over with flashy bits of decadence. It felt wrong, morbid, yet so in tune with the city. Canimere wallowing in layers of filth, even as it proclaimed its glory. This wasn't what Lenora expected. There were supposed to be glints of hope for the future, but thus far, she had found none as she ventured out on her own.

When she thought the show couldn't conjure an act more disturbing than the last, masked men charged the stage, faces hidden behind sewn together patches of animal hides to look like nightmarish amalgams of different species. Fox ears with feathers and tanned leather. A beast covered in beaks. These snarling mockeries of feral men ambushed the show, beating sticks on the floor and waving blades at the actors. Lenora straightened from her seat in terror.

A pair of men with pig snout masks grabbed the conjoined twins. They squealed as they each pulled an arm from one of the twins threatening to tear them in twain. The pinheads were thrown in cages and poked with sticks.

Macabre mashups of dog and fowl tackled the tattooed man. They forced giant hooks into the metal rings embedded in his back, one at a time with high pitched squeals of delight. Lenora could practically feel them as if they somehow penetrated her soul. Each hook a shining beacon of potential agony, and the performers took great care to emphasize them.

With the spotlight secured on the tattooed victim, his captives hoisted him up by the hooks on thick chains above the stage. At first, he struggled. His flailing made scraping clinks on the chains. Then, he seemed drift off; eyes open but dulled with dreaminess. With several loud cranks, the chains pitched his limp body forward to dangle above the crowd. His skin stretched like a wet sheet pinned on a clothing line. Tattooed arms and legs swayed loose over the seated spectators.

A scream. Lenora covered her mouth, but the sound hadn't come from her. Women below dropped in the aisles of faint like gorged leeches falling off a patient. Lenora felt her stomach roll in on itself. The sweat of nausea moistened her palms.

Fogarty came forward with a spring in his step. Rows of fire from various points on the stage were summoned at the slash of his sword. The blazing columns blasted dry heat that enveloped the theater. The flames reflected in his jaw brought the apparatus to life. The extreme grin curled and flexed into ghostly expressions.

The man-beasts scampered backward while hissing at the fireworks. Fogarty spun in glory as the hostages were released, and the audience roared with approval.

Lenora couldn't grasp the message. Surely there was a story playing out before her, but it didn't make sense. Everything she had seen was some variation of appalling.

The finale culminated with an elaborate display. Dancing and singing spiked with more vibrant fireworks. The audience below rebounded from their fright. The fainting women revived, the men cheered, but the jubilation couldn't erase the twisted display from moments earlier in Lenora's eyes. The image of the tattooed man's stretched skin remained burned in her mind's eye.

Fogarty twirled his hat as he gave his final bow. The applause was deafening. The jaw puffed tiny clouds behind each ear as he wound the grin to its highest setting—the grin of a wolf as it savored the victory of the kill. *Was this man capable of murder?* In that moment, she was certain he could kill. *Could, but had he?* The taste of blood flooded her mouth, and she released her lip. In the crowded theater, Fogarty stared only at her.

THREE

As the audience drifted to the exit, Lenora nursed her lip, licking the tear until the iron taste ceased. Fogarty hadn't specified where they would talk or how they would meet after the show. She could have left the box and searched the grand lobby; the glistening chandelier would be a welcome sight in lieu of the empty stage.

However, the residue of the macabre performance clung to her, trapping her in the seat. The private box tightened. The twisted circus displays ran through her head in a repetitive loop. Such heinous scenes, and she was fairly certain whose imagination had hatched them.

No matter how she tried, she found no artistic value in the culmination of strange acts. The best ones relied on tired old clichés of entertainment. The worst, well, those were purely contrived to shock and disgust. What manner of business would her father have with a man who delighted in such bizarre displays?

Rapid thumping noises startled her from her thoughts and her seat. Grunts and the slam of a body hitting the floor followed. The jolt allowed her to break free from the confines of her box. She peeked out from the curtain.

One of the wax-skinned men lay on the carpet. A second usher corralled a well-dressed patron in the far corner of the hall with arms wide to block him in as if confronting a bucking beast in a suit.

Eccentric show aside, this sort of aggression was a shock. Intimidating the audience from the stage could be construed as theater, if only loosely. Chasing them into a corner crossed over from entertainment to brutality. Lenora rushed into the hall spiked with pure adrenaline.

"What are you doing?" she demanded, pulling the spread arm of the wax man back.

She only got a glimpse, a brief flash of the patron trapped against the wall, but that single image bludgeoned her. Rumpled shirt, the shine of perspiration over his features, and hair dangled over his forehead like withered vines. His eyes—wild. Pupils dilated and almost quivering as if the darkness within was trying to break from his soul and spill out.

He moved too quickly for her to react, ramming full force between her and the wax usher's arm to break between them. She felt the gust of air as she was pushed aside. The world turned, spun, and she met the wall then the floor. She hit hard. The blunt pain of impact stunned her as she curled into a fetal position.

The man is the aggressor—the guest—and I naively rushed in to save him.

The sounds of a chaotic shuffle battered the hallway. Screams and incoherent wails. She could feel reverberations through the floor as the wax men tackled the wild guest to the carpet.

Several more of Fogarty's wax men joined the struggle and restrained the screeching man as he rampaged against them. For a split second, his face came into view, pale and crazed. Then they dragged him away.

Pain flooded over her, a heated ache on the side that had smacked the floor. She trembled. That man's eyes—the pure malevolence in them. It was unnatural.

"Do you require a doctor, madame?" the tallest wax man inquired as he pulled out a handkerchief.

The wild man's voice drifted from the stairwell in the far corner. He was on the floor beneath her. They had probably sedated him or secured him in some locked off space, but that knowledge didn't help to calm her. She had been so assured of what was happening, and placed herself squarely in danger on account of that certainty.

"I'm... no, I think I'm alright." She used the wall for support as she managed to stand. "But that man?"

"Agitated Delirium," the wax man said in a flat tone.

The wax man thrust the handkerchief toward her. She refused it. Dr. Brechin had told her the truth; the epidemic was now claiming the privileged as well as the common. Not even the sparkling light of the chandelier could keep the shadows at bay. Nowhere was safe.

The wax man offered the handkerchief again. "But you're bleeding."

"Bleeding?" A thick stroke of vermillion painted the wall.

Had there been a knife? A hat pin? Something sharp amidst the pressure and panic? Blood on her hand. Blood on the lacework of her dress. Bile rose to the back of her throat. The golden wallpaper swirled around her, seized her, snared her in its dizzying weave until she stumbled. Scintillas of flashing lights speckled her vision while the edges of the world frayed dark.

Fogarty muscled his way through the ushers. With an elaborate swing of his arm, he took her hand and flipped it palm up, exposing her wrist. The tubing remained in place, but ribbons of blood poured out around it.

"Aqua Peritia cuffs." Fogarty dug into his pocket. "Such devices are not the glamorous trinkets they are presented to be. They are often downright dangerous."

He wrapped the wound with his red handkerchief. Her blood soaked through it, turning the cloth deeply dark.

She stammered a small *thank you*.

"Always joyful to be of service. Come, we shall care for this injury in my office." He turned to the wax men. "Fetch medical supplies and be quick about it."

Fogarty wrapped his arm around her middle and led her down the hall. A cruel bit of fate, to be so weak in a moment when she needed to be strong—vulnerable in the grasp of a one who might be her enemy.

Birdy rounded the corner, still wearing the slinky costume from her web act. She set one hand on her sparkling hip.

"Weak stomach? Just a bit of blood. Nothing to make such a fuss over." Her high-pitched voice carried a hint of an accent Lenora couldn't place.

"Problems?" Fogarty's eyes went sharp, but his smile remained in place.

"The others are asking if you're coming for the after-show nightcap. Didn't know you had..." she shifted her gaze to Lenora, "company."

"Alas, I have business to attend to. Proceed with the festivities without me. However, I believe introductions are in order. My dear." He lifted Lenora to a straighter posture. "May I present Miss Mary Magpie, informally known as Birdy, performer extraordinaire. Birdy, this is Miss Leahill, the daughter of the distinguished Samuel Leahill." A spurt of steam from his jaw matched with a crisp gear click.

Mary dropped the arm from her hip and adjusted her stance to a more subdued posture. "I… My apologies, Miss Leahill. It's an honor." The tone of her voice tapered down to a squeak.

"Charmed," Lenora managed to say through deep breaths.

"Splendid." Fogarty escorted her forward. "Now, let's tend to your wound, shall we?"

Mary's head sank as they passed. Even winded and frazzled, Lenora noted Magpie slightly twitched under Fogarty's stare. Then she slunk off.

Fogarty's office occupied most of the top floor of Cardend. Likely it had once been a storeroom of some sort, she guessed, based on the lack of windows and low ceiling. Rugs and wallpaper lengthened the room with rich purples. She could fall into that deep purple, but the glittering gold accents gleaming throughout grounded her. Ornately framed portrait paintings of past monarchs occupied each wall. Lush furnishings, rich in fine details, filled the room in a perfect balance between cluttered and vacant. At least six globes placed throughout the office spun at varying speeds. The rhythm of their gears, marching and precise, permeated the room.

Medical instruments and supplies were laid out on a long center table next to an elaborate appetizer spread. At the far end, a glass water jug with a brass spout shaped like a fleur-de-lis shimmered as wax men poured pitchers of clear water into it.

Fogarty led her to the couch nearest the table.

"A strong set of basic first aid knowledge is necessary when running a theater. Believe it or not, we do have mishaps on occasion." He winked as he pulled the handkerchief off. The stitched usher from the entrance popped into her head. "Ah, not ripped. Probably forced loose enough to bleed. Count yourself lucky, my dear. There are far worse atrocities these little follies are capable of."

He cleaned the cuff with swift, graceful movements. No gloves. Obviously, blood didn't have the same nauseating effect on him as it did on her. His forehead wrinkled, brows furrowed but the unnerving smile still played upon his faux lips.

"May I request your honest thoughts on our show? We are proud of each performance, but we're always striving to improve. Were you entertained?"

"It was…" She looked away from the scarlet stained cloth to keep her head cool. She would learn nothing if she showed vulnerability. "Spectacular. I've never seen anything even close to it."

"Spectacular?" The laugh was almost as mechanical as the mouth it came from. "The Sublime Spectacle was spectacular? I have titled it well then."

As he wrapped a bandage around her wrist, her stomach began to settle. His earlier comments about her cuff sharpened now that she no longer fought nausea. So like Dr. Brechin in how distrusting he sounded of the devices. *Just like Father.* The fact all three of them were of the same mind was not lost on her.

She couldn't stop herself from asking, "You don't approve of Aqua Peritia?"

"Approve? What an interesting choice of words. No, I suppose I don't *approve* of them, or most of the Council's infernal devices. Such things are seldom properly tested as they were under the monarchy." He finished the crisscross wrap and tied off the bandage. "All tended to. I would advise you keep it bandaged for at least a few hours."

Wax men scooped up the supplies in a half daze. Their quick, controlled movements in gathering up the equipment clashed with their blank, listless expressions. Sleepwalkers whose bodies knew the work, even if the rest of them drifted somewhere beyond the room.

A puff of steam from his jaw drew her out of her observations.

"Hors d'oeuvres?"

"No, thank you."

"A drink, perhaps?"

He snapped his fingers before she could answer, and the wax men began adding small amounts of deep green liquor in two glasses. Balancing a slotted spoon with a sugar cube on each rim, they twisted the spout of a jug drizzling water into the drink below. The liquid whisked into a milky cloud in the process. Lenora repositioned herself on the couch for a better view. The reaction of the liquor to the sugar water fascinated, like watching fertile green earth blossom into ivory fog.

"Ah, the louche is gorgeous, is it not? The fée verte is renowned for its ability to transform." He handed her a glass.

"Absinthe? Isn't this forbidden?"

"I prefer to think of it as the Council doesn't approve of the drink, primarily because they don't own the distilleries that produce it. They don't approve of my choice of refreshment. I don't approve of their methods." He sipped his glass.

Such casual disregard for the Council. She had never seen someone so openly criticize the ruling party.

"But their methods have brought us advancements." She cursed herself as soon as the words slipped out. It wasn't a debate; the point was to get him to open up.

His voice went sharp. "Like the lovely ashfall? There are many that would forgo the fruits of industry to live once more under a blue sky."

"But now women can work—"

"And thank the Lord you aren't forced into that predicament. Women toiling beside the men that should care for them? Shameful."

Her grip on the glass tightened. She couldn't tell if it was his overt disregard at the capabilities of women in labor or the blatant reference to the forbidden faith's god that irked her more. Obviously, Fogarty was intent on pushing Elsothe back instead of closer to the Age of Awareness.

Then again, she was beginning to get the impression Canimere wasn't nearly as progressed as she thought.

Lenora swirled the ethereal beverage in her glass slowly to cover her silence. He watched with an intensity that crept over her, pulling goosebumps from her skin. Straightening herself she took a solid sip. Anise and herbal notes hit almost too harshly until the sweet tones rose through to comfort the palate—the alcoholic burn stronger than wine, but a flavor more complex than her father's gin.

"It's lovely."

The smile cranked up two notches. "I knew you would find it so. Your father was quite taken with absinthe as well. Our business meeting tradition," he lifted the glass, "a glass for each of us.

"On that note, let us delve into business. Why don't you commence by informing me about what you already know of the venture?" He rose. "Then I can elaborate up to the present state."

Fogarty impressed as he towered over her. Solid in his stance, likely somewhere in his late thirties with substantial bulk. Black hair complemented his surprisingly pale blue irises. Without the fanciful costume, she could easily imagine him a commanding military officer. Perhaps that was how he lost half of his face. She took another drink, slowly and deliberately, savoring the earthiness of it. What business would her father have with such a man?

"Well, Father mentioned…" She clutched the glass. Those that knew her father called him a philanthropist, an intellectual. "Charity. A charity event?" It came out more like a question than she wanted it to.

He leaned over her, sizing her up anew.

Lenora took another deep gulp from her glass to shield herself from him. "Or perhaps that was another associate. I'm afraid I only recently begun to take note of such things. Father engaged in so many projects."

He tossed his top hat on the stand in the corner without so much as a glance. It glided perfectly to the post.

"Yes," he said slowly as he placed his pinky to graze a spinning globe. He let the world rotate around his finger a few times. "A charity event. That's precisely it. A performance to raise funds to combat the spread of diseases, such as the Plague and Agitated Delirium." His speech built up speed in a burst of energy. He spun around to face her, the human part of his face alight. "A charity event so extraordinary as to draw an audience not only in Canimere, but the whole of Elsothe. Perhaps even attracting aristocracy from Laveri and The Isles of Dunfan. Surely, you can see all the potential good we can accomplish with such an event?"

His sudden exuberance unbalanced her. The room became charged and yet flat, like a painting in motion. A wax man collected her glass. As he began the refilling process, she realized she had completely emptied it.

"Now…" His jaw whistled gently, an intermittent piping to accompany the omnipresent rhythmic march. "The performance itself, your father entrusted to me. That was my role. His was to discover where best to put the collected funds to use. You are no doubt aware the Council's scientists and doctors would be of little assistance, if the money filtered down to them at all. No, it is imperative the donations stay in the private sector."

He paced over the darkest rug. Another full glass appeared in her hand. It all felt so fast. She had come to find a means to refute or confirm rumors. She could feel that purpose drifting from her, like specks of sand being thrown off the runaway train of Fogarty's magnetism.

"Your father's part was to find that private sector." He stopped and bounced down next to her. She sipped the glass to lower the seesawing liquid threatening to overflow. "He was well acquainted with a doctor. An independent doctor not affiliated with the Council. He felt certain of the man's brilliance, claimed he was a wonder in both medicine and mechanics. Your father assured me this doctor would inform us on the best routes for our charitable contributions."

The globes seemed to spin faster as the office grew flatter and hazy. The stillness and motion of the room hit contradictory, as if reality faltered. She could feel the blood course through her double time.

"If you deliver me this doctor, our venture can take flight. A lady such as yourself need not be concerned with any of the bothersome details beyond that. I will tend to all else." His shining nose was inches from hers, close enough for her to smell the oiled gears in his face.

"Deliver?"

"Alas, I do not recall his name from when your father mentioned it before. We were in the midst of arranging a meeting when…" He bowed his head slightly. "All I require is his name. You need not bother yourself with attending or scheduling the meeting. Just the name, my dear, and I will see to the rest."

There was clearly only one doctor who would fit Fogarty's description, but his name caught in her chest. Dr. Brechin had many shortcomings, but none that suggested he was dangerous. Brechin was uncouth. Fogarty seemed polished to the point of being slick. *And he could be a murderer*, the thought surfaced against her reluctance to hear it. She didn't make a choice so much as stepped aside and let her instinct take to helm.

"I—I haven't met any doctors." Lenora put her glass down.

Fogarty's frame tensed.

"But I'm still going through all the accounts and investments. I will look," she added.

"It's important. Do better than look." A menacing note rang clear in his tone.

She recoiled farther down the couch. She knew a threat when she heard one. The bullies at Glenn Haven weren't subtle; neither was the ringleader. Nausea reemerged in her stomach. As much as she hated to admit it, there was a seed of truth to some of the rumors. Her father had been dealing with this dreadful man—and she highly doubted their interactions were for any sort of charity.

Perhaps her father's memory wouldn't leave because a part of her always suspected he wasn't the glorified man he presented himself to be.

Fogarty's hand tensed around his absinthe. With a sudden squeeze, the glass shattered in his grip. The lovely, milky liquid gushed between his fingers.

"Forgive me." He shook his hand free of shards. "I forget my strength when I'm excited."

FOUR

The Wilthiem rumbled over the wooden planks of Cyngandor Bridge. Lenora cringed. Staked between the extensive grounds of Foxton Manor and the abysmal city, Dusang Forest cut into the land like a dam to keep any Canimere residue from spilling into the countryside. The red beeches of the forest tended to overgrow, reaching out to those who traveled by with their leafy claws. Horrid trees that sprouted leaves in various shades of red. A canopy of blood and rust and poison—for poison, Lenora reasoned, would be a bold purplish red. To the local villagers that dotted the outskirts of Canimere, Dusang was a hunting ground. To Lenora, the place was the sanctuary of witches and unearthly spirits. A haunted wood. The place to dump a body where the pale flesh would blend in with the white bark.

In the dark hours between midnight and the first warmth of dawn, the forest felt unrestrained—at the peak of its evil power. It didn't help she still lingered a touch in the absinthe haze. She desperately needed sleep after the miserable night at Fogarty's circus. Stories from old books of criminal violence and back-alley bargains went rancid in the spin of alcohol. She had believed those harsh elements to be expired in the coming Age of Awareness. Distressing to find a single trip through Pitchdrift proved her naively optimistic. There was much wrongdoing still in Canimere, and the ringleader had some part in it. She didn't know yet which part he played.

The dirt roads were well worn but new dips and grooves developed after each rain. Jacob took the route with care, perhaps slower than the previous drivers but without the jarring and knocking.

He twisted back to glance at her as he spoke. "This feels dangerous."

"Hmmm? Oh, Dusang always feels that way." She couldn't pry herself from the window. The Wilthiem's lights created shadows stretching out from the foliage; macabre, sharp reflections of bushes and the thick of blood trees saturated the road.

"No, I mean the doctor fella and then the Circus in Pitchdrift. Shady feeling, ain't it?" Jacob said.

"It's been a long night. I'd rather not talk about it."

Jacob should know by now to drive through Dusang in silence. She preferred to sneak through the forest with eyes and ears open, especially now that she sensed her father had enemies. Each quiver of red leaves, each rapid shift in the Wilthiem's lights, she mentally tallied. Nothing is able to ambush one who carefully considered the changes around them. She was silently grateful her father had rarely taken her into Canimere. Before his death, she could count on one hand the number of treks through cursed Dusang after dark.

The words he spoke on that last trip forever echoed in her memory, coming to her consciousness whenever she crossed into the woods. *Not another word on spirits or monsters. I will not have my daughter known as some loon. The Leahills have always been strong of mind, don't make them doubt us. Save your fear for the true evils of the world.* How easily he branded her as mad the instant she didn't perceive the world as he did still stung.

Dusang was teeming with vile, hidden things; no matter what her father had said to the contrary.

Jacob pulled out a knob and twisted it. The lamps positioned on the exterior of the carriage stuttered more intense, the light expanding farther from the carriage, though they remained a soft yellow wash over the road. The glow around the carriage matched thick jaundiced billows of steam clouding behind them. They were lone travelers swatting away predators with weak lamps. Would the wolf from Claire's storybook find them as appetizing prey as Red Riding Hood? The Wilthiem nothing more to the beast than a metal basket of ripe treats?

"And the inside lights, Jacob, please."

Another knob turned and the interior lamps flickered to life, the illumination subdued at first then pitched brighter. An increasing buzz matched the expanding light. She couldn't see the outside. Her window only reflected the brilliant green interior. Unease sharpened to alarm. She couldn't see the shadows, the dark shapes among the vermillion leaves. The lamps hit a blinding crescendo before blinking out with a pop. Lenora yelped.

"Miss? You alright?"

"Just a surprise, is all." Not only a surprise, but to speak of her fear would give it power.

"A wire, maybe the oscillator's jammed. Foreign temperamental heap. Temperature in the tanks looks good." Jacob slowed the carriage. Loose dirt crackled beneath the wheels until they stopped. "Only be a moment, Miss."

Dusang was no longer chasing Lenora—it held the vehicle firmly in the swelling dark. The cabin felt as if it shrunk. A little box waiting like a gift for a child-munching witch. The thin walls both imprisoned her and separated her from the evil of the wilderness. She couldn't shake the growing tightness.

Jacob lit a small gas lantern previously stashed under his seat. Uncertain light, it only managed to darken the area beyond the firelight's reach. He pulled down a plank from the wall of the cabin and cast the lantern near it.

"Hmmmm…" He rummaged inside the wall.

The golden glow of the outside lights snapped out. Now the shadows had full access to the Wilthiem.

"Sorry, sorry. Almost have it," Jacob said as he knocked around inside the exposed mechanics.

Lenora swallowed her panic. *It will be remedied quickly*, she told herself. *There is nothing lurking behind the branches. No vile snarling creatures circling the immobile carriage.*

"Miss, I've been thinking about what my pa says." Jacob dug further into the wall.

A hiss echoed from the trees. Scraping in the thick dark. She rubbed her throat and collarbone begging the vein there to soften its pounding. *Save your fear for the true evils…*

"What of the things your pa says?" she blurted out.

"My pa says I have to be more than a driver. If I take my boss—errr Miss, somewhere, I'm responsible. My job is to get you places and be sure to get you back. That means I should keep an eye open and be smart on the goings on. I've got to be ready to make you safe, see?" After a click from the wall, all the lights flicked on for a second then were gone.

"I see."

She flattened her palm on the cold window to further brace the carriage from the night. Her cuff tapped the glass and the laceration pulsed with pain. She concentrated on the sensation, jagged and hot. Better to feel the physical than to confront the sorcery weaving through the pale trees like ethereal eels.

"So, I've been thinking, the best way to keep you safe is to know what's happening so I can keep you clear of anything that could be a problem."

Branches blew outstretched towards her window like spears coated in the carnage of battle. A single scarlet leaf grazed the pane as if attempting to pierce through the glass and touch the tip of her finger. She shuddered and withdrew her hand. The woods were trying to speak to her.

She held her breath to listen. A faint hum and then a muffled bang.

"Did you hear that?" Lenora whispered.

Jacob froze, tilting his ear to the window. "No. Wind probably." He returned to his tinkering. "Pitchdrift's not a good place for anybody. And so, with the rumors and visiting the circus, it seems only right I know a little more about things. You know, what's going on. To keep you safe and all."

She had heard something; she was sure of it. Something approached, crashing through vegetation towards the road. She could hear the crunch of twigs being trampled.

The lamps came on. The abrupt change in brightness startled more than relieved her.

"Ah ha. A pinch between the—"

The visitor was close. Traveling fast over the moist forest floor. She could smell death on his breath. Jaws full of teeth snapped in their direction. The beast, as it had always been in her nightmares, clawed through the brush in its path towards the lighted box.

"Get the carriage moving," Lenora demanded.

Jacob flinched at her tone then jumped over to the driver's seat. He put his hand on the lever but hesitated to pull it. "So, you will let me know what's happening?"

"There's no need for that. I'm fine." She readied her footing to bolt out of the door and flee from the creature of Dusang.

It picked up speed, racing through the beeches to the manic tempo of her heartbeat.

Jacob swung back and ducked over the seat to face her instead of steering them forward. Instead of driving them to safety. "Only the basics, so I'm prepared."

The humming again but this time louder. Movement in the brush across from her window.

"Yes, yes. Just go," she shrieked.

The bushes parted, and it leapt out onto the road. Erratic galloping. Twisted horns poised to ram anything in its way. Then a thunderous bang and a flash from the dense cropping of beeches. Struck in the throat, the animal instantly flung to the ground within the bright circles of the Wilthiem's headlights. Hooves still running as the creature lay on its side, blood spurting from neck and mouth.

"A deer," she muttered in shock.

Two figures emerged from the forest. Their rural clothes caked thick with dirt. Boys on the cusp of manhood, likely from one of the villages. They hollered with enthusiasm at the downed prey.

"Sorry, mister. We ain't trying to get in your way none," the taller one yelled at the carriage.

"You got 'em good." The smaller one of the pair slapped his companion's shoulder. "Mama gonna be so happy. We got meat."

The thin duo hunched over their kill with gleeful chuckles. Their shirts bloomed out around them like loose sails. Despite their famished appearance, they each wore a Peritia cuff, though rudimentary models. The Age of Awareness was inclusive, welcoming all to its fold—even the common. They had access to the vast collection of printed human knowledge with a simple injection but apparently not basic nourishment. A small shooting pain rushed up her arm from her cuff's tubing.

The one visible black eye of the animal lost the glossy sheen of life and faded to a murky stone. Vitality leaked from the deer, and Lenora realized her father banning her from hunts was a blessing in disguise. The limp corpse settled into the grooves of the road. She gave her handkerchief three quick pulls through her fingers.

As horrid as the sight might be, she was far more concerned with what the taller boy carried. The rifle wasn't the simple type of weapon country folk owned. This rifle had multiple barrels that looked to have a variety of ammunition. Gauges displaying pressure and gas levels protruded from the side of the weapon. The boy could barely lift the gun;

it was a wonder he had managed to fire it. What bothered her most was that the rifle was familiar, and that familiarity made her nervous.

"An Enforcer's rifle," Jacob explained, as if reading her mind. "How did they get one of those?"

He was right, it was the same giant mass each Enforcer carried slung over his shoulder.

Jacob inched the carriage forward, steering around the boys and their kill.

The forest responded with leaves rustling and shaking.

Two Enforcers erupted from the jostling brush. They lunged, one with his rifle at the ready, the other brandishing a long sword directly at the village boys.

Dusang became all movement. Wind? *Applause*—the forest whipped around, eager to witness what the spilled blood had wrought.

The emancipated boys fell to their knees, pale in the glow of the rear lanterns.

With outstretched arms, they offered the rifle. "We're sorry, sirs," the taller shouted as the Enforcer gripping the sword snatched the weapon up.

The Enforcers' masks hung over the boys, violent bursts of smoke from several ports on the suit. They forced the boys to their feet by their collars. The Wilthiem whistled with steam as Jacob pulled levers and pushed buttons. The Enforcers tilted their masks at the carriage creeping away before pushing the boys toward the darkening clutches of Dusang.

Lenora watched, transfixed, nose nearly pressed against the back window. She couldn't process the display. Restless dread clogged her thoughts.

The smaller one tried to run, crying out when the Enforcer grabbed him by the arm and dragged him into the thick.

She snapped to her senses and wrestled with the thoughts flooding in. The scene was horribly wrong. The villages were back along the road, yet the Enforcers headed into the heart of the forest. They were only boys, the gun returned. Surely a warning would have sufficed. Surely the Council would instruct their forces to be fair and just.

"Wait, Jacob. Go back."

Jacob let off the accelerator. The Wilthiem rolled a few yards, hitting every dent in the road. Both hands tightly curled on the levers, his face a shade lighter.

Before he cranked the controls into reverse, the strange hum slashed through the quiet. The noise doubled.

Lenora went hollow. She shuffled around in her seat, searching for shapes in the tenebrous forest.

One bang.

Some soft place inside her shattered.

A second bang.

Jacob flung the Wilthiem forward at full power. She couldn't see the Enforcers and their captives in the night. *This isn't right.* Oppression and cruelty were replaced with enlightenment, that was the intent of the Age of Awareness, yet the shocking silence now engulfing Dusang spoke otherwise.

The trees lined the road like bare bones. A gust of wind ruffled the forest into a stream of flowing crimson. The claws of leaves gave her a last swipe as they passed. Dusang kept the ones it claimed buried in the scarlet.

FIVE

Lenora's sinuses throbbed, and her head pounded. The initial morning after The Sublime Spectacle, she had discounted her symptoms as merely the result of her indulgence in absinthe. However, the headache persisted all through that day and into the next.

Her chambers provided little relief. The flouncy draperies with their tired ribbon bows sagged with age. The wallpaper, featuring wide-eyed sheep, glared at her with faded faces from years in the sun of an open windows. The worn-out remnants of childhood, of the quiet little girl father had wanted her to be. These walls had been her grand prison in those early years before Glenn Haven Academy. Now they felt small, worn, but no less restrictive.

The housekeeper, Claire, brought pitchers of cool water, pots of strong tea, and pastries throughout the day. The hefty servant lugged the trays up to the chambers diligently, but Lenora barely touched anything on them other than water.

Claire slammed the tray down, pleased when it caused Lenora to jump. Either Claire intended to irritate her into limiting alcohol indulgence or was merely enjoying a bit of revenge for all the childhood pranks Lenora had pulled.

"Here are those Aqua vials you requested." Claire tossed them on the tray with a clank. "And a special Council decree," she added as she deposited the Council's vial into Lenora's lap where it rolled into the folds of the blanket.

The old housekeeper strode out without waiting for a reply, which was oddly soothing for Lenora. With all that had changed after her father's passing, at least Claire remained as blunt as ever.

The Council's decree shone a brilliant blue against her lackluster beige bedding. She'd read official declarations before but never injected one. Perhaps this little vial would give her a clearer idea of the Council. Far too long had they been a vague leadership, more akin to an abstract concept than real living people.

The injection disturbed her. The Council remained some omnipresent shadow as the glory of Elsothe's industrial victory struck her full force. Each masterfully executed marvel dazzled and purred, from the newest lines of steam carriages to the Jornstine Airship fleet down to the latest shoe polishing contraptions. Rows and rows of mechanical achievements on the pristine streets of Canimere. Shining, smiling faces on pedestrians. A disturbing contrast to the real city forever under the onslaught of soot.

The imagery shifted—rickety farmhouses, acres of brittle crops, and starving children. A faith house growing giant in the background, spreading a smell far more repulsive than the factories' smoke, like rotten eggs. Holding her nose did nothing, as the stench seemed to invade through her pores. No words accompanied the experience, yet she *knew* the message.

The old faiths led us to ruin. Those that continue to worship them will receive no mercy.

As with the paper decrees, it ended with the motto, *To inject is to know, and to know is to be wise, and to be wise is to contribute to the Age of Awareness.*

Lenora opened her eyes. A harsh warning, but at least one that wasn't aimed at her. She had no interest in religion. It only perpetuated oppressive beliefs. Everyone knew that, didn't they?

She hid the empty decree in her beside drawer as if she could simply put away the way it had unsettled her by removing the evidence. The feeling persisted, so she fidgeted with the remaining shimmering vials. She rolled them next to the water glass letting the light stream through the water and play with the vibrant Aqua Peritia.

Pretty, little, colored bottles with such bleak contents.

Her experiences with both Dr. Brechin and Fogarty made it clear she lacked insight into much of her father's work. It was possible Glenn Haven failed to properly prepare her for the realities of Elsothe's politics as well. At this point, Lenora conceded anything was possible. If the highly respected Mr. Leahill had dealings with the likes of Fogarty, then the rats of Alker Square sang opera during a full moon, as the fable claimed. She had to dig deeper if she was to manage any advancements for the good of the country.

She grabbed a vial at random and set it in her cuff.

This one was technical in nature. How fireworks are constructed and discharged, as well as the mechanics of basic launch systems, but the injection baffled her. It was as if all the technicalities were being transcribed in the Aqua from a different language, the information present, yet foreign. This chemical combined with that. A cog turning lining up with other parts with names she had never heard of. She couldn't grasp a single concept before the imagery changed to the next topic.

Disappointment flooded her. Just like the other injections, she was left with a fleeting gist of the material and a vague sense of dread. All of humanity's knowledge might be accessible to her, but that didn't mean she could master any of it. The innocent sheep seemed to cast disapproving stares at her from the wallpaper, just like father would.

She snatched up the next vial, injecting it without hesitation. This golden vial contained the official history of the Council. She found it vague and blatantly biased. In a meandering flood, she ran through all fifteen members in short biographies. Names, birthdates, notable family, the inventions or businesses that had propelled them to Council member in detail—but nothing about how the Council functioned or how it came to be. No faces, just facts blared before her as she swam through the injection.

So much that she expected to be explained had been omitted. She couldn't recall a time when the Council hadn't led Elsothe; they had replaced the monarchy before she was born. How? What sort of government structure did they have in place? Fogarty's open yet casual dismissal of their worth, the uncanny feeling of the decree injection, and now this skim biographical take made her pause. Perhaps she was missing something. Perhaps there was more to the Council than she had assumed.

Newspaper vials she discovered were all a light rose hue, which she reasoned was probably because they were a mix of white lies and warnings. The only mentions of the Council in the news were in celebration of their greatness or referencing something they accomplished. As for Agitated Delirium, she only found the epidemic mentioned in local hygiene notices and bits praising the Council for their progress toward containing and curing the illness.

The Aqua Peritias proved to be a waste of the day, as well as the cause of further irritation of the tubing puncture on her wrist. She left the remaining vials untouched on her nightstand.

The pounding in her head became excruciating. Too many sensations, too rapidly flashing upon her conscious mind. A jumble of conflicting chaos where she assumed all was settled and stable. She had never been a fan of Burton's Famous Cure-All Elixir, but she was in too much pain to function without relief. It tasted like muddy gin blended with ginger and mint. Revolting, but the tincture did its job. Her head grew dull, if not slightly swimmy, after a dose.

With the headache muffled, she decided she had had enough of the warden sheep and childhood trappings. Other rooms in the house offered new avenues of research.

Her father's private library had been forbidden to her for as long as she could remember. The book-lined walls stretched the length of the west wing, easily dwarfing her private quarters upstairs. Books filled the walls up to the ceiling. Two back-to-back bookcases were planted in the center making a long 'U' shape that returned to the desk by the door. Emptied, the room could have suited as a grand ballroom, but her father never entertained. The electric lighting only covered half the space, leaving the depths at the back of the library veiled in shadow. She kept her search in the light.

She took great delight in rummaging through the library, feeling as if she was almost taunting her father's memory. Swinging from the rolling ladder as she went through the shelves of books, she savored the delicious smell the old volumes gave off. A soft vanilla-like scent, not too sweet yet perfectly aged. The books struck on an array of unrelated topics, bouncing from the forbidden spiritual to business relations to the ills of society to afflictions of the mind.

Lenora started with a small volume titled *17 Cases of Delirium, Agitated: Grunhiver Asylum* by J. H. Peech. Plopping down into her father's chair, feet propped on the desk, she pulled out one of the fancy cigars from his cedar box. She dare not light the thing, but the taste of the oily tobacco wrapper was exhilarating. She was in charge now.

"Cancel all of my engagements. I'm indisposed today," she announced to the empty space, cigar hanging off to the side of her mouth.

Lenora flipped through the book. Less efficient to skim over each page than to inject, but she enjoyed that she could peruse the information at her leisure. Seventeen case studies, all residents from the Pitchdrift area, ages ranged from fourteen to thirty-seven. All had intricate delusionary issues including whole scenarios.

A dull ache raced across her temple. *Another dose of Burton's Elixir, just in case.*

The studies focused on the nature of the hallucinations. Much of the text detailed the particular quirks of each patient: broken or erratic speech patterns documented, abnormal behaviors described, what they drew with chalk—if they managed to draw at all—how they reacted to loud sounds or being splashed with water.

"That wasn't much help," she mumbled through the cigar in her teeth and tossed the book aside.

A figure darted into the shadowed recesses of the library. Lenora spat out the cigar, nearly toppling out of the chair with the start. She had barely caught a glimpse of it in her peripheral but it had seemed so real, so solid. His deep brown jacket, glossy hair slicked back—her father.

She made herself still and quiet. Only the silence of peaceful books wafted from the shelves. Still…

She had been blatantly disobeying, reveling in this place he kept so private. It wouldn't be a stretch for him to walk these spaces. She felt his presence follow her from room to room, from Foxton to the city. Now, he had materialized—actually roaming the library right in front of her. Was it such a crazy thought that the dead would linger if their end was murder?

Or I have an exceptional imagination enhanced with a potent elixir.

She scanned the darkened 'U' of the library again, finding nothing but her own rapid breathing.

A booming knock came from the door. She shrieked. Another heavy rapping.

She gathered herself as best she could, shaking off the image she had surely not seen. "Enter."

Jacob stepped in, hat in hand.

"Ah, Jacob. Come in. Do you need more tools or parts?"

"No but thank you. Just reminding you it's Tuesday, Miss."

"Tuesday?"

"Meeting with Dr. Brechin, Tuesday late in the day." He puffed up with pride. "I remembered."

"Oh, so it is." She scrambled out of the chair.

If a man's office was a reflection of his character, then Dr. Elliot Rothman Brechin was a sloppy jumble of science, engineering, and the morose. Piles of loose paper stacked high with folders and bound books. Mechanical parts were tossed together on a side table. A slight hint of mildew hung in the air, barely noticeable under the powerful floral yet smoky scent she assumed was his cologne. The mess Lenora expected of Brechin; the bizarre décor she did not.

Full skeletons of a cat and a large bird stood displayed in glass cases. Several human skulls littered his desk. Covered in a layer of dust, a battle scene constructed of taxidermied mice with swords and boots sat by the window. The paintings mixed among his awards and accomplishments were crafted to inspire anxiety and disgust. Floating apparitions hovered above a surgery; the doctors intently worked in the open cavity of the patient, unaware of the spirits' laughter. Death, in his tattered robes, reached out of a canvas with snow-white, bony fingers. Cannibals feasted on the pulp of an open skull, while the victim's eyes rolled back in a silent wail.

The wall behind his desk was covered with the largest of the artwork: a horse and rider both stripped of their flesh galloping through a field of poppies. Strangely portrayed in a manner both implying movement yet remaining awkwardly stiff. Lenora felt the hair on her arms rise. The figures watched her. She couldn't shake the feeling the artist purposely painted the empty sockets of the skulls so they could follow her around the room.

On her previous visit, Brechin had hidden his strange collection. This time, he displayed it brazenly.

"I must admit I find your decorations disturbing, Dr. Brechin," Lenora announced.

Brechin peered down through a mounted magnifying glass, screwing a tiny part on the lizard's foot. "That's precisely the point. One should surround themselves with the disturbing. How much work can one get done if they are too comfortable? And it's Elliot, if you please."

"That's ridiculous. One should be calm and comfortable when working." She flopped into a chair.

A cloud of dust puffed up from the cushion as she settled into it. She fanned the air in front of her face while suppressing a cough.

"Not at all. The best ideas are all born out of conflict and pressure. Fear, Miss Leahill—fear drives humankind forward." He twisted the iguana's claw in several directions. "There you are. Should be a firmer grip now."

"You're welcome to your opinion." She rubbed her temples.

"Headache?"

"I'm fine."

He gave her a lopsided smirk as he rose from the desk and crossed the room. His hands gently pressed down her neck, then her upper back and shoulders. She was too jolted by his sudden intrusion of her personal space to say anything.

"Ah, you hold your stress here." He massaged the area where her neck met her shoulders. "Which places pressure on your neck, compressing it. The result is a constant headache without the proper alignment and blood flow."

With one hand under her chin and the other at the base of her neck, he kinked her jaw swiftly up and to the right. At least three pops broke free. Then he reversed his hands and cracked the other side, one loud crunch that both hurt and relieved. The throbbing seeped away, replaced by a lightheaded sensation.

She rolled her head around in astonishment. "Impressive. Thank you."

"You're most welcome. I do my utmost to alleviate pain when I can. I suppose I wouldn't be in this profession otherwise." He slapped his hands together. "Well, now, you do have exceptional timing. We can probably squeeze in a light supper at the Golden Orchard before we head out. Business is always best tempered with a bit of pleasure, don't you agree?"

"Head out? You promised to reveal your findings on the epidemic."

"Precisely. As I've said before, I must show you; therefore, we shall travel to where there are things to be seen." He grabbed a thick coat and a full-face ash mask.

"That doesn't make sense."

"Of course, it does." Brechin tossed her a wide brimmed hat. "This will serve you better than that fancy flowered atrocity. Come, it will be a long night. Some dining is a prudent start."

Lenora twirled the hat around her fingers—not quite as elaborately as Fogarty, but it made a decent spin. "This had better be worth the trouble, Dr. Brechin."

He gave Harold a farewell pat. "Elliot, if you please."

Lenora had to credit Brechin; he wasn't boring company. They started with escargot and the story of how he once managed to wiggle free from becoming part of the Council's "undervalued" scientific staff. Being born the bastard son of an absent wealthy landowner and a seamstress, he stressed that was no easy task. Being free of the Council's restrictions allowed him more choice, but it also forced him to rely on benefactors to float his projects.

He then spoke of inventions and travel, much of which was funded by her father. He studied the people of Renth for their resistance to the harshest of winters. Then he visited the aging officers of Marwich, whom he perfected his mechanical limb replacements on. That earned him enough respect for an honorary rank as a Marwik military surgeon, first class, or so he claimed. As he recounted returning to Canimere, they finished off a cheese and fruit platter dessert.

"And there you have it. I've made myself transparent for you." He popped a grape in his mouth.

"Hardly, but you do entertain with such stories."

She sipped her water, torn between jealousness of his adventures and awe at his ability to thrive despite the odds being stacked against it. Even with her father's help, his circumstances were unique and inspiring. Though it was frustrating to know her father supported this man's dreams while being so obstinately set against his own daughter's similar pursuits.

The Golden Orchard had grown nearly vacant over the duration of their meal. Closing time had already come and gone. A lone waiter stood miserably at the front, checking every minute or so on the straggler tables.

"Where to now, Dr. Brechin?"

"It's— "

"Elliot," Lenora interjected to the doctor's delight. "Where are we going?"

He picked up his glass, swirling the contents as he murmured, "Pitchdrift."

From one of the most expensive restaurants in Canimere into its poorest district?

She flagged the waiter who rushed over to remove their dishes. After being assured they were content with their meal, he placed the check in front of Brechin, who poked at it as if it were some unnatural substance.

"Dangerous neighborhood. And exactly where in Pitchdrift?" Lenora prodded.

"I don't want to spoil the surprise." He pushed the bill over to her.

He maintained keeping the destination secret as they headed south towards Pitchdrift. Jacob grumbled insults under his breath at the helm after each direction Brechin declared.

"I can take the fastest way, if you would tell me where we're going," Jacob said through clenched teeth.

"No sense of adventure in either one of you. *Tsk tsk.* A right at this next corner, if you please."

The streets were serene at night—black ash against black sky with only small globes of light from streetlamps. Without people to confuse the eye, everything was pure in absolute dark. A blank stage. A bare canvas. Lenora enjoyed the potential more than what actually played out within the city.

"Would you indulge my curiosity, Miss Leahill?" Brechin glanced out the window. "Another right, my fine fellow."

The carriage rounded the corner sharply as Jacob had only a split second to react.

"I suppose you're going to ask me whatever it is anyways, so go ahead," she said.

"Why bother? You obviously aren't overly familiar with Delirium or its devastating effects. So, I can't imagine you are as enthralled with my results as, say, another doctor would be. Surely Samuel has many other accounts and business projects that are…" He reached for the right phrase, "less obtuse than mine. Not to mention my account is a drop in the bucket, monetarily. Why bother with me at all?"

"I don't understand what you're asking. I've been sorting through all the accounts."

"In two blocks make a right," Brechin directed Jacob then leaned forward. "What I mean is, if you are looking to garner the praise and admiration of high society, your attention should be elsewhere. Samuel had two law firms in town, a banking empire, and a highly prized fleet of merchant ships. One would assume you would be diligently overseeing those ventures. Yet the talk about the city is you're generally absent from the big Leahill businesses. Instead, you have taken the time to investigate my work. A lowly doctor's work, as it were. Why?"

Lenora glided her hand across her Peritia cuff, tracing the design. A fair question, but one she hadn't given much thought. It only made sense to focus on the big businesses. Perhaps she preferred the streets empty waiting for the day to start. A shred of hope that, to change Elsothe for the better, she could exist beyond boardrooms and paper trails. Or perhaps she was chasing her father's ghost, trying to illuminate the dark spaces he kept hidden and bring them light.

"I find lawyers and bankers to be rather dull company," she finally replied.

Brechin laughed, "Well then, I suppose I can't talk you out of this expedition, can I? A right here after the market, driver."

Jacob growled. "We've gone in a circle. Right back where we started."

"What a clever observation. You have quite the driver. Most would shy away from being so outspoken," Brechin quipped.

White knuckles steered the steam carriage through Canimere. Once they crossed the threshold into Pitchdrift, Jacob only tensed up further, his arms so tight the flesh bulged around his simple cuff.

They ventured deeper than Cardend Theater, to where shops boarded up display windows, and the only illumination came from the seedy taverns erected on every corner. Beneath sagging balconies or against leaning structures the homeless made crude shelters with bits of broken wood or cloth and heaps of ash formed into basic bricks. The residents carried extended canes or long sticks, poking at the mounds of obsidian filth in their path, many of them missing a hand. Each shadowed figure they passed stopped and watched the glowing Wilthiem puff down the road.

"Can't blame them. When you live in a soot-shack, I bet this carriage looks like pure gold." Brechin made a show of looking around the cabin. Down cushions. The rods adorned with brass leaves holding back the curtains. "There will be a safe carriage house, I assure you. A shame there isn't a safe place for everyone."

"You make it sound as if one should pity the thief and befriend the murderer."

She hoped the mention of murder would stir him to speak of his suspicions about her father's demise, but he shrugged nonchalantly.

"I figured as much. Samuel had a unique capability for understanding. I didn't expect you to have the same quality." He ruffled the curtain drawing her attention to the ghastly view of Pitchdrift.

Lenora crossed her arms. "Poverty I understand; it's a sad circumstance those of us in better positions should help ease."

Brechin's spidery fingers drummed on his knee. He raised one eyebrow. "So, you do intend to help them, then?"

"Of course I do." She let her irritation color her tone. "I'm contributing all my energies to the Age of Awareness. Once we reach the true ideal of the age, there will be balance. Such things as poverty will be banished to the past."

"Is that so?" Brechin snorted. "Even if you were able to bring about this special golden age single-handedly, do you really think there will be no scars? Wounds carry through generations."

"That doesn't mean crime can be forgiven."

"No? I daresay most crime of this sort is simply a symptom of poverty." Brechin directed Jacob to make another turn. "The truly criminal are those who commit crimes, not because of need, but out of greed. Injuring others to obtain wealth and power. Therefore, these people are not criminals, merely the product of their economy, don't you think?"

A rather bold perspective. The fact his argument was sound flustered her. *Are they truly criminals if that course is their only option to survive?* Furthermore, he was passionate and sincere, which threw her off balance. She had no rebuttal.

"I grow weary of your philosophical babble. Don't you have anything simple and wholesome to discuss?"

"Nothing is simple. As for wholesome…" He pointed out the window.

Three girls, with their skirts pulled up to expose one thigh, posed outside a tavern. None wore bloomers. They leaned on their canes to further accentuate their bare legs. Whistling drunkards pinched any visible bits of ash-smeared skin. The trio looked significantly younger than Lenora, lost girls in ragged dresses walking the street under the covering of filthy soot.

Lenora pulled her handkerchief between her fingers. "Point taken."

Brechin's destination was a brick beast amidst shivering shacks, a fortress against the noir snow and toxic wind. A solid cube that occupied most of the block with thin slits for windows dimly lit. Ivy had once scaled the giant, but now only the withered veins of the plant remained providing an ideal roost for soot. What resulted were onyx tentacles that groped the brick vessel, threatening to pull it below the rolling ash tide of Pitchdrift.

Lenora shifted uncomfortably in her seat. "What is this? Some sort of lodging? A hotel?"

"I suppose it is, in a way." Brechin chuckled.

"You can't possibly expect me to go into such a place," she snapped at him. Cardend had appeared unkempt from the outside and only skirted the district. This place was practically sinking in the heart of Pitchdrift.

"I don't like it, Miss. Ain't a proper place," Jacob piped in.

"Nonsense." Brechin waved him off. "I've met plenty of proper people at this establishment. Besides, this is only a home base of sorts. Of course, if the Leahill shipping offices are more to your liking, by all means—"

"Don't patronize me, Dr. Brechin."

"Elliot, if you please." He hopped to her side of the seating, reaching over her to retrieve his mask, his face less than a breath away from hers. "And I would never patronize such a lovely woman. Ready?"

The building leered at her. Two old gas lamps flickered on either side of the stained door. It looked like the entrance to a prison or, worse, a dungeon.

Jacob thrust his head back into the cabin. "What about the carriage? We can't leave it out here on the street. Probably best to come back in the daytime, Miss." He added, "if at all," under his breath.

Brechin strapped on his mask. His voice sounded muddled and deep through the respirator. "The carriage house for guests is around the corner. Quite secure. I believe they have some accommodations for the drivers as well, unless you would prefer the carriage to leave for the night and return for us in the morning?"

Jacob practically hissed at the suggestion. "I will remain."

"So outspoken and protective. Rather endearing. Where did you find such an unusual servant? Boldness such as I've never seen before." Dr. Brechin gave Jacob's cheek a playful pat.

The young driver pulled back, his face burning red.

"That's quite enough, Dr. Brechin," Lenora said. She fiddled with the leather straps of her mask to loosen them and addressed Jacob. "Please keep the carriage close by. I have no intention of staying any longer than is necessary."

Jacob opened his mouth to respond then snapped it shut. He slunk back to the driver's seat. "Yes, Miss."

Lenora and the doctor dove into the onslaught of soot. With surprising force, Brechin scooped her up and carried her to the entrance with breakneck speed. He released her in the mudroom. She couldn't pull the hat and mask off quickly enough.

"That was highly improper," she spat.

Brechin dusted himself off. "Not at all. It is best to get off the streets as swiftly as possible. Surely you can agree with that."

"Then you should have taken me by the arm."

"Like a proper lady? And what sort of 'lady' concerns herself with matters of enterprise and science?"

Lenora tilted her chin up. "I'll pretend you didn't say that."

The interior set of heavy wooden doors lacked handles. Unusual symbols covered the portals, thick brush strokes arranged at deliberate yet elegant placements. Tiny works of art, but the organized groupings suggested they were writing. Hanging above the door was a plain sign that read "Ruu's." Dr. Brechin pulled a chain hanging next to the door. A low ding sounded on the other side reverberating through Lenora's entire being.

It was better to focus on her ire, to ignore the growing scratching sensation riding up her legs. *I shouldn't be here.*

"Furthermore, there was no reason for rudeness toward my driver," Lenora forced through her unease.

"He's just a servant."

"Servant or no, he's a person. There's no reason to treat him that way."

"Ha. Now, that sounds like something Samuel would say. I don't consider my behavior rude at all. I consider it an exchange of wits. A gentleman's duel of mental capabilities." The smirk again, fully developed. "He lost."

"You're impossible."

The interior doors swung open with a harsh creak, and an elderly man in red silk robes greeted them. His thin braided chin beard dangled at least a foot long and his unperceivable eyes camouflaged by a legion of wrinkles. He reeked of pungent earth.

Lenora could only assume he was an immigrant from one of the Southern countries, probably Xouai. A group of them arrived in Elsothe as a gift from Xou to the Council. Not as slaves, she had been taught, but as a willing labor force to assist with the expansion of device production. She doubted that depiction was completely accurate. The Xouai worked most of the Council's hard labor positions for little pay. It didn't seem likely anyone would willingly relocate halfway across the globe to scrape by like that.

"Ruu, my dear friend. Manning the door this evening?" Brechin dipped his head in a slight bow.

"Kin Oo not well. I welcome." Ruu pressed his hands together against his chest and bowed. With the severity of his crooked back, Lenora feared he would topple forward over himself.

"Ah." Brechin grabbed Lenora's arm and pulled her toward him. "The lady and I would like to request the private suite, if it's available."

Ruu's deeply set eyes were completely unreadable. After a long pause, he beckoned them inside while nodding. "Yellow room good. Special door?"

"Please," Brechin said.

"Pipe?"

"Afterward, if you please."

The hall felt narrower than it looked, black-lined floral pattern wallpaper faded and peeling. Stepping forward, Lenora's nose was assaulted. Rich smoke layered the upper half of the space with a potent herbal, floral fragrance. She might have found it oddly pleasant, were it not as strong.

The hall ended in a large room divided into sections by brightly colored woven screens. Each section housed some form of heavily pillowed seating where people of all stations reclined, their feet bare and their faces droopy. A single oil lamp sat in the center of every semi-private segment. A constant background hum of sluggish whispers and giggles clouded the space as thick as the smoke. A man's toes wiggled as he smoked from a three-foot long wooden pipe, lit by the oil lamp on the floor.

Xouai rushed about, silently serving the guests. A woman slumped over unconscious in a padded corner section while her friend mumbled to her with an exhale of smoke from a clockwork hookah. Lethargic laugher sounded as if it were being dragged down to the floor.

Lenora had read about these places before. She should have been furious, scolding Brechin for the audacity to bring her, but there wasn't any fire in her pit. On the contrary, she held a strange sensation of empowerment mixed with danger. This wasn't "proper" or "ladylike." Brechin wasn't treating her any differently than he would any other associate— no sugarcoating—and for that courtesy she would overlook his uncouth manner. *Well, so long as he actually has a point at the end of all this and isn't merely toying with me.*

Absorbed in the scene, she nearly stumbled into a shallow pool of milky liquid recessed into the middle of the floor.

"Bath. For feet." Ruu explained.

They left the main room and entered another hallway. The doors lining either side were painted with a cluster of the intricate symbols in the middle. Smoke billowed out from the edges around each door that failed to align neatly. The fragrance became intoxicating once Lenora grew accustomed to it—a musky bed of flowers warmed gently with a high citrus note. Her steps felt lighter, the hallway softer.

Ruu opened the door at the hall's end. Lemon-colored walls and canary cushions. Two long couches faced each other in the middle of the room, with a thin table between. An oversized canopy bed sat in a corner in varying shades of sunshine. The yellow room was an accurate description.

"Good?" Ruu dipped his chin down once more.

"Very good," Brechin replied.

"Come back hour?"

"Yes. Thank you."

The old man closed the door with a small click. Dr. Brechin plopped down on a couch.

"This is an opium den, isn't it?" Lenora nervously examined the upholstery but remained standing.

"How observant of you, Lenora." He rolled himself a cigarette and lit it with the single stroke of a match. "*Lenora.* I'm rather fond of that. Much more fitting than Miss Leahill. That sounds too stuffy, don't you think?"

"Call me what you like, Dr. Bre—Elliot," she refused his offer of the cigarette. "But you still haven't shown me anything. A lovely little trip down to the dilapidated empire of the destitute, to be sure, but I'm growing impatient. You promised me your Delirium results."

Her curiosity had become intensified by the floral smoke. As dozy as she felt, a sense of adventure built. The unnecessary turns on the way to the den, the lengthy lecturing to confuse her purpose, irritating Jacob—he was trying to derail her. This had to be something of grand importance. Something uncommon and profound. Or perhaps this was all a grand joke with her as the punchline? Was he taking her seriously or not? She swiped the handkerchief through her fingers over and over.

He flicked the ashes into a ceramic bowl. "You're truly adamant about that, aren't you?"

"Your funding depends on it."

Brechin exhaled a giant cloud. "Here's the trouble; I'm not sure Samuel would have wanted you involved. You have no inkling of what is happening in Canimere beneath the surface. How could you? What are you, fifteen? Sixteen?"

"Twenty-three, and far more educated than you seem to believe." Her face grew hot.

"I meant no offense." His eyes looked sincere. After a few more puffs he slumped forward to stare up at her. "Some things in this world are impossible to erase from your mind once they have found a way in. I want—I *need* you to be sure this is the path you want to take. The other Leahill industries are safer and, honestly, far more profitable. You don't have to do this. Cut my funding." He winced. "Wait, no, don't cut it. Perhaps turn a blind eye—?"

"Quit stalling. Important stuff, understood."

Even as she tried to dismiss his warnings, fear crawled up behind her excitement. Through her father's larger businesses, she could make a few ripples of change, but she wanted to cause waves. Huge, powerful currents that swept up the country and pushed them to the Age of Awareness. It suddenly dawned on her the scale of progress she desired would involve great risk.

Father would have wanted her to take those risks, wouldn't he?

She crumpled her hat before dropping it on the couch. "Alright, listen, I appreciate the concern. I do. Still, I don't intend to leave here without seeing your conclusions. I promised to dedicate myself to advancing the country in any way I'm able. At least offer me a shred of trust on my father's behalf. Please, show me what you've discovered."

Brechin extinguished his cigarette, twisting the remainder into a mash of tobacco and paper. "Very well, Lenora."

He got up and crossed the room. At the far wall, behind several decorative draperies, he revealed a simple door. Dry wood splintered vertically and bloated as if the old door was tired of holding back the soiled streets. A shot of cold ran from her toes up through her spine followed by a rush of adrenaline. They were going out into the bleak.

SIX

The secret door led to an immense web of tight alleys from Ruu's through numerous aging buildings. As she stepped out, she checked either direction. The left ended abruptly in a wall a few paces from the door. The right stretched long, branching out into various slim passages between neighboring structures like a hedge maze of decaying brick. Miasma filled the corridors and sharp corners.

Brechin handed her a long cane as she donned her hat and ash mask. He assured her the poles were necessary, as the district itself was known to maim travelers. Lenora clutched it like a sword, at the ready to slash down anyone or anything that might lurch out into her path.

The alleys were remarkably clear of soot as the scale of the surrounding buildings sheltered them. Only a thin ashfall descending in a light fog snuck in between the gaps. She couldn't help but wonder why these passages lay empty. They seemed ideal places for the homeless to shelter themselves, concealed from the hazard of the open streets and clear of much of the black blizzard. The metal click of an Enforcer's stride echoed through the alleyways like a pulse, as if these secluded passages were the arteries of Pitchdrift. She suddenly had a pretty good idea why the alleyways remained empty.

At the few low banks of ash found intermittently along their route, Brechin stopped. He gave each pile a firm poke with his cane then paused a moment before pressing on.

Right, right, left, a switchback before another right. The same dingy brick walls lined either side. Scraps of broken barrels and crates discarded from the factories hugged the edges. Each scattering of wood fragments appeared uniquely random and yet indistinguishable. She quickly lost any sense of direction. So long as they were moving, so long as Brechin led the way with such sure strides, she could handle the alarm of feeling adrift.

Brechin halted, throwing out his arm to ensure she did not push past him. He gave a forceful jab at an oddly oval-shaped soot pile. As soon as his cane penetrated the loose ash a blue flame spat out. Brechin jumped back in time with her, as if they were sweeping back in step dancing the Galop. A pillar of fire charred the wall opposite the pile while the mound of soot it originated from deflated and crumpled in on itself. As the flame sputtered from a spear to a dagger, Lenora let go of a breath she didn't realize she held. The shock of the eruption receded leaving a sense of shameful ignorance in its place.

"They explode?" She gulped the dense air inside her respirator.

"Shhhhhh," the doctor replied. He added, barely audibly, "They can, but typically someone releases the built-up gasses long before that point. More often they do this little single burn trick. 'Cinder bursts' they call them."

Why does it always have to be fire?

Lenora's grip tightened on the cane. As they continued forward, she batted and poked at any black pile they happened across, even the minuscule ones. Better to be overly cautious than risk having her dress burst into flame.

Brechin ducked beneath a low awning and pointed. The area lay deep within the labyrinth of alleys. No street access, no existence save for those who already knew where to find it. The building Brechin pointed out appeared more of a skeletal frame than a proper structure. The whole was made of simple poles erected to carry a flat roof which sheltered an area below. Beneath the overlay, a plot of dry earth surrounded by wrought iron fencing. Cut pieces of stone protruded from the ground, the land otherwise in such ruin that it bore rocks instead of vegetation.

Beyond that, the faint outline of a steeple hid beneath the makeshift canopy. The building pulsed a kaleidoscope of colors from the windows, flickering red, gold, and green in rhythmic bright and fade cycles. In time with the colored light, a deep sound kept the beat. The muffled thud pressed against her temples and into her mind, forging images of crude hammers coming down on tenderized meat.

"A-a-a faith house," she stuttered.

"Yes. A church, or at least it used to be."

After Brechin glanced in each direction, he sprinted over to the edge of the fence, dragging her by the arm behind him. As he made his way to a broken space in the fence, Lenora's middle twisted. The realization of what those stones signified froze her in place. *Grave markers.*

A patch of dirt filled with corpses as was the forbidden faith's custom. A horrific display, one intended to memorialize the departed as if they could be reborn through the plants that sprouted from their decay. But this plot yielded no growth. No flies hovered over the liquid decomposition bubbling up from the ground, as she had imagined. Perhaps the bodies didn't rot but shriveled in the barren soil.

Unthinkable, to let the departed lie in some hole.

Her mind raced as the constant thuds from the church boomed louder. Weren't there old rules about walking over the dead? Weren't there tales of bodies rising? *Inhuman fangs. Animalistic cravings. Curses.* The boys at Glenn Haven spoke often of such stories. Elsothe burned their dead instead of buried them for a reason.

"Over to the window," Brechin whispered.

"I can't."

Brechin pulled her down to a low crouch. "You *can't?*" He took stock of the surroundings, peering in each direction. "What do you mean, you can't?"

The mask clung sticky and moist on her skin. "They're dead, underground. What if—? I can't."

Her heartbeat raced past the drone of the faith house. What if all that kept the corpses from rising was the steady thrum beneath her feet beating the dirt down flat?

"A graveyard spooks the great Heiress Leahill? Why? Old ghost stories?" His smirk managed to ooze from his voice. "A rather inconvenient time to get weak."

"I'm not weak." Her voice resonated an octave higher and sounded far louder than she intended.

Brechin whirled to check around them while shushing her. After a lengthy silence, he leaned close enough to address her. "There isn't time for this. I already warned you about how this would be. Are we going or not?"

Lenora desperately wanted to see his face. His mask gave her an unreadable blank canvas. She rolled her tongue over the condensation on her upper lip, tasting the sharp salt of her sweat, and surveyed the defiled earth. *No cracks in the ground. No disturbed soil.*

This was her chance to make an impact—to contribute to researching the epidemic, perhaps even aid in developing a cure. To dissipate the hazy specter of the past from following her.

A deep breath.

"All right. Go."

Brechin shot through the opening in the fence. Lenora rushed after him, focusing on his flapping coattails. *Just watch his back,* she told herself. *Follow his gallop. Step where he steps.* They jumped over one of the headstones. She tried to ignore it, but the faded words 'Here Lies' leapt out to her. She shut her thoughts to it. *Just a barren garden. Empty dirt.*

She tried to keep herself trained on Brechin's heels, but her eyes wandered. Headstones lined up in tight file. A tall cross beside a simple rectangular headstone, both jutting from the earth with a slight lean towards each other as if the cold slabs wished to kiss. Several shorter markers had crumbled to irregular masses. Shadows elongated into crawling creatures cavorting with each toll.

At the rear of the faith house, a chasm yawned. The hole stretched longer and wider than three or four of the graves side by side. Its depths hidden in black, but she could feel the pit calling to her like a banshee's wail. The unwavering eclipse begged her to glimpse inside, to know what horrors lay below.

She nearly slammed into Elliot's back as he stopped short at the church wall. With the gaping hole no longer in view, she could catch her breath, barely. Again, he crouched low, and she followed suit.

Protected from the descending soot by the makeshift awning, he pulled off his mask. She eagerly mirrored the act. The rush of thick, smoldering sulfur made her eyes water. Layered on the heavy pollution hovered a rotting scent. The sort of retching odor that clung around the butchers' warehouses, where the scraps of useless meat piled up in vats.

Brechin waited for her to wipe away the tears with a handkerchief before speaking. "Look through the window but don't linger. The Enforcers keep a tight patrol."

Sweaty palms stuck to her gloves. Lenora shot up swiftly to look beyond the stained glass before she overthought herself out of it.

Giant machinery lined the back wall, primarily three oversized pistons working at the rhythmic pounding. The interior lights dimmed as the pistons rose only to flash as they dropped. Cogs machined with uneven edges. Springs bent and stretched, forcing boxed mechanisms to click and shudder. Tangled messes of wire wove from one component to the next, creating a vile nest for a robotic monstrosity.

The inhabitants felt secondary as the mechanisms dwarfed them. Rows of Canimere's most deprived residents hunched over desks—or what she could only describe as desks. A seat behind a flat surface covered with books and papers. Yet these too were part of the mechanical overlord. Wires reached from the wall to the desks like the extended claws of the device. The people twitched and writhed in the clutches of the machine, reading with pained expressions.

Within the agonized pack, a woman dropped. Her frame went limp, one emaciated arm swinging like a pendulum over the side of the desk. The mop of her greasy hair spread over the book covering all her face except the sharp peak of her nose. A thin stream of blood ran from her nostril down the page.

An Enforcer came from a dark corner beyond Lenora's view. He stomped his way through the cluttered mass to stand over the spiritless body.

Lenora ducked down, biting her lip to hold back the scream clogging her chest. The back door of the faith house swung open. Brechin pushed her flat against the wall. She gripped the façade with all her strength.

The woman dangled over the Enforcer's shoulder like a marionette hanging off the puppet show stage.

Lenora clamped her fingers down harder on the wall, tensing her fingertips into the abrasive surface, hoping to quell the tears of fear with pain so the mechanized henchman couldn't hear them roll down her cheeks.

The Enforcer carried the woman to the edge of the hole, the great abyss, and threw her in. Her body made a moist yet solid smack as it landed. He didn't pause, just discarded her as if she were nothing more than garbage. With a thick blast of exhaust, the Enforcer vanished back inside the church.

Lenora let out in a shaky exhalation. *A vast open grave.* Her hands shook.

The dead woman, her hair like spilled ink all over the desk.

The immense apparatus, those desks... wires, tubing, levers, and the mass of Pitchdrift's impoverished reading.

Reading in agony.

It didn't make sense.

Brechin nudged her shoulder and motioned towards the alley they came from, but she couldn't leave. Not until she understood. She thrust herself past him and returned to the window.

Wires ran from the machinery to each device disguised as a desk. Tubing wound around the seating like rubber snakes that coiled through the mechanics below the seat and desk, up the back of the chair. Several tall levers jutted out of gearwork to the side of the seat. Various knobs and gauge boxes protruded from the top of the reading surface like controls. Each person, unnatural beside the hard-sharp workings. Their jerking limbs out of place among the cold parts ticking and rotating with timely precision, like sparrows trapped in a carriage's engine.

A scrawny redheaded boy near to the window closed his book with a muffled yelp and pulled a lever beside him. As he turned to fiddle with some knobs, Lenora got a clear view of his backside. Her stomach doubled over on itself. The tubing ran up his neck and invaded at the base of the skull. Flesh engorged and puckered around the nearly consumed metal connection, trying to spit the invading worm out. Another lever shifted, causing him to convulse for a moment, and then he opened another book.

The pucker gurgled, suckling on the tube with bubbly scars for lips. Trickles of turquoise fluid ran through it, down the side of the contraption and into a recess housing little glass vials lined up in a row. *Two full, three empty.* The tubing fed into the next empty vial in the line, a drop collected at a time.

She sunk back down. The muscles in her neck tensed as bile rose to the back of her throat. Cold sweat. Hand clenched over her cuff.

Brechin's voice sounded distant. "Aqua Peritia."

The gagging came uncontrollably. Sour acid gushed out of her mouth and nose, purging her insides as if her body could remove the revelation by physical means. Between evacuations, she could make out Brechin's panicked pleas for quiet. Another burst, leaving her core scorching tender. With a final dry heave, it was over.

Brechin wiped the vomit from her face with a handkerchief. He said something about being calm, but his words sounded weak to her.

Tubes burrowed in flesh. The drippings of that boy's brain hitting the vial in a steady flow. The sound of the drops collecting echoed in her ears.

That's what I've been injecting. Her nails bit into her wrist as she clutched the cuff. *From his tubing into mine.*

Brechin seized her waist and bolted forward. Gravestones blurred by. The pounding of the pistons like war drums. Everything spiraled wildly without direction. All she heard was a hum—a hum building like a swelling note.

Brechin flung them to the ground beyond the fence as the Enforcer fired. The shot echoed through the alleys, blistering the brick façade past them. Splinters of the wall pelted her, as a cloud of dust and ash burst in the alley. Brechin lifted her up and tossed her in front of him as the hum rose again.

"Run!"

Lenora stumbled forward into the maze of alleys, racing the hum increasing in pitch. Every part of her being surged blindly forward. *Run.* A right, then a left, another left. One turn after the other without thought. Brick corridors and dark specks.

Her lungs filled the confines of the corset. No mask. The soot sucked into her mouth mixing with the bile and saliva into a gritty paste. The burnt sour trapped on her tongue pushed her body to fly faster.

She slipped rounding the next bend. Her boots glided on a patch of soot. She gripped the wall and pushed into the slide. It flung her around the corner unbalanced, but she recovered and darted forward. Her body agile and quick as her mind went blank. *Run.*

Another thunderous bang. This time farther behind her in the twist of alleys. The sound struck her as surely as if the shot had hit her dead on. She slowed enough to realize the vacancy behind her.

Brechin was gone.

Her arteries still fired away on full even as she stopped. The air rushed in and out of her chest with the same feverish pace. Had that shot downed its target?

Dazed, she took stock of her surroundings. An alleyway, indistinguishable from any other she had traveled that evening. Alone.

Would an Enforcer unload his handgun into her temple or simply snap her neck for efficiency? She took a step backward. Perhaps he would realize she was a woman of means and take her to the Council instead. She clung to that hope, but with what she had seen of the Enforcers, that seemed impossible. They would be quick and merciless.

The thoughts built up steam. One of the penniless inhabitants would come across her corpse in the morning. A lady destined to be a leader for the Age of Awareness felled in her prime. They would strip her jewels. Sell her hair to the wigmaker. She would be naked when someone found her. Or worse, her forgotten corpse thrown into the pit.

Panic rushed her, suffocating her from within. Her eyes swelled moist, the pounding of her heart deafening in her ears.

A hand clasped over her mouth. A warm body against her back. Her knees locked. *This is it*, and she stiffened for the blow.

SEVEN

The hand covering her mouth gave her a gentle squeeze, and the body behind her pulled her close.

"Keep quiet," a man's voice whispered in her ear.

"Dr. Brechin?" She breathed through his fingers.

"Elliot, if you please."

Brechin took her hand and whisked them through the alleyways. Without a celestial display above, Lenora felt as if they were scurrying underground like rats. Elliot took every step with purpose and direction. She let him grip her hand without complaint. Finally, a burst of flowery air hit her as he shoved her through a small, ash-stained door.

Gulping for breath through soot-caked lips, she rushed over to the water basin and turned on the pump. The automated plumbing system in the walls of the yellow room creaked and moaned as the water trickled out. She swished out her mouth and then scraped the gritty gunk off her tongue. It wasn't dignified, but she was desperate to get rid of the taste of the city with its mix of bile and ashes and madness.

Tilting her head back, she gargled another handful of water before spitting it into the basin. The sour-burnt flavor lingered, but at least it was no longer a clinging wad on the roof of her mouth. She ran a washcloth into the stream and then doused her face. After a proper scrub, she soaked the rag again and forced it through the ash-coated strands of hair which had escaped the multitude of pins.

Brechin laughed as he flopped onto a couch.

"I don't find anything amusing in the least right now," she growled through her panic.

His laughter mellowed to a chuckle as he rolled a cigarette. "You resemble a half-drowned mouse."

She threw the wet rag at him, nailing the side of his face with a thick splash before it rolled onto his shoulder. He brushed it off.

"What are you doing? Have someone fetch Jacob. Make ready the carriage. We need to leave this... this... infested hole." Her legs were numb from the chase, but her torso burned with the continued need to fly.

Brechin calmly lit his cigarette. With a curled smirk, he exhaled the smoke through his nostrils. "And how is that to our advantage? The Enforcers are on the hunt for two well-dressed trespassers, correct? Then a remarkably luxurious carriage rushes onto the streets, fleeing the district. We wouldn't make it half a mile."

She despised his relaxed composure almost as much as the fact he made sense. "And if they come looking for us here?"

"Then Ruu will report all of his faithful clientele have been enjoying his services all evening." He tapped the cigarette to make the ashes fall in the tray. "Please, sit. You look exhausted."

No place to run. It's like being trapped in bed, only safe so long as I don't set so much as a toe down on the cold floor. The monsters under the bed can feel it when you touch the floor.

No, it wasn't beneficial to linger on the feeling of being trapped, not when there was nothing she could do to change her situation. However, she could give him an earful for this horrendous evening.

She reluctantly plopped down opposite him; arms crossed. "You nearly got us killed."

He snapped upright with mock shock. "I? Not at all. It was you who made the racket that alerted the Enforcers."

Her arms clenched tighter. "Are you implying this is my fault? After you led me into such a vile situation with lies?"

"Lies? What lies?"

"You promised to show me your findings on Delirium. All I witnessed was—" Lenora broke off, huffing to barricade her anger.

Brechin dropped the last bit of cigarette into the dish as he leaned in close to her. "You're so exquisite when your temper flares. It's a shame you're such a pain in—"

Lenora lifted her hand, poised to slap him when someone rapped on the door. Brechin beckoned them to enter and several Xouai shuffled in. They brought in tea service, including a variety of little cakes and biscuits. Lenora helped herself to a cup as they put fresh rags by the basin.

She dropped in three sugar cubes and then rapidly stirred the cup. The Xouai placed one of the long wooden pipes in front of Brechin, alongside a wadded-up ball of tar in a dainty dish. One of them motioned to an oil lamp he held before he placed it on the far end of the table. After Brechin responded with a few sharp foreign syllables, the workers bowed and backed out of the room.

Lenora snarled at her companion while she sipped the tea. Even with all the sugar, it was bitter, like bits of grass steeped in hot water. Nevertheless, she found it drinkable. She was still alive to taste it.

"I'm sorry to disappoint, but there have been no lies tonight," Brechin said, picking up their conversation as if without interruption.

"Is that so?"

He set to scraping the tar into the pipe. "Those were my findings. What you saw was the way Agitated Delirium spreads. Essentially, those initially infected produce the Peritia that infects others."

Lenora crashed her cup onto the saucer. *Infection through Aqua Peritia?* She swallowed, and the tea went down like a coarse stone, but his words remained lodged in her windpipe. Brechin didn't flinch.

He went on, "Obviously, injection unbalances the humors with the addition of material in the blood, but Delirium is more than that. It's another substance carried through the nervous system. Typically, it requires several doses. One vial alone isn't enough. Seven, eight, perhaps more. With dozens of those Peritia mills set up in the district, each running day and night, there is no way to tell which workers are infected or how many vials are tainted. I still haven't pinpointed the exact catalyst that manifests the full dementia, though. Some combination of lighting and exposure to..."

He continued speculating, but Lenora no longer heard him. The glittering pride wrapped around her wrist had become a weight, pulling her thoughts down toward the faded carpet. The jewel of the Age of Awareness was the poison of the sane mind.

That would mean each injection was a gamble, a possible infection. *And I have injected dozens this past week.* Unchecked, Delirium would spread like wildfire through the cuffs.

That can't be. That leads everything to pure bedlam.

She interrupted Elliot's rambling. "And you haven't mentioned this to the Council?"

Brechin bent his head to the side, looking perplexed. "They already know, of course."

"Then why haven't they done anything about it? Why isn't it in the news?"

Brechin laughed again, but the sound carried a sad note. "So as not to affect their profits, naturally. Likely their positions, as well. Could you imagine the upheaval if the people were to discover the very device they have become reliant upon—the same one which convinced the public to overthrow the monarchy—was responsible for the spread of Delirium? Riots, rebellion, and all sort of chaos would ensue."

The room grew crowded. Everything mashed together in flashes. *The Council aware of the dangers?* Lemon pillows with aged lace fringe. *The monarchy destroyed by Aqua Peritia?* The honey floral fragrance seeping in from the hall. *Riots?* The bulbous pucker at the base of a skull slurping on the tubing.

Brechin took her hand. His confusion morphed into concern. "You really know nothing of the world, do you?"

Lenora noted that his wrists were bare like her father's. Focusing on his hands quieted her mind. *Long graceful fingers with each ring fingernail painted black.*

"Why didn't you just tell me? Why drag me out to see… all this?"

Brechin placed one hand over her cuff, tracing the delicate carving as she had numerous times before.

"Would you have listened? Would you have believed me when everyone else has told you how wonderful these are?"

Lenora wanted to say she would have, that she would have been open to anything he had to present to her with a rational and unbiased head, but that would be a lie. She would have brushed him off as trying to swindle her for funding, or possibly falling into Delirium.

"No."

After a long silence, he withdrew his hands and went back to preparing the pipe.

The quiet between them left her free to spin the sordid details of the night in vivid circles like a tune stuck in her head. She needed something to distract her. His hands worked in clean, sweeping movements. The black painted nail shining like a bit of onyx with each scrape of the tar.

"May I ask you something?" She flicked a rather questionably shaped biscuit across the plate.

"Of course."

"Why are two of your nails painted black?" As soon as she asked, the playfulness returned to his face.

"For anarchy. I find it unnecessary and counterproductive to have any authority system in place. Look at the mess the Council has made of the city, the country. People would fare far better if they ruled themselves, don't you think?"

It was her turn to laugh, even if it sounded meek. "You know, it doesn't surprise me that you would entertain anarchism. Actually, it suits you. But if that's your aim, why not just release your findings? I'm sure there is some rebel group, right? Wouldn't that bring about your anarchic society?"

"If only. Someone else would take up the throne if the Council was destroyed. Still, a man can dream, can't he?" He finished with the pipe and set to rolling several cigarettes. He placed a lit one between her fingers, ignoring her protest. "There is a further complication to my findings, however. Peritia may be the way the epidemic is spread, but it is not the origin of the disease. Nothing will come of revealing how Delirium is spread—well, not for the well-being of the country, anyway. The Council is guilty of allowing the spread but will claim ignorance. Then, we would be discreetly dealt with. To have any impact on the epidemic, we need to discover the source, and we need to find it before the Council. Otherwise, they will declare victory over the disease, and nothing will change."

"*We?*" She sniffed at the burning cigarette; the dry dirt perfume of it irritated her stomach. She tossed the nasty thing in the bowl.

"You wanted to pick up where Samuel left off, then 'we,' if you please." He placed the long pipe between his lips and gently drew the smoke in. The way the smoke held a shape yet dissipated at the same time mesmerized yet unnerved her.

The source of the epidemic. It wasn't the role she had planned to pursue, but any good for the people was a noble course. Granted, she would have to skirt past the Council. The very idea of such treason was reckless, a touch ludicrous, but a risk worth taking. She was increasingly appalled by the state of things under their rule. Everything was in ruins, breaking under the weight of countless specks of filth.

Dr. Brechin, for all his faults, had honorable intentions. If nothing else, she could trust him to be brutally honest. Any other man would have simply told her "a lady such as yourself need not bother with such things" and left her behind. An heiress and an anarchist; she placed the titles side by side. They had a baffling appeal, like two flavors one would think shouldn't mingle yet became magical when paired, like dark chocolate and chili peppers.

"I've come this far. I suppose it's only logical to continue forward."

After repositioning the oil lamp, he offered the pipe. "Then let this be the ceremony to celebrate our arrangement."

Opium was for criminals and immoral persons, but then again she was currently hiding from Enforcers in cahoots with an anarchist. After the faith house, who was to say what was right or wrong anymore.

The opium smelled far more luxurious than tobacco smoke. The offer held her curiosity, but after the smoldering air from Pitchdrift, though, she wasn't keen on trying to suck anything else into her lungs.

"I've inhaled quite enough blight this evening, thank you."

"Cowardice now? After everything tonight, the dragon frightens you?" He chuckled as he pushed the pipe into her palm. "You won't even notice the draw."

The insult stung, as much as she tried to ignore it.

She took a quick suck from the tip of the opium pipe. It was powerful—a thick almost solid smoke that hit her throat with force, the draw as harsh as the pollution of the alleys. She would have growled at Brechin, had her windpipe not been spasming with coughs.

He slipped the pipe from her grasp as she leaned over, hand to her chest in a flurry of unladylike hacking.

Then a calm flowed through her. She let her posture slouch without care. Several neck rolls in either direction eased the tightness in her shoulders. Everything became soft and fluid, as if every blemish had been buffed out of the world. He handed her the pipe again.

The smoke burst from her lips with a blue tinge that enveloped the space like a flood of water. It swam across the brilliant yellow of the décor making rolling hills of grass. The sweet fragrance condensed on her senses; honey coated flower petals wrapped in lemon meringue. She was lying on the grass at Foxton, tasting the essence of summer, miles away from the city.

Another puff, this one more perfumed than the last, or maybe she simply inhaled more. It was of no consequence. She wanted to sink deeper as her limbs grew light. Roll on the grass, her loose hair caressing her face.

Brechin exhaled, letting the smoke glide off his lips in a stream. She tried to do the same but she erupted into a cough after a few seconds. He made what was forbidden seem natural, almost seductive.

Her exhalations came out as thin plumes while his coiled and sprang back and forth, like a man coming to life. The legs formed from the tubular split as the smoke encountered his nose. Then it recombined, an elongated torso stretched into a bulb for a head. The man slowly swayed from Elliot, gliding closer to her face. A thin handlebar mustache branched from the bulb reaching out on either side. She had but to put a smoking jacket on him to make a copy of her father. Ever present, ever unattainable and constantly in motion. *Go away.* She blew at the conjured spirit, and the shape morphed. The line of the torso became soft and sloped. The head grew wisps of hair. But there was no face.

"Why are you always blank?"

"Huh?" Elliot perked up from his slack form.

"My mother, she never has a face." She pointed at the now shapeless cloud hovering between them.

He nodded and then retreated into the yellow cushions. She too slouched deeper into the couch. *Why doesn't she have a face? Why can't I remember what she looked like?* The throw pillow between her hands gave quickly beneath her grasp, her knuckles tight as the pillow flattened. She hadn't even realized she had grabbed hold of it.

She sensed a growing disconnect from her body. Her consciousness hovered, held to the physical by a single rope. The twine wore thin, strands breaking away, and only certain sensations from her body traveled through the tether. The heft of her bones weighed down her flesh. A tingly vibration coursed through her at random moments.

She looked back at the smoke, searching for something to draw stabilization from, but all that materialized was Fogarty's metallic jaw jutting out from underneath his top hat. The grin widened to the point the chin severed from the remainder. *Murderer?* The gaping mouth extended out to devour.

She squeezed her lids shut. *Sleep. Please sleep.*

As if it were that easy. Even with her eyes closed, the images bloomed open before her. Mostly faces, pliable like clay, shifted through the abyss. A couple of the bankers she had noticed; their top hats swayed like cloth in a breeze before mashing together into a single lump. A tombstone. The words *Here Lies* in ink dripped down the cold slab. Then the housekeeper, Claire, grew from the grave. She towered over Lenora, barking like the estate hounds from several stories tall. Another shift into the features of Dr. Wallace, complete with the glasses so dense they could have been clear saucers. He worked on her wrist.

She writhed on the cushions.

Deeper and deeper into her vein Wallace pressed until his cheek and brows began to warp into a nameless boy turning away from her. The back of his head stretched itself open. A bloody pulsing mass of meat within shaped itself into the delicate swirls and putrid accents attached to her wrist. Her own hand reached through the gapped skull towards her, spreading the flesh around the boy's hollow head.

Her eyes snapped open.

"And how is the dance for you?" Elliot's voice was low, as if it crawled along the floor.

"Dance?"

He stretched himself flat on the couch and turned to her, those jade eyes of his even further enhanced by the drifting blues and vibrant yellows of the room. She wanted to rush into them. To escape into the sanctuary of the emerald.

"Why, yes. The dance between the awake and the buried dream. Does it swirl to the music or stumble?"

"I don't care for it."

"Is that because of the dream or the awake? Which vexes you, Lenora?" He was slowing, approaching sleep.

She didn't respond. The nameless faces of Pitchdrift hovered over her, tired and dirty. She watched the shadows stretch and flex on the walls. Fogarty's top hat circled in the dark behind the curtain.

Brechin snored.

She couldn't rest, her ears perked to listen for the Enforcers as she drifted back to Foxton. Ravens flew circles around the bluebirds. *No Enforcers, just birds.* But even as she denied it, on the sunned grass she felt they stood over her, guns poised, ready to blast a hole in her gut.

EIGHT

Lenora kept up as best she could with her father's business empire, which meant she signed the paperwork sent to her. She had become infatuated with the epidemic, the Council, the whole bloody mess. Attending meetings became a nuisance. Hunching over contracts—a chore. She used to hate being stuck within the confines of the manor; now she knew that the city and all its business trappings were even more constricting. Since she could pick her prison, she chose the one lined with books.

Brechin deemed her his silent partner. He expected her to maintain the flow of funds and trust him to dig out the source of the epidemic. The fund allocation was easy; trusting him to find the source on his own was a different matter.

Never one to stand idly by, her own research beckoned to her.

She scoured her father's private library, tapping the spines of each book as she passed to ensure she missed nothing. When the bookcases closest to the front provided no new insight, she shifted her search to the depths of the long half-circle of shelves. The farther she ventured, the less light the electric fixtures and windows reached. The shadows toyed with her, shifting subtly when she turned her head. Still, what lay in the eclipsed shelves may be the salvation of thousands. With a handheld gas lamp in tow, she braved the gloom.

The flame only illuminated a few volumes at a time, forgotten books coated in thin wisps of spider web. Each spine she tapped wore a finger-sized space clear of dust, making it easier to keep track of which books she checked. All else could fade into the distance, the rhythm of daily life restricted to beyond the library door.

After two weeks of book hunting, she happened upon an unexpected goldmine. An oversized book titled *A Fall and a Rise* had been tucked as far from the light of day as possible. A rare survivor after the Council purged the libraries and publishers of religious and undesirable texts a decade before.

Lenora remembered the acrid smell of burning paper as the pile in Glenn Haven's courtyard lit. The edges of a thick volume curled up in blue flames on top of the heap. Lenora found it exhilarating then; the Council destroying works that had no place in the Age of Awareness. She had been young and enthralled with the Council's promises. Now she slid her thumb across the cover of the forbidden book in gratitude for its survival.

Not a volume that would aid much as far as Delirium was concerned, but it could provide her context about Elsothe she severely lacked.

She galloped back to the desk with her treasure and tore into the volume, devouring Queen Evelyn's downfall as detailed in the first half—the monarch's loss of public favor accompanied by pictures, charts, and newspaper articles. Brechin had been telling the truth; Aqua Peritia played a key role in the revolution.

The monarchy hoarded any new gadgetry for themselves, often claiming the devices required more testing before being deemed safe for common subjects. Elsothe had been an agricultural country for generations, and the crown often used religious doctrine to soothe any subjects keen to try the latest mechanical marvels. Clearly, this aggravated the businessmen who aspired to mass produce their devices.

The last straw was Aqua Peritia. The Queen herself wore a cuff for several years yet refused to approve them for public sale. A small group of businessmen claimed the Queen wished to withhold knowledge from the people. This rumor spread wide and fast. Soon, neighborhood resistance groups popped up all over Canimere demanding the "true awareness" Peritia promised.

The people's rage spilled over once Her Majesty publicly declared she required the knowledge available through Peritia as a ruler, while her subjects needed nothing further than faith. The businessmen fanned the flames, providing weapons, funding, and eventually, leadership.

These select businessmen later became the Council.

Little pieces started falling together for Lenora. The Council members' companies received a massive boost once the new drive for the country became industry. The people tolerated Canimere's ashfall, so long as they believed they gained knowledge previously denied to them. Should they discover Delirium was carried through the wonderous Aqua Peritia…

The revelation the church had been linked with the crown startled her. She had been told the Council abolished religion to save the people from false deities. Now she wondered if their motive was more devious, perhaps to ensure the faithful wouldn't demand a new monarch. Or maybe the Council wished to make its own gods of little vials.

The details of the overthrow occupied the second half of the volume. The violent destruction of the palace and its occupants struck her most. The gore seemed unwarranted. The Queen had been hanged over the balcony. A full-page picture showed her corpse swinging over the crowded square like an overdressed bell.

The three eldest Princes and the Princess were all shot by a firing squad in the royal gardens. The picture showed them weeping before the signal. On the next page, the image of their fallen bodies amidst the carnations spoke more of the vileness of the Council than any text could. She flipped the page over quickly.

A knock sounded at the door.

"Enter."

Jacob slipped into the library. "Afternoon, Miss."

"Afternoon. To what do I owe the pleasure?" She skimmed the next page.

He walked over to her desk in an awkwardly relaxed stride, as if he faked comfort. "I thought you might like a drive. Beautiful day today."

She plopped the book down on the desk with a grumble. It wasn't the first time Jacob tried draw her out. His interruptions wore on her.

"I'm busy today. This is important research."

Jacob leaned over to glance at the open pages. The picture showed the close-up of a young boy's face, his bottom teeth dangling over the swollen lips and nose flattened into pulp, with eyes closed in what seemed like innocent sleep.

"Research on badly beaten children?" His face squished up in disgust.

"If you must know, this is about the overthrow," she snapped.

Regret for her tone shot up nearly as rapidly as her anger, but Jacob seemed unfazed. He didn't budge from his spot, pressing his hands together the way he did when he waited for her to continue. Perhaps he already figured out her temper receded as quickly as it seized her.

She sighed and began reading the passage under the picture. "*The youngest Prince, Jacques Henri, age four. He made the unfortunate choice to run from the lineup and was subsequently shot in the back. Revolutionaries silenced his screaming with a club. He bled out shortly afterward.* There, happy?"

Jacob swallowed loudly. "Pretty dark stuff... I'm just saying, it's been weeks, Miss. You've been hid up in here for weeks. Just thought some fresh air was in order, is all. 'Specially with this sort of researching."

Lenora sank into her chair. She rolled her neck side to side, the tension release both painful and blissful. He hadn't forced the issue, but maybe he was right. She had been cooped up too long, chasing phantoms in the dark of the library. Perhaps she was teetering closer than she realized to falling into obsession; letting all her research devour every waking moment. *Is that what happened to Father?*

"Alright, you may have a point." She turned the page to banish the grotesque image. "Get the Wilthiem ready. I'll be out shortly."

He skipped out of the library without another word. She returned to her reading.

The bodies of the royal family had been taken to an undisclosed burial site near the church. The former palace was repurposed as an asylum five years later, after its valuables had been stripped.

Claire knocked, then entered without waiting for a response. Lenora threw the book hastily into the top desk drawer as if it were a penny dreadful she was reading during lecture.

"You have guests, Miss," Claire said as she backed away with the door.

Mary Magpie stepped forward, followed by two wax men. She had layered a simple grey dress with vibrant scarves; a much less theatrical outfit than the pieces she donned for the Spectacle. Metal trinkets and coins clipped onto her belt and strung through her ebony hair chimed as she moved. No wonder Lenora hadn't been able to place her accent; gypsies were rare visitors to Canimere.

Between them, the wax men carried a large item covered in crimson cloth. Setting it on the desk, they removed their hats and bowed to Lenora.

Mary unfolded a sheet of paper and read from it without enthusiasm. "A gift from the humble proprietor of Cardend Theater to the noble Miss Leahill."

The wax men flung off the cloth, revealing an immaculate globe. The land was polished jade, the oceans sapphire, and all of it trimmed in gold leaf. Lenora gulped. This gift screamed opulence beyond any she had ever received. The wax men tinkered with the base and then the globe spun in a rhythmic ticking, spinning to a beat all its own, just as the others in Fogarty's office had. They handed her an additional letter as the men again bowed.

"Just to be clear, this isn't a romantic type gift. He told me so. Just business," Mary chirped.

"I see. I wasn't aware he was courting you."

Mary's laugh was grating. "Get him the doctor, fancy lady. He doesn't like to wait."

She snapped her fingers and the wax men trailed behind her. The jingle of her trinket jewelry echoed as she left.

"Interesting sort of visitors we receive these days," Claire laid the disapproval on thick over her shoulder as she exited the library.

Lenora hissed at the closed door, fully aware Claire couldn't hear her response. Ten years ago, she might have stuck out her tongue as well. Once satisfied Claire wouldn't pop back in, she opened the letter.

My Dear Miss Leahill,

I present to you the world, a treasure few have the capability to truly regard with the immense respect it deserves. In you, I see the potential for greatness beyond the diminished minds that surround us. For you, I offer the world. The world for a name.

With immeasurable anticipation,

Johnathan Fogarty

A chill caught her. She had mercifully forgotten Fogarty or, perhaps, more accurately, she had kept herself too occupied to recall him. The gift thrust her back into the theater where she witnessed the sadistic glee spread across the human half of his face at each macabre scene. If she could erase her father's lingering presence and the rumors of his death, she would distance herself as far as she could from the dreadful ringleader. As it was, Fogarty was a nail piercing her heel—impossible to move forward at a reasonable pace without first addressing the metal burrowed within.

One way or another, she would get to the bottom of the fatal fireworks incident. *Then perhaps Father would stop wandering about in my dreams. Then he would finally be put to rest.*

The faith house had been overwhelming. She hadn't managed to question Dr. Brechin on all the topics she originally planned to after that experience; Fogarty being one of those topics. Clearly, Brechin believed the circus was involved in a non-accidental way, but he was cunning about side-stepping truths. She would have to ensure they talked about Fogarty when next she visited Brechin. The claim of charity for a doctor's name she would keep to herself. She could only think of one doctor, and she certainly didn't feel right about coughing up her recently acquired partner to that overwound grin… at least, not until she could figure out what Fogarty really wanted Brechin for.

She met Jacob in the drive.

"See, a lovely day, Miss." The removal of the hat and bow still appeared sloppy but his manner was improving, at least in public. In the privacy of the carriage, he had grown increasingly inquisitive. She chose not to correct the familiarity as she enjoyed having the confidant.

He fired up the engine. "Where to, Miss?"

"The Marfleur Library, I suppose."

"You suppose?" He pushed buttons and pulled levers easing the carriage into motion with a burst of steam.

"I guess." She tapped her cuff with her nail, making the metal ring. "Did you see them come in?"

"The woman and strange fellas that Fogarty guy keeps? Yeah, I saw them. They give you trouble?"

"A gift actually, from Fogarty. A rather expensive one. It isn't adding up. I don't believe there is any charity event, nor do I think he is charitable in the least. Why does he want a doctor's name? To what end?" She threw herself back into the seat. "It's infuriating I can't find any information on him. I have no idea who or what I'm dealing with."

"I don't understand. If you don't trust him, why not tell him no? Or let one of the bank fellas handle it."

Her entire being erupted in a wave of heat. "Because there's something amiss, and I'm as competent as anyone else to figure it out. If he truly did murder my father, isn't it just that I try to find out why?"

She felt so tight she shook. She wasn't going to let this go—not this time. No stuffy old professor patting her hand telling her not to worry, because one of the boys would deal with it. There wasn't anyone to handle this, not to see it through the way she needed to. No, she was sick of being seen as the scared, weak little girl. She could do this.

The carriage picked up speed, disturbing the soil to kick up that familiar rich, earthy smell. She tried to ground herself with that scent and release her anger. The heat remained, but her limbs went limber and loose. She knew Jacob hadn't meant to be condescending.

"I'm sorry. It's not you…" She busied herself fixing a twist in the nearest curtain to hold back the threatening flood of hot, bitter tears. "I'm sick of being brushed aside while someone else handles things."

Jacob sat quiet for a spell, fidgeting at the helm. She watched the rolling hills of Foxton diminish against the gates of Dusang Forest. Twisted branches seeped their way towards the road.

"Still, I wish you wouldn't bother with him, Miss. I don't think he's safe company. I mean, not that poking about the Council is any safer. It would be smart to drop it all, yeah?"

"Again with 'safe.' Why are you so fixated on that?"

Jacob tightened his grip on the wheel. With a flick of a lever, the carriage slowed to maneuver along the crevices and bumps on the dirt road. An overhanging branch scratched across her window, the sound like metal scraping bone. She drew the curtains closed and rested her head against the seat.

"It's personal, Miss."

"That's not a fair answer. You insist I tell you what's happening with me. You can at least explain why it concerns you so. I highly doubt it's merely a manner of keeping your employer alive to pay your wages. There's more, isn't there?"

His frame seemed to deflate in his seat, a long silent pause—long enough for Lenora to feel the wheels of the carriage roll over the uneven planks of Cygnedor Bridge.

Finally, Jacob cleared his throat.

"Because of my sister, Ebba. She taught us at school, and I walked home with her. Pa said I had to make sure nothing happened to her." He paused as his voice grew shaky and distracted himself with checking dials. In a sudden burst he continued. "But there were these fellas; they did things they shouldn't have to her. They ruined her, took her purity, all 'cause she wanted to teach instead of marry one of 'em. I was a weak kid then, but now, I can do better. You want to be in business; I won't let 'em stop you."

The tremble in his voice hurt. Perhaps she had pried more than she should have.

"I'm sorry," was all she managed in response.

"The city is mean, even meaner to lady folk."

A true statement and a sad reminder. The old faith had been removed in favor of a surplus of mechanical wonders, yet the stain remained. Women were treated as less—*she* was perceived as less—while the expectation to accept cruelty with grace hung heavy around their necks like some albatross. She had been certain the remedy, and the remedy for all other such injustices, would be found in some vial of Peritia. *A foolish hope.*

Still, as horrible as the story might be, Jacob was actively working to ensure such a thing never happened again. His sincere concern warmed her. Mayhaps, if others were as supportive, it would be a step in the right direction.

She ran her handkerchief through her fingers delicately. "I'm glad you told me. It means a great deal that you trust me enough to share something so personal."

Silence again, an uncomfortable sort of quiet when one doesn't know how to break that stillness. Jacob pulled the carriage to the side of the road and stopped. For a moment, he seemed perplexed, as if debating something within himself.

"Miss? If I may... I mean, since this is important to you, my pa's mentioned this Fogarty a couple times. Betting he knows a thing or two about him or at least some other folks who might."

"Really?" Lenora perked up in her seat. "You know, that makes sense. I can imagine Fogarty has quite a reputation. Alright, take me to your father."

Lenora had only passed through the outer ring of the city before, the part referred to by locals as Roudonel. As Jacob steered them onto Roudonel's main road, it seemed much larger than she imagined. Though the area looked fairly shoddy, the residents there fared better than those in the confines of Pitchdrift. This was a place where many of the workers of the city returned at the end of day, a neighborhood without dump vessels, as the soot only came down when the wind shifted west. Some days they had to shovel themselves out of the blackness.

Today, warm sunshine fell on bare faces. Cozy painted houses lined up on ash-stained dirt roads. Stands of carrots and apples sat on the corner exposed to the elements. Not the grey of Canimere, but Roudonel fell short of the full glory of the countryside. The place felt colored with a lackluster palette. One could faintly make out green from blue.

"There's the place." Jacob pointed out in front. "The Dudfield Metal Shop. My pa started it up himself."

More of a shack in a large, fenced lot than a proper shop, but Jacob beamed with pride as they pulled to a halt in front. The yard was littered with parts of every imaginable sort. She could pick out several steam stacks piled up in the corner and piping of all sizes and metallic hues organized in rows. Even in tarnished conditioned, they reflected the light and dotted the opposite fence. The rest of the assortment was a mystery to her, just pieces of metalwork from tiny to gigantic.

A man with the height and build to carry the heaviest of pieces came out of the shack to greet them. He towered well over a foot taller than the average gentleman with a thick neck, broad shoulders, and the slightly rounded gut of age. His left arm, a thick tree trunk of muscle, shot up to wave at Jacob. Where his right arm should have been, the right sleeve ended in a tied knot a few inches from the shoulder so as not to let the empty material flap about. He was perplexingly unbalanced; a brute on the left and lacking a limb on the right. It took her only a moment to match up the brown hair and cleft chin to those same features on Jacob.

"Jake, good timing. Help me pull the canopy over the yard. Looks like there may be some o' the dark stuff coming in tonight," the man said unaware of Lenora trailing behind.

"Sure, Pa, but first we're looking to know about a fella."

"We?"

"Oh," Jacob stepped to the side so his pa could see Lenora. His face shone red for a moment. "I, um, Miss Leahill may I present my pa, Bronston Dudfield. Pa, my employer, Miss Leahill."

Lenora raised her hand as was her habit among the bankers and shipyard managers. The knot of his right sleeve swung around as he walked towards her. She dropped her hand swiftly, flustered with embarrassment.

He pulled up the hand she had receded with his left and bowed graciously. "Good to meet ya, Miss Leahill, not that my son knows how to meet up people proper." He shot Jacob a stern fatherly look. "They call me Beef 'round here, an' you can call me that, too, if ya like."

"It's a pleasure, Beef."

"Well, now, what can I do for a fine lady such as you? Not looking for any parts, I'm guessing." He flipped his attention to Jacob. "Get to the canopy, boy. Make yourself useful while you're here."

Jacob snapped to work, cranking the lever on the side of the shack. A thick blanket of patched cloth rose from the back fence on poles. The gears ran it over the entire lot, shading out the sun. Once in place, Jacob went about fastening the material down along the fence with attached clamps.

"Much easier for the boy, two arms and all." Beef jiggled the knotted sleeve. She felt her cheeks warm as she tried to avoid staring. "Always best to get it in the open. Folks always ask, ya know. Don't you worry none, Miss. It ain't a bother. I left that arm in a Drift factory years ago. Good reminder to not go back."

"I'm sorry for your suffering, all the same." She didn't know what else to say to a man so open regarding his impairments, but then her reason for coming returned to her. "A Drift factory? You worked in Pitchdrift?"

"Been a decade or more but, yeah. Lucky to get out. Not many folks do," Beef said.

"I actually came to find some information about a man in Pitchdrift. A Jonathan Fogarty."

"Why you want to know about that snake? He ain't worth dealing with, not if ya can help it." Beef shook his head as Jacob joined them. "A bit sloppy, Jake, but it'll do."

"It's rather complicated, but anything you can tell me about Mr. Fogarty would be appreciated." She nudged Jacob's back with her elbow.

"Yeah, Pa. It would be a big help," he piped in.

Beef stared down his son a moment, rubbing the stubble on his neck and jawline. "Ya doing right by your boss? Keeping her safe?"

"I swear it, Pa. Actually, you telling us about Fogarty will help me keep her safe." Jacob straightened himself as tall as possible.

"Alright, but I don't see why you want to be foolin' with him." Beef clicked a knob on the fence, switching on dangling lights which ran along the whitewashed boards. "Fogarty's a big name in the Drift. Owns at least a quarter of it. A couple watering holes, a few whorehouses—'scuse the language, Miss, but mostly tenant buildings and not the kind of places ya want to live. Just a room and the rats, but he don't charge much. Can always tell one o' his places by the smell."

"The smell?" Lenora stepped in closer.

"Yeah, pollen. Some folks say it's more of a flowery sort of smell. Just pollen to me. Comes out of the vents. I guess he figured if you gotta live ugly at least it should smell pretty."

There had been a delectably robust floral fragrance in Ruu's, but Lenora doubted that's what Beef meant. As far as she could tell, opium wasn't the top choice of substances for the impoverished, not when they could get a glass of swill for a coin or two. There had been a distinct odor pumped into the theater. Cinnamon? Something akin to that, something of a spicy note. Seemed like a waste of money and effort to perfume rodent-infested dwellings though.

"So how does that make him a snake, Pa? Rent's reasonable, right?"

"It ain't what he keeps, boy. It's how he keeps it." Beef gave Jacob a thud of a pat on the shoulder. "See, he's rough when it comes to folks not paying. Also got his fingers in the protection racket. Every group of thugs 'round the Drift leads back to him some way. If Fogarty don't own it, they still gotta pay him to keep it. As if life there ain't hard enough, the freak keeps a tight squeeze on any money coming in."

She tapped her fingers on her cuff. "Why hasn't the Council stepped in to put a stop to it? Extortion is certainly forbidden."

"He got himself a proper cover with the circus thing. Fogarty gets cozy with Council members at his shows. Besides, who would believe a performer ran the Drift? A fella did try to blow the whistle once, tavern owner tired of the squeeze. Chent or Karnt or something. Heard the Council laughed at him. They found most o' him a few days later."

"*Most* of him?" Lenora closed in further. Anyone walking by might have mistaken them for a pack of gossiping girls with how they clustered.

"Look, I'm sorry. I don't mean to bring up such things. I'm no good at talkin' with gentle-like folks." Beef frowned.

"You're fine. What do you mean 'most'?" she pressed.

Beef scratched his neck scruff again and searched his son's face. Jacob nodded firmly for him to continue.

"It wasn't pretty. They found all o' him but his hands and head."

The crawling sensation from her tailbone to the back of her neck was quadruple the strength it had been when Claire read her scary bits of the storybooks as a girl.

Beef may not have been well-versed in etiquette, but Lenora was confident he was honest. He carried a sincerity that the stuffy bankers lacked. She believed him.

So, he has killed before. She no longer questioned whether the ringleader could have harmed her father, but had he, and why would he?

Beef sent Jacob to fetch her some refreshments while he tried to remember any other details about Fogarty. The ringleader had arrived shortly before Beef's accident, so most of what he knew was hearsay from old friends. She still found his information most enlightening.

Fogarty began acquiring property while the circus traveled the country. By the time he made his bid for Cardend Theater, he was already well-established as a local bullying landlord, even if he was away more often than present in the district. During his absences, his brutes kept the fear flowing for him.

Jacob poured her a glass of fresh lemonade from a pitcher, for which she was grateful.

"If it would be alright, Miss, I would like to fix up a few things while I'm here." Jacob swept his hand in the general vicinity of the yard. At least two of the dangling lights were dim. "Unless you're in a hurry to leave."

"No rush at all. Take your time." She sipped her lemonade.

Beef dusted off an old carriage seating bench for her. Worn, but the stuffing held up well. Jacob jolted into action repairing the light bulbs first and then a loose plank on the fence.

"I made sure he went to school." Beef leaned up against the shack. "Him and his sisters. Merri grew up here, so she and the children lived here with her family while I worked the Drift. That way they could go learn things. How to build things and read things. Does he work good for you?"

"He does. He's improved all the carriages many times over. A skilled driver." She couldn't help but smile. "And a loyal employee."

Before they could say anything further, a shout came from the street. Jacob abandoned his tasks and followed Lenora and Beef out to the gate. A crowd formed on the dirt road. She maneuvered herself between several men to get a decent view.

The Enforcers traveled by horse-drawn cart when they patrolled beyond the city's borders, but in this instance, four of them travelled by long wagon. The man they dragged to their wagon wore half a face of lather. They must have pulled him from the barber's shop mid-shave. He twisted himself free from the Enforcer's grasp only to bolt directly into the primed grip of another. He screamed "wait" at them repeatedly with increasing hysteria.

"Jordan Fleagen? Wouldn't think him for a closed account," a man next to her said to another observer wearing a hat covered in bright ribbons.

"Heard he racked up some card losses. Was going to go face down if he didn't pay 'em. Probably figured he could hold off dem other debts," replied the ribboned hat.

The Enforcers bent Fleagen over their cart, left hand pulled across by chains clamped to his fingers. The sleeve of his shirt cut away to reveal a rudimentary Peritia cuff. One Enforcer pulled the chains while two others pulled his trunk back to keep the arm long. The remaining Enforcer examined the limb, readying a long knife.

"Next week!" the bound Fleagan yelled. "Just one more week!"

Jacob tapped her shoulder. "Please come back inside, Miss. You don't want to see this."

She heard his voice but couldn't pry herself from the scene. They dragged Fleagan out in broad daylight and chained his hand to the wagon. This was medieval. Primitive and unnerving with all the people standing around gawking. It simply couldn't be reality.

Then, without warning, the blade slashed down. The Enforcer pushed the man aside unfazed by the gushing spout of blood from his forearm, his cries of pain ignored. The Enforcer pulled up the chain to examine the hand and wrist still attached to it. With a swift motion, he dislodged the cuff's tubing and fastening bolts from the flesh. Then the cuff slid off the severed wrist easily.

The hand was casually tossed to its former owner's side. Gore mixed with road dust and lather. Fleagen squirmed with low whimpers, cupping the site of amputation. Lenora felt rooted in place as sickness rose from her middle. She swallowed back hard.

"Let's go, Miss." Jacob's hand on her shoulder again.

"They took his hand. Why did they take his hand?"

Beef moved in front of her to block her view, and only then did her legs wobble away from the road.

"To get the cuff off and not break it. They can't sell 'em again if they break," Beef said as he led her back to the bench. "You look white as winter. Here, have a sit."

She eased herself down, willing her stomach to calm. "But why take it?"

Jacob sat down beside her. "Well, most folks can't pay for a cuff all at once. They make payments, so if they don't pay..."

"They cut it off," Lenora said flatly.

Jacob clasped his hand over his own simple cuff. It took a moment for her to realize the fear in his face meant he too had a debt. Her driver could share the same fate. She couldn't hold back her imagination from filling in the scene—

Jacob writhing on the ground, his severed hand beside him, and miles of blood stretching out in every direction.

NINE

"This is the largest of the publishing houses, Miss Leahill, Northlin Publishers," Mr. Cobbet said as they toured the facility.

He insisted on leading her by the arm, like she was a dainty flower he must keep from being tread upon. Lenora let him. His skin was thin enough for the blue veins beneath to show like rivers on a map. He had survived nearly a century, she imagined, based on his hunched shuffle. She could forgive his adherence to the manners of lords and ladies that presided over his lifetime.

With such insistence on etiquette, it was a wonder that the elderly Mr. Cobbet had been accepting of her decision to manage the estate. The younger men, especially Mr. Cobbet's own grandson, 'Cobbs' as they called him, pressed her to hand over the managerial duties.

They suggested a distant cousin or even an associate among their ranks to run the operations. Mr. Cobbet sat quietly in his chair at such length, Lenora was sure he had dozed off. Only when the others insinuated they may have to take the situation to the Council did he speak up. He simply told them to stop wasting time on pointless disagreements and to let her run what was rightfully hers. The others quickly dropped their vocal opposition.

Whether Mr. Cobbet believed in her capabilities or was too old to care was of little consequence. She was in his debt.

Mr. Cobbet led her to the presses. The rusty smell of ink seeped from each machine. With boney fingers, he pointed out the basic mechanisms and costs of operations. His colleagues lagged behind.

They ceased to be openly against her authority; however, that didn't mean they accepted it, either. The group didn't offer advice or information freely, nor did they feel the need to request permission in most affairs. To a degree, Lenora didn't mind. The arrangement worked well to give her flexibility, granting her time to pursue Elliot's elusive Delirium source as well as ponder what role Fogarty played in her father's death. On the other hand, she found many of their decisions questionable. The issue with the publishing houses was among those unauthorized decisions.

"So, you see, Miss Leahill, the cost of running the presses during both shifts, as well as the expense of staff, far outweighs any profits brought in." Mr. Cobbet patted her hand. "This month two more papers have converted to Peritia-only, cutting profits further. It doesn't make sense to keep running the houses any longer."

"And how long have they been unprofitable?" Lenora asked.

Cobbs spoke up. "Well, they have been an expense to the estate for many years, honestly. Of course, Mr. Leahill was quite firm in his belief Peritia would never replace print. Rather old-fashioned. It's obvious that you are more enlightened, with such a lovely cuff and all."

The remainder of the flock joined in agreement, claiming her cuff was elegant and uniquely sophisticated and other such overly embellished flattery. Such an awkward feeling to finally receive the praise for her cuff now that the very sight of the thing colored her with dread and disgust. She thanked them for their insincere compliments while scanning over the scrawled numbers in the file.

"It appears the deficit is miniscule considering all the earnings of the other ventures." She spoke with a deliberately stern tone, the manner she heard her father use with his associates. "And these publishers were so dear to Father. It would seem disrespectful to his legacy to shut them down now, so soon after his departure from this life."

Perhaps "dear" wasn't the correct term, but it would suffice. Shrinking the print available only meant Peritia would become more necessary; a disastrous move for containing the epidemic, not that she could directly say so to anyone quite yet.

"We understand your reservations considering the recent tragedy." Cobbs broke between her and Mr. Cobbet, forcing him to release her arm. "However, we are employed to be the rational voice of the estate. The prudent action is—"

A man charged into the room. Average in practically every sense of the word, height, build, wardrobe, even his face existed in a blandness. A completely unremarkable presence had it not been for the cross of distress and depression layered over him.

"Unacceptable," he spat to the pack of suits surrounding Lenora. "We were given a promise. Unacceptable for you to disregard it like this."

"And you are?" scoffed one of her associates.

"Walter Bartleby, the night manager."

Cobbs met Bartleby with the aggressive stomps of the captain of a ship. "Promises are only kept by those who make them. I'm afraid whatever arrangement Mr. Leahill made doesn't extend past him. If you will excuse us." After giving a curt nod to Mr. Bartleby, Cobbs turned to her. "Let us continue to review the account. This quarter alone the publishing houses have an additional five-percent loss in revenue on top of the deficit from previous quarters…"

Cobbs went on at length. Mr. Bartleby shrunk back away from them. Lenora knew what devastation looked like, and this incredibly average man wore it in the most obvious manner. Head drooped, eyes brimming moist and red, he leaned against the windowsill.

A face popped up outside the window, the coins in her hair swaying in the breeze. Lenora almost murmured, "Magpie?" in shock. On second look, the face had vanished.

"Both are acceptable. Which would you prefer, Miss Leahill?" Cobbs said.

"Prefer?"

"Selling the properties or repurposing them? We could always use more storehouses."

Cobbs stood too close to her. The look he gave felt as if he were attempting to squash her merely by thinking it. She knew the expression. So well, in fact, that it no longer had any effect on her.

She stepped away from Cobbs and toward the window. "Excuse me, Mr. Bartleby, was it? If I may inquire, what was it my father promised?"

He wrung his hands as he spoke. "He promised to place all the employees in comparable positions elsewhere if the house was ever to close. He insisted he wouldn't shut us down, but he promised no one would be without work, if it ever came to that. After all, these are tradesmen. They have spent years, decades, perfecting their skills. Where will they work, if the Leahill house closes?"

The employees around the room perked up, if only slightly, as if awaking from a daydream. Their anxiety suddenly became clear. Men once revered for their trade, men once coveted and employed at great price, cut down to relics of a time recent yet painted as a distant past.

They needed the publishing houses to stay open; so did she.

She addressed her flock of waxed mustaches and waistcoats. "It appears your file is lacking some vital information concerning these houses. The fate of those in my employ should weigh into the decisions regarding all aspects of the company. After all, a business is only worth the character of its workers, wouldn't you agree?"

The group was flustered, scowls aplenty, except for Mr. Cobbet, who cracked an amused chuckle.

Lenora shifted her attention to the whole of the room as she continued. "As a Leahill, I am bound by the integrity of our family. I will honor the word of my father. All the publishing houses will remain open. If, at any time in the future, these doors close, those who have served the house will be repositioned elsewhere without a dock in wages."

The room shot up a pitch. The men toiling at the presses stopped in a half-stunned, half-joyous pause. They scrambled to shake her hand, to thank her. Even Mr. Cobbet leaned in to congratulate her boldness in the matter, mentioning her father would have agreed.

There was no chart the suits could produce that would withstand her claim on family honor. Without anything further, she had Mr. Bartleby walk her out to the carriage.

"Truly, we are most grateful. I'm at your service, day or night. Anything you need," he said before they strapped on their masks.

Lenora found him peculiarly mediocre as he dashed back inside. Still, there was something profoundly warming about gaining his loyalty. The bright faces of the workers gave her a lift in a rather odd way. It cost her so little, yet somehow accomplished so much.

But her mood plummeted when a new challenge strutted towards her wearing a crimson top hat.

Fogarty scooped up her hand before Jacob opened the carriage latch for her. He wore gold rimmed goggles and a brass screen bolted over his mouth instead of a mask. Even in the dotted grey air, the polished metal appendages redirected the limited sunlight, the weak beams not quite blinding but not easily ignored, either.

Flanked by several of his wax men, Fogarty pulled her close. His men situated themselves in a tight circle around them. She was surrounded. Fogarty's frigid kiss on her hand on one side and Jacob anxiously pacing outside Fogarty's men on the other.

"Miss Leahill, what a fortunate encounter." The filter kept his jaw from moving, yet his voice came out unaltered. "My intention was to call upon you later this week, yet you have once again preempted my plans. Your adroitness is a wonder."

He made great use of his free hand, tipping his hat in a grand fashion. She barely noticed the gesture compared to the immobile lips whilst he spoke. She almost preferred the unnatural grin to the dead yet vocal hunk clinging to his skull.

"Mr. Fogarty, quite the surprise." She pulled her hand away.

"A grand, fortunate surprise, considering I am en route to a location I believe will be most enlightening. Come." He waved his arm forward to an inconspicuous, yet large carriage parked in front of her own.

Around the corner, a scarved hip jutted beyond the bricks, matched with a hand gripping the building. Only half of her face was visible, the eye like a dagger. She straightened herself, glaring back at Mary Magpie. Whatever gypsy curse she tried to conjure, Lenora wasn't succumbing to it. Birdy retreated behind the building.

"But, Miss, you have a meeting for tea," Jacob blurted out. His face went red as everyone swiveled their necks toward him.

A slightly raised eyebrow from Fogarty.

If only Jacob could discern when it was appropriate to speak out or, rather, when it was not. He wasn't helping. Teatime was hardly a strong enough excuse to slip from the ringleader's grasp—and Fogarty knew it. His shift in posture from threatening to merely aggressive proved he would take advantage of the leverage Jacob just fed him. She squirmed with anxiety within the rigid squeeze of her corset.

Jacob's fib might have given Fogarty an edge, but he probably didn't need it. A conversation with Fogarty was overdue. She'd been busied with Brechin's work and not given the circus situation the attention it required. If those fireworks were aimed and set loose on purpose, she would know.

"But a minor spell of an hour is all I seek. Have your carriage follow, and you can depart at any point necessary." They walked forward forcing her to either move along with them or be crushed from behind. "Only a sidestep, if you will."

Even through the goggles, his eyes felt sharp enough to pierce. Beef's stories from the week prior were not forgotten. She had been granted access to his flash and dazzle persona at the circus. In the open street, that mask was flimsy, as he probably intended it to be. The spotlight was gone, the makeup wiped off. Flattery had given way to frustration. The realization of this made her legs shake. She was dealing with the criminal. *The murderer.*

"I insist, my dear." Fogarty wrapped her arm through his, leading her as Mr. Cobbet had, only without the old man's gentle stride.

The instinct to resist popped holes in her resolve. She preferred to interact with him on her terms, not his. Since she now knew what he was capable of, the thought of spending any time in close quarters with him petrified her. But if she played along, set him at ease, perhaps she could draw out his true intentions. She made up her mind—she would swallow her fear. Her feet caught the beat of his stride.

"Follow us, please," she shouted back to the flustered Jacob.

The plain exterior of his carriage was a ruse; for once inside, she was surrounded with the emboldened style of his office—plush violets, exquisitely beaded dangling tassels. On the wall, coat hooks fashioned in the form of golden angels raised their arms in a prayer for masks and hats.

His carriage jetted forward as the stale soot thinned and disappeared out the vents and through the piping. The two wax men worked the controls as a team, one to steer while another attended to the levers and knobs. Their unspoken efficiency was uncanny. As she removed her mask, Fogarty drew the privacy curtain to isolate them.

Hopefully Jacob could match their speed.

"Your assistance, if I may." Fogarty thrust a key shaped tool in her palm and then leaned his cheek towards her.

The screen was bolted to his jaw at the four corners, each screw a protruding star. The matching shape indented on the end of the key tool. She flinched.

"Don't fret, although I appreciate your concern. I lack any sensation in my prosthetic, which joyfully includes pain."

With shaking hands Lenora found the first bolt. He may have felt nothing, but she was certain that invisible needles were sliding effortless through her ribcage to the pulsing muscle within. In such tight proximity, she could smell the cruelty his costume tried to conceal. Bitter tea and blood and moist moldy washrags the servants never changed by the laundry. She cranked the tool to the right.

"Other way, my dear." He chuckled.

The imaginary needles reverberated at his laugh, sending the vibration to her heart. He was enjoying watching the nervous twitch he had placed in her. She forced all her weight on the tool to undo the bolt, grunting little squeaks as she fought. Even with all her might it took several rounds of her best effort to begin to loosen it. For the final twists, she went in manually with her fingers, careful not to prick herself on the points of the star while spinning the bolt as fast as possible.

The surrealness of the situation loomed over her; she was unscrewing bits of metal from a man's jaw yet there were no shredded layers of skin nor was a drop of precious blood escaping. Could a man be both monster and machine? A bolt dropped into his waiting palm. The second came slightly easier but her wrists ached after completing the task. The screen slid down hanging from one side.

"My gratitude. I can finish. That side is a tad difficult to maneuver." He said through still immobile lips.

The last two bolts he dispatched with ease. He turned his head to ensure she witnessed his show of how they gave under his hand with little effort. Screen and bolts removed, the mechanism bellowed a gust of steam and wound the grin up as his eyes widened, pulling him long like when a shift in light elongates the shadows on the parlor room wall. He twisted his gloved hands and all the pieces he had been holding vanished.

"Voila!" he exclaimed, jaw whistling.

Lenora shrank back into her seat, unsure if he desired applause she wasn't suppling. "The technology is most impressive."

The scenery outside morphed rapidly. The soot-smeared cobblestones of the city proper softened to country roads. Without a rear window, she was unable to check for Jacob, but felt secure he wouldn't abandon her.

"May I ask where we are going?"

"A fair question. May I answer it with a confession?" He scooped up her hand. "I'm a fool to believe a woman of your caliber could be deceived. As I'm sure you are already aware, there was no plan for a charity event. It was not my intent to mislead. Your idea caught my fancy, and I'm prone to wild tangents. Creative genius can be such a curse. Alas, what Samuel and I had embarked upon was far less entertaining but no less noble." He took her hand to his chest and bowed before continuing. "My deepest apologies."

She wiggled her hand free. "I see. Apology accepted. What, then, was the nature of your venture?"

"An answer to a question." He pulled his glove tight like a surgeon prepping for the incision.

Lenora envisioned him looming over his enemies, fancy hat spins and sleight of hand tricks before he decapitated them. She pictured blood slipping down the metal nose, pooling around his silver teeth while his grin only cranked wider.

The tiny pinpricks in her chest twisted into panicked stabs. She needed to flee. Escape was possible; the carriage door only required a quick pull of the handle. Granted, her limbs would be scraped and bruised. A cold sweat swept over her. Fences whipped past in a blur, shrubs and trees little more than smudges of green streaking past the window. At this speed, she would break an arm or her neck. She pushed the instinct of flight away and tried to focus on what he said. *An answer.*

"And what was the question?" She willed her face to remain as neutral as possible.

He gave her no response. From a secure slot on the wall, he drew a polished red oak cane with golden accents. The handle was crafted into a bird's talon which crushed the globe in its grasp. He tapped the cane firmly on the cabin's floor with a sound thud before leaning over it to set his stare on her with unblinking intensity. He looked like the photograph in her father's collection of a mysterious beast in tall wild grass, readying himself to pounce on his prey. Lenora shifted her weight and sat on her hands to keep them still. Otherwise, she might have reached for the door handle.

The carriage braked in a quick halt. Without her hands to brace herself, she flung forward, nose grazing his cane, and then back roughly enough to bang her head on the seat. Fogarty held firm on his cane.

"Ah, it seems we have arrived." He fetched his hat nonchalantly. "Forgive the abrupt stop, my dear. My drivers seem to require more practice with deceleration."

The slam to her head left a buzz in her ears, like masses of swarming insects. No blood, but a cameo-sized bump rose on her scalp. She gave the tender spot a rub.

The carriage grumbled to a stand-still in a dry patch at the end of the dirt road. They must be high in the hillsides. Only the heartiest vegetation weathered the wind-blasted hillsides, but even those tough grasses grew brittle in the autumn chill. Large boulders baked in the sun without the cool cover of trees. Scales of dry, rust-colored lichen covered the rocks in patches like shingles, a leper colony for contaminated stones.

She liked the view even less knowing her escort enjoyed putting on performances to shock and appall. If this parcel, gasping for its last few breaths, was his backdrop of choice, Lenora filled with dread at what he intended for the main attraction.

Fogarty opened the door and motioned for her to exit.

"Couldn't we talk in here? It looks brisk out there, and I've neglected to bring my heavy coat." She planted herself in the seat.

"You need to see this." Fogarty grabbed her arm and wrestled her out. "I insist."

Outside, the buzzing sound in her head swelled all around her. It rode on the icy blast of mountain wind that blew up her knickers and made her legs shake. It echoed across the perishing land. She imagined rapidly flapping metallic wings ripping through the chill and thousands of stingers searching for a victim.

Lenora jumped as a cutting scream rose above the buzz. Fogarty held tight to her arm as she twisted back towards the carriage. The door rolled away before her fingers could brush the handle.

A dilapidated chateau became visible as the carriage pulled away. Six towers of varied height rose above the base building, giving the impression of a medieval castle. Where a moat once laid, thick wrought iron fencing now secured the area. Discolored drawbridge chains still pinned to the exterior; swaying aimlessly, as if the heavy bridge reached for some lost purpose. In its prime, it must have been a sight to behold.

But its prime had passed. The structure stood firm, but all the ornate details had been stripped from its façade. White stone blocks of the walls looked dappled, textured by decades of neglect. Each of the towers ended in a flat cut off, making them huge, hollow tubes like a paper wasps' nest. Pointed wrought iron fencing wrapped tightly around the premises like a bright ribbon, warning to keep clear of the nest or suffer the wasps' stings.

All the tiny windows were barred, yet hundreds of arms reached out of them, dirty limbs writhing about like maggots. The sound wasn't in her head—the buzz blared out from the belly of the chateau. She split apart the pandemonium of noise; yelled words, unhinged laughter, whistles, all mixed with screams to morph into a single sibilation. The frantic pitch locked her knees. She feared her ears would bleed as the volume rose.

Fogarty squeezed her arm painfully tight before releasing it. He twirled his cane around himself in a wide arch, his grin frozen in place while his brows downturned sharply.

"Behold, one of the Council's desolate homes for the insane, where your father and I began our joint venture," he yelled over the screeching welcome from the captives.

Father, here?

A battle brewed within her. On one side, icy jabs of fright ravaged her at the thought of entering the asylum. On the other, another chance to peel back a layer of the epidemic. What better way to gain a solid grasp of the situation than to see the reality firsthand? It frustrated her to no end that any gains she made required she face nightmares.

Her internal battle was pointless. The force of Fogarty's presence constricted. He would thrust her inside by any means necessary.

Dust whirled up as Jacob maneuvered the Wilthiem in beside them. He jumped out with the engine still puffing at full steam, radiating outrage. She had no doubt he had utilized his full range of colorful language as the Wilthiem failed to keep up with Fogarty's beast of a carriage. His hands curled into fists, likely fully prepared for a duel.

Fogarty paid him little mind. He instructed Jacob to pull the carriage around the back of the building and to collect Lenora's belongings from his servants. The casual dismissal caught Jacob off-guard, and he looked unsure of what to do. He waited, still squeezing his fists tight, until she gave him a shaky nod. Then, he reluctantly retreated to the Wilthiem.

The ringleader drew up her arm in a mock gentlemanly gesture and more dragged than led her toward the building. As petrified as she felt, she let Fogarty pull her to the gate. If her father had managed to visit these wretched premises, so could she.

Fogarty banged on the gate with his cane before anyone scampered out to assist them. He announced himself, and those on the other side of the fence clanked the chains about. One door of the gate opened a slit. Lenora contorted her back so her bustle would slip through. Men in white coats stained russet secured the gate just as efficiently as they opened it. They watched her through side glances as they wrapped the chains roughly. One spit a wad of moss-colored chew on the dry ground.

She was almost grateful when the ringleader ushered her into the building proper without a word.

The air inside carried a strong, moist heat as if the whole ventilation system was clogged. Vinegar, as potent a cleaner as it was, didn't cover the heavy odors of vomit and feces. Her hand went to her nose instinctively.

"As intrusive as it is, you will grow accustomed to the smell rather quickly, my dear." Fogarty pulled the hand cupping her nose down.

"What—?" But her words turned to sand on her tongue as his jaw closed with a sharp snap at her. His teeth scraped as the top row slid over the bottom, the metal screeched with the friction.

"Quiet. Just keep your eyes open."

They stood in a tight entranceway. A few steps away, an admission area opened, separated from the hall beyond by a heavy iron door. Several bulletins which outlined proper interaction with patients, shift schedules, and such were posted around the front desk. Lenora saw them as warning signs, words that might as well have been carved on headstones. *Here Lies…*

A small sign fitted on the wall next to the paper-littered desk read Deklin Asylum.

"The usual visit?" asked a man behind the desk, a pen in his teeth as he peeked up from his papers.

"Of course, Charles."

Charles tossed a thick open book at Fogarty along with the pen he extracted from his lips. Fogarty signed. The man didn't check the signature as he snatched his pen back.

"Wait here." Charles unlocked the heavy door and stepped through it.

Fogarty settled on his cane, only a finger-width from brushing against her. Lenora squirmed. With small shuffles, she put distance between them an inch at a time. The cane came slamming down on the stone floor. She jumped at the noise volleying back and forth in the claustrophobic space.

"Listen well, my dear. Take careful note of all you see here, as this is the only way I can get you to understand." His jaw hissed with a release of steam.

Charles returned with a pale, boney woman, whom he introduced as Miss Tarnell. He explained she would escort them inside. She had donned the outfit of a nurse, but her stance was more fitting for a governess—the kind that raps knuckles.

With an air of annoyance, the stern nurse led them through a set of locked doors. Deeper inside the structure, the humidity rose, salty and musky. Along each side, Lenora could make out the faint numbers beside each cell door that had been worn away by time. The slap of hands reaching out of the bars to bang on the doors blended in with the muffled screams like some sort of ritualist music conjuring the spirit of insanity.

They passed a pair of patients in rags, each strapped into rickety wicker wheelchairs being pushed by white coats. Embedded into their temples, sets of wires twisted like some larval form of the mechanical creature from the faith house. *Council technology*. The same type of wire connections to the head, only this pair didn't appear able to comprehend anything. Their placid faces stared through the world.

It looked more like torture than an attempt at a cure. She shouldn't have been surprised after the church—clearly the Council saw their people as resources to be used up and discarded, like the woman thrown in the pit.

They took a lift operated by Miss Tarnell's key. As they rose, each level seemed to make the elevator creak louder in a shrill whimper. The gears yelped when they stopped—a final cry before the doors rattled open. Fogarty placed his hand flat on her back to push her into the hall.

The cell doors on this floor each had a barred window the size of a head along with a number. No muffled cries reverberated on this level. The sudden absence of noise was jarring. All Lenora could hear was the soft sound of her breathing and the clicking of Fogarty's jaw. The reek of unbathed bodies and urine hung so sickly thick that the floor shone with the condensation of the taint. Lenora had to adjust her walk so not to slip.

A stream of tan, gelatinous material shot out of the barred window of room number seventy-three. The mess hit the floor before Lenora's feet with a steaming splat. She flinched. The dull starchy smell labeled it some sort of porridge.

A soft voice within the cell mumbled, "Why do they keep sending this stuff? It will just sit inside me—inside the empty—and rot. Emptiness can't eat. Rot, rot, and mold. Then the rats come, and crawl into the empty."

Lenora couldn't help but let the words roll around in her head. *Crawl into the empty.* The empty promises of the Council. The half-empty open grave—probably infested with rats. Everything that fell inside would rot, just as he claimed. She bit into her lip. *What's wrong with me that the insane make so much sense?*

Miss Tarnell shushed the man as she motioned to door seventy-eight.

"Call me over when ya done wit 'em," the nurse instructed flatly before returning to the door of the lift and pulling up a stool.

Three hefty locks secured door seventy-eight. Lenora froze. Every other cell was secured with one lock—just one. The solid wood splintered around the bars of the window as if clawed by some unspeakable beastly thing that inhabited the Dusang of her nightmares. Decaying breath hissed out. Fogarty took a sweeping step and knocked on the door.

"Robert? Robert, it's Jonathan Fogarty come to call." The cell remained silent. "Robert? I'd like to introduce you to a distinguished guest."

A bit of rustling came from beyond the door. Fingers ground down to scabby nubs curled around the bars, the scrape of the rough flesh on the metal like roaches crawling around in the dark. Wires weaved in and out of his skin—parasitic filaments that burrowed their way into the tips of his fingers, up his forearms. She couldn't help but shudder.

In the asylum, more than Delirium penetrated the patients; the claws of the mechanical era pierced through as well.

The hands gripped the bars tightly before a ruddy nose poked through them. Coarse skin made dull and dark with layers of grime became visible as the man forced his face against the barred square. He sniffed deeply, like an old hound desperate to catch a scent. Then, a cackle erupted from the man that sparked laughter through all the other cells. The entire hall chortled uncontrollably at some warped, shared joke she wasn't privy to.

Lenora inched back a step. She kept reminding herself these were victims of the epidemic, poor souls who desperately needed a medical solution. Yet, they all looked like monstrous caged things to her, corrupted by wires and cogs.

"You don't smell like the cards I need," the man beyond the door hissed.

The roar of laughter from the other cells rose a pitch.

Fogarty slammed his cane against the floor, and the hall quieted. "Robert, this is Miss Leahill. Miss Leahill, this is Robert Dewar, one of the original members of my theater troupe and costume designer extraordinaire. A rather dear friend of mine."

The nose protruding from the bars continued to sniff wildly.

"A pleasure…" she said shakily.

"Useless card to me. Worthless," Robert said.

"What card?" she asked more to Fogarty than the contained man. "I'm afraid I don't quite follow."

"The winged child of Hermes and Aphrodite, one foot on land, one in water. Stupid girl. It's so simple." Dewar gnawed on his chapped lips a moment coating them with frothy saliva, then he peered at her curiously. "You at least bring me the wheel?"

A few squeals of "wheel" and giggles came from the other cells as if to give his question more urgency.

"Closer." Fogarty shoved her nearer to the door as his jaw clicked into a flat expression.

Dewar's hands pulsed taut and slack on the bars. The knuckles went white and then deep scarlet as the blood rushed back after each squeeze.

"A wheel?" Her voice was small.

"*The* wheel. There is no other way to get in here, or out. Don't know shit about shit, do you?" His nose rubbed against the bars leaving a trail of glossy mucus behind.

Fogarty seemed to sigh, but it was mixed with a whistle of steam from his apparatus. "Robert was quite impressive before. A capitol actor and a gifted designer. After witnessing his decline at the Whindmiere Asylum, I vowed to find better care for his recovery. This facility is far superior, although I know it likely doesn't appear so. Rather luxurious for Council-run. Still, it's apparent there's nothing they can do to restore him to his former self with this level of care. *The Council level of care.* We obviously need a cure, Miss Leahill, but we must also address how inept the Council has been regarding this epidemic. You notice the implants in his hands? I have my suspicions the Council has taken the liberty of testing their inventions on—"

The contained figure jolted forward and slammed into the door with a heavy thud. Even Fogarty flinched. When Dewar resettled, threads of blood dripped from between the dry cracks of his lip.

The ringleader offered him a handkerchief, which the patient snarled at.

"You and all the false airs. Devil!" Dewar licked at his broken mouth. "A kingdom of flies and squat, and here I was, looking for penance. A morsel of the glow. But all you offer is tower."

"This curse will be lifted from you, old friend," Fogarty replied.

Dewar's head slammed back and forth, forcing his extended nose to impact the bars with several clear crunches. Red splattered and ran down the door, rushing from the freshly deformed snout. The creature laughed, a maniacal cackling which gushed out of him in time with the blood. He looked the part of the cannibal from one of Elliot's disgusting paintings. He thrashed into the bars gleefully.

Fogarty sprang to the door to still Dewar's head, and she followed. *He's still a person,* she told herself, *still human.* She fumbled around his chin; blood and spit squished between her fingers. She held it firm while Fogarty clasped both of the man's temples.

The head stopped nearly as swiftly as it had begun its fury. Dewar's hand lashed out like a whip, his scabby fingers securing a firm grip on her hair. The coarse, grated skin of the mutilated fingertips scraped her scalp. She couldn't scream—the hall's stench choked her so only a squeaky gasp came out.

He pulled her locks and bashed her cheek into the bars. He held her there, so close to his face, she could smell the rot of his teeth. "You're not listening, are you, fool? We need the wheel!"

Fogarty thrust his cane between the bars, landing a blow to the patient's chin. Dewar clung tighter, cramming her into the bars so that the bones of her face felt the metallic cold. Several whacks of Fogarty's cane upon his wrist, and he ripped her free. Dewar still managed to take several strands of her hair as keepsakes.

"My sincerest apologies," Fogarty shouted.

She could barely hear him. He wiped his handkerchief on her cheek and neck. It took her a moment to realize he was not only removing some of Dewar's blood from her skin but some of her own from a gash on her eyebrow as well.

Then the laughter. It spread from Dewar all through the hall, each cell caught up in the frenzy of uninhibited laughter. High pitched uncontrollable laughter that pinged from the walls to the floor and ceiling. It sounded more sinister than the hum of the Enforcer's rifles to her ears; an immediate threat born from the irrational. It promised no mercy.

She bolted for the lift. Her sudden sprint drew arms through the doors. Their filthy hands reached to swipe at her as she fled. She could hear the crack of Fogarty's cane lashing out at the arms behind her.

They nearly crashed into the waiting Miss Tarnell. The lift shuddered and then sank down with a quick burst before it settled into a stable decline. Lenora's stomach jumped into her throat. She listened as the laughter gently died as they descended, the monsters saving their sadistic energy for the next visitor. Her cuff felt heavy and constricting on her wrist, throbbing in time with the battered side of her face. All those injections—she could have been among their ranks, wallowing in madness.

What if I already am? What if I am mumbling about a circus and faith houses from the depths of a cell?

"A wet cloth for the lady," Fogarty commanded to the stoic Miss Tarnell.

Miss Tarnell repeated the order to another nurse as they exited the lift. Lenora had no intention of lingering in the asylum. With each door Miss Tarnell unlocked, Lenora barreled through before Fogarty could catch up to her. Not even the weight of her cuff would slow her.

She nearly hit him with the iron door at the front when a nurse chased her down, wet towel in hand. Lenora snatched it with her soiled hand. She wiped her face and neck vigorously without a thank you. The thought of that man's blood mixed with her own made every part of her ill.

"Mr. Fogarty, I do believe you have made your point about the state of this institution." She handed him the crimson-tinged towel and rushed outside.

He ran after her. "My apologies once again, but it was vital to our cause you see what Delirium does. It's not just a touch of madness. It destroys the person they once were and replaces it with that. And the Council *lets* it happen, Miss Leahill. They will let it happen to everyone. Look at the conditions. The Council has no intention of saving them."

She could hear his jaw clicking as it repositioned itself. She couldn't tell which sound was worse, the floor filled with hysterical laughter at her expense or the noise of his falseness shifting.

"I know my view of the Council may seem radical. In fact, I'm aware that if you were to bring my distaste of them to light, I would be disposed of rather quickly. But I believe you can see their failings as well, as your father before you did!" he yelled. She froze at the reference to her father. "Please, hear me but a moment."

Jacob spied her from the corner of the asylum then sprinted out of sight, presumably to fetch their carriage.

"I have suspicions, my dear. I believe the Council not only knows what causes Delirium but have a hand in its spread. That's the real question: What are they doing to us, the citizens of Elsothe? But I have no connection to medical professionals beyond the influence of the damned Council. That is where your father came in." He grabbed her shoulders, his voice launching out rapidly. "He employed a doctor, one not bound to the Council in any manner. This doctor found *something,* and those findings may not only be our salvation from Delirium, but also destroy the ones who ruined our country. Do you understand now, damn it? The fate of the country rests on that name."

Her cuff went tight around her arm, strangling the limb. The bloody Council knew how it spreads, yet they let the epidemic go on. They allowed it to spread further. Still, every part of her being told her Fogarty's goal went beyond the epidemic and the Council. *Some ambition he seeks so vehemently, he would kill for it.* The ringleader and his flattery and intimidation, it was a different sort of madness.

His hands dug into her joints as his eyes pitched manic. "Who is the doctor? Who?"

Jacob skidded the carriage around, throwing up a blast of dust. Lenora pried her shoulders loose. Backing away from the blurry outline of Fogarty, she slammed into the coach door and ripped the handle open. With her jump into the Wilthiem, Jacob tore off, leaving Fogarty screaming on the road.

"The name! The name!"

TEN

Lenora entered unannounced, no knock before she strode into the room. *Manners be damned.* Jacob drove her around the city for well over two hours to be sure Fogarty's beastly carriage didn't follow them. Her reserve of pleasantness ran dry.

Brechin's office was still a chaotic pigpen, yet she could easily overlook all the bits of wire and papers thrown about. *One can't expect an anarchist to be organized.* He sat behind his desk rolling a cigarette with Harold crawling up his shoulder. He looked up in apparent wonder as she shoved a pile of clothes and books off the settee before plopping down, slouching into the seat as if it were her private chambers.

"Couldn't leave it alone, could you, Lenora?" He licked the paper to seal the cigarette. "I do the research; you provide the funds. That was the deal."

"I don't recall signing anything official regarding that."

He responded with a growl which was more a weak poke than a harsh stab. "And it looks like you got a lovely little cut on your brow. You should take more care when pursuing your research. What have you found, if you please?"

"Did you know Fogarty is more or less a crime lord in Pitchdrift?"

He struck a match as she said it but let it burn nearly to his fingers before dropping it in the ashtray. With the unlit cigarette still clinging to his lip, he said, "I told you to stay clear of the circus freak. What possibly possessed you to discover anything regarding that man?"

Lenora sat up straight. "You possessed me. You obviously implied Father's death was intentional, so logically, I figured Fogarty had a hand in it."

Another match struck. This time he brought it up to the tip of the rolled paper to light the cigarette. "I suppose I lacked tact during that conversation. You were about to cut my funding, after all. I wish you would've forgotten him. Honestly, I would have liked if you'd not gotten involved at all, save the funding of course, although I do enjoy having such a lovely partner." He rounded his lips and popped several smoke rings into the air. "Well, I guess there's no point in omitting him now. Fogarty was… an acquaintance of Samuel's, so to speak. I don't know how they met, but at some point, Fogarty claimed he knew for a fact Aqua Peritia caused Delirium. Further, he lamented there was nothing he could do about it without a way to secure legitimate, scientific evidence."

She figured as much. Harold slouched back from a plume of smoke. Making his way down the arm to the desk, the lizard twisted its neck at a severe angle to peer at Lenora with a yellow orb eye.

"And my father hired you for that evidence," she said for him.

"Naturally. No law-fearing freelance doctor would even consider such a task, and Samuel was a patron for many of my projects. We were both rather titillated at the prospect, actually—to have irrefutable proof the Council needed to be toppled from their pedestal. But, as you witnessed, Peritia is the path of the spread of Delirium, not the cause. When Samuel told Fogarty this, he said it didn't matter because the evidence of the spread was enough for his purposes."

"His purposes?"

"I'm as clueless as you are on that account. When Samuel asked of his purpose, he became irate, demanding the research papers, or my name, so he could collect them. Samuel wrote of his numerous gifts, both glamourous and threatening. I do believe Fogarty sent him a box of severed fingers once. It was getting out of hand, to say the least. We decided to back out of the situation. I hid the findings, hoping Fogarty would lose interest or find some other means to enact his scheme. It appears we discounted his intensity on the subject."

There it was—the last piece she required, the buildup before the fireworks. Fogarty killed her father. All those haunting sensations that he was still there, following from Foxton to every small, tedious errand, screaming at her with some wail she could hear only with her the blood coursing through her veins. *His* blood. He was seeking vengeance through her.

"Discounted his intensity?" Lenora stomped across the room, burning from her core. "Dr. Brechin, my father is dead because of this man. *Dead.* And you have the audacity to play it off as though it was merely a matter of underestimating him?"

Smoke rose from the smirk over one eye. "Elliot, if you please. Your blood does fire up with such ease. It really is lovely."

She reached out to slap him, but he pulled back.

The smirk quickly vanished. "I meant no offense. Please, calm down. Samuel meant a great deal to me, too. Let me have a look at that cut."

She gulped for a cool breath. Elliot flattened the nub of his cigarette in the ashtray. The residual smoke thinned. He brushed aside the wisps of hair lining her forehead to get a better view of the cut.

"It's not deep, but I should clean it," he said.

When he concentrated with that expression of concern, he almost looked dashing in a roguish sort of way. She leaned back, letting the desk between them create a comfortable distance.

Harold slithered to the edge of the desk placing his snout on her thigh. She gave him an unsure pet, as if he were a tame dog.

"You said you hid the research papers," she said.

"I did."

"And where are they?"

The corners of his mouth curled back up. "With a friend whose blood doesn't fire up like yours, though I wonder if you are truly angry or if this is how you doctor your fear. Like the way you over sugar your tea," he teased. "You really don't need to hide it. As I said before, fear drives mankind forward."

She tried to brush off the taunt, but truth always burns.

"Where are the papers?" she pressed.

"Safe, but that's a topic for another occasion, when I can add the source to the pages. What of Fogarty and the crime of Pitchdrift?"

"We'll talk of Fogarty afterward." She gave the iguana another pet, this time gracing the scales with a surer touch.

"After?" Brechin snapped his head up with interest.

Lenora pressed her hand firmly on the desk, tilting her forearm so the light caught the cuff and danced across his face. "I want it off."

"Ha." He dug into his tobacco, scooping a few pinches into a fresh paper.

She rushed her hand over the desk, knocking papers out of her path. Then she thrust her wrist at him, squarely aimed at his face.

"You're serious about this?" He cocked his head to the side. "You do realize no one has ever done such a thing before. Well, not willingly, and not leaving the hand and wrist intact."

"But it can be done?"

Elliot took her wrist to examine the piece and area intently. "Possibly. The tube appears to be set in deep. Sutures for the vein might work, although I wonder if the tissue will respond and heal together after such a long separation. It would require an incision to reach the vein. Such delicate bone structure, quite captivating." He wiggled the cuff then flipped her wrist down while pushing her palm flat to flex the injection site. "I've heard of a couple cuffs being replaced before, but never a full, permanent extraction."

"So, you can do it?" She tired of being stretched over his desk, the edge digging into her hips while he rotated her forearm in every conceivable position. "Elliot? Can you?"

His eyes left her wrist and returned to the whole of her. "Think of the scandal you'll cause. The Leahill heiress finally gets a Peritia cuff only to have it removed? You'll be the talk of Canimere. Brilliant. I would do it for the public speculation alone."

"I'm not interested in what they have to say." She withdrew her arm. "I simply want it off, *if you please.*"

He softened for a moment, a brief breath where his eyes lifted from jade to aquamarine and all the angles of his smirk melted into a flowing bend. She turned away from him as she felt an awkward blush bloom across her cheeks. He abruptly snapped upright.

"Right, then. I shall remove it and tend to the cut as well. This way." He led her through the side door in the office. With a tender chuckle, he added, "If you please."

The state of the adjoining clinic-style room shocked her. Pristine in every sense, every item in a logical, organized place from the polished forceps to the crisply pressed and folded linens. Somehow, the abundant dust army from the office was unable to storm through to the clinic. Not a speck settled on the examining table, nor a smudge marred the counter.

She found it impossible that Elliot could maintain such a standard of sanitation. Evidently, a cleaning woman serviced this room but not the shambles of the office. Her heels glided over the waxed floor. *Several cleaning women*, she corrected herself, *and well-paid ones, at that.* At least she could take pride that some of the funds she provided Elliot went to a worthy cause and not just for his indulgences.

"I'll require some time to set everything up," he remarked as he strapped on leather gloves and a matching apron. "Sutures, naturally, and..." he mumbled on rummaging through drawers.

She wandered over to a set of brightly colored jars that caught her fancy on the counter. The labels on each read *Hirudo Medicinalis*. She pulled the red and cream jar toward herself, the contents shifted in a weighty splash that rocked back and forth in the vessel. She barely pinched the lid when Elliot swooped in and grabbed the jar.

"Wise decision. If the sutures stop blood flow in the vein, a couple of these might do the trick. We should have them handy. Best to be prepared in such experimental situations." He placed the jar beside his array of sharp objects. Doctor's paraphernalia or torture devices—they all looked the same to Lenora.

"I'm sorry, *them?*"

"Leeches. Quite helpful in the manners of blood impurity. I attempted to use them to clean the blood from Agitated Delirium for a spell. The result was less than successful." He motioned to the table. "Make yourself comfortable."

Lenora laid down. She could sense the veins in her wrist pulsing with a newfound vigor, as if taking in a last gallop before dropping down into the inevitable abyss. The final gasps of her grand plan to use Peritia to propel herself to the forefront of the Age of Awareness.

Elliot opened the ether, or so she surmised by the sweet yet sterile aroma.

"No ether."

She heard the clink of the bottle as he set it down roughly. "Are you daft? You can't possibly mean to—"

"No ether," she repeated firmly. The vein pumped double time, racing up her arm to her center. "I need to feel it leave me. To know it's gone."

If the poor souls in the faith house didn't get the luxury of ether in their torture, neither would she.

"You will wake up and find it gone. Trust me, it's far better if you let me tend to this while you sleep. Otherwise, you'll move around."

"Strap my arm down, then."

He pounded the cork back into the ether bottle. "You're ridiculously stubborn."

"Not any more than you are," she snapped.

He leaned back against the counter; his arms crossed to match his scowl.

She added, "Each individual to rule themselves, isn't that your belief? Anarchy and all that? Well, I have decided I don't want ether. I want to feel it. Now, strap down the arm."

"I don't like it," he said with a grandiose sigh.

"You don't have to."

"Fine. Try not to scream, will you?" He adjusted a set of restraints tight around her arm.

The pressure caught her off-guard. She glanced over at the cuff, glistening like the false idol it was, to see if her wrist was swelling. It wasn't.

A quick wipe with alcohol in a cool burn around the site.

"Ready then, daft, stubborn heiress?"

He cut the leather strap of the cuff.

"More than ready, arrogant anarchist."

The scalpel sliced in. A burning gush of dark blood oozed out in a dense curtain down her wrist and pooled onto the table. The straps went taut as her muscles rebelled against her will, every sensation ripping through her limb contracting the flesh.

She wouldn't scream. She couldn't, as the boiling within the fresh gash of her wrist clobbered her diaphragm, beating the breath from her. Hot blood rolling over the edge, raining down to the floor with gentle splats. He worked the wound open, scalpel drawn along a hair before the meat tore. She couldn't breathe. He pulled the tube out—she felt every inch of it slither from her. The scene before her speckled black, soot falling before her eyes, and then the curtain of oozing crimson plunged her into darkness.

A woman in an elegant evening gown with lace and pearl accents glided effortlessly through the oversized grass. The blades bent to accommodate her, moving out of her path or collapsing flat on the soil for her heeled boots. Swift and graceful, she dashed through the greenery while appearing to stroll along. Lenora scrambled behind her, crawling through uneven rocks and batting away the blades of grass as they leaned in to slow her progress.

"Mother? Mother!" But the woman wouldn't yield, not a step altered by the pleas.

Lenora toppled forward. Thorns and raw earth rushed up to meet her, scraping her forearms and knees. The woman vanished from her view.

"Mother, wait! Wait for me!"

Nothing but a thin breeze rustling the oversized grass. Lenora righted herself. The trail of the woman now lost in the dense lawn jungle.

The grasses split before her, opening a path which stretched for what seemed like an eternity. Storm clouds whirled overhead. A dozen yards in front of her, a giant lizard leapt onto the newly formed passage. It wore her father's handlebar mustache and hat but peered back at her from one shining yellow eye. The creature's tail whipped across the grasses, slicing the blades. It held up the tail's tip rounded into a globe and dangled it at her.

The woman mounted the lizard gentleman and turned to Lenora, her face blank. The lizard's forked tongue flicked out. They shot off on the path, scaly claws tossing up dirt as they went. She ran after them, calling out for her mother to stop. No heartbeat, just adrenaline racing.

The moist earth fizzled into cobblestone, the cramped buildings of Pitchdrift moaning along either side. The gentleman lizard scaled the turrets of a church, curling itself around the tower. The faceless woman stared at Lenora, glaring with the full absence of any feature to stare with. She rang the bell. The ring so shrill the moaning structures banged into each other, spitting bricks and timber. The very cobblestones shook loose beneath Lenora's feet.

The faceless woman and the lizard's golden eye shone from above as the tubes burst forth from the street below like snakes spewing dark sewage in their wake. She wouldn't let herself scream, curled up with her hands over her ears and her eyes shut tight. *No screams.*

Someone shook her.

"Lenora, wake up. Come to, damn it. Lenora!"

The hazy visage of Elliot. Beyond that, bones. Bones stacked to form a man and a horse in a field. A field with brilliant red flowers. *Poppies.* Lenora shook her head. *That dreadful painting.*

"I'm awake." She rolled over to a comfortable position on the settee.

Elliot swiped a cool washcloth across her forehead. She became aware of her rapid breathing and the abundant sweat that drenched her red hair.

"You had quite a nightmare. Not surprising with what you put yourself through. Are you satisfied? Did you feel it come out or whatever it was you wanted so badly?" He pressed two fingers to her neck, measuring her pulse. Then he tilted her chin towards him. "Look at me. How many fingers am I holding up?"

He raised one finger, the middle one. She meant to slap it but lacked the power to inflict any sting on the offending digit.

Her wrist was a swollen mass neatly stitched up in a crisscross pattern that throbbed with a dull ache. She brought the sutures closer to her face so she could see how the blood had congealed and blackened around the thread.

"I felt it come out. That's enough for me. Are you content with the lack of screaming?"

The cuff was gone, and in its place, she wore a battlescar. She touched the stiches, barely, one at a time.

"I wouldn't poke about that too much. The cocaine will only last so long." He shook his head. "Daft woman. Stubborn and demanding, dare I say spoiled? Are you going to be this much trouble on our wedding day?"

She dropped her arm to her side. "Our wedding day? You mean to say you intend to court me? Now who's daft?"

A soft smirk. "Who said anything about courting? It's an absurd tradition that does nothing to prepare either party for a marriage. Besides, who shall I ask for permission? I rather like the idea of cutting to the heart of the issue without all the dull protocol and nonsense."

"You can't possibly be serious. What about anarchy?"

Buttery Elliot again, wide eyed as if in awe of something. Her middle filled with fluttering of the strangest fashion, like she had swallowed a number of hummingbirds who hovered inside her, searching for an escape.

"What about it? I do as I please. I think Mrs. Lenora Brechin has quite a ring to it, don't you?"

"And then you would have full access to my fortune. You're impossible. Absolut—"

He dove in to press his lips against hers. Firm, but not rough.

She thrust back into the cushions only to have him follow her deep into them, chasing her into the velvet pillows. She was trapped, gloriously and uninhibitedly caught, so as soon as she came to that realization, she gave up the chase. With her surrender, he pulled away, leaving her bewildered at his withdrawal.

He stood up and turned his back to her. "Fogarty."

"What?"

He avoided meeting her gaze, straightening his shirt in a fidgety manner. "Fogarty. You mentioned some connection between him and Pitchdrift crime."

Lenora sat up, her head still wobbly, but she managed to keep herself upright. "Switching the topic, just like that? You are utterly inconsistent and intolerable."

Had she the strength, she would have thrown something at him. He had already crossed the room, hovering over his desk rolling a fresh cigarette.

"Only trying to keep focus on the matters at hand. Tell me."

She settled into the seat and crossed her arms. As she recounted everything that Beef said regarding Fogarty, she couldn't help but feel a sense of violation. Just a kiss. Yet there was more to it than the simple innocent embraces she casually accepted at the academy. None of those boys kissed in such a manner. Theirs had been a quick peck that grazed her and fled. This had been deliberately planted with a feeling behind it she hadn't felt before—passion. She liked it, and that made her burn all the more with aggravation. By the time she finished retelling everything from Beef's story, she felt ready to scratch his eyes out for the forceful embrace.

"Well, then, that must be the source. Ha! I believe you bested me. Well done." He retrieved a dust-coated bottle of wine from the shelf and pulled his shirt from the waistband to wipe it clean.

"Wait, what's the source?"

He searched among the shelves to pull out two wine glasses. They clinked together as he jogged to the clinic. The piping gave a few knocks in the wall and then the sound of running water.

"In the air, of course," he yelled from the other room. "The air he vents into his buildings. Obviously, the floral scent is to overpower the smell of whatever concoction he's made which results in Delirium. Why else would he spend the money to scent the rooms?"

"Bloody hell, you're right. That makes perfect sense. It would be easy to spread, and no one would be the wiser." She slid her handkerchief through her fingers to help soothe as she rolled the idea over in her head but had to abandon the motion at the surge of pain in the stitches. "Well, almost perfect sense."

He returned, shaking the still dripping glasses to spray drops in all directions around him. She managed to stand though the throbbing in her wrist grew into wincing pounds. So much for the medical wonder of cocaine.

"Almost?"

"Why do such a thing in the first place? Frame the Council, surely, but then what? I doubt he has no plans for after their fall."

Elliot pulled out the cork. "I'm damn sure of that as well. From what I've heard, he has some grand scheme in mind." After he filled the glasses two thirds full; he placed one in her hand. "But let us tackle that question after we gather proof of my theory."

"And we get this proof with?"

His smirk had never been higher as he tapped his glass with hers. "With a wealthy heiress, of course."

ELEVEN

Lenora stood in the hall of the east wing staring at the double doors of her father's chambers. In the unspoken manner of so many manor rules, her father's private rooms had always been forbidden. He never specifically said that, there had never been any locks or overbearing servants to bar her entrance, it had simply been so. After dinner, he would retire to his private library or quarters not to emerge until the next morning, if she happened to glimpse him at all.

Once, when she was six or seven, she had worked up the courage to ask if she might join him in the library. His response had been to instruct the governess to tutor her on the definition of the word "private." Shortly after that, her father had arranged for her to attend Glenn Haven Academy.

She hesitated outside the double doors to his chambers. *Was it still improper to enter when death had taken the occupant?* If her father truly did haunt her, intruding here would likely infuriate the ghost.

Her father had a knack for hearing her sneak up to press her ear against the door. As soon as she touched the oak, he would fling the adjoining door open and cross his arms disapprovingly, calling the current governess to come fetch her.

Her hand reached out, wrist still stitched and tender, and let her fingertips drift down the wood. Nothing happened.

With her eyes closed, she pulled the latch and jumped into the room before she could lose her nerve.

She whispered, "Anyone here?" to the darkness but was met with only stillness.

The lights flickered on with a switch of the knob. The quarters were decorated in subtle, simple lines. Her father had been like that, no frills and certainly nothing too brazen. He preferred muted earth tones and polished wood to arsenic green and bright brass. Only the finest leather chairs would do for his seating. A music player in the corner was the singular piece of machinery amidst the subdued furnishings. Even the four-post bed in the adjoining sleeping chambers had a clean, straight structure.

A box of cigars sat squarely on the table with a long rectangular ashtray, awaiting the master of the house to settle in for a smoke. The musk of rich tobacco leaf and warm notes of cedar from his favorite brand had soaked into the carpets.

Above the fireplace, a painting of Father in his dapper attire wearing a serious, flat lipped expression gazing down at the space with neither delight nor dismay. Had she ever seen him smile? Not an honest one that she could recall. She watched him watching her. The eyes of the portrait, ever cold, lashed out. She stood frozen staring at his image, daring it to move while in her view. After a few moments, she melted a touch at the realization of how foolish she was being staring down an image of pigment and oil.

"This is preposterous. I just came to borrow some clothes," she told the painting, which only stared back vacantly in reply.

She shook herself free from the spot.

She set off to find the wardrobe. Elliot had instructed her to retrieve black trousers and a dark shirt. It still didn't make sense why she couldn't have one of her servants purchase them for her in the city. Elliot rattled on about causing suspicion and other such nonsense. She would have to give him an earful when they next met for forcing her to go through her father's things like this.

She snatched up the items as quickly as she could. Trousers, men's socks, and a grey shirt. Her hand grasped the doorknob to leave when she spun back around. A belt. She would require one to keep the trousers up. There were many to choose from, though they all seemed the same with a woven leather strap and brass buckle. She pulled a random one, only to have it snap back like a whip from her haste and knock a frame from the wardrobe. The cracking of the glass pane on the floor filled the empty room.

"Damn it."

Whatever it portrayed, the glass had broken and now she would have to tell Claire to have someone clean it up. As if Claire didn't give her that disapproving look enough already.

The pane was cracked, making a web pattern spreading out from the top right corner, but none of the glass had left the frame, thankfully. A faded picture, probably from an older camera by the fuzzy look of the figures. The man she instantly recognized as her father, though he lacked a mustache, and the deep worry lines that seemed carved in from birth. He stood in a suit next to a woman in a white dress. A woman she recognized from dreams wilted just beyond her conscious thought.

Something moved near the window, like a slight shift of light. Lenora gripped the picture. If ghosts did exist, it would be at a moment like this, with her all alone in the bedroom of the deceased, for one to appear.

A pair of legs swung over the sill, and Lenora felt her heart lurch against her ribs. The legs were followed by a flowing skirt and the jingle of a coin belt.

"Miss Magpie. To what do I owe the intrusion?" Lenora cemented her feet firmly in the carpet. The outrage of Magpie's trespass drowned out the shock of a woman crawling into a second story window in the sheer dark of night.

Mary hopped into the room with grace. The warm spice scent of Fogarty's theater oozed from her. It blended with the soaked-in memory of her father's cigars. The aromatics blended together, complementary, as if her father paired well with the likes of the circus. Lenora found it repulsive. The cruelty of the present world had no right to mix with nostalgia. He had been a poor excuse for a parent, but he was *her* parent nonetheless.

"Dropped off a little package for you. Saw this light on the dark side of the building. I figured must be you. Decided I'd get a little climb in, seeing as I want a word." She shrugged.

The absolute disregard for basic decency in this woman sent Lenora flaming.

"You mean *he* wants you to tell me something. Is that why you've been following me? He sent you to watch me?"

"The package got his words for you." Mary put one hand to a hip she jutted out. "I got my own things to say—my own reasons for watching."

"Then I suggest you go back out to the front door and arrange a meeting with my staff as is proper." Lenora responded.

Lenora tucked the picture between the folded shirt and pants. She put the bundle on a nearby chair, then half circled Mary while maintaining eye contact.

Mary's jaw tightened. "I'm already here. Proper enough. 'Sides, there's no reason for us to do like the gentlemen. Their rules aren't any good for us—we don't need escorts, yeah?"

Lenora advanced a step. "There's a difference between outdated etiquette and simple civility."

Magpie took her own step forward in response, an expression ripe with curiosity played on her face. "What happened to your cuff, fancy lady?"

"What happened to your manners? This unwelcomed visit is over. Will you leave on your own or shall I call—"

"My family are all *Vizi*." She pronounced the last word in her sharpest high note as if it was a threat in itself. When Lenora didn't react, she giggled in her twittery manner. "You don't know what that means, do you?"

"And I don't care."

Mary exaggerated the sway of her hips as she strode forward. "They dream awake. They see things that happened and things that are coming. I can do it too."

Lenora kept her stance, letting Magpie meet her in the center of the room. The ringleader terrified, but Lenora would not let herself fall cowardly in front of a crass woman. She would hold her ground, even as her joints stiffened at the thought of a fight.

"Fortune tellers?" Lenora mocked. "Well, that does seem fitting for you."

"Real Vizi." Mary's voice went shrill. "And I've seen you. Had that dream since I was a child, and it's you. Knew it was you when first I saw you. You're the reason I lose my crown."

The instant the words left her lips, Mary went so tight the dangling beads and trinkets danced at the sudden pulse of rigidity. She elongated, back firm like a board while her fingers twitched in tension. Her eyes rolled back into her head, the visible whites glassy like a porcelain doll. Half words and whimpers squeaked from the taut form. The woman appeared as an apparition in the soft warmth of her father's room.

Lenora growled at the display. This fanciful act was beyond offensive. She steeled herself to wait out the charade. Surely Mary couldn't maintain the posture forever. Yet Magpie remained fixed in her tension at such length her skin went near translucent, and her lips seeped from ruby to purple. Lenora's certainty eroded as the seconds ticked by. There could be no other logical explanation than Mary was performing, and yet, the gypsy's breath dropped so shallowly her chest no longer rose and fell.

A creeping dread spread from a small whisper in her head. *What if?*

Lenora reached out to touch the specter. Mary jumped back by the window like a whip. Lenora couldn't swallow back her gasp.

"You lose me my crown, then you join the men at the table. Playing cards. Wagering their own flesh. Chunks of their bodies as the pot. A tongue. A toe. And you, you ask to be dealt in. You want in!" Mary screeched as she flung herself at the wall with a thud.

She crumpled down into a low crouch. Mary's body, impossibly firm moments before now settled itself on all fours. Her spine bent into a deep slope with the chest curving upwards. Fingers spread wide, digging into the rug. The neck stretched over to the side, twisting her head towards Lenora a breath at a time. A mass of black hair shadowed all her features save for one dark pupil. She no longer looked the agile birdy; instead, she warped into the contorted spider woman.

Magpie's voice went low. "Stay away from him. He's mine. Send the name in writing. Don't come into Pitchdrift. It's my crown!"

Mary scrabbled across the floor then leapt out the window into the moonless night beyond.

Lenora rubbed the erect, fine hairs on her arms to smother the goosebumps. She waited for a scream, a thump, or something to signify Mary hit the ground in a bone shattering crash. Instead, she made out faint taps as Mary scaled down the wall. As soon as the little clanks of Mary's adornments ceased, Lenora closed the window and curtain. She didn't bother to check if Mary found the grass safely.

"Loon." The word came out unsure.

Her father's portrait gazed down unfazed by the gypsy's antics. Lenora pushed Mary from her thoughts.

She grabbed the pile of borrowed items and dashed to the private library in the west wing. There, she placed the bundle of creased clothes and frame on the desk.

There was a heavy knock, and the door opened without pause. She hastily stashed her father's items in the desk drawer as Claire huffed in with an ornate jewelry box.

"Another gift from Mr. Fogarty," she said.

"Oh, um, put it—"

Claire placed the box on the desk with an annoyed sigh. "There you are."

Wrapping paper in gold with violet accents. If nothing else, Fogarty was true to his color scheme.

Claire froze as her face took on a look of horror mixed with disbelief. After a moment Lenora recognized Claire's gaze had fallen on her mangled wrist. Her arm was swiftly pulled from the desk to hide in her lap. Claire recovered instantly and headed toward the door.

"Please, wait. I wish to discuss something with you."

The grey bun snapped around. "If it's 'bout the hunting dogs, I've no idea how they got loose. Jeffrey managed to round 'em all up this afternoon. They're in the carriage house for now."

"Actually, this is more of a…" Lenora reached for the right phrase. "Private matter."

Claire smoothed her apron and closed the door before returning to the desk. Her chin tilted up as far as Claire could crank it.

"I would've thought you knew no one can run this manor like I do. And I do run the manor, not that Welston seems to think so." Her crow's feet dug deep when she squinted down at Lenora.

Lenora couldn't help but smile. Dozens of governesses and butlers and drivers came and went, but Claire had been a fixture in the house, ever frowning upon her when she broke a vase or flooded a washroom.

"I know it. I'm not dismissing you. Please, sit."

Claire backed into a chair.

She scrunched her thin brows at Lenora. "What can I do for you?"

Lenora folded her hands in front of her, then decided that was too formal and separated them awkwardly. She wasn't exactly sure how to even begin.

Finally, she stuttered off to a start. "With all the accounts… It wasn't what I expected, and I need advice on how to manage it. No—how he managed it. I want to know who my father was. I mean who he really was, not his reputation or what he owned. What he was like as a person. How he dealt with all this."

Nothing caught Claire off guard. Not the shrill sound of young Lenora's whistle that had startled all the other servants. Not the vast amounts of missing or half enjoyed sweets. Often Claire had served up a sharp reprimand in response but never a gasp. The housekeeper managed a flat scowl through every prank and unpredictable event, snapping her fingers at the startled staff to fix whatever Lenora had broken. But that moment, for a split-second, Lenora felt sure she had finally managed to shock Claire.

"That's not my place."

"Your place, my place, secrets—I'm quite done with it all. If you won't tell me, whom shall I ask? No one has been here as long. And Father certainly isn't fit for discussion!" Lenora slammed her uninjured hand down on the desk.

"Lenora Elizabeth Leahill, mind your temper!"

The shaky chuckle that slipped past Lenora's lips was unexpected. It wasn't that she found Claire amusing so much as she was astonished by how that tone still choked her with a childish guilt. Ever the stone face, Claire didn't show a twinge of regret at scolding her employer. In fact, her face lit up righteously. A power reversal of the oddest sort, the housekeeper roping the estate owner in line, yet it seemed rather natural.

Lenora set her chin on her hands. "I suppose I deserved that. I just tire of not knowing. Father's reputation is not the reality. How am I to handle all he left without any real idea of who he was?" She swiped her handkerchief between her fingers. The mix of her father's cigar scent with the circus spiciness of Magpie clung to it. They shouldn't pair so nicely. He wasn't that type of man. "No one's willing to be straight with me. I'm getting brushed aside, like I'm still seven. The bankers tell me it's improper to discuss this or that with a lady, and his other associations… well, there's as many wolves out there as sheep. How am I to manage blind?"

Claire let out a small snort of amusement. "You really think people goin' hand you everything? Like if you want answers or respect, they goin' wrap them all nice and put them in your lap? The world doesn't work like that, Nora." Claire's use of her old childhood nickname jolted her. It had been years. "'Specially for us women. Trust me, they won't give you anything easy. Stomping your feet and saying you want things ain't goin' to do shit. The fancy gents just going to laugh. Stop throwing tantrums and start doing."

The words were sincere even if her demeanor was forever blunt. Lenora didn't have a mother growing up, but she did have honest, stable Claire.

"You're one of my favorites, you know?" Lenora sat up and focused on her posture. The governesses had stressed the importance of good posture when making your case. "I'm asking as a favor, woman to woman. Some of his associates are at odds with the type of man he's reputed to be. I'm faltering here. I need to know where he was coming from, where I came from, if I'm going to make any positive impact at all. Please, what was he like?"

Claire fidgeted on the narrow seat. Lenora had softened her a touch. She could see it on Claire's face. "Fine. But you didn't hear a word of it from me."

"Agreed."

"When I first started working the manor, I didn't know much about him. The Lady Leahill hired me. I'm mighty grateful to her for that. A fine lady, your mother. Had upstanding kin and a good heart. Mr. Leahill treated her right. Anything she wanted, she got, no bothering with cost. Seeing as she was a social lady, he held grand galas every year, one in the spring and one at the smack middle of autumn. People came from all over Elsothe." Claire faced the wall, watching some lost image Lenora couldn't see. "Even had some royalty from Laverli come a few times. People staying weeks here, every room filled. Big roast dinners and dancing all night. Your father was a right proper host. Warm, welcoming."

Foxton full of jubilation, entertainment, and company. If her cousins had visited once a year in her childhood, she would've been ecstatic. Never would she have believed her father would host a full house plus more and do so with joy. She couldn't help feeling a bit green that she hadn't gotten to witness it.

Claire came back from wherever her reminiscing had taken her. "Then they were with child, you. Put your father in a bad spot of worry with the lady's life in peril and all."

"Her life?" Lenora ran her handkerchief through her fingers.

The death of her mother suddenly clobbered her. No one ever told her how her mother had passed, nor had she asked. She should have. She should've asked and asked until someone broke and explained it. Yet, she never felt an interest in it or, more likely, had been too afraid to find out. Her mother was gone, a faceless lady slipping in and out of her dreams occasionally. It had been effortless to keep it that way—uncomplicated.

Claire smoothed her apron meticulously before continuing. "Fine women like that aren't meant for childbearing. Their babies don't sit right. Breach babies. But the Council had a device they were testing that turned babies like that right, and it worked for her. You came, and those were the happiest days."

A small sigh of relief. Her existence hadn't been the wind that blew out the flame of her mother's life.

Claire's face darkened. "But good days don't last, Nora. You were three, and Mr. Leahill was havin' trouble with the Council over some business. I think they wanted him to sell 'em the paper mill or publishers or something. He didn't, going off about how horrible their Peritia cuffs are."

Claire shuffled in the seat again, avoiding eye contact. Lenora detested when she stalled like this.

"Go on," she prodded.

The old woman cleared her throat. "Yes, well, Mr. Leahill didn't sell, and the lady of the house being with child again—"

"I have a sibling?" Lenora broke in.

Irrational hope flooded her. She hadn't realized how desperately she wanted that family intimacy she glimpsed in the windows of the houses they drove past. A little sister, or brother, to roam the hedge maze with. Someone to share the burden of the family businesses, kin to come home to, but the downward gaze of the housekeeper shattered all those fantasies in an instant.

"Well, no. As I've always said, fine ladies aren't meant for childbearing and with the Council and Mr. Leahill fightin', they didn't give him the device again."

Lenora collapsed back into her chair with her thoughts cramping up on her. She would have had a sibling, someone to grow up with, and her mother could have been alive to shower her with all the comforts and affections mothers were said to give. Everything would have been as it should if the Council had chosen to be generous and forgiving as rulers should be. The more she thought on it, the more a jagged rage burrowed itself in the back of her mind.

"Mr. Leahill went dark after we lost her. Kept to work all hours. No more galas, and after a couple of years of turning folks away, they didn't come anymore. And, well, he never came back from mourning her really. Pushed all those dear to him away, you see?"

"I do. Thank you, Claire."

The housekeeper excused herself. Lenora didn't notice she had left for a long spell. The anger consumed in an absolute, incapacitating, way. A silent seething that punctured her skull and clung there. Maybe five minutes passed, maybe five hours, she couldn't tell. She had to let the fury melt and settle with deep breaths.

She pulled the picture from the drawer and set it on the desk in the warm light of the gas lamps mixed with the electric fixtures.

"Mother."

Her mother's nose was small and sharp. Lenora traced her own nose; it was wider like her father's but ended in a point more like her mother's did. Her mother had fewer freckles, but she heard those faded with age. High cheekbones that gave her mother a note of nobility. The same small pout of a mouth Lenora bore. The same rounded brows.

She traced the picture over, tears in a sudden overflow down her cheeks. A family taken from her before she was old enough to be aware of the loss of it. She let the mourning pour out, head resting on the desk. The wedding photograph gently cradled in her arm. A family hug that lasted as long as it needed to.

She finally pulled herself upright, wiping the streams off her face.

As much as she hated the thought, it bubbled up regardless; *Fogarty is justified in his hatred of the Council.*

Her father's strange associations suddenly made sense; Elliot, Fogarty—those who wanted the Council to fall. She set the photograph aside and pulled Fogarty's gift in front of her.

A tiny note attached by string dangled from the jewelry box. "The Name" was all it read. She opened the lid, crushed velvet inside to protect a brilliant pearl necklace. Rather oddly shaped pearls, angular and somewhat square. A chill ran up her spine. She pulled the strand out to examine them closer and found they didn't feel smooth and cool as pearls do. Rough like bone.

She tossed them across the desk only to feel fear grasp her from the realization.

It was a necklace of human teeth.

TWELVE

Elliot spied around the corner into the courtyard. The dilapidated housing buildings surrounded the cramped square like authoritarian parents glaring down at the accumulated filth. There was a light flurry of ash in Pitchdrift, practically the sparse fall that occasionally sprinkled over Roudonel. Lenora would've found it a welcome rarity for the district on any other night. At that moment, the thick cover provided by Pitchdrift's usual onslaught of black snow would've been more helpful. She poked a pile of soot ahead of her, though Elliot had already speared it, just in case.

Jacob thrust his way to Elliot from the rear. "Do we really need to do this? It don't seem safe."

"Shhhhhh," Elliot hissed.

Elliot cocked his ear toward the courtyard. Lenora held her breath. She could hear a jumble of noise, feet stomping, a crowd of excited voices, but she couldn't be sure if it came from the main road or if someone still lingered in the courtyard.

Lenora commissioned the entire Haveriture farmer's market for this distraction, a charity event. Dozens of carts overfilled with a wide variety of produce and specialty treats lined the road, rationing out their goods free for residents. Each participant got an equal share. The question was how long this would keep the buildings empty for Elliot's plan.

Elliot thrust his head around the corner a second time then ducked back.

"Did you have to place the carts so close?" he whispered.

"You told me to make sure they drew the people out of the buildings, and they have. And the carts wouldn't go any deeper into Pitchdrift. Do you have any idea how much I had to pay them to come down here? More than the cost of the food they are dishing out, I assure you," she retorted.

"Lower your voice." Elliot pulled the three of them into a huddle. "It appears everyone is out on the road."

"Yeah, getting their fill of a free meal," Jacob said bitterly.

"Charity is proof of the generous nature of the privileged," Elliot snapped back at him.

"Well, my charity will only last so long. They will come back once they have gotten all they can carry, so if you want to do this, we need to do it now." Lenora squeezed between them.

"Or not do it all," Jacob added.

"Why did you bring him along? He's far more of a nuisance than a proper escort." Elliot nudged her arm.

"I didn't think an anarchist cared about what's proper," Jacob said.

"Ha! Very good. A witty response." Elliot nudged her arm rougher. "I do believe your chap is growing on me."

Lenora let out an exasperated sigh. "Enough, really. You two can have at each other another time. Let's be done with this."

She didn't want to linger in the alleys. With each breeze grazing the back of her neck, she flinched. Her previous encounter with the Enforcers in Pitchdrift refreshed in her mind, and she doubted they would deviate from their patrols. Not even for the Pitchdrift Nourishment Charity Event, provided courtesy of Northlin Publishers.

At least she had Cobbs' frustration to look forward to, if all went well. Dumping a hefty sum in the name of the publishers would have all the suits flapping about like chickens with a fox in their coop.

Wearing men's attire added to her unease. It was unsettling to be in trousers. When she crouched low, they gathered between her thighs in an awkward fashion. The lack of a corset had been exhilarating when she first dressed, but now she felt vulnerable and wide. She longed for the security of a skirt. A man wouldn't hesitate to shoot down a trespassing man, but a lady might cause him pause.

"Alright." Elliot took another quick look over his shoulder at the courtyard, "Here's the plan: your driver will take the building on the far left, you have this one." He patted the brick wall they were gathered next to. "And I'll go for Pit's Pot Tavern down the alley there. That way we get samples from a variety of Fogarty's places. The ventilation systems for the housing buildings should be in the boiler rooms under the first floor. Look for a hatch around the back or the side, or an out of place door on the first level. Make sure to keep your gloves and mask on when you collect the sample."

"And what exactly are we collecting?" Jacob piped in.

"The bloody perfume from the ventilator. Weren't you listening on the way here?"

Jacob's voice rose. "I was driving. If you'd give normal directions—"

"Shhh," Elliot broke in. "Get the sample. Should be in a jar or container hooked up to the ventilator. A full dropper's worth, if you can. Slip in, collect, slip out. Easy."

Nothing in Pitchdrift was easy, and Lenora didn't expect that to change for this endeavor. She took the bad omen of the light sootfall as proof enough the district was stacking the odds against them.

"We meet back at Ruu's. Good luck." Elliot dashed around the corner into the shadows.

They had come from the back of the building Elliot assigned her. No hatch at the rear or in the alleyway they stood in. The other side of the building met up with its neighbor, not a full inch between. That left only the first floor to explore.

Jacob tapped her arm. "Should we go together, Miss? First your building, then mine?"

"Not enough time." She scooted along the wall, checking around the corner herself.

"But it'd be safer."

"You promised if I let you come along you wouldn't interfere. Trust me, I can do this. Just get it done. Alright?"

She crept around the building before he could say anything further. Ducking below the windows, she dashed to the doors. They were still wide open from the trample of people that poured out of them moments before.

Without a mudroom to clear off the ash from outside, a black layer coated the walls of the hallway. For a moment she almost thought it was fur, as if the hall were a beastly thing breathing with the breeze coming in from outside. She wasn't sure if the walls beneath were brick or wood, not that the unfortunate people dwelling there cared. A low ceiling made the place feel tight and cramped, like being trapped in a box.

Numbers were scratched into most doors. Other doors wore faintly painted numbers to designate the separate rooms. Several were cracked or broken with big round holes, as if someone had punched straight through. She could peek at the shabby living quarters inside. Boxes for tables, bits of fluff and ripped cloth sewn together for bedding, if the owners were lucky. Most just had rags laid out on bare floors, where she assumed the inhabitants sat and slept. Everything was coated with an oily sheen, probably from Fogarty's fragrance, peppered with bits of soot.

A door at the end of the hall creaked open. She scrunched herself into a tight ball against the wall, squeezing as far into the ash lining as possible. She held her breath.

A little girl with matted hair walked out into the hallway. She had a simple but worn dress and bare feet. In her hands, she cradled a ball of stitched together bits of cloth and carpet as if it were a doll. Her fingers rubbed the ball as she stared blankly ahead with milky eyes. The child couldn't be more than four. Lenora relaxed.

"Hello? I know you here. I hear," the girl said.

Lenora stepped away from the wall. She gently wiggled to toss the ash off her back into a half moon on the floor behind her. The girl tilted her head side to side, one ear to the hall and then the next.

"I hear. Hello?"

"You're blind," Lenora said as the fact hit her. To be lamed at such a young age was a dreadful thing, but even worse in a home among the rats and ash.

"I'm fast. I scream." The girl clutched the ball tighter. "What want?"

Lenora took a cautious step forward. "I'm not going to harm you. I promise. Please, I need to find the boiler-room."

Her head settled to pin an ear directly at Lenora. She pet the rag wad a few times, digging her fingers across the varied textures. "Promise?"

"I swear. I'm trying to help you, everyone here actually, but I need to find that room. Understand? Can you help me?"

Rapid strokes across the ball. "End hall, this side." The child stretched her arm to the left.

Lenora crept forward pausing beside the girl, whose creamy irises gazed off into oblivion.

She slid a handkerchief between her fingers; one of her father's old fine silk ones with *S.J. Leahill* embroidered in the bottom corner. She usually relished the perfect amount of wear on this particular handkerchief. The silkiness matched with a delicate thinning as it had been used over the years. However, as she watched the girl absently pulling her fingers over the rag ball, she couldn't enjoy the silk. It lacked the pacifying effect it once had.

She gently placed it in the girl's hand and said, "Thank you."

The girl dropped her rag ball, running both hands over the silk handkerchief in ecstasy as tears welled up and spilled over her cheeks. The girl rubbed the silk over her arms and face as if it were the essence of life itself. Lenora felt a sharp pulse of sympathy within her ribcage as the girl chanted, "Soft. Soft. Soft."

The last door on the left was marked with a simple *No Entrance* sign layered over the wood with far more nails than should have been necessary. Surprisingly, she found it unlocked. The inhabitants were probably too fearful of Fogarty's men to set foot in the boiler room.

Weak lighting revealed a steep staircase that descended into a dim room. She could hear a continuous sputter and rattle below striking a sour chord when mixed with the blind girl's chant in the hall. She closed the door behind her.

She took each step with delicate footing; in the dark it was impossible to determine if the stairs were secure or merely held in place by some string and tack. Besides a few creaking spots, the whole held her weight easily and she tiptoed into the shrouded boiler room.

Slip in, collect, slip out. Easy. And with the samples they would be one step closer to sparing the people the source of Agitated Delirium. Any way to ease the suffering of the those trapped in Pitchdrift was worth the risk. *I can do this.*

Lenora couldn't smell the fragrance being piped in the building through her mask, but she could see and feel it. Thick billows of vapor streamed out from cracks and loose joints in the deteriorated piping. The cool mist collected on the back of her neck and up her sleeves, giving her a brief chill. The ventilator knocked as it ran, dials fluctuating between metrics she had no conceivable idea as to what they measured. With the glow from the coal furnace, the scene looked like a cheaply assembled crematorium warming up for the next corpse.

Setting up the little collection kit Elliot provided proved no challenge. Finding the container of the perfume took longer, as there wasn't an obvious large jar set out filled with thick mucus liquid like she had imagined. She circled around the rumbling ventilator a half dozen times, the minutes ticking down in her head. Time was of the essence and each lap around the machine kicked her anxiety up a notch.

If she hadn't tapped the repurposed milk bottle with her toe, she never would have found it tucked at the rear of the machine. Barely a smidgen more than enough clear fluid to fill the syringe. Her hands shook with a second wind of adrenaline as she transferred the sample to the test tube, however she filled it without a drop spilt. Capped and packed in her pocket.

Easy, just as Elliot said.

The door at the top of the stairs swung open. In a sheer panic, she leapt under the stairs. Heavy footsteps pounded down the steps. Nowhere to go but deeper into the crevice, she wedged herself between the coal bin and a pile of loose tools. The steps ceased at the bottom. She felt her heart beat erratically, unsure if it had hit a manic rate or couldn't keep a steady rhythm.

She must have been sloppy and overconfident, leaving a trail for the Enforcers to follow. Or the blind girl directed them to the boiler-room to drag her out into the street or snap her in half. In this dungeon below Fogarty's slave quarters, there was no escape. She covered her mouth to muffle the sound of her hyperventilating.

She caught a sliver of the man's shoe in the dim light—polished dress shoes reflecting the boiler fire's glimmer. A slight relief. *Not an Enforcers' boot.* Still, polished shoes meant it was unlikely to be the poor fellow in charge of feeding the boiler.

The footsteps made their way towards the ventilator. Tinkering sounds of glass tapped together, then the dribble of a steady stream of water joining a pool. Lenora leaned out of her spot to make out his back. Between the crimson jacket and top hat, his neck flesh bulged with a waxy sheen. He worked on the bottle she had emptied, filling it in an efficient manner. She ducked back into the shadows.

She had nearly believed this plot would go as smoothly as Elliot predicted; instead, she had trapped herself in the boiler room with one of Fogarty's wax men. The refilling liquid a constant trickle piercing her ears like a bolt twisting into the eardrum.

Impossible to gauge how long the process would take but there wasn't time. The food carts would grow empty, and people would shuffle back into their rooms. She would be spotted as a suspicious trespasser as soon she stepped into the hall. They would scream out and attract an Enforcer or perhaps tackle her themselves. On the other hand, trying to duck out as the wax man went about his work terrified her. If he saw her, surely, he would chase after her and deliver her to his ringleader. Far too great a risk.

Frantically, she felt around through the pile of loose tools behind her. Any sort of weapon would do. Fight or flight instinct propelled her into action. With a shaky grasp on the handle, she stepped out of hiding and crept forward on light feet. Her breath heavy but even, her pulse pounded in her head.

Her stealth must have been less than impressive, for the wax man spun around immediately to confront her.

Startled, she swung the wrench wide giving him plenty of time to dodge, but in his evasion, he dropped his near full jar of fragrance, shattering shards of glass across the room. The wax man lunged at her, gripping her throat with both hands. The fingers like clammy putty held in shape with solid rod bones. A rough squeeze and she yelped.

He relaxed his hold. "A woman?"

She took the opportunity to swing again, this time lifting the wrench above her and striking it down on the top of his head. The skull cracked on impact and a bulge of grey mass spit out of the split. The oily skin of his face went chalky with bewilderment, then the cheeks slackened, and the eyes dimmed. He dropped. His body flopped on the broken glass with several snaps and pops before settling limp.

The wrench, splattered with the moist spray of his cranium, slipped out of her hands and hit the floor. The sour tang of bile hit her tongue. *I didn't even hesitate.* Blood spatter on the lens of her mask ran down in straight lines, slicing the world into segments separated by gore. *I killed him.* She took the stairs two at a time and ran out of the building into the night.

THIRTEEN

"And you really thought you were going to sneak up and knock him unconscious?" Elliot chuckled. "You're incredible."

Lenora pulled the blanket tighter around her, even though it reeked of opium, and the course embroidery itched. Jacob said something about nothing being funny, but Elliot only roared with laughter harder, forcing it out from his belly directed towards her driver.

The yellow room should have been comforting. She survived yet another venture into Canimere's cesspool, the dulled canary surrounding her was proof of that. Somehow the room didn't calm, rather it colored her terror with the shade of cholera and cowardice.

"And what was I supposed to do? He would have found me eventually," she said.

Elliot lit a cigarette. "I would imagine so. However, you actually thought he wouldn't notice? A Pitchdrift man that creeps about the district as part of his occupation, being pounced on by a girl who hasn't been in the slightest brawl before? Ha!"

"I slapped a boy once," she snarled back. "Besides, they all seemed so absentminded at the show. Like they didn't know where they were. I figured he—"

"You went to the show? The circus?" Elliot shrieked.

"I told you that."

"No, you didn't. You said you researched him. Researched, damn it." Elliot rolled another cigarette with the lit one still clinging to the side of his lip. He sucked in and then blasted out a storm of smoke from his nostrils. "That makes our entire situation worse. Shit."

"Watch your words. A lady is present." Jacob paced behind the couch, shooting vile looks at the back of Elliot's head.

Jacob had lit his own cigarette. The dry tobacco smoke overpowered the floral opium smell which usually filled the room. Lenora coughed and then made a show of clearing the hovering cloud in front of her. Jacob blew his next exhale upwards but sped up his pacing.

Elliot cocked his head to stare Jacob down. "We are far too deep in for pleasantries. Sit down, damn it. Having you hover isn't helping."

"Fine." Jacob grabbed a chair from the corner and planted himself in it.

"Why does it matter? So, I met him. What of it? We got the samples." Lenora wiggled in her blanket cocoon.

The blood had been wiped from her clothes, but the stain on her soul remained. Elliot only ground into her black mood further. She just killed a man, or something that seemed like a man. Her intention had never been to harm, and yet in this contradictory city of ember snow, she struck a deathly blow on the course for a cure.

The flares of smoke from Elliot's nostrils coincided with his breath. Fast, rhythmic puffs as if from a train engine, as he continued to roll a pile of replacement cigarettes. "Met with him? Privately? On how many occasions?"

Lenora sunk further into her Xouain blanket retreat and set her eyes pleadingly on Jacob. The driver gave nothing in the way of reassurance.

"Well, come on. Spit it all out," Elliot said through a cloud of smoke.

"Privately after the show, yes. He wants the name of the doctor Father had working on Delirium." Lenora winced as Elliot threw the cigarette down into the bowl. "I didn't tell him. I swear."

"And nothing more?"

He lit another one and thrust it at her. She took it and set it between her fingers to mimic the way he held them. The inhale was nothing like the sweet opium. The tobacco hit the back of her throat like fire and tasted like scorched earth. As soon as the smoke invaded her lungs, her body forced it out. Elliot waited for her violent coughing to end without a word. A sip of water, then she sucked on the cigarette again with little better results. However, she felt airiness in her head and a tingling calm spreading through her.

"He took me to an asylum to see what became of people with Delirium. I still wouldn't tell him."

"And?"

"And…" she dug through the blur of the past several weeks. "And he sent gifts. Quite expensive ones at first, but then—" She managed a weak draw without hacking. "The last one was a necklace made of teeth."

"He sent Samuel gifts as well. Severed fingers and such."

"You didn't tell me that until after I had already met him. Perhaps you should've been honest about everything from the beginning," she snapped defensively.

"Perhaps I should have, but that doesn't help us get out of the disaster now. Does it, Miss High Horse?" He surpassed her yelling by raising his voice twice as loud.

"Alright. Alright. Calm down. It's already done." Jacob jumped up from his chair.

Elliot struck a match and held it to another cigarette. He sat back into the couch, grimacing at the floor. He dispatched the smoke in four deep inhales. The fury in his face dimmed as he lit himself another.

"I don't think you two fully grasp the situation we've found ourselves in." Elliot said evenly. "Fogarty will find one of his men dead, while filling the scent bottle no less. Now, if that is indeed the source, what do you think he will conclude?"

She didn't have the slightest idea. There was never a course on the thought processes of criminals at Glenn Haven. It appeared people die in Pitchdrift every hour. She doubted the ringleader would grieve anything more than the loss of a worker when he found the wax man.

Elliot rubbed his forehead in annoyance at her lack of an answer. "He will see this as a threat to his plan. He will rush forward. He will put more pressure on you to deliver me. Let us not forget how that ended for Samuel."

Panic crept into Jacob's expression, but Lenora didn't share his apprehension. A frigid gloom set in. Not fear so much as dread on her shoulders weighing her down, like ice blocks dropped on her from above.

"Shit. Well, at least we know he hasn't had you followed thus far, as I would already be exposed," Elliot said more musing to himself than addressing either of them. "Doesn't mean he won't send someone to watch you now. Especially if he suspects you know who I am. We should keep our distance. At least until I test the samples. Perhaps have you leave the country for a while. I can follow shortly after, that way we don't appear to be travelling together."

"I won't leave."

Being a murderess she could learn to deal with. Being responsible for the possible doom of the city at the clutches of the man who murdered her father? Absolutely not. *Father would never let me be if I were to flee now.*

His neck snapped toward her. "None of your stubbornness. Not this time."

"We can't leave. What about all the people being poisoned here? What about the spread through Peritia? What will become of all those people if we run?"

Jacob settled back into his chair, "Miss, it's not—"

"Safe." She finished for him. "I know. But it's not safe for anyone in this damned place, is it? Elliot, how long will it take to get results from the samples? A few days?"

He pinched the bridge of his nose. "I'm honestly not sure. A week, maybe two?"

"A week. We can work with that, right? You send word once you find what we need in the samples. Then we can plan what to do next. I'll keep busy with the businesses. Even if I'm watched, there will be nothing for them to see. Just the heiress managing her estate."

Elliot slumped forward, elbows on his knees, chin in his hands. "I'm not thrilled with the idea."

"Jacob will be with me to keep an eye on anyone watching," she pressed. "It will be fine."

A long-winded sigh from Elliot. "Fine. If that's what you want, but if something goes awry, even in the slightest, we leave. Deal?"

"Deal."

Five days after she dropped the wax man, Lenora fidgeted in her seat. Canimere Central Bank's conference room had an oversized table regularly filled with overinflated egos. She sat at the head and listened to them bark.

The only decorations were portraits of other bankers, probably deceased, lining the walls. No detailed landscapes in brush strokes for her to mentally retreat into. These business meetings had been annoying and tedious when she first took over the estate, now they were a poor excuse for a distraction. She packed the past five days with as much business, time-wasting rubbish as possible, but it only brought her father's name to the constant forefront of her mind. He was there, circling every meeting, silently wailing at her as his murder roamed the city freely—and there was nothing she could do to remedy that at the moment.

There was no way to tell if Elliot had discovered anything from the liquid they collected. Knowing the doctor, he would sit on the results, even if he had them, for the full week simply to spite her for altering his plans.

"As much as I agree on the importance of good will, this *charity* event was overall a disaster," said a banker with thick bristly sideburns.

"A disaster may be a bit over exaggerated, don't you think, Marlin?" Mr. Cobbet spoke in his usual calm manner.

Sideburns grunted. "Not at all. The whole event wasn't properly publicized, so no potential customers of the publishing house even heard about it."

"Not all charity is solely for appealing to customers and profit." Lenora tapped her pen on the file in front of her.

"Of course not," said a deep voice from the other end of the table. "However, if one is going to orchestrate such an event it's in the best interest of the financial backer to gain a generous public image for their investment."

The table dissolved into a mumble of agreement with heads bobbing down each side. Her eyes drifted over them vaguely. A pale face stood out from the rest, his cheeks sallow, mouth drawn long, open in inaudible suffering. *Father?* She snapped to attention to look again. He was gone, but the jagged urgency he forced into her wouldn't vanish so easily. Twice he had come. *Twice.*

She steadied herself, trying not to thrust all the paperwork off the table and scream. None of this business babble mattered. It was a flimsy distraction that she could sense deteriorating by the second.

"Perhaps the event can still be utilized for public image. What would you say to spreading news of the event after the fact? Build up Miss Leahill as so charitable that she didn't even feel the need to attract attention to her good deeds?" Mr. Cobbet piped in.

"Or the public can interpret this as the blunder of an inexperienced leader," Cobbs hissed.

They continued squabbling back and forth. As much as Lenora appreciated Mr. Cobbet for his loyalty, she couldn't engage with the debate. Every corner, every scrape of a chair moving along the marble floor sent her teetering further towards darting out of the room. *It was Father; I'm certain of it—and nothing positive ever came from a visit from Father, even when he was alive.*

Thoughts ran through her head on a constant loop, no matter how she tried to dispel them. Tubes running up the back of a chair into a neck. The crunch of Dewar's nose against the cell bars. The most vivid and terrifying—the irregular crack of the wax man's skull, and the way he convulsed on the ground making those awful clanking noises on shards of glass.

A younger gentleman from the front of house staff slipped in, unnoticed by the grumbling assembly of bankers. The gentleman slinked over to Lenora, bowed slightly to speak solely to her.

"Miss Leahill, a Mr. Fogarty has arrived and requests to speak to you." His breath ruffled the hairs of her neck which suddenly stood on edge.

Her stomach dropped. Nearly half a dozen packages and three letters from Fogarty sat unopened at Foxton. She had anticipated he would send more with the potential discovery of his plot looming. The possibility that he might visit the manor had dawned on her as well, which was why she strived to be out on business every moment she could. The idea that he would come directly to her in the midst of a meeting seemed too bold a move even for the ringleader. In hindsight, Lenora realized she shouldn't have underestimated his determination in the matter. The man had murdered her father in public on a warm afternoon, after all.

"I'm afraid I'm indisposed for the remainder of the afternoon. Tell him he will have to call on me another day," she shakily whispered back.

The young gentleman squeezed his hands together. "I told him you were in a meeting, but he said he would wait. He is very insistent he speak with you today."

Lenora clenched her pen to stop herself from biting down on her lip. She could imagine Fogarty intruding into the conference room with his grandiose theatrics, demanding she step aside. His metallic grin blinding. The pressure of his sharp aura flooding the space. She was in no condition to face him now. Not with her father already setting his cold stare over her.

"Where is my carriage presently?"

The young man, stunned by the question, stumbled over his answer. "The carriages, they are in the...yours is in the carriage house, I believe. In the rear of the bank."

"And there is a back door that leads there, I assume?"

The gentleman nodded. Lenora quickly stood up and knocked on the table. The suits fell into a hush.

"I'm afraid an issue demanding my immediate attention has come forth. I'm sorry, but I must leave you. Mr. Cobbet will head the rest of this discussion in my absence." Her legs shook when she spoke, but she hoped the firm voice she mimicked from her father would flatten any opposition from the men. She need not have worried; they were all too happy for her to leave them to their work.

She leaned in toward the young man's ear. "To the carriage house, please."

He escorted her down halls and past the impressively heavy looking safe door. They crossed behind the tellers clicking away on counting devices while customers with wry faces shuffled their feet in queue. She caught a flash of Fogarty's hat spinning in mock amusement in the lobby. She turned her face away from the room, hoping he hadn't made her navy-blue dress out among the black and brown jackets. Clenched fists at her side, she quickened her step, out pacing her escort. If she was lucky, Fogarty would settle on his cane expecting the young gentleman to return with a message. Luck hadn't been on her side recently, she noted to herself.

They rounded the corner and slipped out of an unmarked exit. Lenora didn't bother to strap on the ash mask as she could make out the carriage house a few yards away. The gentleman was still at the door preparing an umbrella when she shifted into a run, yelling a "thank you" without looking back.

Nearly blind in the onslaught of soot it took her a minute to ram into the carriage house. Three men abandoned a round of cards to close the swinging door behind her and latch it. She shook the ash from her hair and face but kept moving forward, desperate to escape even if the threat wasn't in pursuit.

Carriages parked in rows. Benches, old wicker chairs, and barrels for makeshift tables strewn about anywhere there was room. Some of the drivers lay on piles of straw with their hats pulled over their eyes. Everyone perked up to stare at her as she wiped her ash-coated tongue with a handkerchief. The coal taste didn't bother her as much as the gritty texture—it felt like Pitchdrift.

"Jacob," she called.

He jumped up from a bench. "Miss? Is there trouble?"

"We have to go. Now. Start the carriage."

They scrambled to the Wilthiem, which was parked at the end of the line. Jacob yelled that he needed to back out and a few men in overalls got in position to open the barn doors behind them. They screeched out of the house before she even realized the engine was running.

"He's here. He came demanding to see me."

Jacob tore through the streets, swerving around any traffic by riding halfway on the sidewalk. They were inches from the carriages at a standstill while tactfully avoiding any pedestrians on the other side. Once he maneuvered them out of the downtown area, the streets widened, if only slightly, and the people shuffling on the edges thinned.

Jacob could drive the carriage faster here with fewer obstacles, working the levers. "He really came? What did he say?"

"I snuck out. I know what he wanted though. I hope he didn't see me as I left."

Lenora wiped the smudged soot from her face. No matter how many trips she made into Canimere she still couldn't get used to feeling constantly dirty. Hats, masks, umbrellas, they all did little to keep the black from clinging into crevices and tainting her strawberry hair a few shades darker. They travelled towards the edge of the city in frantic silence. Each of them doing whiplash searches through the Wilthiem windows.

"Where should we go?" Jacob deflated the quiet.

"I'm not sure. Perhaps, for now, the—" Something hit the Wilthiem with a rough bang, and they were thrust forward.

The knock tossed Lenora off her seat. As she attempted to sit up, they lunged forward again with a second crunching bang as a carriage rammed the Wilthiem from the rear, knocking the rhythm of her heart off a pace as the terrible realization of what was happening spread hot through her.

"It's him!" Jacob yelled back to her.

FOURTEEN

Fogarty's carriage sped up to ride close to the bumper. The wax men at the helm stared expressionless as they worked the controls for another ramming maneuver. This time, Lenora braced herself by gripping the seat tightly as they rocked from the impact.

"Go faster!" Lenora commanded. "Don't stop!"

Jacob remained silent as he fought the controls of the Wilthiem, trying to stay on the road.

The street widened as they rounded a curve. The stoic wax men took advantage of the opening and moved to the side, slamming into the Wilthiem with enough force to cause the carriage to veer sideways into the window of a nearby bicycle shop. The plate glass window displaying a pair of unicycles for sale shattered as the Wilthiem's right flank struck it. The bell-like ring of breaking glass echoed off the cobblestones and bricks of nearby buildings.

Jacob struggled to regain his seat as he pulled on various levers in a fury. With a surge, the Wilthiem bounded forward, throwing shards of glass up in its haste. The dense steam from the Wilthiem's exhaust filled the air behind them like a tail, temporarily obscuring Fogarty's carriage. Jacob spurred the carriage ever faster, pulling the turning handle sharply. Two wheels lifted off the ground as they made a sharp turn down a tight alleyway.

Lenora slammed against the opposite wall, clinging to the curtains as the carriage skidded around the corner. With a thump, the wheels met the surface of the road. The force tossed her back into her seat, ripping the curtain off the rods.

They flew down the narrow alleyway, the spinning wheels throwing out sparks whenever they contacted the brick walls.

"What are you doing?" Lenora screamed as she clawed the seat trying to recover her stability.

"We can't outrun 'em, so we're going to try to lose 'em. They're too wide for the alleys."

Lenora craned her neck, searching through the rear window for any hint of Fogarty or his beastly carriage. The fact she was unable to spy him only fueled her fear. If this was the same carriage that had taken her to the asylum, it was incredibly fast. Coupled with the efficiency of the wax men, evasion would not be as simple as Jacob seemed to think.

She prepared herself, holding firm on the seat as they approached the alley's end.

Fogarty's carriage rounded the corner towards them as Jacob catapulted out of the alley and swung the coach to ride along the road. The beast gained on them easily, forcing Jacob to veer the carriage down another alley. Lenora kept her bustle on the seat, but her upper body whipped with the turn. This alley was a hair wider, to her relief, but halfway down the carriage bumped sharply as the cobblestone gave way to dirt streets.

They shot across the next road. Jacob drove directly into the next alley, skipping the Wilthiem over the dented dirt like a stone on the water. The alley flashed by in a rush of dark bricks on either side.

The shadow of the alleyway broke into light. That moment in the open was all it took—the barrage of confusing banging and metal crunching metal as Fogarty's carriage careened into the side of the Wilthiem. The carriage flipped over, rolling across the ground as the sides slammed into the rutted dirt road with each revolution.

Lenora felt weightless as the carriage spun around her, curtains flapping like caged birds, yearning to be free. In that instant, she didn't ponder her possible death. No bright moments of her life cycled through her thoughts. All that struck her was something a boy, whose name she had long since forgotten, said at Glenn Haven about his distrust of sky ships. *Birds fly not simply because they have wings, but because they know how to land.* Those words struck her in that panicked half-breath.

They know how to land.

Gravity took hold, and she smacked into the wall and next the seating. Each impact a blur as the windows and ceiling danced around her. She was too stunned to feel the battering from one hit until she tumbled towards the next.

Then everything stopped.

Lenora found herself on the floor of the coach, though she wasn't been fully aware of how she had ended up there. Everything ached, but a signifigant pulsing yet deep pain erupted on the corner of her forehead. She touched the spot, feeling the sting as her finger poked the cut. Blood trickled over her eyebrow and down her cheek. The engine still sputtered, but they were still. A rather poor landing, but she had managed.

"Jacob?"

He slumped over the controls, moaning as he rolled his head side to side. Past him, the silhouette of Fogarty's carriage parked sideways in a haze of dust and steam.

"Jacob? We've hit them. Jacob!" But he was still shaking himself from the crash.

The door swung open, and a gloved hand ripped her from the floor by her bodice. Fogarty slammed her onto the exterior of the carriage, his jaw against her neck with a high-pitched screech as the silver teeth ground together.

"A rousing round of hide and seek these past few days. And quite the invigorating chase, but the time for games is over," he snarled.

He clenched her face, fingers digging into either side of her upper jaw as he forced her to look at him. There was something frightfully unhinged in his eyes—something beyond greed or malevolence. A hard sharpness as if the blue eyes were a scalpel that only knew to cut. She scratched at his arm and arched her back to push her body off the carriage only to have him slam her down harder. The blow to her bruised backside sent waves of sharp pain. Tears and blood streamed down to her heaving chest.

"I could nip that pretty little nose off in a single bite, and that would be but an hors d'oeuvre of the agony I could unleash on you. I can introduce you to a whole new spectrum of suffering. A veritable rainbow of torture. Do you hear me?" His fingers pressed deeper into her soft cheeks. "But what a waste of precious time and effort. I would rather you just cough up the damn name. Out with it. Who is he?"

Gunfire.

A spray of displaced dirt as the bullet struck the ground only a few feet from where they stood.

Lenora suddenly took note of her surroundings, dry earth under foot, the lack of ash fall, and quaint but basic lodging lining the road. A cart selling lemonade next to Kent's general store. In front of the shop, folks gathered to gawk at the wreckage.

Roudonel. Clever Jacob, in a crisis he made his way home.

Beef stood in front of the gates to the metal shop, shotgun raised in the air, barrel opened. He reloaded, utilizing his stump to squeeze the gun to his chest while he slipped in the shells. A brisk snap shut, and he squared the muzzle off at Fogarty. The ringleader glanced over his shoulder at the weapon with an air of annoyance.

"Let the lady loose," Beef said.

Fogarty tensed his hand into her for a second before releasing. With a flick of his wrist, he tipped his hat at her and backed away. "We're not finished, my dear."

One of the wax men leapt out of the carriage to open the door for his master.

"Gideon?" Beef called out letting the gun dangle at his side.

With Fogarty secured, the dented carriage spun off leaving Lenora gasping for breath. The relief of escape faint. What she had seen in his eyes wasn't the soul of a man; she saw the monster that dwelled within the flash and dazzle.

Jacob rolled out of the carriage and flopped onto the ground next to her. "I believe the doctor summed this one up—*shit.*"

She shrank into herself, receding until she was curled up in the fetal position on the ground. She felt Fogarty's bitter breath cling to her hair and the pressure of his fingers still jammed into the tender spots in her cheeks. She shivered uncontrollably, watching a small yellow bird settle and land on Beef's fence. How could she soar if each time she landed nearly broke her?

Curled up on the old carriage bench turned temporary metal shop seating, Lenora allowed the encounter minutes ago to steep in her mind. Then she wandered beyond the last encounter, to the weeks that had somehow blurred into one horrendous mass of stitched together nightmares she carried around in a blind daze. Each atrocity another stitch of the scar on her wrist. It had all been real and yet not. This madness consumed her every thought, destroyed sleep, and yet she dreamed as she walked. The adrenaline boost was going dry.

For the first time since Elliot jumped into her carriage, she wished she had just tossed the funds at him and gone about her business. She wished she had never visited the circus, never set lips upon absinthe or opium or cigarettes.

Never felt the crack of a man's skull.

"How's your head, Miss?" Jacob asked, sitting down next to her.

The amount of blood had been overwhelming. Before they stopped the bleeding, she was certain that she would require a doctor. After she cleaned up, she found a tiny cut, maybe two centimeters long. Sore, but not life threatening.

"Fine. I'm fine."

"If you don't mind me sayin', ya don't look fine to me. Palest lady I ever saw." Beef pulled up a large square chunk of metal and sat on it. "But I bet I don't look much better."

Beef looked well enough to her, at least in skin tone. Tanned cheeks and callused hands rarely looked frail. However, he slumped down in an odd way as if he had run from one edge of Canimere to the other and was near collapse. That hadn't stopped him from lecturing his son. Jacob received quite an earful, though there was gentleness to it. Almost as if Beef had been telling him to toughen up while wiping away the tears.

"Who is Gideon?" she said to the hunched Beef.

"Hmmm?" Jacob gurgled through a mouthful of water. He swallowed and put down the Mason jar turned cup.

Lenora wrapped her fingers around her water jar like a warm, soothing cup of tea. "Gideon. You said 'Gideon' when Fogarty was leaving."

"I did." Beef grabbed his own jar and downed the clear contents.

Lenora and Jacob leaned in. Beef set the empty Mason jar down. They waited while the big man took a few deep breaths, his eyes misting.

"Ain't nothing to be thinking o' now. Ya don't got the time for that," Beef refilled the jars from his cracked pitcher, his eyes downcast.

Lenora wouldn't pry, not after he freed her from Fogarty's grip, but she made a mental note. She would dig for that story later.

Everyone sipped their water. To Lenora, they sat as ladies of feuding houses at a tea service. Everyone glanced up occasionally with nothing to say and hoped to drink enough, without taking obvious gulps, to have a legitimate reason to excuse themselves to the privy. The difference was she actually enjoyed her current company. The open air, too. Birds swooped in to peck at scraps while the sky was clear. Their chirps cut down the silence some, but the songs couldn't erase the dread.

At length, Beef stretched his arm out and spoke as the sun drifted into the late afternoon. "By the looks o' it, you got big problems in the Drift."

"That's one way to put it." Lenora didn't mean to sound bitter, but the words came out that way regardless. "I suppose going about my daily routine isn't an option any longer."

"You gave it a try, Miss, but, as much as I hate to say it, I think Dr. Anarchist had the right idea," Jacob piped in.

"I can't up and leave. It's cowardly," she mumbled weakly.

Cowardly and humiliating and weak... and Father would follow. I would see him everywhere. He would hound me with that silent scream no matter where I went.

"One of those Anarch men that don't take orders from nobody, and a doctor to boot?" Beef slapped his knee as he laughed. "You aren't what I 'spected from a fancy lady. You knows all kinds of folks I figure the rich steer clear of."

Jacob crossed his arms. "This one came to her. He's a clever one, I'll give him that. Not the nicest of men though. All this mess is his fault. He should have to clean it up."

Beef had returned to his jolly demeanor. The same couldn't be said for his son who kicked at the ground.

For her part, Lenora slouched into her seat. Laverli for a season, perhaps explore the feral Ongal and search for the weather magicians the boys of Glenn Haven talked about. A respite from Canimere. It sounded so easy, yet she couldn't. The city was a asylum, Foxton a tomb, and she felt trapped in both.

"I didn't expect you to put stock into any plan of Elliot's," she said.

Jacob sneered. "I'm not fond of him, but I believe it's for the best, especially after that chase, and Fogarty being rough with you. You would be safe. Ms. Claire could run the manor, and the bank men would handle business. You could come back when things are better."

"And when will things magically be better?" she flared.

Lenora was quick to catch her temper. A few cool sips of water helped to smooth out the burn from her breath. Jacob rolled a pebble around with his foot while he waited.

"I'm sorry. I just don't see rushing out of the country as a positive solution." Lenora rubbed her pink wrist. Not quite healed into a scar yet, but she had managed to remove the sutures without damage.

"You did make a deal with him. The slightest bit wrong, right? I will gladly forgive any grudge I hold for the doctor if he were to take you away from this Fogarty. Keeping you alive and well is what's important," Jacob said without an ounce of taunting.

Beef refilled their jars quietly. Still, Lenora could see a slight glow of pride at hearing his son speak his mind. Sometimes, Lenora wondered if Jacob realized he could dodge her defenses. A young driver turned personal confidant on his first employment. He was smarter than she gave him credit for.

"Well, any discussion of leaving will have to wait. We can't go back to the city in that." She pointed to the battered carriage Beef had pulled in front of the shop. The bumper and side dented inwards. Two of the steam stacks had snapped off, and a third was bent nearly into a slanted capital L. The Wilthiem reeked of a dying fire, all smoldering, acrid embers. "I'll have to send an errand boy to Foxton and have Fern fetch us. Perhaps in the morning, I'll go see Elliot."

"I can fix it, Miss. It won't take long with the parts 'round here. If that's alright with you, Pa." Jacob jumped up.

"Whatever you need, Jake."

"Won't be longer than an hour," Jacob insisted.

"But what of my things? I can't travel without at least the bare necessities—and funding." Her excuses were thin, frail things.

"Oh, um. We can stop at the bank, and you can get all the money you need. Then you can buy things later. Shopping on holiday, that's what people do, right?" Jacob tapped his fingers together at a manic rate while searching around him at the piles of metal.

He had already galloped off. After circling the slanted carriage, he gave it a rough push to glimpse at the underneath.

Beef chuckled. "Jake's always had spirit. Best work he done's when he was in a good mood."

"I've noticed as much."

"If he's this happy to get ya out o' the city, then it means a lot to him. Means you mean a lot to him."

Jacob rushed back past them and flung an assortment of tools in the Wilthiem's direction.

Lenora nodded back to Beef. "I suppose that's what friends ought to do. Care about each other and such."

Beef rubbed his chin, itching the cleft at the center, "A rich lady like you, friends with my boy? You is an odd lady, Miss Leahill, but you is the good kind."

She didn't feel like the good kind, especially not after killing a man. She bit her lip. All her efforts, and she hadn't managed to do a bit of good. She dug her teeth deeper into her pout. If she was to leave, it required she concede to Elliot. The thought of his smirk on account of her submission wound up her anger, but she could manage that. In fact, she would rather focus on how Elliot irritated her than the growing feeling that the evils residing in the city were inevitability closing in on her. Like how she was about to walk away from a candle soon to catch the draperies aflame.

Everything will go up in flames, and it will all turn into ash. Me, the city—all of it, just blackened ashes. Gone. Just like Father.

FIFTEEN

Lenora didn't bother knocking. She let herself in. Elliot scribbled furiously on some papers oblivious to his surroundings. Harold noticed her entrance, one bright yellow eye winking. He rose from his perch on the bookshelf and clinked his metallic limbs down the side, kicking up stale dust along the way. The iguana crossed over the desk. After giving Lenora a slight bob of his scaly head, the creature crawled over the papers directly in Elliot's way. The doctor slammed his pen down and cursed the lizard before realizing he had company.

"Obviously you have issues with following a simple plan—and you cut your head again. You really should be more observant of where you're going." He leaned back in his chair.

Lenora sat in one of the seats facing his desk. "Each person to rule themselves. I wanted to come, so I did. And my head's fine, thank you."

"I would say that I can't argue that logic, however we are in a predicament that can have severe consequences. Like bodily harm." He drummed his fingers watching her briefly then sighed. "If you must know, yes, I have found a substance in the samples that leads to symptoms identical to those of Agitated Delirium. Similar to Mercury. Not a perfect match, but it will work for providing proof of the source. I only had mice to work with and a short period of exposure, but others can further test the substance later."

Lenora shrank back into the seat. "So, it is him."

"It is. Deliberately poisoning his tenants."

Shivers rushed up her back. Little flashes of memory sliced through her. *Fogarty's grand hat twirl. The morbid show. The feeling in her stomach when the messenger delivered the news of a fireworks display gone terribly wrong.*

"Well, aren't you going to ask?"

"Ask what?"

"Why, of course. Why he's doing it."

"I… I don't…" She started weeping against all the protests she hurled at herself. Streams flowed forth. She was cross at herself for letting them go. For being weak. "I don't give a damn what it is he does so long as he stays away from us."

"Ah." He was soft again, lifting her tense ball of a body from the chair to stretch her out on the settee. "Something happened, did it?"

Angry blubbering— "He ran us down with his carriage. He…he hurt me. Threatened me, right in the middle of the road."

Elliot had joined her, curling his body around the fetal position bulge of her back. She cried. A cry like in childhood when she let every emotion spill out unrestrained. Heavy, hot tears burst open every mental barrier she laid in their path. Just as she thought the outburst was subsiding, another flood rushed over her.

He held her and stroked her head. The undulation of his chest with each breath soothed her. She felt rolled up in a conversation that didn't require words, for it was blissful in its silence. Inappropriate and profound. Had she ever been held in such a way before? Her cheeks gradually dried as she fell into a sweet sort of numb. It didn't matter. None of it did, at least for those few minutes.

Lenora closed her lids to moisten her eyes after the burn of a long cry. She could fall asleep. His long fingers loosened the combs and pins until her curls spread out down her back where he twirled them delicately one at a time.

"I want you to wear your hair down for our wedding. Just like this." His voice carried a note of firm authority draped in velvet to melt her.

Her frame tensed.

"What a selfish assumption. When did I consent to being wed?"

"I don't recall you saying no."

She wiggled out of his embrace. He took her arm to pull her against him.

"We have a deal." He turned over her wrist to inspect the healing. "We should probably leave as quickly as possible."

She wrestled free and sprang up. "And what of the findings? Fogarty? He can't get away with this. And the Council letting Delirium infect countless people? You want to run off?"

Elliot snickered as he stood. "Five minutes ago, you didn't care about Fogarty, so long as he left us alone."

"I was angry."

The sweet smirk. "Exceptionally angry. Gloriously, passionately angry."

Lenora saw the approach in his eyes before he moved, splitting her open with the grazing of his lips on hers. Breath. Sweet and warm, and he dove deep, only to be met with resistance. She couldn't drift into him completely. Part of her longed to plunge deeper, but there was a different sensation ignited by his arrogance. She hated him—she hated that she didn't hate him. The longer he lingered, the more her outrage swelled in step with her need to be lost in the kiss. With a surge she pressed back, trying to push his body off her. His hand curled around the nape of her neck, hooking her into the moment.

The conflict in her broke like waves on a cliff. This wouldn't happen, she wouldn't allow it. Too much was at stake to get distracted by the lure of passion. Opening her eyes, she grounded herself with the filth of the office. The disarray of papers and the heinous taxidermied dioramas rose above the embrace. The horrible poppy field painting stretched overhead, and with her focus on it she severed the kiss.

She broke away. Their heavy breathing pounded in her ears. The corners of his mouth rose, but before he could reach the full smirk, her hand swung out hard on his cheek. The high note of the palm against his face startled her out the swimming music of their bodies so close.

His expression reflected her anger. "What the hell was that for?"

"You think you can kiss me, and I'll just bow to your whims?"

They stood primed for a battle. The shape of her hand rose in an irritated pink on his cheek through the stubble like war paint. The room charged with enough growing electricity that the dust hovered in anticipation for the coming lightning storm.

"I kissed you because I wanted to." His fists clenched. "But we're leaving, make no mistake about that."

"Really? With what money? I make the decisions." She threw another slap at him, but he caught her arm mid-swing.

"Why can't you just…" The hurt was plain in his eyes. He released her slowly, lingering as he had with the kiss. "Fine. So, we just wait to die then? Grand."

He kicked the bookshelf on his way to the desk. An avalanche of aged papers and random mechanical parts crashed on the rug.

He lit a cigarette and forced the smoke out of his nose in a great menacing puff. "Or do you have some brilliant plan, my liege?"

She sat down on the settee, feeling the burning of her fury dwindling in the question.

"I'm not sure yet," she admitted.

The dust settled. Harold crawled down from his high point on the curtain rods. His clicking limbs the only noise in the room. Elliot went about his chain smoking in silence, coating the room in smoke until everything looked as if she was viewing it through a dingy lens.

"Don't light another one of those things. My eyes are burning." She wiped the moisture from her eyelashes.

"Good. My cheek burns." The words had no bite. He set down an unlit cigarette and took a breath. "At least hear me out. Try to see reason for a blasted minute. This scheme of his has been years in the works—longer than Delirium has plagued the city. Obviously, it is more than merely obliterating the Council. I am certain Fogarty will stop at nothing, and we can't take the risk. We don't know his plan, his motives. At best, we can thwart him by removing the findings from his grasp. That will have to suffice. Perhaps we will be able to do more later, but first and foremost we must subtract ourselves from the equation."

She had to admit his points were more than logical. Still, there was that sensation, that knowing, that was worming its way through her center. They were already caught, already backed into a corner by the monster, by the ghost. How did he not feel that?

She shifted on the settee. "And the findings on the source?"

"With the others. My good friend without such deliciously burning blood keeping them well concealed." The tease came out weak.

She swept the hair off her face. The hesitation still clung, but she was becoming increasingly eroded. No alternatives made as much sense. Staying could mean Fogarty would make good on his threats. Operating on sheer feeling wouldn't do—the sane functioned on reality, facts.

"It's cowardly," she said weakly.

"It's smart. Who gives a damn if it's cowardly?" He smirked, almost as if the slap never happened. "Just need a few items here, and then we depart."

She hadn't agreed, but he already sprinted into action. He leapt about the office tossing random things into an oversized suitcase before she could say anything more. Harold watched the erratic actions with caution. The iguana slithered to the back of his owner's chair, spine raised in high alert.

"Don't fret. You're coming as well, Harold," he said as he rushed past the reptile.

She crossed her arms. "If we are going, we have to go now. I need to stop at the bank before it closes, if we hope to have money on hand."

"Of course." Strapping the suitcase closed, he slowed and blinked, as if something dawned on him. "I need to make a stop as well, briefly."

"Where?"

Elliot turned away from her to talk at his stuffed suitcase. "Ruu's. Not for too long. Actually, this will work perfectly. We can relax tonight and then slip out before first light to catch the dawn train at Muvlite station."

"Wait, what? Why would we go into Pitchdrift? Fogarty has that district pinned down, and he nearly killed me. No. You'll have to do without your nightly smoking pleasure." She would be furious if she wasn't exhausted, her tender backside probably developing a darkening bruise.

"It's not for the dragon. You see, we will need travel papers."

She exchanged a confused look with the lizard before responding. "Of course we will. Traveling papers are for travel. The Council issued them in April."

His hand slicked back his hair. "Right, that's the crux of the issue. As you can imagine, anarchy isn't particularly appreciated by the Council, and I denied a post as a Council scientist. So, my papers haven't exactly been approved for travel this last renewal. Doesn't mean I'm a criminal exactly, just they would prefer I didn't go beyond the region. To keep tabs on me, I assume."

Lenora rubbed her temples. "Then how are we supposed to leave? This was your big idea, and you can't even manage it?"

Elliot tossed a hat on top of the luggage. "Ruu provides many services. Opium, laudanum, forbidden imports, and occasionally an alternative set of traveling papers to the ones provided by the Council."

"We have to go into his lair to get your false bloody papers?"

Elliot's face lit up with a devious glow. "One last evening at Ruu's. Come now, Fogarty would never suspect we're hiding right under his nose. If anything, he thinks you have returned to your posh manor, trembling with fear. Consider it the highest insult to the man before we escape."

It didn't feel like a jab at the ringleader; it felt like walking into a deadly trap.

SIXTEEN

Fern pulled up to the curb outside Elliot's office in the carriage nicknamed the Brown Back. Her father had assigned the carriage for the servants to use on shopping trips and various errands. Although the Brown Back kept the same maintenance schedule as any of the other vehicles in rotation, the carriage showed its age. Brown leather wrapped the coach, worn down to a fine sun-blasted, straw hue. The wooden seats had grooves from the weight of the hundreds of bottoms that had sat on them. As if that wasn't reason enough for Lenora to loathe the old carriage, it was also exhaustingly slow.

As the Brown Back creaked up the street, enormous shots of dark steam sputtered from the stacks like coughs from the ancient fellow's rusted throat. At least the crawling rate of the carriage had given them ample time to visit the bank and return.

"After I leave for this urgent business trip, I want you to retire the Brown Back. Have the staff use the Develton Edition from now on," Lenora directed her servant.

Fern bowed. As far as she knew, the boy was mute and illiterate which worked in her favor at the moment. Besides the local messenger they paid to fetch him, no one else was aware of the carriage switch or her sudden departure. Jacob would deliver her official orders via an instruction letter once she and Elliot were already miles away on the train.

Jacob and Fern exchanged the ignition rings for the carriages. Fern quickly fired up the damaged Wilthiem, eager to head back.

Once Fern drove out of view, Jacob said, "I hate driving this thing. It handles horribly."

"And I'm not fond of the fact I will be riding in it, but we are striving to avoid suspicion." Elliot huffed from his ash mask. "Though I agree this is exceptionally pathetic. Exactly the kind of atrocity that commonly rolls around Pitchdrift."

"You would be the one to know. You're the type that travels that district." Jacob swung the door open for Lenora and held out his hand to hoist her inside.

After fiddling with the seat to adjust it for his height, Jacob swung in.

"Wait, my bag." Elliot called out.

"I'm sure you can manage." Jacob slammed the cockpit door.

The coach rocked as Elliot tossed the bag inside with one hand, the other curled over the lump in his waistcoat containing Harold. The passenger door slammed in similar fashion to the cockpit.

The Brown Back groaned to life, taking several minutes to whisk out the drifting ash. She pulled off her mask only to consider putting it back from the stench of sweat that had soaked into the wooden seats. Elliot clicked his tongue on the roof of his mouth to Jacob's groaning irritability.

"If you could both at least pretend to tolerate each other for the rest of the evening, I would be grateful," Lenora said.

As miserable as she was with the situation, the pissing contest was piercing her last nerve.

"I would, if he would stop putting you directly in danger every chance he gets. This is a bad idea. A stupid idea," Jacob grumbled.

Elliot responded with a nonchalant yawn. He freed the iguana, who ascended to the shoulder of the doctor in a few sharp clicks. Lenora shifted on the hard bench. Her bustle dug into her back, so she switched to a sidesaddle position for relief.

The Brown Back inched forward. Dusk was likely upon them, but in the ash fall, Lenora had grown accustomed to noticing that the dark only got darker. The day never transitioned into a sweet sunset. Night simply arrived.

Through the winding roads, Lenora couldn't help but notice a change in Elliot. The way he set his hands on his knees, each finger placed with purpose, was unlike his usual sloppy manner. His eyes skipped from the window to her lips and then his fingers dug into his kneecaps.

She ran her fingers over her scar. She wanted to feel absolute hatred for Elliot, but a hole developed inside her instead. He hadn't treated her well, or even civilly. Yet, their spat vexed her. Something about how he didn't handle her like some delicate thing. He knew she wasn't made of porcelain. There was more than the arrogance and rudeness he presented the world. She felt certain that somewhere in there, Elliot had a heart.

"What was that about, in the office?" She adjusted against the hard seat.

"What are you on about now? We decided on a plan. What of it?" he said through clenched teeth.

"That's not what I meant, and you know it."

He stared at her for a long spell in a weak attempt to get her to drop it. He gave her big, wounded eyes like he was a mutt with its tail between its legs.

The curve of her lower back cramped from the uncomfortable seating compounding the bashing from the Wilthiem crash. "Well, are you going to say something or just sit there spineless?"

"What do you want me to say? That I don't know how to get deeper?" He slammed his hands on the bench on either side of his legs. "Because I don't. There. Happy?"

He set Harold on the bench next to him and pulled the tobacco pouch out of his coat. Several pinches of loose tobacco were crammed into a paper. He rolled it too tightly, and the paper burst open spraying the crumbled brown leaves all over his lap. He threw the wasted paper on the carriage floor and started the process anew.

Harold slid on the bench as the carriage turned. Lenora picked up the lizard and set him securely in her lap. "Deeper?"

Elliot's tongue ran over the paper of the second cigarette to seal it. He seemed to diminish a tad, as his chest sunk in when he leaned back.

"I can get down to the bone with a scalpel. You go straight in, cut a direct line to where you want to go." He closed his pouch and put it away. "But that doesn't work with people off the table. I never get past the surface and—I don't know, maybe no one is supposed to connect with anyone else."

That strange fluttery sensation engulfed her middle again. "I don't believe that. Everyone wants to feel like a part of others. Maybe try again and take it slower. Or at least refrain from using something sharp."

A small smirk, but she felt it was enough to soothe the frayed ends their argument created. However, that sense of truce was short lived as the carriage jutted into Pitchdrift. A feeling of dread returned to her. Fleeing was wrong; she knew it in every wisp of her soul.

A spray of small thunks came from the roof of the carriage. Pitchdrift had a nasty spell of ash chunks in the autumn. Something about the way the warmth was sucked from the air condensed the powder into little hail bullets. The harvest shiver swept in, and Canimere's miasmic weather bowed to it.

Even amidst the spray of noxious projectiles, people roamed the streets. Each amputated wrist that passed choked her. The Council robbed them of limb and sun. Fogarty stole their sanity. The seedy pubs became a retreat. The theft and violence a necessity. Her flesh itched as if the phantom fingers of the district scratched at her for salvation.

"This isn't right." She clutched her pink scar to her chest.

Jacob slowed the carriage to a hobble as he eagerly searched for a place to turn around.

Elliot put his hand on her knee, telling her to breathe. Just breathe. But the people kept coming, stalking the street, one toe in the grave and the other foot in the asylum. Bodies twitched as each soot-lump pelted them. *Ashes, ashes, they all fall down.*

"We can't do this. We can't leave them."

Elliot shook his head softly. "This compassionate streak you've developed is touching, but there isn't another option. It will be worse if that maniac gets my research."

The carriage rounded a corner, then another. A row of shanty style housing on the left crumbled under the coal hail. Pieces of shelters succumbed to the harsh blows of the bleak balls, falling into piles of rubbish. A whole community avalanched by the dark. Men held up the most resilient roofs with pure muscle as women and children gathered beneath.

Lenora pushed Elliot's hand off her skirt. "He'll find another doctor or change his plans. And the Council, what about all their faults? You want to leave these people to the wolves?"

He sat back and lit his cigarette in defiance of carriage etiquette. Smoke filled the cabin in a rush.

"And you suddenly have this grandiose notion they can be saved? What, with your utopian Age of Awareness? It's not going to happen. This cause is pointless so long as there is someone above them. The Council, the bloody Queen—what difference does it make? Someone will always be in power with the people so blind and beaten down. There's nothing more we can do here right now." His grumble sounded more like he was trying to shake her into agreement, as if his faith in his opinion depended on her supporting it.

"That's not true. The Age of Awareness can still happen. We just have to make it happen."

Jacob drove as the tension grew as heavy as the collecting smog of burning tobacco. Each puff he took cranked some mechanism within her tighter. It couldn't be as hopeless as he made it sound. There had to be a way out of the madness. Nightmares cannot be eternal.

The Brown Back grumbled to a clunky stop. Outside, Ruu's sank even deeper into the onyx sea of Pitchdrift.

"Jacob, I said I'm not leaving," she snapped.

Jacob tensed his fingers on the lever then let his hand slip down to his side. "He's right; there's nothing more you can do here. Leaving the country is the best way to protect yourself."

His words were a hot knife in her back. Elliot trampling over her opinion was one thing, but Jacob? The shock of it sent her limp.

Elliot seized the moment to strap on her mask before his own. Harold tucked into his coat and thick umbrella at the ready, Elliot thrust her out of the door. She stood in the street watching Jacob limp the Brown Back towards the carriage house. Her servant, her friend, abandoned her knickers-deep in the consuming black.

Elliot took her arm, and they pulled their legs through the rising tide of soot. The withered vines gripping Ruu's spread thick and heavy with the ash storm. As if whatever beastly thing that wrapped its tentacles on the building threatened to break the surface and devour the structure whole.

Elliot pulled her closer to him as a howl of wind sprayed chunks from the west. The tilted umbrella deflected them like a shield. As the gust piddled down, Elliot rushed them double time. The compacted ash molded to her shins and then cracked into deep canyons as she battled through it.

They neared the entrance. Her hand curled around his arm in a tight squeeze. The building cackled, giddy in its slow decent into the abyss of Pitchdrift.

She caught her breath. No, it wasn't the building. The round of rough laughter came from a trio of decently dressed men exiting Ruu's. They leaned into each other for support in a slow walk. The polished shoes focused on each step together as a unit, while the man in the center chuckled to himself as his head bobbed gracefully.

Elliot patted her hand, and her grip relaxed a degree. "Someone was having such a good time that he's now tardy to supper," he whispered to her with a teasing tone.

Elliot tipped his hat to the three as they strode past on the right. Only the man on the far end acknowledged the gesture with a nod in return.

Another man blindsided them on the left. Elliot took the full brunt of the hard shove and slammed directly into her, tossing them both into the heap of soot lining the entranceway. As they fell, the crunch of the condensed ash echoed in the night. Lenora scrambled to her knees, adrenaline pumping, ready to fight off whomever had descended on them. To her surprise, no attack proceeded.

The offending man made great strides down the street, already several paces away underneath one of Ruu's outdoor electric lamps. He turned briefly, ignoring a sharp wind of ash pellets spraying his front, as if he felt nothing. The sweat beading beneath her mask collected into a stream on her lip. The salty taste dried her mouth of words. He lifted a thin syringe in front of his oversized mask. The sharp metal caught the light and shined like a bolt of lightning. With a small twist of the wrist, he waved the needle back and forth like a metronome. Then he resumed his confident stride into the darkness of the district.

Elliot pulled on the hem of her dress. "Inside," he said through labored breath.

On shaky legs, he managed a few supported steps before Lenora had to drag him to the door by his upper torso. He slumped into the enclosed ash room, in a twitchy rush to remove his mask. His breathing loud and erratic, but it was the look on his face that sent Lenora into a panic. He was frightened, truly frightened. He shuffled off his coat, wrapping Harold in its folds. She jumped up to ring the gong with repetitive hard pulls of the cord.

"Stop," he commanded, but she yanked the cord harder still.

Fabric ripped as he tore the shirt's sleeve off from the shoulder seam.

"Stop. Come here." The words sounded weak and vibrated in their low octave.

She pried herself off the cord, a finger at a time. Overflowing tears helped to lubricate her grip. Sounding the gong was a call for help. To release it meant… *It's too late.*

She settled next to him. His eyes already glazed over into that frenzy, into the madness. He tilted his arm so she could see the injection mark. A tiny red dot, blood barely bubbling up to a garnet blemish.

"The research…" He paused, a small drip of drool leaking from the corner of his mouth as his eyes darted to different areas of the wall. He snapped back and thrust the wrapped Harold into her lap. "Papers, here."

"Here at the den? In Canimere? Pitchdrift?"

"Here," he repeated with force in his voice.

"At the office?"

He slammed his fists down at the floor. His head nodded then shook, and each movement sent out a spray of joint cracks and pops. Only grunts escaped his lips as he slunk into the corner.

Lenora backed away, cradling Harold.

"Elliot? Don't—stay with me. Alright?"

He battered his back against the corner. The wall shook, flinging bits of clinging soot and peeling wallpaper over him. *We're sinking.* She could feel it in the cold brick floor, in the vibration hanging in the air. He thrashed again. The building was being swallowed up and they would be sucked down with it. Anchored to the depths of the black sea. She gulped, forcing the scream back into her gullet, reeling in her wild imagination.

"Dr. Brechin? Dr. Brechin!" She finally screamed at him in desperation. He went lax, letting his backside slouch down the wall. "Say it! Say, 'Elliot, if you please.' Brechin!" But the man in the corner only growled in response.

A faint orange glow rose from the east as the Brown Back sputtered out of Pitchdrift. Lenora squeezed Elliot's jacket with Harold inside as the carriage hit every groove in the road with a harsh knock.

"I hate this damn ride," Jacob said as they hit a rough turn.

"Take it apart then or burn it if you like. It doesn't matter."

What a stupid comment after the night she had. As if the Brown Back was of any concern. They had toiled through the midnight hours, well into the bleak hollow span after two a.m., attempting to wake Elliot from his delusions. He went through cycles of calm, but they were brief. In one of his manic moments, he tackled Jacob to the floor and sunk his teeth deep into her driver's forearm. Jacob insisted Elliot had purposely chosen him, but that was unlikely. Delirium was unpredictable.

"You think Ruu's people will be able to keep him under control while we're gone?" Jacob said with a softer tone.

"They'd better."

She had her doubts. She hoped they would, at least long enough that they could search the office and return. The papers had to be there. Ruu promised her Elliot left nothing for them to hold, and they plowed through the yellow room to be sure. As the dim haze of the morning light fought to strike the cobblestones, Lenora gave the wiggling iguana bundle some soothing pats. The sun was as likely to penetrate Canimere's dense soot storm as she was to happen upon Elliot's research. Still, they both had to make the effort. Every effort.

Jacob pulled around a slower carriage, jostling her in the seat. "Why would he do that? Fogarty wanted the doctor, yes? So why—"

"Just drive."

Another bout of crying threatened, writhing its way from her chest. She quelled it with anger. *Be furious.* Books had shown her that warriors turned to rage to overcome unfathomable odds. That's precisely what she needed to do. To stoke the flames of her fury. Let all the other emotions scatter and hide as she boiled. She could bawl to her heart's content later. She could figure out how to handle arrangements for Elliot's care afterwards. She could tremble and wallow in self-pity once the papers were neatly folded in her hands.

Jacob shifted the Brown Back to an uneasy halt outside Elliot's office.

Three men filed out in a single line. The waxy flesh around their ash masks swollen, threatening to devour the leather straps into the shimmery skin. Each carried armfuls of folders, papers and any other various items they could grab from Elliot's office. They threw them into half full crates on the sidewalk.

The row of them all seemed to notice Lenora's arrival in unison, tilting their folded blobs that were once chins up at the carriage. More leapt from a wagon carriage parked ahead of the Brown Back and rushed to load the crates. The last crate swooped up as she made out the jar of leeches balanced precariously at the peak of the haphazardly packed pile. They thrust the bounty into the back of the wagon carriage, then jumped into the vehicle. The last man barely got his foot in before it lurched forward and raced down Webbs Street.

"Damn it." She stomped her foot.

Jacob flinched as did the iguana whose snout rose above the linen. Harold snuck out of his temporary housing and began scaling her arm. The chill of the metallic claws pinched up her shoulder. It took all her willpower to keep from shaking him off. *Hardly the creature's fault his extremities have such a foreign feel.* Not that she was accustomed to any reptile clinging to her.

"Maybe they didn't find them?" Jacob's question sounded meek.

"Are you a simpleton? Of course, they found them. They probably knew exactly where to find them. I've been naïve from the start."

As soon as she spat the words, his face twisted red, huffing with bulged veins. He sprung out of his seat, ramming through the soot flurry into the office.

Lenora tossed the coat over her shoulder, loosely covering Harold, and followed Jacob inside at a gallop.

He stood glaring at the interior. Furniture flipped over and gutted. Shelves emptied. Artwork tossed onto the floor. The taxidermied solider mice knocked down on their board like fallen chess pieces, never to finish their courageous miniature battle. The place was even eerier in shambles—a scraped out shell with the grisly bits of meat left clinging within. Even his scent had been obliterated. A pungent mix of chemicals from the devastated clinic hovered in its stead.

The condition of it all stunned her. Elliot's office was a reflection of who he was. This offensive shamble? This was what he had been warped into.

Jacob kicked the pieces of a smashed chair.

"Jacob, calm down."

"No. We did all this for those papers, and he got 'em. Your father, the doctor, crawling around the Drift, dodging Enforcers, collecting smelly stuff, for what? Just so that bastard could get it all." He slammed his hands against his temples. "All this work, keeping you safe, and that snake won."

"Alright. Let's think about this for a second." Lenora placed a hand on Jacob's shoulder although the calming effect she hoped for was minimal at best. "Elliot said he left the results with a friend. Someone who didn't have the hot-blooded temper I do. Therefore, the papers might not be here in the office. Fogarty may have stolen a bunch of useless junk."

Jacob jabbed one finger at the large painting above where the desk once stood. The skeletal man and his meatless equestrian companion in a poppy field. The wax man sliced the whole thing through, top to bottom. That in itself didn't bother her. She detested the painting. To see it ruined was hardly upsetting, save the fact it was another part of Elliot destroyed. Beyond the gash in the canvas sat a small square recess in the wall. Lenora walked closer to get a clear view of the dented wall safe door dangling by a single hinge. Harold settled his head on her collar bone, his face lying on her neck.

Jacob stiffened next to her. "That painted skeleton friend doesn't have any blood at all."

Her heart sank. "No. No, that can't be."

It was her turn to be emotional, smashing the bits of chair beneath her foot. Anger, fear, helplessness—it all congealed into an uncontrollable outburst, and she obliterated the waste under her feet without rhyme or reason. Harold's claws dug into her skin to brace himself as she stomped. Once that unrestrained part of her was satisfied with the splintered results, she calmed and smoothed the material of her dress.

The three of them stood in front of the sliced painting, glaring at it as if it were a betrayal.

Lenora stroked Harold a moment then her tired eyes grew wet. "Then he will know that we know. He will know we took the samples. That we know he's the source."

"Then you have to go. Devonton Station isn't far. You can make it before they bring the papers back to Fogarty." Jacob grabbed her arm, trying to lead her back out of the room, but she stood firm.

"No."

"Are you mad? You have to. He'll kill you." Jacob pulled harder twisting her torso towards him. "The doctor wanted to leave. Your father planned to leave."

Lenora pried his hands off her. Elliot claimed her blood boiled. If that was ever true it was at this moment. Fury—fear, it all burned the same. "And neither of them are here, are they? Fogarty won't let us get within ten yards of the station. Don't you see, there's no way out."

Jacob's eyes went wide with realization.

With all the murder, disease, and plotting, Fogarty must have quite the performance planned. He had her confined to her private box. Nothing left to do but prepare herself for what lay beyond the curtain.

The ashfall grew lighter as the dense chunks of the night before were replaced by feathery flurries of fine powder. The Brown Back crept through the shuffle of Pitchdrift's morning workers. They filled out the narrow roads like corpses attached to marionette strings. The factories were gorged with them, spilling into the street. Jacob had to inch the carriage past the crowds. Not too long ago, she would have considered them dutifully working towards the Age of Awareness. Now she saw them as unfortunate souls that had their wills torn from them.

"We should leave him." Jacob pulled the lever to speed the carriage once they passed the glutton of workers.

"Absolutely not. You don't know what they do in those asylums. I won't suffer him being trapped there."

Harold's metallic legs suddenly felt like bars against her skin. She set Harold down on the bench beside her.

Jacob rounded the corner.

A soot-stained white carriage sat outside Ruu's. The solid shape of a blue tree painted on the side. Supposedly, the symbol of stability and longevity, but that tree promised neither. An asylum carriage.

The elderly Ruu's bent frame stood at the door, his wrinkles flattened in frustration as several rather unsatisfied customers yelled at him. One wore a torn coat with his hair roughed up. Elliot must have slipped out from the yellow room. Once the other patrons knew, someone was bound to rat Elliot out.

Ruu glanced up at the Brown Back with a slight apologetic nod. Behind him, two asylum workers in their tattered aprons wrestled a fighting Elliot out into the street.

"Shit." Jacob worked the controls to speed the carriage up a notch. He passed Ruu's as Elliot was thrown into the rear hatch of the asylum carriage.

"Wait. Stop."

Jacob continued at the leisurely pace. "No point, Miss."

Some unnamable emotion seized her—not completely passion nor anger nor any other flavor Elliot conjured in her before. A pure instinctual rebellion from reality. If the city insisted on insanity, then she would seize upon that expectation. She slapped on her mask and leapt from the carriage. The layers of soot caught her as she rolled, sullying her with the filth of the city. Jacob yelled out, but she wouldn't hear.

She ran, forcing her legs to kick through the mounds of ash as she darted forward. Even as the Asylum carriage pulled away from the curb, she ran. Her heart pumped bitter arsenic to every muscle, the burn propelling her further.

The carriage carrying Elliot drove onwards, but a blurry face popped up in the back windows to spy her desperate sprint. *Did he see me? Will he have the driver stop?* The sullied white carriage slowed but kept a quick enough pace that she couldn't catch up, only trail behind. The back door swung open. One of the orderlies leaned out and flapped his arm in a gesture for her to shove off.

"Wait! I'm—" she fought for breath to continue. "—his employer. Where are you tak—"

The man ducked back into the carriage, remerging with something in his hand. Perhaps he was attempting to pass something to her. Lenora clawed out any remaining reserve of energy to spring a touch closer, only to recoil once the object the orderly held became clear.

A gun.

He wasn't aiming it at her though. The barrel tracked the nearby sidewalk as if patiently waiting for the necessary prey to come into view, but there was nothing there. Empty walkways littered with rubbish and a lone bulbous soot mound protruding from the base of a streetlamp like a distended gut.

Cinder bursts they call them, Elliot's words repeated in her head. He said they mostly just shot out a singular flame, but sometimes... they explode.

The gunshot rang out as she dove toward the center of the street followed by a thunderous boom. A spray of hardened soot balls and debris pelted her, stinging like a thousand needles raining down. She took cover in the soft layer of ash, wiggling her way beneath it like how she snuck under Claire's blanket after a nightmare.

Just as suddenly as the cinder burst had erupted, an eerie stillness took the street. She sat up. The echo of the explosion raced outwards, leaving only the cloud of wafting dark dust surrounding her. A squalid fog impossible to see through. She watched it slowly separate, falling away like candy floss dissolving in water. By the time it had cleared, the asylum carriage had long since fled.

Elliot was gone.

She sat in the blackened street staring in the direction she had last seen the carriage head in a stunned stupor. It was wrong—all of it. Nothing she had believed of the world had been true in the slightest. Even those from the so-called health division had tried to kill her, and for what? All she wanted was to know where they were taking Elliot. Maybe they were wrong, maybe it wasn't some chemical perfume that sparked Delirium, maybe it was simply the city itself. A massive hole being buried in charred remains.

Tears pooled low on the lens of her ashmask, and the street distorted in the fluid. All the shades of night blurred together, and Lenora screamed into them.

SEVENTEEN

Perry Bohely lifted Lenora's wrist for the third time. The man had incredible patience. They had been practicing all day, and not once had Perry used a sharp word or scornful expression as he repeatedly explained the proper way to fire the gun. He reloaded for her after she placed the bullets in backward and readjusted her grip, without the slightest hint of annoyance.

The little clear patch of grass they occupied was wedged between the rear gardens, the carriage houses, and the wooded acres of the estate. Until Perry suggested it for their practice, Lenora hadn't known of its existence. She rather liked it. A concealed and secluded area yet big enough for a picnic; a wide-open hiding spot. Pungent gunpowder masked the smell of dying grass and rotting leaves. She was alive here. That feeling made all the more exhilarating as her internal musings were silenced by the sharp bang of bullets. No worries, no dread, just action.

"The pepperbox is longer, see? So, you need to be sure your wrist is strong. Don't go limp," Perry instructed, angling her wrist to align the barrel at the target.

Lenora held her arm as steady as she could and squeezed the trigger. The gun pulled back. The bullet whistled through the air followed by an echoing crack. The projectile struck more than a foot from the center-painted circle in the haystack. She was having the damnedest time adjusting for setback.

She felt like each time she made a plan, it came with its own form of unexpected kickback. Three days since that dreadful night, and she was still trying to recover. Every time she closed her eyes, she saw Elliot dragged into the asylum, sometimes by Fogarty's disfigured wax men, other times by the clockwork grip of the Enforcers. The cells on either side of him roaring with manic laughter. The arms clawing at the bars, hands bloody and bent from scraping against the walls.

Elliot, unreachable in his own dank cell where not even light could provide him grace.

The wires embedded in the temples of wheelchair-bound patients, the implants in Dewar's hands, plagued her dreams. If they were experimenting on patients, it was only a matter of time before Elliot would be prodded and examined. The thought made her ill in her soul.

She had attempted to approach the Council that horrible morning to find out which asylum they'd placed him in. It could take weeks or months to document Delirium patients for public record in any asylum, but she held some lingering hope Elsothe's rulers had access to patients no one else did. As the carriage approached Pinfork Hall, she had broken into a cold fever. The Enforcers standing guard snapped their helmets to scrutinize the Brown Back as it had crawled to the curb. She had felt them watching her, their cold stare pierced her, even through the carriage walls, as if they knew she had taken actions intended to harm the Council.

How thoughtless of her to come.

Even if no wax men had tailed her to ensure she didn't tattle to the Council, surely there would be no mercy from the men whose Enforcers severed hands for debt and shot down children. A single step out of the carriage would sign her death certificate, probably Elliot's too. She had screamed in panic for Jacob to speed away before they were recognized.

As much as it sickened her, Elliot was safer as just another Delirium victim than exposed as her accomplice. The possible punishments at the hands of the Council's Enforcers were insurmountable, making her weapon feel impotent.

A wisp of smoke from the pepperbox revolver hung in the air. Lenora lowered the weapon to her side. She never realized the muscles of her arm could tire just by holding them up at length.

"A fair shot. Well done, Miss Leahill," Perry said with sincerity.

"Well done? I wasn't even close to the target."

"You hit the target, just not the bullseye. Don't worry. It will come in time. No one can master the skill in a day." Perry held out the box which Lenora gladly filled with the heavy weapon.

"I think I would much rather stick with the derringer. It's lighter and easier to handle. And it's small enough to tuck in my boot. Isn't that where dangerous women keep their little guns? In their boot?"

Perry smiled, managing not to laugh at her. "I'm not sure if a boot is where I've heard they stash it, but it will do."

Claire had been wise to suggest Perry as an instructor. It was possible Claire was merely ensuring the gamekeeper remained useful considering the switch from a master who enjoyed a good hunt to a young mistress with no interest in the sport. Even so,

Lenora found his cheery disposition refreshing.

Perry brought the derringer back out of the case for her to examine. She couldn't help but think of it as a gun sized for a child. The stubby barrel was made all the shinier contrasted by the ivory handle carved with swirls of little leaf designs.

"The derringer can be handy, but it has some major drawbacks. For one thing, you will only get one shot. The pepperbox has six. The derringer is meant for close range only, really. Last resort weapon. Aim for the gut. The pepperbox does much better at keeping an enemy at a distance, don't give up on it. Trust me; you'll get the swing of it in no time. We can give it more practice tomorrow, if you'd like."

Lenora sighed but agreed. The reprieve from her fears faded as quickly as the gun smoke cleared. She would need bigger firepower once Fogarty made his move. Bright and early the next morning, she could start fresh. That is, if the world hadn't fallen victim to Fogarty overnight.

Three days and Fogarty hadn't done anything with the results. Each day she sent out a servant to the city every few hours with some excuse. Someone to fetch some files from the bankers, or she changed her mind for dinner, and someone needed to run to a specialty shop in Canimere. She then developed a sudden interest in self-defense and needed several pistols and ammunition purchased. They would return telling nothing new in town. The city dragged on as every day before.

The anticipation was emotionally incapacitating. Every hour crawled by with cold sweat gathering on her collar. The tension made her stiff.

What was he waiting for?

She could do nothing but wait for Fogarty to do something, but she was absolutely terrified of what he might do. If the ringleader planned to silence her before enacting the next part of his plot, he was going to have to come to her—and that was a real possibility.

She decided to take the long path back to the manor to soak up the last warmth of the afternoon and try to cool her mind. This route would also have her pass by the carriage houses and the mechanic's cottage. Jacob would be tinkering somewhere in the area. He promised to keep an ear to the ground, or more distinctly to have his father keep a look out in Roudonel for the slightest news from the city. A nice gesture, even if he wasn't exactly on good terms with her. His blatant disobedience at her orders was not forgotten. Had he just turned around, Elliot wouldn't be crawling about like an animal in some matchbox cell. Had he stopped, she could have intercepted them and placed Elliot into a private facility.

Two gardeners walked past her, a look of puzzled shock as their mistress roamed the green paths. She nodded at their polite "Good afternoon, Miss Leahill," but kept a brisk pace. The curious stares of the staff wore thin on her already taut nerves.

Even Claire poked at the topic of her newfound interaction on the grounds and sudden disinterest with traveling into the city. A bright one, that Claire. The housekeeper noted the first day that Lenora's mood was altered.

She couldn't deny a shift within herself. No more trembling late-night searches in the library for answers. The time for observing and investigating had expired. She was preparing mentally and now physically for the impending attack as best she could. *Father and Elliot both fell. What are my chances?*

She came to the three hulking carriage houses that hung back from the well-traveled path. Her father had quite the collection of carriages, though she found them to be all steam and no comfort. Everything in them skimped down to accommodate bulking machinery. Jacob once pointed out a particular carriage he claimed could travel as fast as if a hundred horses were pulling it. Lenora walked past it, imagining the phantom of her father racing through the ash led by a hundred invisible stallions.

Following the sound of metal hitting the ground, she came upon Jacob. He pulled parts from the old Brown Back with glee. With the wheels removed the carriage was a sad sagging shell. Engine pieces spread over the grass like a load of clean laundry blown off the clothesline. The steam stacks leaning up against the cottage. Jacob never looked so giddy to dismantle anything before. She debated inquiring if he'd heard anything from Canimere when she noticed Beef hunched over the spread of parts.

"Beef, such a pleasure to see you again." She lifted her skirts enough to jog up to them on the damp earth. "Any news?"

"Af'ernoon, Miss Leahill." Beef tipped his dull bowler hat.' "'Fraid nothing for ya from town. Yet."

Jacob wiped his grimy hands off on a rag reeking of old grease. "Pa was looking to buy some of the parts off the bucket."

"I'd take 'em all but mostly the stacks. What cha want for 'em?" Beef knocked on one of the steam stacks. The bright ding was sufficient to make him nod with approval. "Yeah, can use the stacks."

"Take whatever you want. Call it payment for the parts Jacob used to patch up the Wilthiem. As well as your hospitality," Lenora said.

Beef rubbed his chin stubble, looking as if to haggle with her generosity when Claire arrived behind them.

"Miss Leahill, you have a visitor," she said sternly.

"I told you to turn away any business associates for the time being." Lenora waved her off. "I'm not seeing anyone. Oh, and did you sort out the feeding issue with Harold, the iguana? I won't have the poor creature starve to death under my roof."

"The thing has been fed, though I don't see why it has to stay in a guest room. Should be with the other animals outdoors." Claire shot her a slight disciplinary scowl then smoothed her apron. "And Mr. Fogarty demands you speak with him. He won't shove off 'till you do."

So, he had finally come. Even with all her mental preparations, the news he had dared to seek her out in her own home sent a shock through her. *Straight posture. Steel will.* But her heart plummeted into her stomach regardless of her assertive stance. She would have been in a pure panic had she not already laid out a plan.

"Inform him I will be with him in a moment; have him wait in the Current Parlour. And bring in a tea service. Thank you."

"The Current Parlour?" Claire raised an eyebrow at her employer.

"It still works?"

"I don't see any reason it wouldn't." Claire eyed her in that old witch stare for a moment, then straightened as Lenora held firm under the gaze. "That bad, is it? I'll have a couple of the big men waiting too."

Claire took off back to the main house, swatting at any winged bugs that dared to get in her space.

"What still works?" Jacob stepped up next to her.

A pity she had Perry store the guns for tomorrow's practice. It would have been prudent for her to keep at least the derringer on her person, should the Current Parlour prove ineffective.

"Jacob, I'm in need of a weapon."

Jacob stared back blankly. "He came to Foxton? What is he going to do?"

"A weapon, Jacob. A small hammer or something?"

"You're not going to meet him, are you?"

"Are you listening? A weapon." Her boot sunk into the mud swallowing the dying grass as she stomped it. The smell of moldy earth cut into the crisp autumn air.

Beef chuckled. "You be one of a kind sorta lady." He pulled a knife from his pocket. The handle wrapped in a dirty cloth over the worn smooth wood. "It ain't much, but I keep it sharp. Gotten me out o' a problem or two. Go for the belly. Go deep. Or slash all wild like. Makes 'em confused."

Beef handed her the knife, which made Jacob cringe. Heftier than she expected, but the cloth gave a good grip. A full four inches of blade, dingy but in otherwise good condition. She turned it around in her hand uneasily. This would require being closer to the ringleader than she wanted to be. She wished on the lazy leaves blowing around them it didn't come to that.

Lenora stopped outside the parlour. She arranged the folds of her dress skirt around the blade to conceal it as much as possible. Hopefully, the scarlet and black stripes of her dress would help it blend into the stiff cotton unnoticed. Fingers wrapped firmly around the cloth handle. She wanted to feel powerful holding it, but instead she felt nauseous at the thought she might have to use it.

Steadying her breath, she checked her overall appearance in the hall mirror. A slight pink painted the bridge of her nose and cheeks. In the future, she would wear a broader hat when out shooting. That is, if she had another chance to do so. She didn't look intimidating, but she didn't appear frightened either. That would have to do.

Jacob squirmed farther down the hall. He squeezed his hat in his hands. She told him to remain outside, but in his typical defiant style, he trailed behind her anyways. Beside all the large men Claire had gathered for extra protection, he looked like a guilty child. He roughed up the hat a few more times, then stepped back to let the others with manual labor muscles guard the parlour doors.

"Don't come in unless I call, but stay close," she whispered to the men.

She preferred to do this on her own without the possibility of endangering any of the staff. That didn't mean she was silly enough not to have backup security, just in case.

The men gave her nods of reassurance while they adjusted their stances to prep for action. They were ready. The thumping of her heart reverberated through her body. Her legs trembled. Shoulders back, head up.

I may die today.

One of her men swung the door open when she signaled, and she entered.

Fogarty rose from his seat at the tea service. His jaw set in a reasonably mild smile. A grand bow. Lenora gripped the weapon tighter, reminding herself she held it.

The Current Parlour always left a nasty, moldy bread taste in her mouth. The dusty pink and lilac color scheme appalled her in its overdone femininity. A man's idea of what women found pretty—flowers, paintings of mothers cradling cherub faced infants, seating with an excess of stuffing which looked more like puffy clouds than chairs. Disappointing that somehow her father thought this would be the ideal setting to put his enemies at ease. Still, the pink mockery gave her an opportunity to defend herself.

The wires running from the wall appeared to be intact. She followed them out of the corner of her eye. They blended into the maze of the swirling pattern drawn on the hardwood floor, unnoticeable if one didn't know what to look for. No cuts or fraying. The wiring fed into the center carpet embroidered with dozens of metallic roses that lay beneath Fogarty's feet.

Lenora checked the miniature reproduction of Venus on a pedestal next to the wall. All it would take was a simple pull on the Venus disguised lever and electricity would jolt through the wires into the carpet. The voltage would send her enemy to the clutches of all those he had murdered. It all appeared to be well maintained. She could only hope it worked as well as it looked.

"My dear Miss Leahill. Such an honor to be graced with your presence once more," Fogarty spoke with his charismatic charm. "Especially after the unpleasantness from our last encounter. I do hope you will accept my deepest apologies for that. Occasionally, artistic geniuses such as myself are prone to extremities and eccentrics."

She felt slightly off balance. Where was the direct attack? The cruelty of the man on the dusty road of Roudonel? The blade graced the back of her thigh and the sensation, even through the layers of her dress, propelled her into motion. She ventured a few paces farther into the room and rooted herself near the Venus.

He continued, "Please, shall we sit and discuss the—"

"Your deceptions are pointless." She made herself loud without being shrill. This was her father's killer. A mass poisoner. Elliot's corrupter. She forced an outward collected demeanor while the fingers around the knife clamped down tighter. "I am not a fool."

His jaw clicked up a notch with a blast of steam. He eyed her intensity with a nonchalant wave of his hand, and he eased back into the chair. "Such a gorgeous parlour. I particularly enjoy the floral wallpaper. Roses?"

"Enough. We are far beyond pleasantries. What do you want?"

She held her weaponless hand tight against her waist. She only had to reach out and pull the Venus. A quick tug. Yet she hesitated, writhing in conflicting emotions. She had taken one life accidently. Was it just to end another intentionally? She bloody sure wanted to. If he would throw that first attack... If she could believe it was self-defense...

The grin cranked wider. "Always a step ahead, my dear. Cutting to the quick, but you are correct. To the point of my visit. I hear many bits of talk in the theater. Such is the unfortunate nature of our location. Excuse my forwardness in this matter; I'm curious of the truth of a particular story."

"That story being?"

"I mean no offense, my dear, but it's being said you were seen at Ruu's enterprise in the company of a young gentleman. A doctor, so they say, and this doctor fell to Delirium during that visit. Is it so?"

Lenora slid her finger across the blade, slicing it open to hold back the flood of panic. "It is so."

Fogarty tapped his fingers together. "Am I to assume this doctor was the one your father employed on my behalf?"

"What the hell does that matter now?" she yelled, but this only caused him to relax further into the chair.

She gulped for calming breath. She wasn't a killer, but the impulse wouldn't recede. It lapped at her ethics, at her center. If his demise would save countless others, wouldn't the death be justified? He had threatened her, shouldn't she defend herself?

All I need do is pull the damned lever.

"Such a tragedy when young talent is taken by illness. And the Council does nothing. They are a danger to the people of Elsothe." He snatched up his cane and stood. "But fear not, we are but the strike of a match from relieving them of their position and saving the city from this evil epidemic."

"Are we?" The blood from her slit finger drenched the knife's wrap. She pressed the cut hard on the handle, using the painful pressure as a distraction from her internal struggle.

"Incredibly close. All that's required is the final piece." His eyes bulged as steam spewed from both corners of his jaw.

Staring right back at him, she rolled his words over in her head a few times. A sudden relief washed over her, then a warped sense of joy barely contained. She nearly giggled at the realization. "Your men didn't find what they were looking for in the office, did they?"

The grin remained, but the voice behind it dove deep and coarse. "Where's the research?"

It was her turn to wind up a ridiculous grin. "I don't have it. It seems you have played out this little charade for nothing, Mr. Fogarty."

She rushed to the Venus without thinking. The whole nightmare would end, and she would strike the finishing blow. And she felt happy about that, absolutely ecstatic. Rage and joy. A crazed whirlwind of morbid delight. *He deserves this. He deserves to suffer and die—and the epidemic will die with him.*

She pulled the lever.

EIGHTEEN

Lenora squeezed her eyes tight, certain when she opened them, Fogarty would be twitching as every muscle convulsed with the electric current. She could even smell the burning flesh as his body smoldered and smoked. Yet, when she lifted her eyelids, he remained unchanged, casually perched on his cane.

Mortified at his impossible resilience, she flipped the Venus statue back upright then slammed it down a second time. Then a third time, and a fourth. Fogarty picked up his top hat from the table and flipped it on his head in an exaggerated swoop. He laughed at her. Malicious laughter spiked with the click of his silver teeth.

"How… I…" she mumbled.

He crossed the rug with little dance twirls and skips. "And here I thought you wouldn't have the spirit to follow through. Bravo, my dear." With the cane tucked under his arm, he gave her a round of applause. Each acute clap ringing in her stunned head.

"But…"

"Your father was rather proud of this ingenious little contraption. After a couple glasses of absinthe, he was more than willing to gush about the details of the design." Fogarty kicked the severed wires out from under the edge of the carpet.

His cold shadow crept over her as he strode forward with the confidence of the grim reaper coming for the mortally wounded. Her breath became so deep and rapid, the laces of her corset creaked and tore. It seemed he could sense her fear, his clockwork jaw reset in the grin of the deranged, eyes hard with sadism. Each step weighted with cruel intentions.

She pointed the knife at him. Her arm shaking wildly with terror, flicking drops of blood from her finger before her like the first sprinkle of rain. The strong red contrasting the weak pink of the wall. He stopped to cock his head at her and chuckle at the tiny blade.

"After all I have shown you, and you still refuse to aid me in my noble cause. Have you forgotten the asylum? How can you turn away from such suffering? Don't force me to remind you of our last conversation. What I'm capable of. What is in my power. Where are the research papers?" He slid his teeth together after the question, casting blinding sparks with the squeal of metal scraping against metal.

She lifted the knife higher, pointing it at his face, but she lacked any power behind the threat. Her heels inched backward on the polished floor.

After a moment of her silence, he pointed his cane at her. A thunderous crack and a plume of smoke came from the tip of the pole. The bullet stuck the Venus, shattering the sculpture into bits that exploded in every direction. With a piercing shriek, she crouched into a ball to shield herself from the shrapnel, hands over her head. The four-inch blade dropped and abandoned. A firearm concealed within a walking stick—how terrifyingly appropriate for the ringleader.

She went tight, curling within herself waiting for the next shot to burrow through her body. Any moment the bullet would split her open, and her life would spill out like blood across the room. But no second shot came, only the sound of stomping shoes and the grunts of men in struggle.

She unfolded herself to find her servants tackling the ringleader, striking punch after punch to his jaw and gut until he crumpled to his knees. Steam spurting erratically from one side of his face. Grin lopsided and whining as broken gears ground on each other.

She managed to pull herself to standing with Jacob's assistance. The men dragged Fogarty near the door.

"Wait!" She found her footing and her breath. Still shaking, she made certain to meet his gaze. "As I recall, you were in desperate need of a name. That name is Doctor Elliot Brechin. Our business is done."

A derangement of gurgled vowels and the screech of jammed gears came from the broken smile. A faint hint of burnt oil emanated from him. No words managed to form, but Lenora understood him perfectly well as he bucked his weight forward in her men's hold. He wasn't finished with her. Even though she lacked the papers, he wasn't done tormenting her.

They forced him out of the parlour, his shined shoes dragging the severed wires from the rug along with him. The terror he caused began to flee with him. She had emerged unscathed.

"Are you alright, Miss?" Jacob said.

The echo of Fogarty's exit reverberated down the hall with thuds and grunts to match the squeak of shoes on polished floors. The pieces of the Venus lever crunched under her foot. The fear of moments ago faded into obscurity, as a bitterness settled over her palette like a mouthful of spoilt milk. He had been toying with her in her own home. Every word designed to drive her to that lever. She pressed her tongue on the roof of her mouth, trying to suffocate the imaginary flavor. Her anger and fear had been manipulated into a weapon and turned against her.

And I pulled the lever. The thought haunted her. That wasn't the action of someone desperate to preserve their own life. She had *wanted* to kill him—and that was pure madness. Fogarty may have killed for pleasure, but not her.

"We're not the same," she mumbled to herself.

"Not the same?" Jacob led her to one of the chairs.

The pastels and the pattern roses disgusted her. A bunch of pretty, delicate decorations failing to do anything substantial. Jacob motioned for her to sit down in a strawberry cushioned chair.

She slipped out of Jacob's escorting hand and told herself, "There's too much to do to be lounging about. He will find the papers eventually, and I can't let that happen. I must do something—figure something out. Father will be cross otherwise."

She stomped out of the parlour. Jacob stumbled over himself to keep up.

"Wait, what? He doesn't have them? They weren't in the safe?"

She kept a rapid pace down the hall, letting whatever ideas that sprouted come out of her mouth. Maybe, if she talked herself through it, some plan would emerge. "A friend without hot blood. So, a person. Can't be Ruu. A friend, a friend. Someone with cool temperament. Another doctor? Someone he corresponded with? Maybe there are some letters or something left in the office. I'll have Fern drive me out and—"

"Fern and not me?" Jacob jumped in her way. "I'm the driver."

"Is this some sort of romantic territorial thing? Because if it is, be assured I'm not interested," she snapped at him.

Jacob's mouth hung slightly open; his face a couple shades paler. "That's not... I'm not like that." His face warmed up, sprinting from white to red. "I mean, Fern can't—You're just like my sisters. You never listen to me, and all I'm trying to do is protect you."

"Protect me? No, what Fern and Mr. Reeves and all the other men did today in that parlour was protecting me. They didn't try to stop me from doing what I had to. They know I'm capable of handling things and came in only when I needed them to. Your idea of keeping me safe is locking me in a business bubble where I can't do anything at all."

He couldn't have looked more surprised if she had pulled out a sword and ran him through. He stood wide-eyed, as if she were a remarkable stranger. After a long breath, he moved from her path and leaned his back against the wall.

"I didn't mean it like that. I thought," he paused as his eyes pooled with moisture. "I thought I was helping."

She backed up to the opposite side of the hall. Tilting her head back, she set the top of her head on the wall. It was easier to battle with someone when their honesty wasn't so disarming. Not that she liked fighting with him, or anyone, but it seemed to inevitably end up that way. Her temper, her ambitions, they always got the better of her. The view of the ceiling was bland and lonely.

"I know you were trying to help. I just don't understand your idea of protecting me. If I don't do anything to better the world, what's the point?"

"The point is terrible things won't happen. If Ebba had listened to me and kept to our regular way home, she would've been safe. But I'm just the little brother. I'm the tagalong. She knew damn well to tutor that boy she would have to pass those heartless men. She knew, and she did it anyways. If she just kept to the path she knew was safe…" His voice was gruff, not angry but sore. "You don't know what they did to her, what they'll do to you."

Quiet, then the sounds of his shoe scuffing the carpet as he kicked at the floor filled the space. Lenora waited until the hall became uncomfortably cramped with their energy, watching the shadows of the past play over his face.

"You said your sister went to tutor a boy. Did she keep tutoring him?"

Jacob snorted. "Yeah. Said she wouldn't let them stop her from giving him a proper education."

"I like the sound of your sister. I would like to meet her someday," Lenora said. Uncertain of what to say next, she paused.

Jacob stopped his fidgeting leg to give her a look of serious thought, as if considering a poem in a new light, the verse unfolding in layers of meaning he only skimmed before.

"I suppose there's no point in trying to steer you the safe way now…but I can do better protecting you. I promise." He stiffened as if something dawned on him. "I mean, if you still wish to keep me employed, Miss."

She couldn't resist a chuckle. How typical of Jacob to forget his position until after his outburst. It felt good to laugh.

"Dismissing you would mean I'd have to do some paperwork, and you know how I hate that. No, I need my driver, if you're up to the task."

"That I am, Miss."

Elliot's office had undergone another round of ravaging since the last time they had been there. Every scrap of paper had been made off with, including any books, labels, and the collection of loose maps which once occupied a corner of the desk. Each painting had been slashed to rags of canvas. Upholstery eviscerated. Fluffs of stuffing rolled about at the slightest movement or breath like dandelion seeds cast away by the wind.

The settee, the one Lenora and Elliot had once folded into each other on, was gone. Lenora had to dig through the spread of rubble on the floor to realize that particular piece of furnishing had literally been hacked into palm sized bits. Her eyes misted only a moment.

She patted the pepperbox settled on her waist; holster wrapped over her shoulder. A loose-fitting jacket and anyone walking by was none the wiser, but it gave her a tiny shred of security in a city set on destroying her.

Jacob picked up a splinter of a frame and then tossed it. "Looks like there isn't much left for us to look through."

"They don't have any idea of what to look for."

"And we do? Some offhand comment about a friend without a temper." Jacob dug through a pile flicking fragments after examining them.

"Just keep looking," she grumbled.

Jacob might not have thought the clue was much, but it was her only advantage at the moment.

"Are you sure we weren't followed?" she said.

"Pft. Do you really need to ask?"

To be sure they wouldn't be able to keep track of her comings and goings, Lenora began running all carriages on a rotation in and out of the city, two or three at a time. At first, she made ridiculous requests of purchases and errands to get the carriages out. Claire was quick to put an end to "such wasteful nonsense," as she put it. The old housekeeper set up a proper schedule of shifts for the carriages to make trips to random parts of Canimere. Naturally, she insisted the drivers receive a small bonus to spend on leisure or dining while they were out. The housekeeper didn't even ask why Lenora wanted them constantly running. For how stern her temperament seemed, Lenora couldn't conceive of anyone in Elsothe more capable of running Foxton than Claire.

By the time Jacob and Lenora passed through the gate towards Dusang Forest, Lenora felt confident the wax men had abandoned any attempts to track each departure. At least, it seemed highly unlikely they would continue following every carriage that rolled away from the manor.

The clinic had met a squall. All the drawers tossed out, their contents of scalpels and syringes flung everywhere. Dirty footprints blackened the floor. This was where Elliot's good work for humanity had been done, and they soiled it. The scene pulled at her in a surprisingly potent way. She had to take slow, calculated breaths to ward off the threatening tears. Elliot wasn't perfect, but he did his people proud with all the medical advancements he provided. That night shouldn't have happened.

Lenora backed away from the defiled clinic to where the desk had been. In the left corner, an impressive array of taxidermy oddities lay in a miniature rubbish pile. A pair of kittens posed and clothed in death as if dancing. Three toads wearing britches in the midst of a game of leapfrog. An owl with a mustache and waistcoat. Each scene secured neatly to a solid wooden base. Morbid whimsy. The depictions of innocence played out by death made her cringe. Even the wax men had been too put off to bother obliterating them. What manner of man would sit dozens of hours stitching doll clothes on tiny corpses?

"These things don't have hot blood." She picked up a pair of pigeons playing cards for Jacob to see.

"Not anymore they don't."

She flipped the tasteless thing around at all angles. A flip upside down revealed a burnt signature branded on the bottom of the base. She examined the frogs and owl sets, same signature.

"They were all done by the same man. A Cyprus C. Waites. Might be a possibility. Do you think they might have some record of him at the library?"

Jacob abandoned his scavenging with a snort. "No need for the library. I can take you right to him. He's in Roudonel."

"You know him?" A flash of hope. Lenora clung to it.

"Course I do. Everyone around there does. He's sort of a hermit. Lives in the big place on Kurtswell. Pa says he makes those type of creepy displays. Sells them as art, I guess."

Lenora pushed all the lifeless things aside and stood up. The excitement was quick to escalate. She could sense it in the wiggle of her toes as she paced the floor. "Is he the calm sort?"

Jacob rubbed the cleft of his chin, mirroring the motion from his father. "Never met him. Honestly, I was too scared to go near the shop much. Seems a bit off to sit around gutting dead animals and then propping them up like real folk. But word around is he's quiet. Keeps to himself and doesn't bother anyone."

Lenora's fingers strummed the gun beneath her coat. "So, it's possible he's the friend. No temper and such, right?"

"Worth a look, Miss."

The transition from city to the outskirts never failed to perplex her. The ash spray became sparse and then ceased altogether within a few yards. Lenora imagined the pollution descending upon the city was some supernatural weather cursed upon Canimere. Occasionally the area would shift with the seasons, but for the most part, the boundaries of the city were clearly defined. An enclosed area of gloom. The last few inches of soot made a sweeping curtain which opened to the world once the carriage passed through it.

Jacob took the coach past Beef's shop. She couldn't see him, but the gate stood wide open ready for business.

They drove several blocks down and then turned up to a parallel street. At a distance from the density of the city, the buildings moved farther apart taking up more space, occasionally gaining a second floor. The businesses in this sector of the district shifted as well. Beef's scrap metal yard stood near a grocer, a barber, and a modest café. On Kurtswell Street, Lenora made out The Sister Marie Orphanage beside Toddle Seamstresses. Not the sort of places one goes to browse.

Then a row of buildings with shadowed interiors and signs too worn to read. Deserted shops whose only patrons were browning, overgrown grass. The opposite side of the street contained The Book and Hook. Its windows boarded up and a cobweb coated *closed* sign nailed to the door. Another casualty to The Council's Aqua Peritia.

"The school's up there, right on the corner." Jacob pointed as he slowed the carriage to stillness. "And this is Waites' place. Not much to look at, but he never lets anyone do any outside work for him."

Waites' place, a simple two-story house, looked far bigger than the others lining Kurtswell. Perhaps once the mayor's mansion, now it was a sad relic from a time when Roudonel had been a thriving rural village. At one point, it might have been baby blue, but Lenora couldn't be sure when all she had to go on was peeling sun-bleached paint. The picket fence had missing planks every few paces where weeds jutted though like a barrage of arrows. A small sign on a front post swayed in the breeze: *Cyprus C. Waites, Creator of Curious Collectables.*

From the rear yard, three boys slipped out of the fence. They gleefully counted bits of shiny coinage in their palms. As they came around the front, their faces fell solemn when they caught sight of Lenora. Somehow, she shadowed the day like ominous weather. Must have been her dress. She had unconsciously been adapting to the darker palette of the city. Her deep plum-brown taffeta skirt and velvet coat stood out as the style of a sinister sorceress compared to the subtle hues of the countryside. The trio passed her by in a hurry, never peeling their skeptical side gaze away from her.

"He lets children roam his property?" Lenora said.

"Kind of. If you find a dead bird or rat or whatever, you can bring it to him. He has a little door in back for the drop-off. You knock and put the dead thing in the basket. If he wants it, he'll pay a bit. Enough for a sweet or two. Can't go out killing them, though. My old chum Ralph tried. Dropped a bunch of sparrows with his slingshot. Waite wouldn't buy anything from him after that."

Lenora folded her hands and watched the boys run out of sight. "So, he deals in dead things but doesn't want them to be killed for him. I'm not sure if that seems kind or crazy."

"Both? I mean, you don't get to see him or talk to him when you drop off the things. Just the basket. I tried to get a peek once or twice. It's like the lower half of a door cut out. He waits for you to push in the basket and closes the door. Then he opens it back up and kicks out the money basket, so you don't see him. It's good pocket money, and he doesn't want them doing any harm, just a bit…"

"Eccentric," she finished for him.

That wasn't necessarily a bad thing, though thoroughly creepy. It made all the more sense that this was the friend Elliot spoke of. A recluse that detests violence.

Lenora bunched up her skirt and pulled it to the side to travel through the yard. The thick weeds were prickly, catching on any loose fabric that dangled from her hold. Either the flora reached out to try to save her from the hermit or was protecting the isolated man from the darkly dressed lady bringing the evils of the city to his doorstep. Either way, it unnerved her. She wished she'd kept one of her father's canes in the carriage. Having something available to swat at such obstacles in her path would have been wise.

She stood at the door unsure whether to enter as if this were any other business or to knock as if at a private residence. A profession such as this wouldn't receive a large clientele. Jacob stood beside her, just as uncertain. He reached out to ring the bell then withdrew his hand with a shrug. If he wasn't going to do anything, she would. She gave the door knob a tug. *Locked.*

"Funny. Never thought I'd be going into Waites' place of my own free will. Ralph would be laughing." He rang the doorbell with an unsteady hand.

They waited a few minutes as the tangle of thorns and field grasses stretched further toward the sun. A thin mail slot in the door snapped open. The inside drenched in too much shadow to make out any eyes, if any were there to be found.

"May I help you?" practically a whisper as the voice was so soft.

"Yes, I'm Miss Leahill. This is my escort, Mr. Dudfield."

"And?" the voice replied.

Lenora cleared her throat. "We wanted to talk about some of the pieces you make."

"Ah, a special commission. Yes, please enter, enter, enter," the voice from the slot said. The repetitions of 'enter' were smooth, yet they sounded restrained as if he wanted to continue.

The door creaked open a quarter of the way. They had to slip in sideways. The interior plunged them into darkness. Every window blacked out. The sudden blindness kicked her other senses into a heightened state. She could taste the staleness of the air. The dry smells of dust and age with a hint of something acidic that hit the back of her throat. The tick of a clock, precise and crisp, counting the seconds of solitude. She felt like an intruder in a place undisturbed for a lifetime.

As her vision adjusted, vague shapes developed in the darkness. A simple sofa or a crouching beast. An altar with a spill of some alchemist's concoction flowing down the side or a table with a lace tablecloth hanging off unevenly.

"I'm going to light a lamp now. I want to prepare you. My, my, my appearance is... unusual. I am afflicted. A severe back injury, injury. Don't be afraid." Waites spoke in a quiet and soothing manner, even with the echoed words.

The match sparked a small flame with a whiff of burning sulfur. Even in the faint glow, she could see the fingers manipulating the match. A nail painted black on each hand. A sweet blast of relief breezed through her at the appearance of those fingernails.

Another anarchist. This had to be Elliot's cool tempered friend.

As the lamp's wick caught the glow expanded. The sight caught her off balance as she tried not to gasp at their host. She pegged him a hunchback but quickly realized there wasn't a hump, only a sharp angle that folded him forward between the shoulder blades. Like his spine had been bent into a human cane or an upside-down L. The shoulders drooped forward and down. Chin against his chest. Face stuck staring at the floor between oily strands of thin hair.

His appearance disturbed even with the warning. Had this man been a character in one of Claire's fairytales, he would be the evil warlock ready to curse the innocent princess. She made her posture hold firm. She had to give a first impression that inspired trust. Even if she could not rationalize how this man was alive. His back had to be completely broken. Even by a simpleton's logic, he should have been bedridden at the least.

Jacob made no attempt to conceal his shock, mouth dangling ajar. She threw him a stern look, and he snapped his jaw closed with a muffled pop.

"At least I can always see, see, see where I'm stepping." He cast his eyes up at them, a halfhearted laugh tacked on at the end.

"I suppose that's true. Always a silver lining." Lenora wanted to believe that, but there wasn't a silver lining here. Not for Canimere and probably not for the deformed Mr. Waites.

"Come, come. My workshop is back this way. I shall show you, you, you the quality of my work." Waites took a cane in one hand and the lamp in the other.

They followed the crooked man down the hall. Glimpses of the house came to life as the lamp's illumination touched upon them. Then they drifted back into the shadows as they passed by, like being pulled away with the tide. Skulls on shelves spied on the visitors. The empty sockets seemed to wake with curiosity as the light played with the holes' depths. An old family crest displaying a majestic dragon curled around a shield hung by the stairs. A display case of carved wooden horses. Everything they passed dulled with dust and long abandoned spider webs. Obviously, Mr. Waites was as keen to let a maid tidy up for him as he was to have a gardener.

They entered a long hallway. The pictures lining each side were reminiscent of Elliot's collection; vivid carrion in various poses that implied some artistic message she couldn't grasp. To her, it all looked like suffering portrayed in its most gruesome forms. Nothing beautiful or meaningful beyond the gore.

A perfect miniature replica of the skeletons in a poppy field painting that used to hang over Elliot's desk came into the light and then vanished behind them. The subject matter still disgusted her but seeing it gave her a smidgen of cheer. They were on the right path. No doubt lingered in her mind Elliot had found some sort of kindred spirit in this man.

"Interesting artwork," she noted.

"I'm glad you enjoy, joy it. I mostly dabble, but I have managed to, to, to, to sell a few." He shuffled to a heavy door at the end of the hall and held it open for them.

A soft glow settled in this room, like the way the gas lamps on the streets lit up pools of fog at night. The lamps concentrated on the main work bench at the center, with a thin dispersal of illumination that spread out beyond the focal point but never reached the darkened corners. No windows. However, thin slivers of sunlight shone through the outline of a short door at the far back. The pungent smell of ammonia mixed with a variety of other offensive chemical odors saturated every inch of the space. It filled her lungs like poison, making each breath burn.

A large raven on its back spread its wings over the table. The fowl posed awkwardly, frozen in the preflight posture with breast thrust forward and beak raised to look upwards. Unnatural posing, and yet the raven looked strangely serene, as if it had opened itself to let death pull the soul from within it. Small tools and bits of wire and string circled around the bird as if set for a ritual.

Jars of the obtrusive smelling chemicals filled the top shelf along the wall. Bits of fur and bone, wire and glue, littered the lower shelves. A variety of rusty scalpels, thin dentist-like picks, and small, dull saws scattered everywhere. Her sternum tightened. Never interested in taxidermy, she had been more than content to be uneducated in the procedure. By the look of the tools, it seemed as gruesome as she had imagined.

As a child, her father had purchased a piece featuring three foxes posed as hunters aiming for a fleeing mouse. He found it amusing, as did his associates. Lenora often watched the horrific thing from the corner, eyes never straying in an attempt to catch the creatures moving. As if the foxes would turn their glass eyes on her and shoot when she wasn't looking.

This room held more glass eyes staring at her than she could count. The dim light reflected in each pair to pierce the gloomy edges of the room, like stars. Rows and rows of death, yet they did not stay frozen in their positions. In time with subtle brass clicks, several of the pieces moved in a set series of motions. A goose spread its wings and lifted them towards the sky then reversed the gesture in a repetitive loop. A ballet of field mice spun incessantly. Two kittens in military uniforms shook hands in a never-ending greeting. She felt ill. Repulsive, the way these corpses had been defiled for amusement.

"People, people, peep love this." Waites motioned to the automatic creatures while trying to catch his repetitive tongue. "They find it whimsical. Lowly animals, animals mimicking us. Things that bend over and crawl on all fours standing erect. Like real, real men."

Mr. Waites shuffled the tools on the table to create a clear space. He winced as the point of a wire punctured his finger. He examined his wound. Only a tiny drop. He wiped it away.

The lifeless creatures that surrounded them watched. Lenora could sense they were envious. Hungry for the blood he wiped away as if it meant nothing. Even the deer standing on its hind legs like a man appeared ready to pounce. The transition from beast to mocking animalistic humanoid was enough to cause fangs to break through the gums. Displaying death in such a manner had nullified the natural order. Squirrels with violins, bathing chickens desperate to protect their modesty, they all appeared ready to strike.

Lenora tried to shake off her disgust. The harsh burn of the potent ingredients hadn't faded. The room felt crowded, lacking in air. Each deceased atrocity plucked a new nerve of unease within her. Together they rose to a terrifying symphony singing to her nightmares.

The taxidermist fetched a clean sheet of paper to take up the cleared spot on the work bench. Pen in hand, he slightly tilted his head to address her.

"I find it best, best to get a visual representation for commission pieces. Do, do, do you have any specifics in mind? A preference of subject or, or scene represented? I have recently come into possession of a lovely swan specimen, from that river by Dusang. Quite a beauty, if you are looking, king for something more elegant."

Lenora squirmed at the thought of such a majestic bird stuffed and mounted in some ridiculous false tribute.

"I, we, are actually here on account of a friend—Dr. Brechin." She finally managed to choke out.

"Ah, yes. Dr., Dr. Brechin. A fine man. I have done many pieces for him in the past. Is this a gift for him? If that's the case, the case, case, I have many ideas I can show you which I'm sure will please him."

Lenora shifted her weight, rubbing the scar on her wrist. "I'm afraid Dr. Brechin has recently been taken with Agitated Delirium."

Waites dropped the pen, neck cranked towards her as far as he possibly could, thick veins protruding from his neck. "Please tell me you say, say, that in jest. I saw him not two weeks ago. In perfect health."

"It's true," Jacob piped in.

Mr. Waites let his head sag even further down.

She titled her chest to shift her corset allowing bigger gulps of breath. Everything felt too tight, as if this room strangled any living being who dared enter.

"He was poisoned," Lenora pressed further. "On account of conspiracy." She swallowed roughly. "The culprit is seeking out his research papers."

Waites took a few moments to gaze inquisitively into the stiff raven in front of him. Then he spun around towards them. His face forced up as far as he could manage to see their expressions.

"And, and who poisoned him?" The tone was still mellow, but his brow sloped down into serious eyes.

"A man in Pitchdrift." Jacob stepped forward to position himself as a shield for Lenora. "A Mr. Fogarty. The circus fella."

Mr. Waites went rigid. His expression blank and unyielding, like the glass eyes of his creations. "Fogarty."

"You are acquainted with Mr. Fogarty?" The ammonia made her increasingly dizzy. Slightly nauseated and disoriented, she inched herself back.

"Of course, I am. Am I, I not a freak? Freak," Waites said as if it was a simple fact. His calmness became frightening. She wondered if he felt any emotion at all.

She scooted back a little more but held her casual demeanor as best she could with the room shifting so fast in a queasy blur. A blend of toxic fumes and brittle feathers and fur.

"I'm not, not, not getting involved in this. The circus is a bad place. Bad people. No more of that, that for me. If you, you want the key, bring Dr. Brechin to claim it himself." Mr. Waites advanced, driving them back into the hall.

Lenora felt the world tilting. The deformed taxidermist defied gravity as his body appeared to swing back and forth like they were on a ship at sea.

"He left you a key?" Jacob asked.

"Never mind that. Be gone from me. I am crippled, not stupid, id. Fogarty is trouble. I work for him no more." The thinning peak of his skull came at them like a battering ram.

Sweat pooled into her collar. Nausea clamped down on her organs. She could even taste the bitter volatile concoction he used to warp the departed into stiffened toys. Death surrounded them in portrait form. There was nowhere to avert her eyes that didn't make her want to gag. Mr. Waites continued forward, coming towards them like a bull readying his charge.

"Now, just a moment. We are trying to stop Fogarty." Jacob retreated another few steps. She leaned onto his back. Breathing heavily into his shirt to regain control of her senses, but it didn't help.

"And what are you trying to stop him from doing?"

They were back in the dusty dark of the front room. Old dust, dry and choking. Lenora pushed herself off Jacob and wiped her wet brow.

She swallowed the taste of rising bile. "He is planning to frame the Council, so he can..." She reached for the thoughts, but they scattered from her cold sweat. "...do something."

"You don't, don't even know what it is you are trying to stop? Am I to believe this? Dr. Brechin did not send you." Waites pointed his cane at them. "Be gone from me."

Three loud pounds hit the door and startled her. Even Waites froze in place with them to listen. The condensation of sweat on her neck ceased to swell and drip. The specks of dust hovering in the air stopped swirling as they too held their breath. Footsteps tapped around outside, movement, the shuffle of crisp paper, more steps, and then silence.

"He couldn't have followed us. There's no way," Jacob whispered.

"No. No Fogarty. I'm not involved," Mr. Waites stated flatly.

He pushed past them, against Jacob's protests and swung the front door open.

NINETEEN

The sunlight burst in and momentarily blinded her. A perfect rectangle of light. No shadow of a man twirling his top hat. No melting wax-faced usher reaching in to snatch her up. Just the warm glow of afternoon.

Lenora bolted out the door into the fresh air. The robust scents of autumn leaves over damp earth and clean, sharp gusts of wind. She inhaled deeply, clearing her sinuses of the putrid acidity of ammonia and whatever else Waites used to ward off animal decay.

"Anyone?" Mr. Waites lingered inside, carefully concealing his twisted spine behind the door frame.

The vacant yard stretched out to respond with the hissing whip of weeds in the wind and the soft crinkle of paper. Some official looking notice tacked to the door rustled.

"Just this." Jacob stepped outside and removed the paper. He waved it in the darkened doorway.

The dangling strands of hair bounced as the crooked man gave Jacob a slight nod. "Read it."

The chill of the air cooled her head. The individual thorns of the prickly weeds returned to a clear point instead of a blurred smudge. She inhaled without an overwhelming need to heave.

"Wayward children of Elsothe, the desperate plight of your souls has not been forgotten. God—" Jacob paused at the word, then he repeated it slowly. "God has not abandoned you, the lost lambs of our mighty Lord. The humble Church has not abandoned you. Take heart. The time to bask once again in the salvation of God is nigh. Pray upon bent knee. Redemption is nigh."

The paper fell to Jacob's side, his face twisted in confusion. "But religion is forbidden."

"God." The word felt foreign on her tongue. The enemy of science, of the Age of Awareness, or so the Council claimed. The idea of theology's return pounded on her temples.

The door creaked closed and locked with a gentle click. Lenora rushed at the house, pounding the portal with the full force of her body.

"No, Mr. Waites. Just listen for another minute." But she could hear the faint shuffle of his feet treading away from the door. She gave the wood another frustrated slam with her fist. "Shit."

The coarseness of the old paint flakes against her fingers increased her frustration. Each time she neared the goal, it was pulled further away from her. Even if she could manage to wring the key from Waites' hold, there would still be the matter of the unknown lock that was its mate. The myriad of complications and deceit was exasperating.

Jacob collected the religious proclamation he had dropped. "He's right you know. We still don't know what Fogarty wants, 'sides framing the Council."

"Then we need to find out." She swiftly marched out of the yard, trampling through the thorny brush as it snagged her dress and ripped little holes in the fabric.

She hopped into the carriage while Jacob rushed to catch up with her. The crumpled paper crunched in his balled fist. He took his seat at the helm, then fired up the engine with a fierce roar.

"And should we be worried about this?" He tossed the wad of paper on the controls.

Before she could answer, a thud slammed on her side window. Her heart leaped over a beat, but she kept firmly planted in her seat, only tilting her glance in the direction of the noise. Nothing was going to catch her off guard again. A determination built in her to expect everything with a calm resolve. The course of her life since her father's death had proven nothing could be trusted at face value.

Between the soft lines of the curtains, a copy of the religious proclamation pressed flat on the glass. The thin paper reminiscent of a cup of tea overloaded with cream with the dark shadow of a hand holding it to the window. An untrimmed jaundiced nail tapped on the pane, adding a scraping noise beside the note, as if the Church planned to scratch and claw its way back into Elsothe one window and door at a time.

Outside, an old priest withdrew the notice. He set a withered expression of forced calm on his round face. Palms pressed together in prayer, he bowed to her his shiny bald dome inches from colliding with the window. Each slight shift in his muscles controlled with a precise timing and placement to create overemphasized tranquility. A fake smile, intended to pacify, spread over pallid lips. She twitched with the uncanny familiarity of the expression. Something about his presence sent a ripple of repulsion across her skin. With a flap of his black cloak, he stepped out of view.

"Yeah, that." Jacob tilted his chin to the empty street where the priest had vanished. "The Council isn't going to like that."

Lenora straightened her skirt, examining how all the runs caused by the weed snags made irregular vertical strips down to the hem.

"I'm not fretting about what the Council thinks. I'm more concerned with what this means."

"Means? It means the priests are trying to bring back the church." Jacob propelled them forward.

"It just seems—I don't know, off. Why now? Why not ten years ago? Or twenty? Why stir up the old faith now?"

"I figure they think it's been long enough away is all. I wouldn't waste time wondering why too much."

But the visual of the priest lingered, as if stained in the material of her mind. The way he intruded on her carriage with unearned authority, presumptuous in the manner he assumed she was required to give his document her attention.

Her mind percolated well into Dusang. The forest floor a flood of red leaves with splintered trunks of ivory reaching up for breath. A dried blood carpet spread over the earth made all the eerier by the natural theatrics of the atmosphere. *Theatrics.* She snapped erect from her slouched recline on the seat. Dusang was morbidly theatrical, as the priest had been. Overly deliberate in each movement, every adjustment of a wrinkle. *Just like Fogarty.*

Her middle went hollow, but she couldn't be sure if it was from dread or from the excitement of revelation. There was a link, she was certain of it. The priests played a role in his plan. She merely had to find the connection. Before the carriage even pulled to a full stop at Foxton, she tore out of the coach and sprinted to the house. Religion and the ringleader, co-conspirators to pull the Council beneath their own ash.

"But what then, and how?" she mumbled to herself as she nearly tripped over the carpet of the private library.

She rushed to light the gas lamps in quick succession, then headed to the dark recesses of the library that remained shrouded in gloom. In the faint radiance of her handheld gas lamp, she scrambled to the long end of the shelves she had previously ignored. Books that hadn't seen the glow of a candle or the delicate caress of a finger in years, tucked forgotten in the farthest back rows. Books of faith. Of God. She gathered them up, using her skirt as a hammock for them. These volumes were added to the mounting clutter already spanning the surface of the desk.

She spent the long night hours in the flickering gas light, too absorbed in the material to bother with the electric bulbs. The sweet herbal mustiness spiked with a hint of vanilla from the old books smelled of comfort, but she felt devoid of such simple pleasures as contentment. This wasn't a midnight for pleasure reading, lingering in the open spaces of the page. This was a witch hunt through a continent of faded fonts. Somewhere in the blackness of the darkest hours between midnight and the glimpse of dawn, the lamps dwindled down their fuel and went weak. She reminded herself she could click on the electric fixtures, but the soft wash of light soothed her tired nerves.

Her father's shadow passed over her. The silhouette kept the same cadence as when he walked the hallways to his chambers or private spaces. The rich smell of his cigars wafted over the pages of her book. She paused as if she were still a child curled up under one of the hallway decorative tables reading, fearing he would discover her and shoo her back to the governess. Or when he would, on a rare occasion, walk behind her as she studied, making her flinch in the middle of an arithmetic equation.

She didn't dare look up; she knew there would be no physical figure. He came and went, just as he had in life. A memory her imagination conjured into brief glimpses. An apparition set on remuneration for his demise. She could accept either of those possibilities—because the alternative frightened her most. She wasn't losing her hold on reality. She wasn't drifting into the madness that bled from every crevice of the city.

He's a ghost born of recollection, nothing more. I'm fine.

Still, her hand trembled as she turned the page. He had morphed since his departure from merely a feeling looming over her shoulder to a presence she could fleeting catch with her other senses. Was that not insanity? How many tainted vials had she injected?

"I'm quite fine," she announced to the empty library, finally looking up from the book. "I'll have all this sorted. I will."

No response, just the dwindling gas lamps' light burning a dismal glow over the space. There was no time to entertain any disfunction in her mind. Better to believe he was there, driving her forward. She tore back into her reading, digging deeper into the words until she could think of nothing but the ink and paper laid before her.

She wasn't even aware she slept until a hand tapped her shoulder. Jacob's voice told her to wake up.

"What hour is it?" she mumbled in a half haze.

"Three, Miss."

Claire slammed a tray on a side table, the clatter of china hit every pressure point down her spine. "Afternoon tea."

"Is that necessary?" She rubbed the sleep from her eyes.

"Gots to be someone making a bit of mischief, as I remember a wee girl keeping everyone on their toes before. Might as well be the old maid now, ought it? Your hair looks like a bird's nest. Might want to tidy up." Clare put a jolly sway into her step as she left.

Lenora ran her hands over her head. Thick sections of hair flopped out of the bun from the night before in all directions. The entire left side had fallen out, draping over her shoulder. Instead of trying to tame the red beast, she pulled out the pins and let the curls fall where they pleased.

"Did you find what you were looking for?" Jacob said.

"I'm not sure," she grumbled into her cup. "Some of the texts lead me to consider the priests might have returned for some event which supposedly frees the initiated from strife. Fravashi, prophesized in many of the later writings, but the numbers don't add up for me. The dates are all wrong. Although, I suppose I could be mistaken. Still, that doesn't provide any connection with Fogarty."

"Fogarty and the priests?"

"Mmmhmmm." She downed the last of the cup and handed the empty vessel to him. "Do you know anything about the old churches?"

Tea trickled from the pot at a steady rate while Jacob tapped his foot. He returned a fresh cup to her with a dainty cucumber sandwich.

"Just that they were run out of the country shortly after the burial services for the royals."

She maneuvered around the clutter to retrieve the sandwich and knocked her elbow on a stack of books before she could take a bite. With an exasperated huff, she slid everything off the desk. Books and paperweights dropped into a heap to the side. "Bunch of bollocks that isn't getting me a bit closer to figuring out anything. Old forgotten faiths and dead crowns."

She froze mid-chew. Mary Magpie mentioned a crown. A jolt of alertness shot between her temples, but the flash was brief. She forced the crisp cucumber down in a hard swallow. *Crowns, Magpie's crown. What did it mean?* She gazed downward to the pile and practically jumped out of her seat.

"Miss?"

She pointed at the floor where the book, *A Fall and a Rise*, lay open. The youngest prince's mangled face presenting itself to them. Even without the color of the moment, Lenora could smell the blood.

"Are you seeing what I'm seeing?" she said so quietly it was a feather above a whisper.

"I see a dead child."

"No, look."

She bent down on all fours, digging through the mess to pull out an advertisement for The Sublime Spectacle. Fogarty's sinisterly impossible grin front and center. She placed the flyer next to the prince's picture. The line where the lower half of the face had been bashed in on the prince. The line of Fogarty's mechanical replacement. The eyebrows. Slick dark hair. Jacob crumpled onto the floor next to her, staring in utter disbelief.

"The youngest prince—what if he hadn't died? You said the priests buried the royal family. What if they found him alive?"

"Are you really suggesting Fogarty is Prince?" Jacob said.

The lethargy of waking had left her entirely, but she still felt trapped within the clutches of her nightmares. A man who could stoop to the depth of poisoning the wretched, of killing for control, made a king. Her hands shook as the seed of panic grew to an overwhelming need for action. That grotesque grin as monarch struck her as more frightening than a night alone in Dusang. The fact there was an actual means for him to achieve it—a shot of pure terror.

"The priests are here to legitimize the bastard's heritage. To proclaim him undisputed king," she said as if the wind was being knocked out of her.

The parts of his performance were coming together to create the complete drama. Frame the Council by claiming Aqua Peritia causes Delirium. Once the populous rebelled, the priests could reveal his lineage. With the people's rage aimed at the Council, he could easily claim his birthright. Gone would be the hope for a true Age of Awareness as Elsothe would be plunged back to the times of the monarchy. Knowledge restrictions. Limitations on scientific discoveries which clashed with religious views. Everything sucked into the depths of ignorance and oppression with a sadist on the throne.

The panic seemed contagious, and Jacob shuffled about like a caged tiger. "What do we do? We can't let him crown himself, not after what he's done."

The images of Fogarty anchored them into the room. The boy that should have died beside the monster he'd grown into. The resemblance impossible to deny, which made the contrast all the creepier. How often could one see the exact moment when innocence dies, beaten to a new shape, next to the hateful beast that crawled out of those wounds?

"We stop him, Jacob. We have to."

Twenty

Pulling up to Mr. Waites' mansion the second time, determination filtered Lenora's perspective. Waites wasn't a gentleman to be wooed into assisting her any longer. She would slash through his resistance, like an ax tearing through the weeds. This house stood as an unkempt obstacle, a decrepit shack concealing a recluse, nothing more. She pinned a nosegay of fragrant begonias on her collar to ward off the atrocious smells of the taxidermy room. Shoulders straight and will hardened, she stepped out of the carriage.

"What if he doesn't let us in?" Jacob held back a section of prickly weeds with an unopened umbrella.

"He will."

She hiked her thick skirt up to her waist and pulled all the fabric over to one hip. Beneath, she had taken the liberty of forgoing knickers and instead wore a pair of men's trousers. The branch of a thorn bush just missed smacking Jacob's cheek as he dropped the umbrella in shock.

A deafening whistle came from across the street.

A group of adolescent boys on the other side of the dirt road snickered at the sight of the woman pulling up her dress to march up to Waite's house. Half of the little cluster already had Peritia cuffs attached, which wound Lenora's resolve tighter.

Rather than waste her words on them, she ignored them and stomped to the front door without so much as a single snag. She dropped the ball of material. The skirt fell back into place with a grand swoop.

She banged on Mr. Waites' door before Jacob fully collected himself and joined her.

The boys dispersed, leaving two dawdling by a massive oak. One pulled two bright yellow vials of Aqua Peritia from his pocket. They leaned against the tree as they injected. By their warm smiles, she imagined they were enjoying something fanciful or perhaps a bright bit of poetic verse. The sight was heartbreaking; two youths curled up in the arches of a tree's roots in the afternoon sun, taking in a full book possibly tainted with insanity. Had they known the dangers of the imaginary visions, they would certainly crush those little vials beneath their worn shoes. Tragic that they wouldn't believe her if she warned them. Not yet, at any rate.

The snap of the mail slot opening redirecting her back to the task at hand.

"May I help you?" It sounded like a perfect repeat of their last visit; calm, soft tone coming from the slot.

Lenora crouched close to the opening, keeping her words as quiet as possible to avoid being overheard. "Mr. Waites, it is with urgency I implore you to aid us. Please, let us—"

"Be gone from me, me, me. I'm not involved," the voice said in a melancholy hush.

"But you are already involved," she shot back as the flap of the slot tapped shut.

The only reply was the sound of his shuffling footsteps backing away.

She raised her voice far louder than she had intended. "He is planning to make himself king."

The footsteps ceased. Stillness from within. Lenora caught her breath and held it. Jacob gave her a nod of encouragement and poked his fingers through the slot to give her an opening to speak through.

"Did you hear me? *King*. He would control everything and everyone. You know how terrible that would be, don't you? What kind of despicable man he is? Please, Mr. Waites, just give us a moment of your time."

The staleness of the inside leaked from the slot onto her face. The ancient dust desperate to escape the confines of the old house. A hint of the ammonia smell carried through with it. She let the disgust roll off her like drops of rain. This took priority over her weak stomach.

"Mr. Waites?"

Another round of footsteps tapped around within and then the click of a lock turning. Her relief in that instant could have filled the sails of a ship and carried them across an ocean. The door once again held a quarter of the way open for them to squeeze in. She took a long lingering breath of fresh air before slipping in, followed by Jacob who closed the door behind them.

Mr. Waites bent before them clutching his single gas lamp between his palms, a silhouette in the surrounding blackness.

"We talk about this, this quickly." He turned and took two steps toward the hall leading to his taxidermy chamber.

Lenora cringed at the thought of the dead faces in the back room. "Can't we speak here?"

He was already vanishing down the hall, taking the only faint light with him. "No lamps here," he said over his shoulder.

Nothing she could do but follow him. Invisible threads of spider web drifted across her face. Dust settling in her hair, itching her scalp. In the dark heat of the room, the faint particles felt like a sandstorm. She batted at herself with a handkerchief. Amazing how the dark exaggerated everything, except reason.

She kept her vision limited to the crooked Mr. Waites, avoiding the full scope of the corpse collection in his workroom. But the incessant click of the animatronic pieces wouldn't let her forget they were present. The chemical stench seemed thicker than the last visit but pulling the nosegay bouquet to her nostrils kept the spins at bay. The only unavoidable glass eyes were of the raven on the table, now propped erect and eerily captured in a perfect moment of impending flight.

"Will, will he come here?" Waites' voiced carried the shaky timber of apprehension.

Even with her flowers shielding her from the smells, the room felt overpowering. As if each rotten carcass that had graced his table left some of their weight in the air.

Jacob compensated for the way the odor had robbed her of her tongue. "Maybe. We don't know. He'll be looking for the papers, and if he thinks you have 'em, he might."

Mr. Waites frowned or at least that's what she assumed from the small part of his face she could see. "Fogarty can't be king. He's a bad, bad, bad, bad, bad man."

She pushed aside the creeping sensation of dead animals watching her back. Nothing could be done to revive the dead, but insanity could be held at bay. Fogarty could be derailed. Her resolve returned long enough for her to seize upon it.

"Precisely why we need the key Ell—Dr. Brechin gave you. If that fell into his hands, the whole country is doomed. You have to trust me."

His face tilted up to her, eyes peeking through the oily strands of hair. He wanted to believe her, but there was something else clouding his expression. An old, familiar fear. Whatever history Waites had with Fogarty left a deep scar on this man. She may not have known the details, but she knew enough of the ringleader to understand the pain he inflicted ripped to the soul.

Lenora reached out, ready to place a soft hand on Waites' crushed back, when the bent form suddenly shook.

"Fogarty hurts people, but I, I think you already know that." He wrung his hands. "Do you promise to stop him from taking the throne?"

"I will do all I can, with my very life. I promise."

The soft nod of his head flopped the strands about, concealing his downcast face once more. From his waistcoat pocket, he pulled out a brass key. No elaborate design, a bare circle attached to the straight key.

He handed it to her trembling uncontrollably. "I'm not much of a, a man, but what little man I am, I consider on the side of what's good."

She clutched the key like the most precious of jewels, too elated with having it in her possession to even begin to wonder what it unlocked.

"I think you're a fine man. A full man." She teared up, key curled up in her palm. Not even the exposed fangs of the taxidermied creatures smothered the warmth in her hands.

"You really think so?" Mr. Waites beamed at them.

Jacob nodded in agreement, and Mr. Waites lit up a broad smile exposing each rotten tooth without a hint of self-consciousness.

A cracking shot shook the room.

Mr. Waites' smile dulled; his eyes searched about in confusion. A mouthful of blood oozed from his lips down his chin. He slumped over on the table, a bullet hole in the center of his back.

Shock froze her like an arctic wind. Dead, without any warning. Another specimen ready to be stuffed and mounted. It didn't seem real, more like something from the warped visions of opium.

Fogarty stepped into the room, the tip of his cane still spewing gunpowder smoke. A high screech of steam sounded as Fogarty's grin wore down to a flat line. The broken side of his jaw had been repaired and fastened with patches of steel. He tapped the cane firmly, and three wax men entered from his rear to flank their master on either side. Each servant with their weapon drawn and trained directly on Lenora.

She shrank back next to Jacob, who puffed up his chest with grinding teeth.

"Cyrus, I must say I'm quite shocked." He mocked the corpse. "Not only have you continually refused my generous offer to rejoin our successful troupe, but now I find you with such obstinate company. I'm starting to wonder if you have some vendetta against me."

Lenora ran her finger over the pepperbox but dropped her arm gently observing the wax man's steady aim. As tense as every muscle in her body felt, she was under no delusion that she could draw her weapon, aim, and fire before Fogarty and his men had already filled her with holes. All she could do was clench her fists.

Trapped.

Fogarty kicked the body and knocked the table on its side along with the limp Mr. Waites. The body made a heavy thud accompanied by the sharp taps of glass eyes and wires scattering everywhere. Lenora shrieked.

Fire.

Waites' lamp toppled over with the worktable, its flame touching upon the bird's wing. The whole fowl caught in a burst making the stuffed bird a burning phoenix upon the rug. Lenora shrunk in tighter to Jacob when Fogarty turned to her, cane pointed at the ready. An orange glow on his face striking off a bolder hue from his jaw.

"It is apparent you still do not fully comprehend the situation, Miss Leahill. Did you really think this freak would protect you from me? Him and his pathetic Anarchist Guild?" He stepped forward; his gloved hand stretched open to receive. "Now, the key and the location of where the research is locked up."

Her fingers curled up around the key so firmly the fingertips throbbed with the lack of blood flow. Glimmers of firelight in the countless glass eyes around them. Singeing fur and the crackle of growing flames on the wooden table, and the stiff creatures seemed to lean in to watch.

"No," she hissed.

"Let me make this crystal clear for you." He raised his cane.

Her eyes squeezed tight. She didn't want Fogarty's face to be the last image she saw. The cane fired once again. As the sound of the bullet rang through the room, Lenora felt sharpness in her stomach. Then that sharpness faded, and there was no pain. Grabbing her dress, she found it unscathed. No holes and no moist blood.

Jacob bent forward onto her, grabbing his shoulder. The bullet hole gushed blood down his front as he transcended pale and went translucent.

"Jacob! No!"

Across the room, the wax men scrambled to force their master back through the door. The flames spread from the lifeless fowl to the carpeting and walls.

"What are you doing? I'm not finished here!" Fogarty screamed as his cane discharged a third time, striking the far wall inches from Jacob's head.

Fogarty fought to bring his cane back in line with Jacob and Lenora, but the wax men had him by both arms yelling "fire!" as they muscled him away. Flames crept up the wall beside the struggling men, making them dark silhouettes against a swirling orange backdrop. Fogarty twisted free long enough to turn on his men. Flinging the cane at them and shooting wildly. He managed to hit one wax man before the remaining servants wrapped themselves around him and held the cane to his side. The injured usher collapsed where he stood like an umbrella. An unnatural descent that only added to the vulgar theatrics of the struggle.

A heartbeat later, the shelf of chemicals combusted into claw-like flares. Jacob's arm dug into her middle as they dove to escape the explosion. An enormous blast from the ignited chemicals burst out at them in an expanding rush of blinding orange. Flares of magenta, teal, and amethyst shot out as individual chemical bottles popped like the vibrant spirits of the desecrated creatures freed.

Once the blast retreated into the roaring fire, Fogarty and his remaining henchman were gone.

The hallway vanished in a thick wash of putrid smoke that choked. The glowing orange all around them.

She rolled over to be met by the soulless gaze of Fogarty's fallen servant. The skirt of her dress ripped under her as she thrust back away from him. With her rear pressed against the wall, she couldn't bring herself to turn away from the dead man's face. The sight of him punctured her bravery, forcing her body to seize up with fright. The skin melted clean off his face, exposing the flesh and bone beneath it. Nothing plump and fresh under the wax façade, only withered stringy fibers held the skull together. Wound through the muscle and around the jawbone were thin dark veins like jellied wires. As the inferno gained momentum the light bounced off them, and they seemed to passionately dance.

Each moment that elapsed gazing into his empty sockets stoked the flames higher. She pried her vision from the waxless skull.

"Jacob!"

He lay face down. His back was as coated in wet blood as his front. The bullet must have passed through him. His arm alight, fire crackling as it burned through the coat and shirt. She rushed to smother the flames with her jacket, pressing down on the seared limb to be sure it was extinguished. His body remained limp as she fumbled to drag him closer to the wall away from the spiking red and gold heat.

The one doorway in had become a solid row of flames. Had there been windows? No. All dark within. All dead flesh and chemicals. The smell of burning fur as the animal corpses were freed from their macabre displays. Lenora coughed.

She pulled Jacob deeper into the room, knocking over the upright deer. Her fingers searched around the wall as the breathable air was rapidly sucked from the room. Eyes stinging. Body coated with a layer of perspiration. *It has to be around here. Please.* She patted the paneling in a wide circle. *Please.* Finally, her fingertips landed on a crevice. The half door.

With all the might she could muster she rammed that spot on the wall. The little door gave way, toppling Lenora forward onto overgrown vegetation. One full inhale of clean oxygen, and she poked herself back in. Wrapping her arms around Jacob's chest, she wrestled his body out into the open yard.

A few paces away from the half door, she spread them both out, gulping at the blue sky. The weeds massaged her back, welcoming her into the fresh air.

Jacob was breathing. Labored breathing, but he was alive.

The ring of the fire marshal's bell sounded in the distance, but she only listened to the rustle of the grass. The breeze cooled her sweaty skin. A blue sky stretched out ripe for gazing.

She laughed nervously at the passing clouds. *We survived.*

Then a cold shadow crossed over her, blocking out the sun. A shadowed figure of a man in a top hat stood above her. Rays of sunlight crashing off the metal at the back of his jawline. Before she could scream, her mouth was stuffed full of cloth, her arms twisted behind her and bound. Fogarty's eyes matching his insanely wide grin as her exhausted body struggled with the wax men. Coarse cloth pressed up her nostrils. The smell of ether. Then darkness.

TWENTY-ONE

"I don't like it. Too risky. They shouldn't have brought her here," a scratchy male voice said from a distance.

Chilled, smooth floor under her cheek. A tension ache as her shoulder blades pressed together. A blurry crimson wash.

"And where else would you have taken her?" a deep voice replied.

"I would have offed her," the scratchy man said. "She doesn't have the papers, or she would've already given 'em up. She isn't worth the bother."

"Is that so?" another male voice said. "I think she damn well knows something 'bout where they're at. I think ya just a meater. Big man acts like a mouse."

The scratchy man hissed. "I just don't see the point. She's got nothing we need. I'm sure of it."

Lenora blinked. The crimson curtain. The sleek stage floor. Cardend Theater. She tried to keep her breathing even and her body relaxed while the voices from stage left continued.

"Don't listen to him," the deep voice taunted. "Ole Jasper is as tall as he is cowardly. Spooked by a little lady, are ya?"

The two men burst abruptly into a fit of laughter drowning out Jasper's protests. They quieted as footsteps approached. A sudden thud tapped down on the floor.

Fogarty's voice came out sharp and clear. "Enough. We have business to attend to."

"You want me to dispatch her for you?" one voice piped in. "I have the perfect dumping spot. She won't be found for weeks."

Lenora could hear the gears of his jaw turning, clicking away, echoing across the stage. "No, my friend, we have much use for Miss Leahill. As stubborn as the girl has been, everyone has a breaking point. She will tell me where the papers are hidden."

"And what if she doesn't know anything?"

"Oh, she does." Fogarty tapped his cane again. "And if I'm wrong on that account, there are other uses for her. A wealthy benefactor is a rare commodity indeed."

"Make 'er sign over all 'er money," one of the men snickered.

Jasper cut in again. "She's a problem. She could talk. Why not just kill her and start again? There are other doctors and scientists and such. I'm sure we could find one to—"

Fogarty cut him off. "You know as well as anyone else we don't have time. If the papers are indeed out of reach, I will make other arrangements, but at this point, we need to avoid that situation at all costs. The priests have already gathered. Each day the threat of discovery rises. My patience grows thin with you, Jasper. Don't question my judgment again."

The binds cut into her wrists, making her young scar burn. Her neck tweaked at an uncomfortable angle on the stage with her arms pulled back. She shifted herself slowly holding her breath. Hopefully, they were so enthralled in their conversation they wouldn't notice.

"Ah, it appears our guest has awoken." Fogarty's boots stepped towards her followed by the footsteps of the others. "I'm sure the mode of travel isn't what you are accustomed to. However, you realize you forced my hand."

She bit down on the gag. He didn't deserve a response, especially a humiliating muffled one. Boots shined to a blinding sheen stopped an inch from her nose. Those boots remained a moment, showing her where she was; beneath the foot of another.

Some of the men pulled her up. Set on her feet still weak from the ether sleep, the two men held her up by her biceps. Their faces were unfamiliar. Lenora recognized the man they called Jasper by the tattoos covering every inch of his skin. On his backside, he bore the embedded hooks used to hang him over the audience during the second half of the circus. Lenora felt her belly twist at the memory. Fogarty gave Jasper a nod, and he rushed backstage.

"It has occurred to me that you, my dear, are unaware of your role. Look where you are: *the stage*. This is where we all are. The acts unfolding around us. Some we play an active part in, while others we stand at the sidelines waiting for our entrance cue. The performance is only a successful, coherent piece if everyone assumes their roles properly. You aren't playing your part. Naughty, naughty." He tapped the handle of his cane on her forehead. "However, I can forgive you as I have come to realize you never got the script. From the very start, you have been unaware of your path. It's proof enough you chose to take up your father's position. A woman doing a man's job instead of seeking out a suitable husband to step into that role. Again, I can't fault you. Ambition is an admirable trait. You desire a bigger part in the performance. Still, you can't simply steal lines from someone else."

Jasper trotted back out with his head down. Behind him, he pulled long chains which attached overhead. Dangling at his thigh, the chains ended in hefty metal hooks. A razor's slit of terror sliced through Lenora's grogginess.

"Now, I am prepared to offer you a most prized gift. I will change the script. I will give you the reputation you so desperately seek. Your name will forever be remembered as one who helped save Elsothe from oppression. A hero. Surely your dream part is worthy of a small bit of cooperation. Of course, if you still cannot grant me the information, those pesky little research papers I require, well... then I will have to show you the unfortunate consequences of jumping into a part other than your own." Fogarty cranked up his smile in a sputter, the clinking gears made a horrid cackling sound.

The two men holding her joined in laughing.

His offer ripped through her. What had once been all she craved felt shallow when forced through false lips. *What kind of hero would she be to assist in bringing about a broken age?* Still, a part of her longed for that dream. No one patting her head or talking down to her as if she couldn't grasp the simplest of concepts. Treated with the same respect as her father, or any other man with a great lineage. To add her link as worthy as any other in the chain of the Leahill legacy.

But is it worth it?

No, not like this. There could be no heroes in Fogarty's fever dream of a future.

"Jasper plays the hanging man well. He has the necessary skill and body modifications for the part. The rings ensure he will dangle over the audience each night without issue. No mess. You, my dear, may find it a far more agonizing feat." Fogarty snapped his fingers, and the gag was yanked from her mouth.

He crept close to her, rotating Mr. Waites' key around slowly before her eyes. "Now, be a good girl and play your part. What does this open?"

Jasper dragged the hooks towards her, his face covered in sweat. Sharp points that thickened into a U-shaped curve. They swayed side to side. The shimmer of the steel chains clashed with the brass of Fogarty's extended grin. For a moment her heart collapsed in on itself. Breathing in rapid bursts. Then Lenora caught how the stage lights made his eyes twinkle like fireworks. Blinding, lethal fireworks.

She tilted her chin up even as every part of her trembled. "I do apologize, but I'm a dreadful thespian."

The mechanic of his face clanked with a spout of steam. The smile vanquished. "What a shame."

They released the ropes, though the harsh manner with which they pulled the fibrous material over her wrists was less than a relief. They held her firm, fingers digging into her arms. Unnecessary roughness in her weakened state as she was still limp at the knees. Someone jostled her corset about from behind. The snip of scissors through starched material. Jasper cutting her bodice and corset, stretching them apart to reveal her bare back. Lenora's lungs unfolded utilizing the newfound space with inhalations that went down to the belly first before rolling up the chest. Slow exhale.

This is going to happen, and I must let it happen or I'll rip apart.

"Last chance." Fogarty lifted her chin with the cane to meet his gaze. She didn't provide what he was hoping to find in her expression. "Very well then."

Fogarty went about the deed in a meticulous manner, pinching a good chunk of her skin away from her shoulder and setting it on the hook. Just the tip. Barely enough to break the skin and he held it there, letting her feel the point. This lacked the perfect sharpness of Elliot's scalpel, with its jagged, slightly dull edge meant more to tear than slice.

She closed her eyes and tried not to flinch in her anxiety. *This will hurt, let it.* Her mind was made up, but that couldn't dampen the waves of terror crashing over her.

He pulled the hooks through her flesh one at a time. It felt as if her entire back was being pulled open, like the hooks each dug into a seam running parallel to her spine, unravelling it to expose the raw meat below.

Something between a scream and a growl erupted from Lenora. Hot tears on tense cheeks. Fogarty gave the last hook a rough tug before releasing it. The ripping pain replaced with a feeling of pulsing skin being pushed aside to accommodate the hooks. Like being stuffed in one spot.

Lenora flattened her heels drawing some solidity from the floor.

Laughter. Maddening laughter from the men.

The curtain drew open. A myriad of wax men occupying the seats. Her feet held her upright, but she didn't feel stable. The stage rocked like a ship. Like the merchant's vessel *Gloria* of her father's fleet. She could almost smell rotting sea spray. One trip down the coast, and she had gone green in the face. She willed her stomach still.

The hooks pulled taught spiking fresh torment from her wounds. The skin of her back stretched with the invading objects. Heels rising off the floor. Feet hovering over the polished stage as her arms were released.

Don't struggle.

The tension blinding, inescapable. Lifted and swung out into the seating. Her skin pulled away from her whole, settling in with the sensation of tiny rips and blood draining down the curve of her back.

Rows and rows of seats rushing back and forth beneath her. The wax men gazed up at her expressionless. Blank heads like mounds of clay still not fully shaped. No delight nor dismay from the crowd. Each agonizing swing over them, they sagged more formless into their chairs. A blur of butter melting on a windowsill.

Another swing, and her father sat front and center, watching her sanguinary performance with his usual disapproval. White, blotchy skin punctuated by two hard ebony eyes. Never there to assist or support her, just the stern figure watching from a distance.

Then why are you here?

As the hooks lurched her back in a fresh bout of suffering, he was gone, but she couldn't let him dematerialize so easily. She willed him to reappear, searching the wax faces as her blood ran down her spine. Still, the fickle ghost refused to return.

"Why do I always have to chase you?" she groaned through the tears.

Flashes of swimming light in her vision.

He had always been off in the distance, unattainable, no matter how she reached out for him.

Another swing, and she yelped at the shift of the hooks in her flesh. The holes were worked wider with each sway over the audience.

I'm still chasing Father. He's not haunting me; I'm haunting him.

"I thought you were wiser than your father." Fogarty's voice echoed across the theater. "To accomplish great feats, you must be willing to do whatever it takes. You must be willing to pull that lever—and we both know you are capable of that. Would you rather die as nothing? As even less than your father?"

"My father made his own choices," she yelled back. "And I am not him. Just as you are not your mother or her monarchy."

A roar came from the stage.

Her body throbbed. The pain spread outward, sparking at her scalp and the tips of her toes. The mass of melting faces blurred into one generic mask that each audience member wore.

Fogarty stomped down into the aisle beneath her.

"You're wrong," he bellowed, flogging her legs with his cane. "I'm the son of the royal family, heir to the throne. Only I have the intellect and tenacity, as bestowed by God, to rule. I and I alone. And the Council will pay for the transgressions upon my family honor. Their vile little contraptions will face judgment, as will you, you worthless pinchcock. I am ordained by the Almighty to rule over all!"

Her calves swelled deep inside the muscle from the pummeling with his cane. The skin of her back pulled thin, begging to rip and spare her anymore agony. Yet, even though she felt nothing but pain, there was a part inside of her proud. Fogarty thrashed around enraged like never before. She had gotten under his skin.

Her father always insisted she be courteous and pleasant, as a little lady should be, but she wasn't seeking his approval any longer. She was battered and bleeding and on her own, so she might as well make use of her sharp wit.

"It appears to me that I'm currently in a position over you."

The cane cracked across her jaw.

The audience blinked out with not even a whisper of applause.

TWENTY-TWO

The curtains remained parted. A few wax men lingered in their seats, but the majority wandered off to other tasks. Either her torture was in intermission, or the performance had run far beyond the attention span of the audience. Silence occupied the lobby rather than cheery voices toasting the night's entertainment amidst Fogarty's spice-scented air. The vents blew nothing warm or sweet. Only the fading hints of the last audience's combined musk and lead-based stage makeup remained—spiked with the coppery scent of blood.

Her feet pressed down on the polished stage as the hooks forced her to stand. Blood collected between her toes, slick and tepid. She was soaking in the flow of her internal workings, the oil which ran her gears. Inside out and on display in the harsh spotlight, her labored breath reverberated in her ears.

A wash of throbbing pain occupied all her backside. The pressure of the individual hooks was no longer perceivable, yet the exhaustion of her legs grew increasingly intolerable. Each attempt to slump her frame and relieve the burn on her muscles pulled at the wounds, opening the gashes fresh with trickles of blood coursing down to the floor. Her arms dangled free but useless with her back fastened to the set. The pain she could handle; it was the exhaustion that was wearing on her. She felt like she had aged fifty years since her father's passing. She wanted to curl into herself like an old woman slumped over a cane.

Good posture is the sign of a fine lady's upbringing. A whisper of a giggle escaped her lips at that thought. *Good posture indeed.*

Fogarty had stopped questioning her some time ago, but he still hovered somewhere in the wings, watching, critiquing her damsel in distress performance. Faint clear breaks in her bleary view revealed his unflinching stare. She wasn't portraying the victim to his liking.

A second figure stepped onto the wing. The lengthy shadow filled up space next to the ringleader's hazy form. The echo of stormy words rang through the theater. An argument brewed, but the meaning eluded her. The stress on her flesh deafened her to the world beyond her soliloquy of suffering. The spotlight blanked out all the details outside the growing puddle of blood which spread beyond the hem of her skirt. Wide brush strokes of color moved around the seats like leaves blown about in the wind.

The voices grew louder, crashing across the stage floor.

"This isn't what I signed up for. I'm a performer, damn it. I won't have some bricky girl die on my hooks. I'm not getting involved no more. Have your deformed lackeys do your other work. I'm just cast." Jasper's words became more gravely as his volume rose.

"You are as I say you are. We're all in this!"

Her left foot slipped on the ocean of ruby red beneath her, yanking her body off balance. The chains above clanked as a searing sensation roared down her. A fresh stream of warmth flowed down her spine. She forced her aching muscles to secure the foot. Little ripples haloed around the heel and toes as she recovered her balance. *I can't maintain forever.*

"She's going to bleed to death. What then? Will you be satisfied?" Jasper sounded shrill, yet his voice was fading, like someone yelling at the Wilthiem as they sped away. Syllables swallowed up in the trailing steam and hum of rolling wheels.

Her vision dulled as if in the gloom of Elliot's smoke.

"She... will... break..."

Fogarty's statement became a hiss on the wind. A ghost's whisper in Dusang where her bare feet flattened the damp carpet of fallen red leaves. The metallic taste of blood coated her lips as the moon beamed down on her, banishing the skeletal bulk of the beech trees into the dark. Cold. She shivered, too wet and afraid to move from the lunar glow of protection because the forest moved. The Dusang of her childhood nightmares stretched out in all directions.

Nowhere to go. Nowhere to hide.

The grunt of the beast prowling beyond her sight and the smell of gunpowder hit her with a jolt. All her senses startled awake. The freezing wind stung. The ivory bark reflected the glow of the moonlight like icicles in bewitching detail. Each exhalation hung like fog before her with the sharp taste of blood. The gun in her hand contrasted the frigid air so strikingly it felt nearly molten. Wisps of smoke curled into the night from the barrel. She sensed the vibrations as the monster scurried around her.

It's coming for me. It's always been coming.

She turned her head to a flash of the figure as it darted outside her peripheral vision. Just the still shadows turning the bare branches grey where the darkness clung. A growl cracked out of something behind her. As she spun around, a glint of billowing fabric ducked into the thin fingers of trees. Her pulse quickened. The creature waltzed with the pale trunks, circling closer and closer.

The dense clouds of her breath formed a long train into the woods.

Another snarl in the black. The rustle of disturbed leaves.

The gun went heavy in her palm.

The nightmare was coming to a head the way it always had in her youthful slumbers. The climax—the attack. Her eyes squeezed shut.

"Stop!"

The inside of her lids flashed a swirling orange. Her body pulled back in space like she had her feet snuggled into the sand as a wave retreated from the shore. That sensation of being yanked towards the land as the beach stretched out in response to the sea pulling the swell back. Traveling without moving until she collapsed into soft cushions.

She reclined on the couch in Ruu's yellow room. The air made thick with the essence of tobacco and opium. Those herbal and floral scents mixed, and it smelled like him, like when she laid helpless in his arms on the settee in his office.

Madness.

Her entire being twitched. Is this what insanity was like? Shifting from one place and time to another in an impossible yet somehow abstractly accepted manner? Perhaps this is what Agitated Delirium appeared to be from within one's own mind. Wild searches for research papers and being hunted by fallen princes.

"How is the dance for you? The dance between the awake and the buried dream. Does it swirl to the music or stumble?"

Elliot sprawled over the opposite sofa in a posture meant to signal relaxation, yet he appeared stiff with his ankles crossed and body drawn long. His brows and smile lines softened in a calm more akin to classic sculpture than a breathing man. She much preferred him as this fixture of the yellow room than the pathetic wretch they dragged away to an asylum, even if she knew it all illusion.

She dared not look too deeply into the space. If the details were skewed, if the pillows or water basin were out of place, surely, he would vanish along with the fantasy around her. He sat up, though there had been no movement to justify the change of position.

"I still don't care for it," she replied.

She hoped her words would evoke the feeling from that first night at Ruu's, the thrill of it all being new and unexplored. When she had leapt towards the Age of Awareness full steam while tucking her fears into her coin purse until the time payment came due. But that feeling didn't return to her. After all she had seen, she couldn't deny Canimere wasn't heading in the direction of the Age of Awareness she had been promised, *her* Age of Awareness, where every mind was open with knowledge, and none suffered.

He stroked Harold, who had cuddled up on his lap. She wanted not to miss Elliot, to dismiss him as merely a professional in her employ. Yet the expanding gloom the lack of his presence cast over her was undeniable. They had been partners in this endeavor— and possibly more. Much more than she wanted to admit.

"Perhaps you are using the wrong steps for this song. Or perhaps you shouldn't let your partner lead. You lead."

"A woman leading the dance? How ridiculous."

He chuckled while exhaling a thick puff of smoke in an upward swirl. The blue tint of it spread out against the yellow decorations, sending shimmers of wafting emerald over the draperies and cushions. He rolled cigarettes, offering her one.

"Why not? You haven't exactly followed protocol so long as I've known you. Make the dance yours. Lead."

"Lead."

"What?" a voiced squeaked.

Flat darkness. The stench of animal dung assaulted her nose, tempered by the sweetness of freshly clipped plants. Straw. The crisp hay cushioned her palms and cheek. Her back throbbed but felt tight, as if folds of her skin had been rolled in and tacked. She touched the area gently. Her fingers ran over the dried blood. Bits of it cracked and flaked off onto her hand. The show was over, the stage gone, but that realization brought only momentary relief. No doubt Fogarty kept her alive only to torture her further later.

Beyond the vertical bars nearly touching her nose, the zebras shuffled in their cramped pen. An elephant's trunk reached into the enclosure, spooking the striped herd as far to the left as possible. Their pens were only inches apart. Three monkeys bucked in their cage as the zebras packed together right next to them. Mounds of feces-cluttered straw covered whatever floor was beneath her. She sucked in a breath through her teeth.

Pushing herself up to a seated position was slow and tender. The flesh threatened to tear open with each slight movement. Her scalp grazed the bars on top of her cage. A hefty iron lock fastened the lid. Lenora gave it a yank. Solid as a rock.

A twittery laugh rose over the grunts and stomps of the animals.

Mary Magpie squatted down on the outside of the cage. "Lead? That's what you say? You're more a caged animal than a lead performer. Fitting though. Miss High and Mighty in a box. Not even a pretty one."

Magpie crept closer. The tangled mess of black hair and trinkets matched her wild expression. A rush of adrenaline smacked Lenora. *This insufferable woman again.* She puffed her chest up only to relax into a slouch when the slashes bit into her from the strain.

"I have nothing to say to you," Lenora snapped.

Mary laughed again, only this one hit gruff and solemn.

"That so?" Mary swung an iron key from a chain. "Want to talk now?"

Watching the key swing back and forth sent fire shooting up from Lenora's core. This heinous wench had the upper hand on her. She stoked the anger and let it melt away any residual terror. She thought clearer with ire.

She heard her father say the word only once, but it was the only thing her tongue would create. "Bitch."

"Not so proper now, are you? You don't listen when it'd be smart to, either. Told you not to come here."

"Does it appear to you that I came of my own volition? I was obviously dragged here, you simple—"

Magpie grabbed her by the bodice before she could finish. A blade pressed against her neck. She couldn't swallow her shock for fear that would cause the knife's edge to sink into her throat.

What now, Elliot? Plead for my life? No response came. Just the crunch of hooves on straw and soft utterances of the monkeys.

Mary hissed out each exhale. The blade pressed a hair deeper. This wasn't a woman that would listen to reason or employ mercy. Magpie was the type that only responded to threats.

Lenora settled herself into a composed position. "Playing the gypsy Lady Death, are you? I call your bluff. You wouldn't want to talk if your intent was only to murder me."

Her heart leapt over a few beats, but her frame remained still. Mary pressed her face against the bars. They were close enough to kiss. So rarely in her youth had Lenora been able to interact with girls her own age; she always wanted that sisterly kinship she saw between the other girls. She hadn't realized until later other women could be cruel to each other. Mary showed her just how brutal they could be. *Sisters or enemies, no in-between.*

"Show me your spirit. In the eyes," Mary whispered as she angled the knife slightly up to put pressure on Lenora's windpipe. "Do you have any desire for him at all? Any want to be at his side? To be his queen?"

Lenora stared directly into Mary's black irises. "If I had my preference, I would place all the oceans end to end between me and your precious Fogarty."

Something in Magpie wavered, some glimmer of satisfaction. The knife withdrew. Lenora rubbed her throat with silent gratitude the skin there remained unbroken.

"Then what 'bout this?" Mary drew a small white square from her belt.

A silk handkerchief dangled from Magpie's fingers. *S.J. Leahill* embroidered on the corner. Lenora went cold.

"It's my father's. He must have dropped it here," she sputtered.

"Liar. The girl said a lady gave it to her. A proper lady. Now, the li'l blind imp couldn't tell me what this lady looks like, but it says it right here. *Leahill.* Right here!"

As Magpie's voice crested at an ear piercing note all the beasts panicked in their confinements. A whimpering sound from an elephant's trunk matched the neighing of the zebras.

Think, Lenora. She couldn't admit they had been scurrying about Pitchdrift for evidence of Fogarty's treason. That would certainly land her into disaster deeper than she already drowned in. Yet, Mary hadn't mentioned anything of Agitated Delirium or Peritia. Could it be possible she knew nothing of Fogarty's plot? Perhaps Magpie was merely a bit of pleasurable company for the ringleader. Company with a jealous streak. Perhaps she knew nothing. After all, she hadn't asked once about what Waite's key unlocked.

Lead.

"Well, what do you think happened then?"

Mary pointed the tip of the knife in her direction. "You met with him here. All secret like."

Lenora eased forward, placing one hand on the chilled metal bar. She needed to select her words carefully, keep her tone sincere. "Yes, I admit to that. We met."

Mary retreated to the corner, contorting down like a spider confronted with a thick newspaper. Envy oozed from her.

"He proposed!" Mary shrieked.

A renewed flurry of knocks came from the cages after Magpie's shouting. A spray of straw kicked up around her as the zebras bucked. The circus beasts understood the signs of oncoming violence well. Magpie seethed in the corner. The shadow of her untamed hair spread over the walls into a nest of thorns.

Lenora kept her voice as even as she could muster. "Discussed, as if it were a business proposal. He's interested in the Leahill family's reputation and estate."

Magpie scraped her fingers down the wall, silencing everything as the scratch slowly ground its way to the floor. "That bastard."

Lenora's other hand graced a bar. Her arms gently poised in surrender. "He wasn't thrilled with my rejection. That's why he kidnapped me, you see. To force the matter."

Magpie snapped upright, knife at the ready. "And this key? The one he keeps talking 'bout?"

Lenora swallowed hard. "To a safe. One of my father's hidden safes. He, he happened to save some of the old jewelry from the monarchy during the overthrow."

The ringing clash of the trinket belt swaying as Magpie bounced off the wall to stand over Lenora once more. A fresh wad of dung plopped down in the elephant's pen. The steam rising off it perfumed her lies appropriately. She kept her hands resting on the bars, wide open in submission, but her chest heaved. Each breath aggravated the lacerations.

Mary twirled the blade in her hand. "And why not tell him where it is then?"

"Do you think he would release me after that? I don't."

Magpie loomed over her. Her head tilted sharply; one beady eye looked down on Lenora from the profile. "I should kill you."

"That would cost you his favor. He won't make you his queen if you betray him like that. Isn't that your prophecy, that I will cost you the crown?" Lenora lifted her chin.

The knife spun faster in Magpie's palm. Each revolution of the blade accelerated Lenora's pulse. Mary took her time thinking. Lenora could only wait as the blade kept the rhythm.

The knife stopped. Magpie's thumb pressed into the hilt. "And what would you do if you escaped?"

"Flee the country. What other choice would I have?"

"Hmmph," Mary responded and walked out of the room.

The jingling exit made cracking stone of Lenora. She had escaped death, at least for now, however her cramped prison remained. Her forehead rested on the bars. Tears threatened. She couldn't let them free, not when Fogarty wasn't finished. Not when she knew he would stop at nothing.

She bit her lip until it bled to feel anything but despair. There had to be some course of action. Perhaps she could irritate the animals into breaking the cage. Surely the elephant had the strength. The question was if she would survive the trunk's bashing. Not likely.

The clattering of the coins and ornaments returned. Lenora straightened as Magpie rushed towards her. A sheet of paper and pen landed in her lap.

"You want to leave. I want you gone. But I want the safe too. Write where." Mary swung the key savagely about. The knife secured in her belt.

Lenora scribbled some nonsense address on the paper, some street named Falront near the shipping yards. Then added, "in the back-left corner office, underneath the desk" at the bottom. She folded the paper into a condensed square in the manner of the notes she penned and passed at Glenn Haven.

"Let me out first, then I'll hand over the paper." Her fingers squeezed down on the note in her hand.

Magpie jutted out her hip. "Ha! Don't trust you that much, fancy lady."

"Considering I'm wounded, and you have a knife, I doubt your concern. Do I frighten you that much, even in this state? Flattering." Lenora gripped the tiny square until she could feel the exact spots where the corners pricked her palm.

This sort of ego poke worked wonders on the boys at school. However, she wasn't at Glenn Haven, and this wasn't some bratty school chum. Mary didn't rush to prove herself unintimidated. Instead, she stood contemplating with the key slicing through the air like a flail winding up to strike. The collective breath of the animals brushed on Lenora's neck as if they were engrossed in the drama.

"As you say, but don't think I won't gut you if I have to." The key clicked into the lock; the façade of the cage dropped onto the moist hay with a muffled pound. "I'd bleed you for laughs."

Every layer of her back erupted in flames as she willed herself to stand. The sensation penetrated so deep that even her bones wailed. Being back on two feet, however unstable the straw ground seemed, was relieving.

"That safe." Mary held out one hand ready for the paper to be deposited, the other closed over the handle of the knife.

Lenora hesitantly brought the folded paper almost to Mary's fingertips. Close enough that, had Mary been a worthy adversary, she would have snatched it. But Mary was cautious when she should have been quick. In an abrupt flick, Lenora tossed the note towards the far wall, past the pens. When the knife rushed past, Lenora stepped back. It grazed the lace of her bodice and nothing more as Magpie tumbled forward. The monkeys hooted as one of them scooped the little paper square from the floor. Mary flung at them full speed and contorted herself on the cage, smacking at the creatures as she clawed for the prize.

Lenora reclaimed her proper posture. Spine straight and head level enough to balance a book on. She rewarded herself, briefly, with the spectacle of black tangles and cheap trinkets battering against the trio of chimpanzees.

Lenora walked sorely to the exit. She ripped some cloth from her dress to use as a makeshift ash mask. Anything would serve better than a bare face, yet she could still taste the soot. She shuffled into the streets at a steady pace through the storm of onyx. The ash collected into the loose bodice and stuck to her tacky wounds. Chunks pelted her at every angle, but she didn't feel them.

There was nothing left to feel.

TWENTY-THREE

The young Xouai from Ruu's turned a cramped carriage onto the long driveway of Foxton. The trip had been a blur. Lenora recalled briefly scanning for any possible wax men trailing behind. There had been none as no one rammed the rickety coach off the road to drag her back to Cardend.

The memories of her care at Ruu's were vague at best. The Xouai had been gracious, even after all the trouble Elliot caused in his Delirium rage. Sad to realize that all the supposedly upper crust flocked to Fogarty's deranged circus when the poorly received Xouai proved far more welcoming hosts. In the future, she would have to find a way to repay their kindness.

The little cup of hot bitter liquid Ruu's assistants served her was the last thing she could remember clearly. A few exotic leaves and thin scraps of bark floated in the brew. After that, time skipped forward at random intervals and the parts she could remember were fuzzy and numb. She less recalled what she had done and more watched a distant view of the events surrounding someone else who looked identical to her. For that, she was thankful. No point in dwelling on much of anything for the moment.

Coming up to Foxton, time was still choppy, but pieces came together in a dribble.

Claire met her at the door along with the butler and a slew of housemen. She was whisked away, calling back to the housekeeper to make sure to pay the driver for his services.

In her room, she lay on the bed as maids undressed her. Their soft gasps of shock at her condition remote.

Claire's voice, "Two men at every entrance point. I want a constant watch. No gaps."

Warm towels run over her tired skin. Bandages wrapped around her.

The smell of the grass from a cracked window.

A night shirt and then bedding draped over her.

Her head falling into the down pillow.

She almost sunk into sleep, but Claire's voice rose again. "Am I to believe you are far too deep into whatever you've stumbled upon to simply walk away?"

"Yes."

Claire sat on the edge of her bed, brushing the hair from her face. Attending to her like when Lenora was small and ill.

"Rest now."

Lenora drifted off into a dreamless slumber.

The sun poked at high noon when she woke. She struggled to lift her torso. Everything hurt. Even the lobes of her ears pounded and ached. She managed to bring herself to one hip debating whether standing up was worth the effort or if this was as far as she could push.

"Two days," Claire said from the corner chair.

"And you've been here the whole time." Lenora's voice was hoarse. She shifted farther onto the hip to reach for her water pitcher with shaky hands.

"Mostly. I had to attend to other duties occasionally." Claire took the pitcher and poured a glass. Lenora guzzled it down. "I'm sure you wish to know the state of things.

Your wounds are clean and well trussed. It appears your foreign friends are quite skilled at mending. The estate has been secured. Four intruders were dealt with the first day, but since then it appears whomever you angered has kept their distance. Your business associates have been told you have a dreadful fever and not to come calling."

Lenora put the glass down gently. "I see." Then a face rose to mind. "Jacob, my driver. Is he being cared for?"

"He has been. Fidgety boy has been trying to get in this room since you came home."

"Send him in then."

Claire grunted. "Really?"

"I've no time left for tired etiquette. We both nearly died." Lenora winced. The firm tone caused a shooting pain through her chest.

"I don't care about the etiquette. You aren't well enough yet for the lad to be riling you up." Claire smoothed her apron.

"I'm the mistress of the house, and I say I am."

The housekeeper sighed as she shook her head, "Nora, being the head of the estate means more than making demands. Think about the staff, about the people who depend on you. Trust us to help you."

The old woman's lip trembled. For a moment Lenora considered all the times Claire had given her a stern talking to, and caught her mid-leap between couches in the sitting room, and waited on her in sickness, and called her in from the rain before she was soaked through. She didn't have to do any of that. Looking after the child of the manor was the role of a mother, of the governess, not part of a housekeeper's duties. Yet Lenora couldn't recall a single governess who had any lasting effect on her at all.

Perhaps giving birth wasn't required to mother.

Claire flattened her expression to the tight-lipped grimace that she always wore. "At least one more day in bed. The manor is safe. Give it another day to heal."

Lenora laid back down. "Just one. It's more than I can spare, but it if you insist."

"I do." Claire refilled her glass.

Lenora rested the day as Claire instructed. With regular doses of Laudanum, she drifted in and out of sleep. Blissful, untroubled sleep. Still, the city and the darkness within it weren't vanquished. The Council still produced case after case of infected vials of Aqua Peritia. Enforcers mutilated and murdered the innocent. The asylums overflowed with the raving Agitated Delirium patients packed inside, Elliot among them. The little blind girl was still being poisoned through the vents of her dilapidated home. Fogarty lurked out there in the thick of Pitchdrift, relentless in his pursuit of the paperwork she had never set eyes upon. In between unconsciousness, they all circled around and screamed at her.

The Age of Awareness far from her reach.

She woke the next morning coated in salty sweat, heart leaping bounds around her rib cage. The room was still besides earthy bursts of air from the window. Claire dozed in the corner chair, hands flat over her lap as if she was straightening her skirt and apron.

The skin on Lenora's back felt tight, but she found that gently stretching herself forward was possible without the sensation of ripping. Just raw tension. Almost as if the hooks still pulled her up. As soon as Lenora wrestled herself to standing, the old housekeeper roused herself out of the nap.

"You're up." Claire creaked with each joint that moved as she stood. "I suppose I can't convince you to rest any longer?"

"I'm afraid not."

"Well then, I'll fetch your driver."

Jacob pulled out a random tool from his collection, tilted it to examine its length, then tossed it back on the bench. He wasn't working on anything, but he kept his right hand busy. The left arm wrapped in a sling, immobilizing it so the bullet wound on his shoulder could heal. She couldn't be more grateful for the fireman who came upon him on Waites' lawn and brought him home.

He wanted to talk in the gardens. As if the prettiness of nature would be able to smooth over the ugliness of her tale, but the fragrant beds of lavender, usually a vibrant deep purple, were now all skeletal, withered and brown. She insisted on his work shed.

Jacob circled around outside before returning to fidget with the door, testing its stability. She wished he would settle in one spot. His movements made it harder to talk as she had to follow him about. As her story went on, as what she endured unraveled onto the dry grass outside the shack, he paced and plucked up various items faster. He didn't want to look at her.

Two crows darted over the shack as Lenora finished. The birds' shadows ran across the ground racing their aerial partners.

"I'm alive and the manor is secure. That's at least something." Lenora stretched her torso. Her flexibility was returning gradually, even though the throbbing remained.

Jacob kicked the green carpet of grass, caking the toe of his shoe in mud. "But I wasn't there to help. I failed you."

"Failed me? Don't be absurd." Her posture slacked. She rubbed the scar on her wrist before adding, "I put you in peril. As your employer, I should be more cautious. I failed you."

Silence between them. A crow dove sharply towards the rear of the shack. They both flinched. She waited for it to smack against the far edge of the roof, crashing in a solid splat. The bird transitioned to a glide a moment before impact and flew on into the brush.

The circling crows cawed roughly at each other before migrating towards the rear of Jacob's shed. A shiver ran through her.

"That's a lot of crows. Are there always so many?" she asked as the tilt of her head followed the swarm of birds into the trees behind the shack.

"Actually, I never see them. Sometimes a few perch over by the vegetable patch on the other side of the property, but never over this way." Jacob switched his gaze from the ground to the sky. "Wonder what they're after."

Lenora walked over to the side of the shed, staring into the browns and oranges of the trees. Something was off. She could sense it in her core. The wooded area rustled with the flutter of wings and the click of beaks. A hint of fragrance rode on the breeze, both pungent and sweet. She drummed her fingers on the shack's wall.

"Jacob, what's back here?"

He came up behind her. "I'm not sure. I think it goes into the hunting grounds."

"The hunting grounds are past the hedge maze," she said as she made her way through the first cluster of trees, one hand on her holstered replacement pepperbox. "There should be a fence somewhere here. Father built one around the main buildings of the estate. I thought he was being paranoid, but…"

Jacob matched her step for step into the foliage. She positioned her footing with care, keeping her spine tight with each step to soften the stress on her sutures. A small dry branch snapped as she pushed it forward out of her way. The whoosh of flapping wings burst up but settled without a single crow taking to the open sky. The land sloped down farther in, and the trees thinned.

Just ahead she could make out an iron fence covered in shifting shapes of slick black feathers. Their clicks and caws clear on the sharp breeze. A putrid odor spilled through the sparse trunks in rich, offensive waves. The birds perched on something dangling from the fence. The group muscled around each other in winged aggression for their spot. They feasted upon this form hanging with ravenous pecks. A familiar form. A human form.

Lenora screamed.

A flurry of onyx feathers thicker than Pitchdrift ash took to the air. The flapping wings forcing gusts of rotted meat stench through the brush. Lenora clung to a trunk and shielded her face. The murder departed in a swift and violent burst.

They left behind the corpse swinging by hooks in each of the poor victim's temples. A naked body pecked unrecognizable. As the chains looped around to swing back, the skull split open at the empty sockets from the weight. The mass hulk of the corpse dropped to the leaf-coated floor with a wet thud. The top of the skull remained aloft on the hooks.

She screamed again, but no sound broke through into the physical. The screech of terror was trapped in her head.

Wild black hair swayed from the skull cap, little coins and trinkets braided into the locks sung like a wind chime in the breeze.

Mary Magpie had lost her crown.

TWENTY-FOUR

Lenora dropped the sixth sugar cube into her cup. The murky tea spilled over the rim and flooded the saucer. She knew Fogarty was a murderer, Beef had made that point clear. However, there was a drastic difference between knowing how grotesquely he killed and seeing the evidence firsthand.

And she had a hand in that murder.

All she ever wanted was to advance Canimere forward—to show them what she can do. She'd failed on an epic scale. For all her grand intentions, she had become a murderess and a liar with no research papers to show for it.

"My deceptions resulted in *that*." She stirred the tea and a tide of liquid sloshed on the desk. "I left so proud. Why didn't I realize what I'd caused? What else would he have done with her when he found out?"

"You didn't do that. He did," Jacob said while pacing the library.

Dear Jacob, always holding her in such high esteem, but she couldn't ignore her hand in Magpie's end. The death of the wax man weighed on her like a boulder of guilt strapped to her back, and that had been in self-defense. Fogarty goaded her into pulling the lever in the Current Parlour. Her role in Magpie's demise felt dirtier somehow, like Fogarty's cruelty had crept in and corrupted Lenora. The taint writhed just under her skin, itching and burning.

As if his madness has seeped into her pores.

The electric fixtures blinked on. She hadn't even noticed how dark the library had been with all the curtains drawn. Jacob broke his constant pacing and squinted at the brightness. With a clearer view of the mess she had made of her tea, she pushed it to the side. Funny how wreckage could seem so minimal until a light shone on it.

Claire deposited an Aqua Peritia vial in shocking sapphire blue on the desk. "Another decree from the Council."

Lenora didn't need to inject it to know its contents. The last such message clearly warned against involvement with the old faith. This vial surely repeated that message with added force. Fogarty's priests were making a show of agitating the people. The Council naturally retaliated. Even without the research papers, Canimere stood on the cusp of a riot.

The globe Fogarty gifted her ticked like a metronome. The noise had become a fixture of her late nights in her father's private library. She should have thrown it out, yet having the reminder fueled her in her searches. A steady click that wound down the hours. This evening it felt louder and reverberated through the floorboards. Her wounds pulsed with the rhythm. She was running out of time.

Claire took the disaster of a tea serving from Lenora and placed a fresh one in its stead without a word.

She tossed a sugar cube into the new cup, and then another. "He isn't going to stop."

A third cube thrown into the cup followed by a rapid mix with the spoon to match her speeding thoughts. Poor Waites slumped over his table. Blood on the polished stage floor, reflecting the spotlight. No, Fogarty would never cease his destructive quest, each atrocity added to the grotesque performance.

"He's a snake. A slimy, hateful snake," Jacob spat before resuming his directionless patrol.

A fourth sugar cube bobbed in the tea then sank as it dissolved. The way the coins in Magpie's hair drifted in the wind, tinted red with blood, stuck in her mind's eye. That wasn't what death looked like. Death was pale and quiet, not the raw, vibrant hulk that swung from the fence. Her pulse pounded.

Lenora pinched another cube between her fingers. Air rushing into her lungs in hard swallows like punches.

Claire stood solid on the other side of the desk. In that moment, the look the housekeeper gave Lenora held the undying confidence a mother has for her child when they face one of life's harsh challenges. That expression of "you can handle this because you have to." Lenora had no mother, but she had been mothered nonetheless.

Chin lofty, Claire tapped her temple with her pointer finger.

The sugar cube dropped from Lenora's hold back into the dish.

"Right. Hysterics won't serve me now. There must be a way to sort this situation out. He thinks I know where the papers are. That's… good?" Lenora chewed on her lip. "Yes, that's good. If he didn't believe I had valuable information, he would have already—so he won't go to extremes."

"But he has. Everything he's done is extreme." Jacob took a sharp turn behind the desk after walking the length of the long 'u' shape of the library. The rows of books made a cluttered background for his aggressive pacing.

Lenora ignored him and went on, thinking out loud, "So, I don't do anything which would give away that I'm as ignorant as he is about Waites' key. I can't go searching for any locks. Not while I'm certain he would simply abduct me again as soon as I left the gates."

Jacob's fist came down on the desk. The teacup shimmied in the saucer sending the powerful sweetness up in steam to wake her palate.

"He won't be getting his hands on you 'gain. I won't let 'em." He sounded like Beef, powerful and sure.

"Jacob, you're one man. He has dozens, if not hundreds, at his disposal in Pitchdrift. And the priests." She slumped back into her chair.

The tea smelled too sweet. She preferred it that way as a child, but now it reeked of candy-coating and the rich tea fragrance was lost. She pushed the cup away.

Jacob stomped around the desk. "That snake. No, he's worse that a snake. He's some slithering, cold-blooded, reptilian thing that shouldn't be livin'. A monster…"

Cold-blooded. He went on, but Lenora couldn't hear him anymore. She was somewhere else—that night in Ruu's entrance way. Elliot's eyes wild, his body erratic and violent. The doctor she knew being consumed from the inside out by Delirium. Barely clinging to the last threads of sanity, he had shoved Harold into her lap. *Papers, here.*

She stood up, slamming into the desk with the sharpness of her ascent. The teacup bounced off and crashed to the floor. Jacob froze. If he had still been speaking, her jolt silenced him.

Claire smoothed the splatter of tea off her apron calmly. "Nora?"

Lenora didn't respond. *Could it really be that simple?* She tore out of the library at full charge. *It's been right here the whole time. I just wasn't paying attention.* Barreling up the stairs, she nearly knocked over a maid with a full load of laundry in her arms. The guest room at the end of the hall, that's where Claire said they set him up. The hall carpet slid up beneath her as she tore down the corridor. The soreness in her back no longer relevant.

The door banged against the interior wall as she dashed into the guest room. With a quick twist of a switch, the room flooded with soft, electric light. A bare floor except for fragments of fruit and lettuce spread around a tray. No wonder the maids had removed the rugs. She stepped over the bits.

The bedding lay flat and clean. She ran a hand over it to double check for any hidden form snuggled under the covers. Nothing. A lift of the bed skirt yielded only a few scraps of some root vegetable.

Alarm rose in her throat. Did he get out? Then she spied him clinging to the bedpost with metallic claws, glossy yellow eye peering down at her.

"Harold." She kept eye contact with the iguana as she backed away to the door and gently closed it behind her. It took her a second to catch her breath to continue. "Now, I know I haven't been the best hostess. I should have come to visit you sooner. I'm sorry, but I need your help now. Please."

She couldn't look away, as if he would dart into a hole like a rat if she wasn't watching. Some bit of left-over vegetation squished beneath her boot as she made her way to the bed. Harold kept his grip firm as if he had been frozen solid on the post. Only the dark dot in the golden iris moved to follow her.

She sat down on the bed rubbing her temples. "And now I'm talking to a lizard. I really must be going mad."

Perhaps a broom would coax him down. Or a fresh platter of food. She was desperate enough to toss things at him if that's what it took. Luckily, extremes wouldn't be necessary; she heard the click of Harold's legs as he scaled down the post. He walked deliberately over the duvet. Each claw placed with precision and purpose. She half-believed he understood her.

He placed one claw on her thigh. A moment's pause, as if the animal was sizing her up, or perhaps attempting to decipher her flushed appearance. He gradually crawled into her lap, spreading himself flat. Legs spread stretched in all directions and neck cozied down on her dress. She stroked him a few times, gawking at the awkward position.

"Oh, I see. This is how Elliot trained you when he worked on your legs?"

He blinked in reply.

At first, she didn't know where to begin, so she continued to pet him while observing the mechanical limbs in detail. Each of his extremities had been torn at different angles and lengths. The mechanics were secured beneath the scales into the remaining flesh. Pistons linked from there on either side of a tube with a hinge sort of piece that acted as a wrist. Elliot was truly brilliant. There didn't appear to be any sort of engine. Each leg was fueled by the natural movement of Harold's stumps, or at least she assumed as much.

Her timid hand ran over the nearest hind leg. Harold remained still. His belly soft. She explored further, pressing her fingers at the hinge and at the joints of the claw. Nothing transformed or moved but Harold was still calm, which prodded her to use a tad more force.

Pushing on the tubing of the forearm, it gave with a snap, swinging open. She let out a gasp and a nervous giggle. A small scroll slipped out of the tube onto the ivory bedspread. With a burst of newfound zeal, she went through the tube of each leg, extracting its paper treasure within before clicking the metal pieces closed.

With all the paper in a little mound beside her, she hugged Harold. The lizard wiggled in the embrace like a child in an overzealous aunt's arms. "Thank you, my friend without hot blood."

Harold rushed off her lap and moved to a spot on the bed where the sun cast a yellow square for him to bathe in.

With the papers unrolled and unfolded, she found them filled with the details of Elliot's experiments on both front and back. From the specific chemicals he had extracted from Aqua Peritia and the manner it affected the blood through injection, to Fogarty's vent fragrance and an overview on how they acquired the samples with dates and addresses. Some of the medical and scientific terminology read a bit foreign, but the overall meaning was intact. Undeniable proof.

Lenora flipped through them in an elated daze. Two letter-sized pages on the spread through Aqua Peritia—the research her father had paid for. Two more labeling Fogarty the source. She stacked them only to flip through each paper one at a time again.

"I have the papers," she said gleefully. Then the warm glow of discovery faded. The papers became heavy in her hands. "Bloody shit, I have the papers."

She finally held all the evidence to end the epidemic. Yet the question remained how to use the research. So much blood spilt, so many lives shattered. All those hands reaching out from asylum cells. The truth crinkled between her fingertips. *What now?*

Fogarty sought these pages with such brutal resolve. Before, there was nothing he could possibly do to force the research from her hands because she didn't have it.

Lenora scratched the scar on her wrist. Something needed to be done. Otherwise, these same pages that could be Canimere's salvation would elevate the sadistic ringleader to ruler.

She could surrender the research to the Council. They would deal with Fogarty in the harshest and most permanent manner. But, that option filled her mouth with a sour, stinging taste. The ashfall. The swarms of dirty faces outside the factories in Pitchdrift. Punishment dealt out by Enforcers in pain before mercy. Profit before people. And she couldn't forgive what they had done to her mother.

Wouldn't handing them the research be another way of surrendering Canimere to their oppression? Not an inch closer to the Age of Awareness?

Lenora rubbed the paper between her fingers noting the coarseness of it, the officialness of it.

What would her father have said? Probably to figure it out for herself, she supposed. He always sent her to the main library or had her write out her options whenever she asked for advice.

Elliot? Her dear doctor had been vague at best when coming to any decision regarding the papers. Each to rule themselves, but no idea how to reach that point. Beyond his anarchist vision for Elsothe, he hadn't mentioned any particular path to achieve his goal.

They left her with the means but not the way.

Out the window, the green reached out into a thick strip in front of her. A grassy ocean which separated Foxton from the cruel places. Dusang Forest, the dark that occupied the space from just past the gate to the horizon. Beyond the forest, the bleak grey of the soot cloud hovered. In the light of the late afternoon, the plume of ash became the mast of the gigantic warship that was Canimere. Full to the brim of decay, corrupt captain spinning his top hat at the helm, the vessel raced towards her emerald refuge.

Jacob vocally accosted some chambermaid in the hall, demanding to know where Lenora had gone. His voice pulled her from the window.

This was a heavy decision, a shame she had to decide for so many less fortunate. It wasn't only her country and her future at stake, after all. *Why should I alone make the choice?* A spark of inspiration surfaced.

To inject is to know, and to know is to be wise, and to be wise is to contribute to the Age of Awareness. She now knew many things she hadn't before, and yet she didn't feel any wiser—but maybe there was still a way she could contribute to the Age of Awareness. She folded the papers neatly and gave Harold a final nod before heading to the door.

Jacob scrambled next to her before she closed the guest room.

"You alright?" He was raspberry red down to his collar and panting as if he had run through the layout of the manor at full steam, twice.

"Quite. Make my carriage ready, and fetch Perry Bohely. I plan to leave immediately."

He scuttled behind her down the hall. "Wait, what? I thought—"

"I want to arrive at the publishing house when Mr. Bartleby starts his night shift. I have an important document that needs to be reprinted."

TWENTY-FIVE

Lenora twisted in all directions. The left window, the rear view, then the right and back again to behind them. Not so much as a stray dog since they left. Rather than put her mind at ease, the calm only served to fuel her paranoia. The forest stood too quiet. No sway of branches from the wind. Not a single rat feasted upon the mass of roadkill on the side of the dirt path. A silent Dusang, but she could feel someone watching from the recessed shadows between the trees.

Jacob winced as he gave the rudder a twist with his wrapped arm. The other hand worked the levers furiously. He dashed through the uneven road with impressive mastery, swerving through the dips and rocky patches like he had memorized each yard before him. As remarkable as his driving was, Lenora couldn't ignore the grunts he tried to muffle with compressed lips.

"I should have had Bohely drive me. You need more time to heal."

"Not a chance, Miss. I won't fail to protect you this time." Jacob gave the carriage a burst of steam, and it shot over the bridge like a fox fleeing the hunter. "Besides, we needed him for the other carriage. He probably lured those creepy circus fellas halfway down to Jemci by now."

As much as she wanted to believe Bohely in the decoy carriage had lured all the ringleader's forces into following him, she doubted it. Fogarty was too sharp to go all out for a single shiny coin when he could divide his forces and triple the profits.

Lenora's hand rested on her coat pocket, the research papers tucked away within, safely folded in half. All she had to do was stay alert and keep her head. She squeezed the pocket before spinning back around to check the rear. Still clear.

"I don't see anyone following us." Jacob cut around a slow carriage.

"But they're out there," she muttered.

With the end of Dusang in sight, Jacob threw her a small victory smile over his shoulder. "I think we're in the clear. He's probably too busy with the key to bother with you, Miss."

The mention of the key sent ripples of guilt expanding in her head. Waites had been a decent man. Probably misunderstood, but she believed he had a good heart. How awful he died for a key that didn't lead to the research. A terrible waste. They sped through Roudonel, the town less one reclusive taxidermist.

The first puffs of soot hit the windows, barely a sprinkle of little lazy fluffs. If she didn't know better, she might see beauty in the ash. Tar flakes drifting down like the first moments of a snowstorm. But the soft flurry lasted only briefly. Before them, a thick curtain of ash came down like a waterfall, the true entrance into Canimere.

Lenora held her breath. The stars twinkled in the rear window. She knew it may be the last time she saw the clear sky. The odds that she would wind up a corpse buried in soot were greater than she wished to acknowledge.

She stretched her spine. The lacerations on her back aggravated and alert in her constant twisting from window to window. She put herself in the center bullseye of the target, but who else could be hit in the blast? Jacob? Mr. Bartleby? All those in her charge, depending on the Leahill enterprises as their means to survive? She bit her lip.

The back window went dark as the carriage crossed into the full ash fall.

She reclined in her seat. Too late for second thoughts. Not that she could have turned around after she left Foxton's gate, but riding into the inky clutches of the city hardened her resolve. The ringleader was on his way. She must arrive before him.

Around each bend, she braced for impact, heart racing. Yet, no beastly carriage steered by wax men rammed into them. Not even suspicious hats following the course they drove with shadowed eyes. Only the sidewalks thin with pedestrians and sparse carriages flanked them. She clawed at the cushion of her seat. *What is he waiting for? It can't be this easy.*

Northlin Publishers. A weak stream of working-class grey bonnets and bowler hats trickled along the road from the market around the corner. The ash settled on rooftops and streetlamps.

The carriage bucked as Jacob skidded to a stop right next to the door. They had made it without incident. Without so much as a sighting of Fogarty's men. A surge shot up her spine. She leapt out of the carriage, fists clenched. No need for an ash mask with the door only a few steps away. Her body rushed forward on its own. *Just get inside.*

She yanked at the door, but it only groaned and knocked as the bolt banged in its latch. Her knuckles went white on the knob. Again, she pulled, and then again. The door held firm. Her pulse beat like her veins boiled. She matched each jerk with heavy bangs from her other fist. She pulled with all her strength until her gloved fingers slipped off the knob.

She stepped back, heaving soot-tainted breaths. "We're here before Bartleby. Bloody shit. We're here before the night crew."

One hand gripped the pocket and the other on the pepperbox. *This was a stupid idea.* How careless and reckless of her not to consider the gap between shifts. Of course, the bankers would insist the house shut down completely in those hours. *Those idiotic men and their obsession with pinching every coin possible.*

She swallowed down the sour riding the back of her throat. *Not now.* This was supposed to be her moment; all she had to do was get inside and hand off the papers to Bartleby. She took a few deep breaths that tasted like burnt cinders. The ash dissolved on her tongue. This must be done one way or another. She had to pull herself through. Fogarty wasn't going to stop his incessant torment until she did.

Jacob emerged mask-less from the front of the carriage, her ash mask tucked between his bandaged wing and his chest. He had enough sense to retrieve protection for her lungs but neglected his own. "They'll be here, just wait—"

A wax man popped up behind Jacob like a deformed Jack-in-the-box. With a knife at his back, Jacob stiffened.

Three more swooped in on them, the tips of the pistol barrels peeking out from their sleeves lazily faced Lenora's direction. Early to her victory, but right on cue to face a monster in a top hat. Probably an inevitable confrontation, yet the pressure of it threatened to crush her. This time, she actually held the papers. This time, he could claim the prize.

She straightened herself, pressing down the panic within as far as it would go. The wax men didn't speak. They didn't have to. They weren't meant to exchange words with her, only to detain. She softened her hold on the pepperbox. It would do no good to expose the weapon if she wasn't prepared to use it, and her main target hadn't arrived yet. The flow of pedestrians swirled around them like eddies in a stream.

Jacob lifted the ash mask, prepped to hand it to her. Then his frame twitched, and the mask retracted. She couldn't see the blade but assumed by the forward slant in Jacob's chest the tip had broken the threads of his coat and vest, if not the outer layers of skin.

Turning the corner, Fogarty waltzed up the walkway, flagrant in his catch. His cane twirled in the air as he tipped his velvet top hat. He exuded aggression beneath the playful steps; an anger which conflicted with the impossible grin secured in place by the screen. Lenora could taste her own demise, bitter-sweet and mixed with soot.

"Why, Miss Leahill, here on business are you? Rather odd for the mistress of the estate to be in the city so late. Then again, I have noted that you seem to enjoy stepping out of your role." He pointed his cane at Jacob. "And this driver of yours. Certainly seems a loyal, if not unconventional, fellow. A friend, perhaps? Pray tell, what are you up to at such an hour?"

It took all her willpower not to shake visibly, but her mind shuttered. She wanted to be done with fear, numb after being stung by terror over and over, yet the feeling only grew more acute each time she felt it. That smile locked in place while the voice still rang out clear. *Don't look at it.* Avoiding his face only led her to confront the loaded cane pointed at Jacob's ribcage.

"Leave him alone." The words shot from her lips like dragon's breath but lacked the anger she intended. More shaky hot air than fire. "He's of no use to you."

"Is that so? I'm inclined to disagree." Fogarty ushered them to the side of the publishing house out of the flow of traffic. "Your devoted driver has certainly been of great use thus far. How else would I know which carriage to follow? I dare say if you rotated drivers, your little fleet of vehicles coming and going would have proved quite the obstacle."

The shock on Jacob's face flashed for a moment only to burn down into agony—utter devastation tore a hole in his spirit. He tried so hard to assist, to keep her safe.

"I appreciate the help, my dear boy," Fogarty said, closing in on Jacob. "Well? Come on, servant. What do you say when a superior man thanks you?"

"I..." Jacob faltered. Fogarty jabbed the cane in his side, prodding him to continue.

"I said leave him alone!" That time her voice carried the sharpness she intended.

The threats, the torture—she could take those from the ringleader. She chose to get involved with him; the consequences were hers to accept. Not Jacob. He was in her employ, in her care, and only tangled in this web by proxy.

"Awww, emotional attachment. A flaw of the weaker sex." Fogarty bent in closer, the cane tip grazing Jacob's Adam's apple. "Are you ready to cooperate now, my dear?"

Fogarty lifted the cane's end to Jacob's forehead. He flinched.

She needed to say something, anything to distract him from Jacob.

A sharp inhale, then she blurted out, "The Council falls?"

Fogarty raised an eyebrow as he sized her up anew. "Pardon?"

"If you were to get the research, then the Council falls? You would stop them from hurting the people?" Lenora said.

"On my word. My honor." The smile barely contained by the screen, ready to snap open and devour.

She slipped her fingers in her pocket feeling the rough paper. *Elliot's research. His words in his handwriting.* Her pointer finger separated the pages, counting them. Elliot was trapped inside a nightmare in his own head because of these papers. The bile and contents of her stomach rolled.

"And you will let us be?"

"Of course. I have no desire to be cruel. It is merely out of necessity that I have done so. Now, what of the findings? The papers, Miss Leahill. Where are they? What does that key unlock?"

Dry lips. Bitter belly. Salt sweat dripping down her neck and tar in the air.

Fogarty practically convulsed with anticipation under his skin. His eye twitched. Flicks of his fingers. He yanked the screen off. The bolts shooting out and scattering into the crevices of the sidewalk. Even though she had mentally prepped for the theatrics, she jumped back.

"Well?" He rushed in, inches from her face, so she could see the jaw reposition to the flattest line within its capacity. A serious expression, no hiding behind the smile.

Her legs weak, but her heels dug in firm, she slipped two folded sheets out giving them a gentle press before offering them.

"Wait. No," Jacob growled.

It was done. The papers crinkled in Fogarty's hands. The ringleader read over them with undignified starvation. Teeth ground together, frantic in his merriment. A mix of laughter and gear clanks echoed down the street. The jaw twittering in such rapid unpredictable movements that thin streams of oil spurted from the corners and raced down his throat.

Lenora inched back a pace. The world fell away.

"It's all here. Just the way I need." He giggled to himself. "It's finally here. The day of reckoning has arrived at last."

Lenora slid her hand into the waist of her coat. The pepperbox was warm against her side—ready. Her fingers curled around the trigger. It would only take a moment to draw it from its holster and point it at the deranged man inches from her. *Easy*, she breathed to herself.

Then Fogarty snapped back into control in a sudden straightening of his frame. The shift from lunacy to composure was uncanny. His attention shifted from the papers to her. "Now, was that so difficult?"

Remember, squeeze the trigger.

With gusto, the papers were refolded, and then he made them disappear with a sleight of hand. A cackle to accompany his slight bow, and he backed away with his men in step.

She eased off the gun.

"Thank you, my dear." And he vanished behind the corner from whence he came, leaving them to stand in the descending bleak like alabaster statues.

"You gave him what he wanted, after everything we've been through. Why would you do that?" Jacob slammed his back against the wall and slide down the brick defeated.

"To keep you safe."

He pressed his palms to his temples. "What? No, you shouldn't have to—You're Miss Leahill of *the* Leahills. And I failed you. I led him right to you."

She settled herself next to him, careful to keep her tender back from pressing against the wall. "Don't be ridiculous. You did everything you could for me, so, I did the same. My life isn't worth more than yours. In fact, from now on, I'm making it an official rule that we keep each other safe. All of us, everyone that works with me."

Jacob released a deflated attempt at a chuckle. "That's a beautiful rule."

Even in the dark, Jacob always managed to light a candle. This one may have been small, but she only needed the tiniest of flames now that she had grown accustomed to the shadows.

"And what about keeping them safe?" He pointed at the oblivious pedestrians around them. "What will he do to them once he rules?"

With the specks of soot settling on her lashes, the people appeared splattered with ink. Walking bits of paper marked and stained. A little girl in a smudged blue dress clinging to her father's stubby forearm cranked her neck back to watch the elaborately dressed lady without a mask. The others ambled by without so much as a glance in their direction, but the girl saw her. And she knew the girl would suffer most under Fogarty as he stripped the country's last bits of prosperity for himself.

Farther down the road, a man walked towards them. His stride neither rushed nor leisurely, but with steps so unremarkable he seemed more a part of the background than an actual living person. *Bartleby.*

Lenora pushed off the wall. "Come on, we've got work to do."

"Work, Miss?" Jacob stood up, offering her the ash mask like an afterthought. She refused it.

"Fogarty got his research papers. Exactly the ones he requested." She pulled the remaining two pages from her pocket for Jacob to see. "But we did some research of our own."

TWENTY-SIX

The only window in her father's private library faced north away from the city, which spared Lenora the vista of Canimere. If visible at all from other windows, the city only appeared as a dark, far-off bump on the horizon, but her imagination often toyed with her eyes. If the streets burned, as she knew would be the case in an uprising, she would envision tiny specks of bursting flames at the edge of her view. In the library, she was safe from such self-induced visuals. Still, her mind wandered.

The scene played out before her, Fogarty making his grand entrance onto the political platform, hat spinning and jaw polished. A slew of robed priests standing behind him, giving merit to his claim on the throne, as the city unravels around them in the chaos of the Delirium findings. Bricks thrown through storefront glass ushering gusts of ash-polluted air into previously pristine shops. The tiny shelters in Pitchdrift ripped apart, their splintered planks held as weapons by the mobs of enraged inhabitants.

Lenora spun a tiny violet vial of Aqua Peritia on the desk as her mind conjured the scenario in excruciating detail. The opal iridescence of the liquid glistened in the lamp light as the vial rotated. The otherworldliness seemed fitting as the vial contained the Grimm's fairytales she never found time to inject. She desperately wanted to fall into those stories, where evil always perished and good prevailed. The "happily ever after" inevitable from the first page, the reader just had to get past all the scary stuff in the middle. The waking world didn't have such certain endings.

Fogarty had his proof, but it was his papers against hers. Bartleby and his crew at Northlin publishers worked all night creating copies. Jacob had hired dozens of men from the outskirts on her behalf to blanket the city in prints of the condemning evidence against the wayward prince. They assured her they adhered them to every door in the wee hours of the morning. She sent the truth to the people; it was up to them to decide what to do with it.

Maybe they thwarted Fogarty before his plot gained any footing; the people rising to defend themselves from his tyranny, the truth more powerful than Fogarty's deceiving flash and dazzle. Maybe it was too late, and the ringleader led the people of Canimere in a charge on the Council's chambers to place himself on a throne. Either way, the city would boil with riots.

She caught the vial mid-spin and pocketed it.

The sun would rise soon, framing the scene of carnage. The tick of Fogarty's globe seemed to increase in volume. She lit the match in Canimere; had it caught?

Elliot would have thoroughly enjoyed this. His dusty office curtains flung open at long last to witness people lashing out at the rotten core of the city while he smoked his rolled cigarettes one by one. Perhaps he would even join in on the destruction. After looting and frolicking in the mess, he would retire to the yellow room, drawing from his pipe and spouting anarchy for all.

Her father would sit opposite Elliot, an oversized cigar wrapped loosely in his hand. Their sweet floral and wooded coffee scented smokes converging in the room. She indulged in the scenario, picturing herself with them. No more shooing away for "little Lenora." Instead, she sat with the men discussing the important topics—government, conspiracy, war.

A deafening explosion shook the library. At first, she was not sure if the sound was only something her imagination had conjured to frighten her, but the noise was followed shortly with a splatter of crackling. More deep booms that gave way to twittering fizzles.

Fireworks. Lenora sprang out of her seat.

The view from her tiny window revealed the outside staff scattered like water on a hot skillet. A burst of blue and white sparks amid smoke. They were launching wildly at the manor, sending the fireworks as if they were cannon balls.

"Find where they are launching from!"

"There! There! Get 'em."

"Stop him!"

A wax man raced across the grass trailed by several of the new hires. No more fireworks rushed towards them, but the screaming continued.

"The carriage house is on fire!"

"More water!"

"Hook up a hose to that water pump!"

An orange tint lit up the edge of the window. The carriage house lay beyond her limited range of view, but she had a clear view of the dry grass spotted with flame, as if each fire were a tiny goblin staking a claim on the lawn.

He used fireworks. She was too livid to physically react. *Fireworks!* An attack as much about ripping open the scar of grief as it was about destruction. *That bastard.*

The door to the library swung open, propelled by a sharp kick. Fogarty stood in the doorframe, disheveled, and perspiring profusely. His whole being expanded and retracted in a hulky mass of heavy breathing. A rabid man, metallic teeth bared.

"You tricky, little bitch," he snarled.

Lenora reached for the pepperbox at her waist. Fogarty unloaded from his cane. Two bangs. The smell of gunpowder and blood. Pain struck her forearm as she pulled out the gun, sharp yet hot. The arm fell limp. The pepperbox slipped from her grasp, flung somewhere unseen. The second shot struck the bookcase behind her.

The world unbalanced. Black smoke. The pain spread across her arm, but her middle remained intact, the corset unscathed. The bullet hadn't made it through her limb but had successfully disarmed her—the pepperbox lost to the depths of the library. *No time to find it.* Fogarty drew a pistol from his side and aimed it at her. She dodged, rushing to the right as he fired.

"Do you know what you've done, you insignificant child?" he charged. "You've deprived Elsothe of her true king!"

Adrenaline flooded her body, and the wound went numb. All sensation but the need to move evaporated. She groped blindly for whatever she could grab. Something heavy. Her fingers met cold metal. *The globe.* She swung it with full force at his face. The blow knocked him back onto the floor.

He didn't stay down for more than a moment. Back on his feet, his jaw warped like a crumpled sheet of paper, dangling by a single bolt below his ear. The gears twitched making a gush of black oil mingle with blood where the dented metal joined his flesh. He gurgled, guttural vile sounds from something less than human. His piercing eyes saw her and nothing else, even though he must have been dazed by the impact.

"Monster," she whimpered.

The globe slipped from her grip as she darted past him out the door. She burst into the hall and tripped on something big and warm, landing hard on the rug. Behind her, Jacob lay on the gleaming parquet wood of the passageway. Blood leaking from his temple drenched his hair and concealed his features in a glossy mask. As she stared, frozen for moments that seemed an eternity, his chest rose and fell. He breathed, so she stumbled to her feet.

Fogarty barreled out of the library and into the wall, sending hanging paintings of her glowering ancestors crashing to the floor. A long, serrated blade dangling from one hand, pistol in his other. She took off before he righted himself, running the halls like she had as a child. Only this time, the evil chasing her wasn't imaginary.

Lenora burst outdoors. Smoke blanketed the manor grounds heavy like the Grim Reaper's robes. Bodies flashed before her in a blur, a rush of movement in the suffocating spread of the flame's exhaust. The landscape of Foxton purged into the morbid greys of the city except the dawning east lit up in fierce golds by the carriage house fire.

Her arm shone with gore. She blinked the sight away and scrambled forward. People rushed every which way, but she was a ghost to them. The shriveled grass danced with flames that licked at her hem. She pulled the skirt up, batting at the smoldering edges. She screamed, but it only added to the chorus of shouting voices.

Fogarty thrashed his way out of the manor behind her. The remaining mechanics of his lower face clattered as they wound up and down in vain. Without his false humanity, he became a howling creature clawing at the earth. Brandishing the hefty blade like a snake showing its fangs before the strike, he lunged towards her.

She surged with a new burst of energy, the instinct to live charged through her like lightning. She ran without direction. No glances behind, undiluted momentum. Each yard her lungs screamed out, unable to quell their thirst for air. Veins punching outwards as the blood rushed through her. Her wounded arm swung like a rapid pendulum at her side, scattering droplets of blood like seeds. Her heels crunched the uneven ground. She ran like a madwoman as if Delirium seized her feet and drove them on and on until her legs shook beneath her. Minutes, hours—it all melted away as the chase rode her past exhaustion.

Finally, with her muscles spent and her body gasping, she crumpled to the ground.

Vermillion leaves crackled under her weight. She desperately gulped the air, her pants a painful wheeze. His low grunt echoed nearby, as if he was everywhere.

Lean skeletons of red beech trees surrounded her. The morning fog obscured their brilliant leaves. The trees stood as bleached bones erected upon a flood of crisp red. Batches of green and black moss crawling up the trunks glistened like rot clinging on the dying remains. The musk of moist leaves decomposing hung heavy on the air. A fresh corpse of a forest.

Dusang.

"No, not here," she whispered.

She swiveled around on the forest floor to get her bearings. Trees in every direction, matchsticks emerging from a blanket of red above and below. Distracting. Disorienting. A flicker of movement out of the corner of her eye but then all was still with a turn of her head. A kick of breeze ruffled the scarlet. A reverberating snarl from all directions. The sound of her heart beating like the deafening pounds of the Peritia factory pistons.

Lenora crawled between two young twin beeches as if they were armor and pulled herself to her feet. Memories crept in with the mist, just like the nightmares that haunted her childhood. The coarse bark bit into her palm, reminding her this time it was real. The thing chasing her had every intention of disemboweling her.

She crouched low and snatched up a fallen branch with a shaky hand. Slimy soil caked on the stick squished between her fingers. Each exhalation hung like a high note to match the deep thud from her heart. *Slow it down. Muffle the bass. Still, quiet.*

Her biology wouldn't obey.

Her tired legs darted to the next cluster of beeches. Then the next, only pausing to set an ear to the forest. The faint creak of a hinge swinging free. Lenora held her breath. A footstep on dried leaves, then a series of vaguely familiar clicks.

Reloading.

She sprang to a nearby bush for cover as two shots whistled behind her. Rolling, stick in hand, she dove backwards swinging with all her might. She hit nothing but empty space.

Silence again.

The fog crept over her legs, her torso. The terror paralyzed. In her dreams, this would be the moment when it would descend upon her, gnawing and mauling. The crimson of her blood staining black against the brilliant burgundy of the forest floor.

Hooks and tubes penetrating flesh. Glass eyes of the taxidermied bird in flames being brandished by an Enforcer. Wails from the asylum, hands wrapped in snake-like coils of wires stretched towards her. A kaleidoscope of Aqua Peritia vials leaking together into a rusty fluid, the color of blood, as it mingled with the fallen ash.

And his grin, cold and solid, spreading wider and wider to swallow it all.

The branch slipped from her grip as hands came to her head. *This isn't real.*

Fogarty jumped on her. The knife gouged at her collar bone, then the top of her left breast. No impossible grin—his mechanical jaw dangled to the side to reveal the mangled meat behind it. His tongue flicked wildly from the nub of bone that once formed the base of his jaw. Guttural noises seeping from the hole as he stabbed away. Her bicep. The shoulder.

She screamed, squirming in agony flat on the earth. She twisted to shove him off and grabbed at her boot. With the derringer freed from concealment, she aimed the barrel upward as his knife came down again.

One shot. The gut. Squeeze, don't pull.

A sharp bang rang out with a sickening pop at the end. A spurt of blood from the fresh hole below his armpit splashed on her neck. She hit his side, not his gut.

Bloody shit, I missed.

The knife stopped as his hand went to the wound. No suffering in his eyes, only surprise, the beast momentarily stunned.

I won't die in this forest. I won't die here.

She fumbled around the ground, her dress, anywhere her hands could reach for something. In her pocket, the vial rolled beneath her fingers. The knife rose up, ready for the next slice. She wouldn't let it come down again. The vial smacked into his metal teeth, breaking it in half. The fluid soaked his tongue, and he gagged. With a final thrust, she plunged the jagged edge of the glass vial into the side of his neck.

The piercing stare went panicked. His hands flew up to cover the wound. He toppled off her and slithered back in retreat while the gurgles turned moist with blood and Peritia. She collapsed back into the leaves as the fallen prince stumbled off into the maze of Dusang.

The trees rained red, and all was still. A ray of morning light shone from a break in the canopy above. All else slipped away. The sun, vast and warm, slowly ascended beyond her view, but she took solace in the fact it did indeed rise.

TWENTY-SEVEN

Lenora stared up at the members of the Council in their elevated desks. Raised at least five feet, they peered down at her from a half circle. Besides the Council members, only a single record keeper occupied the room. He hunched over a typewriter on a slight platform behind her. The clicks from the keys echoed through the long hall.

She felt small. Not so much like a child, but someone whose stature was being ripped from them, like a rug pulled from underfoot. Surely, the Council planned this to inspire a feeling of submission.

The hefty Lord Gout itched his temple with a pen before speaking. "My fellow Council members and I have thoroughly examined the particulars of the Fogarty incident for the past three months. While we disapprove of some of your actions, Miss Leahill, we chose not to fault you on them. Being such a young lady with limited experience in society, we can understand how you could have held off the prudent course of action, which would have been coming directly to us. Rather, you chose to chase a bit of excitement. Youth is prone to such reckless fancy."

Heads bobbed and muttered around the crescent in agreement, except for one Council member on the far left. He ran a hand over his oiled beard with displeasure.

She found some relief in Lord Gout's words. If the actions of the Enforcers indicated anything about the Council's sense of justice, she feared the harshest of penalties. She had slipped Claire a will dividing up her fortune, just in case. Thankfully, that precaution proved unnecessary. She would walk out on her own two feet. Yet, his proclamation of no fault on her part didn't completely quell her unease.

Weak lamps kept the Council's faces in partial shadow. That bothered her—not because it made them appear threatening, but because there was something wrong with these men. She had researched them. Lord Gout was in his early sixties. Lord Artifell, nearly seventy. Not one under fifty-five, yet the men before her wore not even a streak of grey in their hair. The necks of the clean-shaven members were lean and smooth, without the telltale sag of age. Skin stretched so taut over their faces that the subtle lines in their bone structure seemed overly pronounced. If someone would bring in some proper bloody lighting, she could get a clearer view. As it was, she steeped in a sense of the uncanny that the obscured faces above created.

The bearded member at the far left cleared his throat to quiet the others. "I wish for my disagreement on this matter to be noted on the record."

"Of course, Lord Malhon. Speak your mind," Lord Gout said.

Malhon rubbed the back of his neck with a handkerchief roughly then stood up. The added height made him appear formidable. Like a giant fowl spying a mouse.

Taller means easier to knock down, she told herself in a weak pep talk.

"Much excuse has been granted due to Miss Leahill's youth. I fear our assumption of naïveté in this case is unwarranted." Lord Malhon gripped the front of the desk, leaning forward to address her directly. "I do not believe you are an innocent-minded girl, Miss Leahill. You displayed cunning and the capability for deception in this failed coup that would supersede many experienced gentlemen. I have my doubts you intended to protect this Council or the best interests of Elsothe. Please, convince me otherwise."

The clicks of the typewriter rang out in a flurry.

Lenora had to choose her words carefully. There were rumors the Council kept a machine to ensure only truth came from those they interrogated. It inflicted severe pain for anything that even hinted of dishonestly.

"I'm flattered you believe me so clever, but I only did what I thought would help," she started. "Considering it all in hindsight, I certainly would have done things differently. To be honest, I mostly acted out of fear, but I swear I am fully devoted to Elsothe and the Age of Awareness, your lordship."

The member to the left of Lord Gout scratched his hand while chuckling. "There you have it. Satisfied, Malhon?"

Malhon scraped the back of his neck with the handkerchief again and backed into his seat. The constant itching and fidgeting, unbecoming of those considered rulers, managed to be rather unnerving. The urge to scratch her own arms seized her as phantom tingles rode up and down her limbs.

"Any other comments for the record?" Gout made a show of checking both sides of the semi-circle before continuing. "No? Then it is settled. As for your requested information—"

Malhon hissed, nearly shaking her off balance. The rest of the Council ignored him. After Lord Gout cleared his throat, Malhon relaxed and stroked his beard.

"As I was saying, we are unable to speak of most of the information you requested publicly. Protection of the country comes first, you understand. We are all grateful you brought to our attention how our glorious invention was being misused to carry this awful disease, however the specifics of Aqua Peritia production and the manpower workload details are topics we will not discuss with you," Lord Gout said.

So, they were going to play ignorant about the spread. Not surprising, but it still burned. It took concentrated effort to keep the utter disgust from showing. She could pretend dumb too. All the better, actually. If they suspected she knew they ignored the spread for profits, the Enforcers would have already killed her.

"As for your doctor." Gout held up a sheet of paper and rubbed his cheek. "Brechin? Ah, yes, Brechin. Rest assured he is receiving the utmost care in one of our asylum facilities."

Blocked, as she expected. The Council kept their secrets, but it had been worth the attempt.

She took a step forward, light but noticeable. "My lords, if I may? I only wish to know the location of the asylum treating Dr. Brechin. As my associate is in such a perilous situation, I feel obliged to visit him in his time of need."

Grumbling conversations stirred among the men. They took the sudden noise and movement as an opportunity to scratch their various itches, as if a plague of fleas and ticks had swooped in on them.

Lenora took another step, this one surer. "Please, my lords, my colleague and I have suffered dearly protecting the country. It would bring me great comfort to see him."

Malhon's voice rose above the others. "You lack faith, Miss Leahill. Our scientists are working diligently towards a cure. You will be reunited with your doctor in due time. Besides, such a *genteel* creature as yourself shouldn't be exposed to the harsh realities of Delirium."

His condescending tone grated on her.

"I'm afraid I must concur," Lord Gout followed. "For your best interests, we insist you leave this doctor to us. In lieu of your requests, we wish to offer you something as a repayment for your services. A society is best judged by the quality of its members of the fairer sex. Our country has made great progress under our leadership. Today, I propose another advancement—situating a woman into a government position. Elsothe needs a diplomat in Laverli, as well as some possible representation for local issues. Your accomplishments in discovering the source of Agitated Delirium are known well beyond our borders. Perhaps this position will appeal to your adventurous spirit? Take some time to consider it."

"Thank you. I will."

She couldn't think of anything else to say. The offer stunned her. Never in her wildest dreams would she speculate such a position could be proposed to a woman within her lifetime. She arrived expecting a swift death; their offer in lieu of that fate was a complete shock. Surely, it would place her as one of the groundbreakers leading Elsothe towards the Age of Awareness. But would that shift the country in the direction of her Age of Awareness, or theirs?

"Oh, and Miss Leahill? I would be happy to replace your cuff. Only the finest quality, naturally," the man to the right of Lord Gout added.

She ran her fingers over the fresh scar Fogarty gave her along her collar bone, making a show of it so he noticed. "Most kind of you, but I'm afraid I wish to avoid physical discomfort for a while. I do believe I have had quite my fill of it recently, but thank you for your charitable offer."

They fell into a round of falsely sympathetic nods while madly scratching.

"Quite understandable, after what a lady such as yourself has endured. When you feel ready for the cuff, just send word," he replied with a patronizing lilt.

"Good day, Miss Leahill." Gout closed the meeting with a rough scratch of his scalp.

She needed time to process. A Council post—the unexpected offer should have elated her. Yet, it somehow felt like a backhanded compliment. She hadn't received any of the information she came for, but at least she gained some notoriety. It was a touch bittersweet. Before Elliot climbed into the Wilthiem to shift the course of her life, she would have counted the post as a grand step towards securing her legacy. In light of all she had seen, that seemed an impossible path. The Council's oppression was so clear to her now. Joining them would not be the best route to better the people's lives.

The Council descended from their high seats and disappeared into the shadows. All except Lord Malhon. He sat motionless—a falcon watching his prey. His hands curled over the edges on the desk, tight skin making his knuckles look like bulging tumors.

As she turned her back on him to leave, he called out, "Did you know, Miss Leahill, that acting contrary to this Council's requests is strictly forbidden? Being as innocent and inexperienced as you are, I feel obliged to inform you of that, just in case you had any urge to seek out your doctor against our decision."

She forced her voice to sound as light and sweet as she could muster. "I wouldn't dream of such a thing."

"Good."

She rushed to quit the hall before he could say anything else.

Outside, the ash fell in light spurts. Jacob leaned against her newly refurbished Wilthiem and puffed on a hand-rolled cigarette. She wondered why he only smoked in the city but decided it would be rude to ask. She had imposed on Jacob far more than she should have already. The cigarette sprayed a burst of red sparks on the ground as he tossed it down. He snapped erect to help her into the carriage.

The engine roared to life, and the soot flushed out of the interior in a whoosh from the vents. Both of his hands gripped the controls, but he didn't pull forward.

"Well?" he twisted his head back.

"Well, I wasn't detained." She rested her head on the cushion.

"I see that. The doctor?" He grabbed the lever but didn't pull it.

"They wouldn't tell me. In fact, I'm forbidden to even look for him, which only strengthens my suspicions. They want to keep him, although I'm not certain why. I suspect there's something going on in the asylums. Fogarty mentioned experiments on the patients."

Jacob fidgeted in the seat. "Yeah, but that snake was a liar."

"I wish it was a lie, but you weren't there to see the interior. Wires and such poked into people—and Elliot is in one of those places. Who knows what they're doing to him." She kicked the side of the wall. The carriage rocked like a canoe on a lake. "Infernal Council and their contemptuous bullshit. Didn't tell me anything useful, but they offered me an ambassador's position, as if that would make up for it."

Jacob spun around completely in his chair. The surprise on his face matched her sentiment on the matter.

"Really? Well, you did save the country from that lunatic," he murmured more to himself than to her.

"I suppose, but I didn't improve anything, either."

Outside the window, two boys built a castle from a mound of ash. One had a mask three sizes too big for his face. It jiggled around as he shoveled piles of vile soot on top of the tower. The bare-faced older boy shaped the mass. A sweeper shooed them off, waving his broom and knocking the tower over. Further up the street, two old women coughed arm in arm with their baskets swinging at their sides. They passed a lone man injecting outside the barber shop. No laughter, no enthusiasm for life, just filth constantly raining down on dull cobblestone.

All she had endured, all she had done, and the ash buried them all just the same as before.

"The Council are deceivers. They promised the Age of Awareness: prosperity, peace, and access to knowledge for everyone. I have every intention of making that age a reality." She drummed her fingers on the carriage wall to aid her pondering. "Perhaps I'm being too hasty about this Council position."

Jacob sucked in a long breath that whistled through his teeth. "What are you on about? I know that look; you have plans that are going to get us nearly killed."

He pulled the lever, and the Wilthiem rolled onwards, leaving the scene outside her window behind. New soot-stained faces appeared over every yard they traveled. She wouldn't pull the curtain on them, not anymore. Each ash-burdened shop and sickly passerby in full view, she saw them all.

"You can't beat the Council at their own game," Jacob advised.

The city hummed with forgotten promises like whispers from a ghost. Words contorted in the dark crevices. A shrill prophecy in Mary Magpie's voice.

Men playing cards… wagering flesh…

She traced the scar running down her wrist. "Not unless I sit at the table and have them deal me in."

ABOUT THE AUTHOR

Van Essler tinkers with devious devices and macabre magic. She writes a signature blend of dark edged, cross-genre fiction, creating fantastical settings to expose real world societal issues. Her work appears in *Like Sunshine After Rain, Story Emporium Magazine*, and Zimbell House anthologies and she won the Founder's Award from the Professional Writers of Prescott for fiction. She holds a Master of Fine Arts in Writing Popular Fiction from Seton Hill University. A tarot deck collector and believer in cat naps, Essler makes friends with all her dreams, whether they are sweet reveries or nightmares. She lives in the Seattle area with her family, and spoiled, ginger cats. You can find her on the instagram account VanPunkAuthor or her facebook author's page.

www.ingramcontent.com/pod-product-compliance
Lightning Source LLC
Chambersburg PA
CBHW031233260626
47169CB00007B/2281